D1004158

VENGEFUL GAMES

VENGEFUL GAMES

Jeff Menapace

MIND MESS PRESS

2013

Copyright © 2013 by Jeff Menapace

Published by Mind Mess Press

All Rights Reserved

VENGEFUL GAMES

ISBN: 978-0-9888433-1-8

All rights reserved. Without limiting the rights under copyright above, no part of this publication may be reproduced, stored in or introduced into any retrieval system, or transmitted in any form or by any means (electronic, mechanical, photocopying, recording or otherwise) without the prior written permission of the copyright owner or the publisher of this book.

This book is a work of fiction. Names, characters, places, and incidents are a product of the author's imagination or are used fictitiously. Any resemblance to actual events, locales, or persons, living or dead, is coincidental.

CHAPTER 1

Chicago, Illinois
Autumn, 2008

Although the interior of the house was black with night, Monica could have slinked her way upstairs and into their bedrooms eyes closed. She had been in their home—alone—several times already. Her job demanded this kind of tactile homework. She had to be perfect. Always. But it was never a burden. She loved her job. It was why she was so good.

Monica never cared to know the reasons behind her assignments unless they were critical to the job. Reasons meant little to her. It could be a terrorist hiding in suburbia, or a school teacher having an affair. She didn't care. It was the work itself she prized. Her first solo assignment at nineteen was carried out with the exactness of a veteran—her hand never shook, her movements never second-guessed.

At the top of the landing, Monica made an immediate right into the boy's bedroom. He was a freshman in high school. Five-foot nine. Scruffy brown hair. Skinny. She'd studied him on his way home from soccer practice. Every day after school until five. He walked home.

Monica now stood over his sleeping body and withdrew a pistol from her leather bag. Teenagers were always so easy. They slept like the dead. The boy snored deeply, his mouth ajar. She smirked at the opportunity and placed the suppressor of her Glock into his mouth. The boy never opened his eyes, even when the two quiet thumps bounced his head and turned the back of his pillow red.

Mom and dad were down the hall. She didn't have to hurry with this one, and that was just fine by her. Quite often a job would require a quick in and out with little time to savor and enjoy. But with this one, she could (and would) secure the situation, and then take her time.

She glided into the master bedroom, hung at the foot of the bed, watched their sleeping silhouettes. She felt the familiar tingle flutter its way down her spine until it made a pit-stop in her belly, swirling hot and bad, waiting for the chance to continue its exquisite journey south.

Monica had once read that Adolph Hitler would often ejaculate while delivering passionate speeches to his minions. A crazy notion to most, but she understood the moment she'd read it. She desired sex as often (she assumed) as most women did, but achieving orgasm was near impossible no matter how earnest the man's efforts may have been. But when an assignment like tonight's allowed her to take her time? She was able to explode with ecstasy—multiple times.

One poor fellow unknowingly volunteered to be her first successful effort at sexual gratification when Monica was only twenty-two. The young man was not an assignment, just another random penis stepping up to the plate in hopes of hitting one out of the park. Unfortunately, the man, despite his efforts, could not even manage a bunt, and in a desperate attempt for fulfillment, Monica—she on top, he still inside her—reached for one of her instruments (always hidden close by) and slashed his throat.

Staring down at disbelieving eyes, a mouth gurgling red, and frantic clawing at a throat that no longer worked, she came instantly.

Future sexual encounters of the same nature occurred, but they were infrequent. More sport than anything else. The job satiated her appetite with far greater satisfaction.

And so now, just as the female subject (40, dirty-blonde hair, five-foot two, Pilates at twelve on Tuesdays and Thursdays) lifted her head off the pillow to likely obey the blind suspicion subjects sometimes had—the suspicion they were being watched—she did not receive two quick bullets like her son had. Instead she got a lightning-quick injection to the side of the neck that put her back into a deep sleep. The husband (42, brown hair, five-foot ten, work hours eight to six, happy hour with colleagues on Wednesdays and Fridays from six to eight) barely stirred, even when he received an injection of his own.

Monica left the sedated couple, entered their bathroom and hit the light. Her reflection in the stretch of mirror above the dual sinks was exceptionally kind: dark, seductive eyes, full lips, healthy dark hair that usually bounced at the shoulder (now pulled back tight for job efficiency), and a body that defied the majority by being slim and tight in the usual trouble spots, full and firm in the oft-desired.

These physical gifts were accentuated—and coveted by every female eye she passed—by a powerful and sophisticated aura, product of conditioning from years in the most elite of boarding schools. If she were wearing a power suit instead of the unassuming but apt attire needed for her current assignment, she could easily pass for a seven-figure knockout parading down Wall Street.

Monica placed her leather bag on the sink, glanced into the bedroom at the couple, and felt the familiar tingle begin its feathery dance down her body. Now she would take her time.

* * *

Monica sat on the edge of the bed and lit a cigarette. Inhaling deep, she glanced over her shoulder, searching for the remote. It was on the nightstand next to the wife's corpse.

She stood, strolled past the chair that held the husband's bound and mangled body, flicked an ash on his scalp, picked up the remote from the nightstand, and returned to her spot at the foot of the bed.

Crossing her legs, she took a second drag, leaned back on her elbows, and blew a long stream into the air. She tweaked the toes of the dead woman next to her, then clicked on the television.

The news was replaying a top story from a few days ago. The incident had caught her attention the night it aired, and she had given it a brief glance. Multiple murders in the sticks of western Pennsylvania. A place called Crescent Lake. Torture. Sick games. Something out of a movie, they had said.

Now they apparently had the whole story.

She turned up the volume and looked on with the casual eye of an athlete watching their own sport. She hoped this local station had the balls to air recordings of the aftermath. The breaking report she had witnessed days ago on assignment in New York had given her nothing but a woman with a bad dye-job blabbering in front of a cabin in Bumblefuck, Pennsylvania.

For the moment, this one looked to be no different. Same bullshit drama in front of a cabin. A man reported this time, one with a bad toupee and capped teeth. He carried on as though auditioning for a Hollywood role.

Four murdered . . . two men responsible . . .brother. . . one of the brothers eventually killed in an act of self-defense . . . the other brother critically wounded and in custody.

Her casual interest was waning.

The reporter disappeared, and Monica was finally rewarded with a brief shot of a large black body bag being carried out of a cabin and into an ambulance.

She rolled her eyes. Painfully unfulfilling. She took another drag of her cigarette and blew perfect smoke rings.

Toupee returned for a brief moment to provide new details about the naughty brothers. And then, for the first time, their pictures—side by side headshots that took up the whole screen.

Monica sprang upright, the remote falling from her hand, the battery casing breaking open as it hit the rug. She leaned forward and gawked at the screen. The brother on the left—the one they'd declared dead. He looked exactly like her.

The finished cigarette burned her fingers and she cursed and dropped it. She quickly stubbed it out with her toe, pocketed the butt, pushed off the bed and rushed close to the screen. A lock of her thick, dark hair came free from her ponytail and fell over one eye. She slapped it away from her face as though it were a bug.

The other brother, the one that was still alive and in custody, there was a resemblance there as well. And then she heard the word and her open mouth gaped wider.

Adopted.

Both brothers had been adopted. The pictures disappeared and she snatched at the screen as though she might be able to bring them back.

Toupee stood in front of a lake now. More cabins rimmed the corners of the screen. If he had been auditioning for a Hollywood role before, he was now trying to take home the Oscar with his dramatic recap:

"Once again, an idyllic autumn getaway becomes a nightmare for an innocent family, as two psychotic brothers subjected these unfortunate people to unspeakable horrors for their own sick amusement . . ."

A photo of the family's cabin, and then of an isolated house where apparently further atrocities took place.

". . . the family survived the brothers' wrath, even fighting back and taking the life of one of the sadistic brothers in a heroic display of self-defense . . ."

A solitary picture of the deceased brother now—the one that looked like her. Monica touched the screen, caressed his face.

"The same cannot be said for the four victims here at Crescent Lake, whose lives were brutally snuffed out for unknowingly playing the role of obstacles in the sick games the brothers were orchestrating . . ."

A repeat shot of the same black body bag being taken out of a cabin and into an ambulance. Her fingers fell from the screen, dropped to her side.

"Ironically, it would later be known that one of the survivors of that night of horror was actually the adoptive mother of the two sadistic brothers. A widow, this elder woman, whose name is being withheld, was tragically unaware of the evil she was raising until it was too late. She too proved to be an obstacle, and is now in critical condition . . ."

Toupee on his own again, in front of the lake, pouring it on.

"What compels men to do such things? How does one develop the urge and ability to torture an innocent family for their own enjoyment? To slaughter four people without pity? Attempt to take the life of their own adoptive mother who, along with her now deceased

husband, lovingly took these boys into their lives out of the pure goodness of their hearts . . . ?"

The side by side headshots leapt forward again as the commentary continued. She caressed the screen with both hands this time, one for each.

She knew. All those questions they were asking. The whys? The hows? She knew why. She knew how. *God* how she knew.

Monica rushed towards her leather bag, fished out her cell, dialed.

A male voice picked up on the first ring. "Code in."

"Neco. 8122765," she said.

"Waiting for voice authentication . . . clear. Everything okay?"

"Fine. You can send the cleaner in an hour. I want you to check something for me first."

* * *

Monica "Neco" Kemp hung up after ten minutes then dialed a second number. It rang twice.

"What's up, baby girl?" A male voice, deep and powerful.

"I found them."

CHAPTER 2

**The Western Pennsylvania Hospital
Pittsburgh, Pennsylvania**

Two days later

"Hey, Fannelli, are your hands clean?"

Arty Fannelli ignored the officer. He'd learned over the past week that the officers assigned to him for the night shift could be chatty, and not in a *how 'bout them Steelers?* way. Day shift weren't exactly benevolent watch dogs either, but at least they kept their noses in magazines most of the time.

"Hey!" The officer snapped his fingers. "Earth to stupid! Are your hands clean?"

"I've heard that one before, asshole; I'm not holding your dick for you while you piss. And don't call me Fannelli . . ." Then, to himself more than the officer: "I don't *have* a last name."

The officer stood and kicked the base of Arty's bed, rocking it. "You better watch who you're calling asshole, *Fannelli.* Wouldn't want another 'accident' now, would we?"

The officer strolled towards the bathroom, eyes fixed on Arty the whole way. He left the bathroom door open, dropped his pants, and slapped his bare ass for Arty while he took a leak.

The hospital room door swung open, a nurse entered, and the officer quickly hiked up his pants. Arty smirked when he saw a quarter-sized stain on the front of the officer's trousers. The officer caught the smirk and heightened his previous threat with a glare.

"Medication time," the nurse said.

The officer grunted, took his seat next to the hospital bed, and lifted a *Sports Illustrated* up to his face.

The nurse gave Arty his medication and did a quick check of his wounds. She was sure and methodical, neither rude nor friendly, despite her patient. Days ago, Arty would have made a lewd comment to the attractive nurse. However, recent knowledge about who Arty and his late brother truly were had changed all that, and the energy for such juvenile comments grew depleted; rage had siphoned it all.

"How's your pain?" she asked.

Arty just nodded and the nurse left.

The officer put his magazine down. "Let me ask you something, Fannelli. I heard that a *woman* kicked your brother's ass. Is that true?" His grin was huge. "I heard she stabbed him in the fucking balls with one of those metal nail files." The officer grabbed his own pair and winced. "What kind of pussy would let a woman do that to him?"

Arty looked away and said nothing. This only spurred the officer on.

"Why'd you shoot your mother, Fannelli? Was she kicking your ass too?"

"She's not my real mother," Arty said to the wall.

"Yeah, but you didn't know that at the time, did you?" The officer started to chuckle as he spoke. "You thought she was your *real* mama. That was your whole big thing you kept babbling about when you got here, wasn't it? You and your douche bag brother were *born* to nice people?

Raised in their *loving* home? Yet both of you turned out to be psycho fruitcakes, so you thought that somehow made you special? Nature versus nurture and all that bullshit?"

"Shut up."

The officer's chuckling grew to soft laughter; he struggled finishing his sentences whole. "What . . . what was it you called yourselves? Exceptions . . . exceptions to the rule?"

"*Shut up.*"

"You thought . . . you thought you were gonna be placed in some cushy hospital so shrinks could study how *diabolically unique* you were? Like you were fucking Hannibal Lecter or something?" The officer put a hand to his mouth to stem further laughter. "So really . . . why did you shoot your mother, Fannelli?"

"She's *not* my real mother."

The officer continued, his laughter now back to periodic chuckling. "I know, I know . . ." He then shook his head, disappointed yet still amused, as if hearing about a great party he was forced to miss: "*God*, how I wish I could've been here when you found out. Your face must have been fucking gold." He grinned. "But still—when you shot her, you thought she *was* your real mother. So what gives, Fannelli? Oh wait . . . you were 'freeing her,' weren't you? Isn't that what you told everyone? Poor mom's suffering from dementia, and you think it best to 'free her' with a bullet to the chest?"

Arty said nothing, kept his eyes on the wall.

"What really happened, Fannelli? Did mommy find out what you and your naughty brother were up to, and take a paddle to ya? Did you end up having to fend off an old lady with a gun like the pussy you are? Come on Fannelli, tell the truth."

"I told you not to call me Fannelli."

"Right, right," he mocked. "Such a touchy issue with you. So what *should* I call you then, Fannelli?"

Arty finally looked at the officer. "I don't know. What's the name of the guy your wife is currently fucking?"

The officer leapt from his seat and punched Arty in the face.

* * *

Monica Kemp put on a modest pair of horn rims with fake lenses, strolled into the Western Pennsylvania Hospital, and headed towards the east wing.

Her attire for a registered nurse was spot-on: navy blue scrubs, ID badge, sneakers, hair pulled tight into a bun, fingernails clipped short, stethoscope around the neck. But these tangibles, while crucial, weren't the deal-sealers that made her innocuous to the staff. It was her trained intangibles. She knew when to smile and when to look away. Who to speak to and who to avoid. And, in case of emergency, when to become a phantom and vanish. Most people spend their lives trying to be noticed. Monica Kemp was a master at being invisible.

Her contacts had told her everything she needed to know. What floor he was on, shift rounding, medication schedules, and of course, where his adoptive mother was being treated.

Maria Fannelli's wounds that night had been critical. Sharing a hospital with the son who had tried to kill her was irrelevant to the EMTs on the scene—proximity was crucial if her life was to be saved. The nearby Western Pennsylvania Hospital would have no choice but to house *both* Arthur and Maria Fannelli.

And that was just fine by Monica. Two birds, one stone.

* * *

Arty held one hand over his throbbing eye.

"You're lucky that's all you got . . . fucking wise-ass." The officer hoisted his belt and puffed out his chest.

The door opened again, and the officer took his seat and picked up the *Sports Illustrated*.

"Medication time," the nurse said, making her way to Arty's bedside.

The officer put down the magazine. "Huh?"

The nurse kept her back to the officer and repeated: "Medication time."

"He just got his medication a half hour ago."

The nurse glanced over her shoulder, barely giving a profile. "I have a STAT order from the doctor for a UTI."

"A *what?*"

"UTI—urinary tract infection."

The officer shrugged and picked his magazine back up.

The nurse handed Arty a small piece of tissue paper. "Take this."

Arty didn't look at the nurse. He just frowned and took the tissue paper from her hand. There was writing on it, small but clear. The nurse removed her horn rims as Arty read:

Read this quietly and know that what I write is true. People will suffer for your misfortune. I swear this to you on the same blood that runs through our veins. I am your sister. And before long we will have exacted a vengeance of unthinkable horror onto those who dared cross our family.

Be patient, big brother; our time will come.

Faithfully yours,
Monica

Arty's frown was now sardonic. This note. A lame attempt at humor from the nursing staff no doubt. He finally looked up at the nurse, keen on crumpling the tissue paper, tossing it in her face, telling her to fuck off. Except what he saw robbed his lungs of even a gasp.

Arty was looking at his own flesh and blood. Of this he was surer than the pulse that now hammered his chest. This woman could have been his dead brother's twin.

His breath returning, Arty went to speak, but Monica placed a hand over his mouth, took the delicate paper from him, and placed it gently between his lips.

"Come on, take it," she said, handing him a glass of water. "It's for your own good."

Arty quickly chewed the tissue paper and chased it down with the glass of water.

Monica smiled, leaned in to fluff his pillow, whispered: *"I'll be on the telemetry unit in a few moments. I believe Maria Fannelli is being cared for there. How would you like me to handle that?"* She stood upright and stared at him.

Arty smiled genuinely for the first time in days. Monica smiled back, nodded once, and then left the room.

Arty began whistling a tune.

"Shut the fuck up," the officer said.

Arty smiled genuinely again. "Yes, sir."

* * *

As she exited, Monica winked at the young officer seated outside her brother's room. He blushed, smiled sheepishly, and quickly looked away.

Fish in a fucking barrel, she thought, putting the horn rims back on and heading towards the telemetry unit.

* * *

Monica stood next to Maria Fannelli's bed. The room was dark and quiet save for the consistent beeps of Maria's heart that see-sawed white lines on the monitor's black screen.

The woman's eyes were closed, her mouth open a crack, the occasional snore flapping from her throat. An IV snaked its way out of her arm and attached itself to a free standing infusion pump on the side of the bed where Monica stood.

Monica wanted to wake her. Wanted the woman to know what was about to happen. She wanted to savor it; look deep into this woman's eyes and watch the life drain from them. After all, this was something new—the first step in their path to vengeance. Who knew what ecstasies it might bring?

But alas, this could not be one of those times. Years of discipline extinguished such blissful thoughts, and self-preservation immediately took hold. She was not in someone's home where she could take her time.

Monica snapped on a pair of latex gloves, hit stop on the infusion pump, withdrew a syringe from her pocket, took hold of the intravenous port, and administered an IV push: a lethal and undetectable injection of potassium into Maria Fannelli's vein.

* * *

Monica was halfway down the hall when she looked over her shoulder and spotted a young woman from the nurse's station hurry into Maria Fannelli's room—no doubt hoping that the one of many monitors she was observing was simply incorrect, and that Mrs. Fannelli had not flat-lined. The last thing Monica heard before she exited the hospital was the commotion surrounding the Code Blue that had just been called.

Upon reaching her car, Monica paused, lit a cigarette, and blew a long satisfying plume into the dark autumn sky. "Resuscitation is futile," she smirked. "That bitch is dead."

She entered her car and drove off without suspicion.

* * *

Arty was asleep when the doctor entered the room. The officer on duty was fighting off sleep himself, periodically dropping his head into his chest before it would pop up suddenly as though someone had startled him. When the doctor entered the room, he hopped to his feet and made a subtle attempt at wiping the sleep from his eyes.

"Mr. Fannelli," the doctor said.

Arty didn't stir.

"Mr. Fannelli," the doctor repeated.

Arty spoke without opening his eyes. "Don't call me Fannelli."

The doctor exchanged looks with the officer. The officer shrugged.

"I thought you should know," the doctor continued, obviously deciding to forgo a second guess at an acceptable moniker, "that your mother has succumbed to her injuries. There was nothing we could do."

The doctor left the room.

"*Bra-vo*, Fannelli," the officer said, clapping slowly. "Your mother's dead . . . and *you* killed her. I'd say that just about puts the last nail in your coffin, wouldn't you?"

Despite the pain it caused his wounds, Arty rolled away from the officer and lay on his side.

The officer grinned and took his seat again. "What's wrong, Fannelli? You gonna cry?"

Truth be told, Arty was trying not to laugh.

CHAPTER 3

The Alaskan Wilderness

One week later

John Brooks watched the homeless man devour the bowl of stew at his kitchen table. "Good?" John asked.

The homeless man lifted his head, stew dripping from his mangy beard, and smiled like a child eating ice cream.

John smiled back. "It's one of my specialties. Snowshoe hare and fox. Can't get along out there—" He pointed out his cabin window "—but put 'em together in a pot with some veggies and they get along just fine, don't they?"

The man lifted his head and smiled again, wider this time. His front teeth were gone.

"More?" John asked when he noticed the man had now abandoned his spoon and begun scraping the inside of the bowl with his fingers in order to sop up every last morsel.

The man licked his fingers and handed the bowl to John. "Yes—please."

John took the bowl to a small white stove in the corner. Simmering on one of the burners was the black pot that held his specialty. He ladled two big helpings into the man's bowl and placed it before him again.

The man's appetite, strong as it was, had not completely vanquished his courtesy. Even as the steaming bowl sat beneath his runny nose, he managed polite small talk before diving into his second helping. "So you live all the way out here by yourself?"

"That's right."

The man chewed, swallowed, burped into his fist, then dug in again. "Year long?"

"Pretty much," John said. "Unless I'm working."

The man took a mouthful bigger than he could handle, and after a few noble attempts of getting it all down at once, resorted to pulling a chewed hunk of rabbit from his mouth and placing it back in his bowl. "What do you do?"

"Hunter."

The man kept his eyes on his food as he spoke. "So then what brought you all the way into town today? You need ammo or traps or something?"

John smiled. His black eyes sparkled. Softly, he said, "No."

For a man as physically imposing as he was, John Brooks could play the big teddy bear when he wanted— embodying a serenity that seemed to oppose the hardened edges of his rough but handsome face; a physique that suggested he bench-pressed oak trees and dead-lifted boulders.

The homeless man finished a mouthful of stew and made eye contact with his host. "So what were you in town for then?" he asked.

John smiled again—the same accommodating smile he'd flashed for his guest when first leaning to his right and opening the passenger door back in town. "Call it an urge," he said.

The man shrugged and went back to his stew.

John went to the window. The sun was strong, reflecting off the snow and ice covering the earth. John squinted through the glare and looked further out. He saw that even dim, congested areas of forest were pierced with light in various spots. "*Perfect,*" he whispered. The lighting was perfect. Perfect *now.*

John turned back towards the man. "How you coming along?"

Smiling, the man held up and displayed his empty bowl, and once again John likened him to a child.

"Excellent," John said. "Feel good?"

The man nodded.

"Feel strong?"

The man nodded.

"Energetic?"

The man paused, his smile now more polite than genuine, and nodded again.

"Think you can give me my money's worth?"

No nod this time. Just a quizzical face. "What do you mean?"

John reached into his pocket and pulled out a stopwatch. He pressed a few buttons and placed it on the kitchen table in front of the man. The watch was set for ten minutes.

"That's how much of a head start I'm going to give you," John said. He reached forward and pushed a final button. There was a faint beep, and the stopwatch began its countdown.

The man looked up at John. "I—I don't understand . . ."

John didn't reply. He walked to his gun rack fixed next to the mounted head of a grizzly bear, considered his selection, then chose his custom-built Remington.

"Mister, what are you . . . what are you doing?"

John stayed quiet, but found it impossible to fend off a small smile as he began loading the rifle.

"Are you . . . taking me hunting with you?" the man asked, eyes fixed on the Remington.

John laughed softly and shook his head. The tranquil demeanor, despite his rough exterior, was still there, but the eyes . . . the eyes were different now. Intense arousal had dilated his pupils to an extreme, making them more akin to the black marble eyes of the grizzly on his wall. Akin and relevant: both were lethal predators.

John slid the bolt on the chambered round, brought the rifle to his chest and asked: "How much time you got?"

The man stuttered, producing nothing but quick, frenetic breaths. His eyes volleyed back and forth between John's face and the Remington. Wet stew still hung from the beard surrounding his open mouth, his filthy layers of clothing unable to hide the shakes of his body.

Rifle still in both hands, John poked his chin towards the stopwatch on the table. *"How much time?"* he asked again.

The man looked fast. "Seven—says seven minutes."

John booted the man from his chair, sending him hard to the wooden floor.

The homeless man stared up helplessly at his once-generous host. He stared at the now lustful grin that was close to leaking. He stared at the blackest of eyes that were useless windows to a soul that didn't exist. He stared at it all, unable to look away, his face contorted, frozen—an effigy of absolute fear.

And John rejoiced. He laughed, wiped his mouth, and pointed the rifle towards the front door. "You better get a move on, sport."

* * *

The homeless man darted through the Alaskan wilderness, his frantic lungs machine-gunning clouds of breath. Branches smacked and sliced his face, the dense underbrush like cruel wooden hands trying to snatch an ankle, making him stumble more than once.

Calls for help were futile in the desolate environment; he knew that, but it didn't stop panic from shunning reason and trying all the same. So he cried out. A bullet answered just above his head. It thumped into the large spruce behind him, splintering the bark and producing a hole the size of a dime.

Two more shots thumped into the girth of the spruce, one on each side of his head—a perfect triangle if one connected the dots.

He screeched like a wild bird and dropped to his stomach, eyes closed tight, cheek and body pressed hard to the earth in hopes of somehow sinking into it for cover.

The evil man had missed him on purpose; he knew this fact to be as sure as the ice and snow that was now biting into his cheek and ear. He was being toyed with. The stopwatch, the head start, it was for the evil man's own amusement, not some race against the clock where life was the prize should he outlast his pursuer. Death was not a possibility; it was a certainty. It was all just a matter of when.

And so there, pressed flat on his belly in the freezing underbrush, he gave up and began to cry.

* * *

One hundred yards away, through the custom scope of his Remington, John Brooks watched the man resign and begin to sob. The image was satisfying, but at the same time disappointing. Tears of dread were always nice—but giving up? Accepting fate? What the fuck kind of pussy shit was this? Perhaps some pain would inspire his prey and resume the chase.

John steadied the Remington, peered through the scope, held his breath.

* * *

A distant boom. The instantaneous whistle of a bullet slicing air. And then a wet thump that carried an explosion of searing pain into the homeless man's leg. He rolled to one side and gripped the wound, his hands coming away a mess of wet red.

Yes, the evil man was toying with him. Yes, he intended to kill him. But apparently he had no intention of doing it quickly.

The homeless man struggled to his feet, his leg producing a wave of agony unparalleled to that of anything he had ever encountered during his hardships as a transient. He hobbled through the snow, leaving a thick dotted trail of blood behind him. His tears had stopped for now; the pain of the wound had ironically stemmed them.

The man's destination was unknown. He was simply buying himself minutes before he was ultimately murdered, and he knew that. Was that a purchase he really wanted? Yes. He had accepted fate earlier and had paid an excruciating price—his leg was now a throbbing log of useless meat.

Inevitable fate be damned, he was going to try. Try and *succeed*. Disappear in the forest. Lay low until it was safe, no matter how long it took. He was a homeless man living in *Alaska* for Christ's sake; he could endure the elements. And when it was safe he would find a way back to town. Go to the police. Tell them about the evil man. Beg them to listen for once. Yes—he would go to the police, and the evil man would be punished. Yes . . . yes, that's what he'd do.

The homeless man hobbled with a purpose towards a thick mass of pines.

* * *

John was pleased. His shot to the man's leg had done its job and restarted the game—sort of. Likely, the shot had hit the femoral artery on the man's leg, and if he managed to hide for the remainder, the man would slowly bleed to death somewhere—*the equivalent of fucking for hours without coming,* John thought. He could never allow such a thing. He would rather come quick and accept *some* joy than cope with such an excruciating disappointment.

So let's just go for the headshot and call it a day, shall we? After all, the man's terrified expression in the cabin would sustain him for a little while. And the girlish screech followed by the cowardly sobbing *was* kind of funny the more he thought about it. Nothing great, but it was something.

John waited patiently for the man to finally stop and catch his breath. He was deep into a mess of pines, almost assuredly invisible to anyone looking from afar, but from the custom scope on his Remington, John felt he could reach out and tickle the man's chin.

John smiled. Zeroed in on the man's head. Aimed between the eyes. Held his breath. And then watched the homeless man's head snap backwards, spraying the pines behind with red chunks before his body crumbled to the ground.

Except John never pulled the trigger.

He turned fast over his shoulder, the echo of the mystery bullet still reverberating throughout the forest. Monica Kemp stood ten yards away, her own custom-built Remington gripped tight in both hands.

"Hi, Dad," she said with a smirk.

John grinned and placed his rifle on the ground. He went in for the hug. "How's my baby girl?"

* * *

Monica sat at her father's kitchen table. She kept her heavy wool coat on. "It's *freezing* in here, Dad. How do you stand it?"

John placed a hot bowl of stew in front of his daughter. "Getting soft on me are you?"

She pushed the bowl away. "Thank you, but I think I'll pass on your critter stew. God knows what's in it."

John took the bowl away and dumped it back into the pot. "Well then what *can* I get you, your majesty?"

"Coffee would be nice."

John went to work in the cubicle of metal and mess he called a kitchen. "It's going to have to be instant."

"As long as it's hot."

He filled a pot of water, lit a burner, set the pot on the stove. "It'll be a few minutes."

Monica took out a cigarette and lit it. "What's going to happen to your little buddy you were playing hide and seek with?"

John took an ashtray from one of his cupboards and placed it in front of his daughter. "The wildlife will have a snack to look forward to. Circle of life, kiddo. One of the bonuses of living out here."

"What about the bones?"

"The bones will take care of themselves. Worse comes to worst I'll pick them up myself in a week or so." He took the jar of instant from the cupboard. "So tell me about Pittsburgh."

Monica took a pull from her cigarette, blew a thick stream of smoke into the air and gestured towards it. "Air looks like that. Worse than L.A."

He waived the smoke away. "And yet you voluntarily inhale the shit."

The pot started to boil and John turned away for a moment to prepare the coffee. Finished, he turned back and placed it in front of her.

She took a sip and cringed. "Fucking hell, Dad."

"Sorry, I'm afraid my espresso machine is in the shop." He set a small bowl of sugar on the table that she waved off. "All that money and travel has turned you into a snob."

She smiled. "A snob who got the drop on you a few minutes ago."

"You don't think I knew you were there?"

"I *know* you didn't know I was there. You're getting old, Dad."

"Old, my ass." John took off his flannel, rolled up his short-sleeve, and flexed a cannonball bicep.

Monica feigned childish awe. "Daddy is so strong."

John frowned and muttered, put the flannel back on, then picked up her modified Remington resting against the table. "Jesus, look at this thing. It looks like a goddamned M40A3. Could hit a fucking beetle in Anchorage with this thing." He gave her a curious look. "I know you didn't get this from a Marine . . ."

She batted her eyes and waved both hands towards her chest. "Don't underestimate a perfect pair of tits, Dad."

"What the hell's wrong with you? You don't say shit like that to your father."

She brought the coffee mug to her lips to hide her complacent smile. "Sorry."

"Pittsburgh," he said.

She took a sip, set the mug down. "I established contact at the hospital. He was shocked at first, but I gained his trust quickly. He gave me the thumbs up to finish off the adoptive mother. She's very dead."

He smiled, nodded, and took a seat across from her. "How'd he look?"

"Weary. He was stabbed a lot; it looked like much of the fight had gone out of him. I think seeing me might have ignited a spark though. And I'm sure knowing his fake mom is dead certainly won't hurt his mood."

"You weren't spotted by anyone?"

Monica pursed her lips and frowned.

John held up a hand in apology.

Monica took a final drag of her cigarette then swirled the glowing tip into the ashtray until it was dead. "How do you want to play things for now?"

John's face fell grim. He hung his head for a moment before lifting it. "We're sure the other is . . . ?"

Monica nodded, equally sullen. "He was killed that night. His name was James."

The father nodded. He took another moment before saying: "*Arthur* and *James*, huh?"

"Was that our mother's idea?"

"Who the fuck knows? Doubt it. My guess is that it was the adoptive parents. Your mother probably would have named them *Jack* and *Daniels*. Named you *Meth* or something." He spit on the floor. "Good riddance, bitch."

"What would you have named us?" Monica asked. She looked sincere in the inquiry.

He shrugged. "Don't know. Every time I'd come home on leave, another one of you was gone. Don't know why I kept fucking her. Guess you spend so much time fucking Asian pussy, you start to crave some good old American poontang, no matter how fucked up they might be."

"Nice way to talk to your daughter, Dad."

"Getting even for the 'tits' thing." He rocked in his chair. "Either way, you hit the fucking lottery with that family that snatched you up. It's like you're a goddamned Kennedy or something. And I like the name Monica. It suits you."

"So are we going to be calling him Arthur then?"

"Up to him I guess."

Monica stayed quiet and sipped her coffee.

"So what are you telling the Kennedys you do for a living these days?" John asked.

"International banker. Lets me travel on assignment without suspicion; keeps their lofty status in tact. You know—brilliant, wealthy daughter traveling the world and all."

He beamed. Monica had tracked down John when she was only fifteen and still in prep school. Summer vacations allegedly spent in the Hamptons with a classmate's family, winter vacations skiing with friends in Aspen, spring breaks in Tortolla—all time spent with John, learning, training, following and obeying the deadly impulse that was ingrained in their bloodline. On her eighteenth birthday, when most women were blowing out candles, Monica blew a hole in her first human head from fifty yards away. They even stuck a candle in the hole afterwards, laughing hysterically when the man's hair eventually caught fire.

"Why are you looking at me like that?" she said.

"Like what?" His beam became a grin.

"Like the cat with the cream."

"I can't admire the product of my tutelage?"

"Oh get off your high horse, old man. My education didn't exactly stop with you, ya know. Maybe one day you'll let me introduce you to the twenty-first century."

He barked a laugh. "Thanks, but I think I'll leave all the geek shit to you. My education stopped at *Donkey Kong* and *Pac-Man*."

"Shame—you'd get hard over something like *Call of Duty*."

"There you go with that fucking mouth again."

She grinned. He frowned. And then neither grinned nor frowned; their faces fell into somber masks of rumination, the subject of that rumination instantly shared when they eventually locked eyes.

"They were off the radar, Dad. Even if that fucking family and their doctor hadn't buried the adoption—and believe me, I dug—it's obvious Arthur and James inherited our control; they would have avoided the limelight. Only pathetic serial killers want to be caught so they can have their fifteen minutes. James went out on his shield."

John nodded once, stood, and walked towards his kitchen window. He gazed outside, the now-setting sun reflecting in his unblinking eyes, his mind lost in a fantasy of things to come. He spoke in a low, dreamy tone—a haunted voice emanating from deep within the darkest chamber of his core. "It's time to bring Arthur home. Let him know what real family is all about . . . what we're truly capable of . . ."

"We will," Monica said. "We just have to be patient, Dad."

He nodded slowly, still unblinking out the kitchen window, still seeing nothing but the fantasy.

"In the meantime, I'll start gathering the necessary intel," she said. "We want to wait for things to die down some anyway. Everything is too raw now. Too acute. We want to wait until they feel some measure of safety again. As if things might finally be getting better." She licked her lips. "That's when you and I start to play."

John turned from the window and looked at his daughter; his pupils were his whole eyes. "Before this is all over . . . they'll be praying for death."

Monica licked her lips again. "Yes they will."

CHAPTER 4

Valley Forge, Pennsylvania

Three months later

The Lambert family had survived hell. Not only survived, but managed to kill one of their two evil captors.

James "Jim" Fannelli was dead.

Arthur "Arty" Fannelli, however, was alive, but had been severely wounded during the ordeal, and was now in custody of the Allegheny County Police in Pittsburgh, awaiting trial.

Patrick and Amy Lambert, along with their two children, Carrie and Caleb, did not come away unscathed. Patrick had been badly beaten and stabbed, and Amy had been shot in the chest from close range. And then there was the psychological damage, to which the toll seemed unforgiving.

Immediate counseling for quiet suburbanites like the Lamberts after such torment was strongly recommended, and, when offered, Patrick made one of the doctors laugh when he said it was like asking a sailor if he wanted to get laid after being away at sea.

So for the three months that followed the harrowing incidents surrounding Crescent Lake, the family had been attending frequent sessions with a psychologist.

To the surprise of no one, things were shaky from the start. Dr. Janet Stone explained that their psychological trauma would assuredly hit peaks and valleys for awhile, but in time the bad memories would become just that— memories. A thing of the past to which the old chestnut rang true: Take it one day at a time until each passing day carries less impact than the last. Even seven-year-old Carrie, who had been plagued with nightmares from day one, would soon follow suit, Dr. Stone assured—youth was on the little girl's side.

This logic proved especially true for four-year-old Caleb. The incident seemed a lost memory a mere week after arriving home. It was almost as if the boy had never been subjected to such horrors in the first place. That was until he put more than a dozen thumb tacks into Amy's slipper one night, tearing her foot to shreds. A joke little Caleb thought Mommy would find amusing. She did not. A particular child psychologist referred by Dr. Stone was immediately contacted. Caleb Lambert's appointment was scheduled for 7 p.m.

CHAPTER 5

Dr. Bogan initially wanted to speak to Caleb with his parents in attendance. Carrie was in an adjoining room being entertained by the doctor's wife with an array of books and toys.

The first half of the session (Caleb seated on his mother's lap, her stroking his fuzzy brown head of hair) had nothing to do with the events surrounding Crescent Lake. It consisted of the doctor asking the Lamberts fundamental questions in regards to milestones achieved by their son during his developmental years, in addition to behavioral patterns in his daily life.

Amy and Patrick answered frank and with zero hesitation; they were in fact, somewhat proud as they sensed that each answer they provided was almost assuredly positive:

No—there were no abnormalities before, during, or after childbirth.

No—our son did not suffer any head trauma at any time throughout his life.

Yes—our son walked when he was expected to, spoke when expected to, and no, our son never wet his bed; he was actually potty trained in less than a week at the age of two.

A few more questions:

Cruelty to animals?

No way.

Unusual signs of aggression?

Nope.
Poor impulse control?
No, sir.
Irritable temperament?
Quite the opposite.
Lack of empathy towards others?
Again, quite the opposite.

Dr. Bogan closed one notebook and retrieved a second. He then asked Amy and Patrick if he could speak to Caleb alone. The Lamberts hugged their son, told him they loved him, then joined Carrie and Mrs. Bogan in the neighboring room.

* * *

Although acquaintances with Dr. Stone, it was not uncommon for Dr. Bogan to receive referrals from doctors he had never met. He was that good.

Dr. Bogan believed that working with children was a special craft; the younger the child, the more subtle the approach. If the doctor cozied up to the child with sunshine eyes and a syrupy tone, the child would likely shrink further into his or her shell, only poking their head out once the blatant bastard had disappeared. And while his peers sometimes scoffed at the notion that children of such an early age were capable of identifying—and therefore rejecting—such deliberate behaviors in adults, the good doctor liked to remind them that children often cried when they sat on Santa's lap, even with their parents close by.

And so now, alone with the boy, Dr. Bogan had but one thing he wanted clarified. Caleb had already stated that he put thumb tacks into Amy's slipper because he thought his mother would find the prank amusing. What Dr. Bogan wanted to know was if Caleb, after bearing witness to the brutal games orchestrated and enjoyed by two grown men (despite any anguish it caused his family), did what he did because of his age, and thus, his inability to understand the ramifications of physical humor? Or did the boy, perhaps already armed with the terrifying ability to exhibit convincing deception, injure his mother because there was a part of his fledgling mind where a sinister need festered . . . and Caleb himself thought the prank would be amusing?

The former seemed likely; the latter frightening.

* * *

The session was over. Dr. Bogan opened the door to the adjoining room. Caleb walked past the doctor and made a bee-line towards his mother who stood talking to Mrs. Bogan. Patrick sat on the floor reading a book to Carrie, her head on his lap.

Amy instantly leaned down, kissed and hugged her son. Patrick told Carrie to sit up, then got to his feet. Both parents looked at the doctor. He smiled and gestured for them to follow him into his office.

* * *

Dr. Bogan is short and exceptionally thin. His bald head appears disproportionately large above the skinny neck that supports it. Yet it took less than five minutes in the man's presence before Patrick realized that Dr. Bogan was a titan. His insight seemed capable of demoting even the most advanced text to amateur status, and is contained within a calm, assured manner without the slightest hint of arrogance.

Despite his considerable size, Patrick soon felt the smaller of the two men, but never once felt threatened by this revelation. It only added to Patrick's admiration for the man—he was brilliant, and without a condescending bone in his body.

"Caleb is just fine," said Dr. Bogan, not one to practice the oblique approach, the moment they were all seated. "I'd still like a few follow-up sessions if that's okay, but other than borrowing the car and paying for college, I'd say you have little to worry about in the years to come."

The doctor's levity was unexpected but appreciated. Both Amy and Patrick sunk into the sofa and simultaneously exhaled.

Dr. Bogan smiled across from them, legs folded, notebook on his lap.

Amy and Patrick then exchanged looks. Amy started. "So why did my son do what he did?"

"You already know that—he thought you would find it funny," Dr. Bogan said.

"Yeah, but . . . how could he think such a thing?"

"Because he saw two men enjoying themselves while they were tormenting you both."

Patrick stuttered, his eyes becoming confused slits, trying to comprehend. "But, they were—they were *hurting* us. He saw that. He was *crying* because of it."

Dr. Bogan shook his head. "Caleb is too young to comprehend what actually transpired at Crescent Lake. He is still in the ego-centric phase of his development. That means it's difficult for him to see something from anyone's perspective but his own. It's not a bad thing; we all go through it."

"But if he saw his mother and father hurt and crying . . . " Amy said.

"He was crying because *you* were crying. Because Carrie was crying. It had nothing to do with the physical abuse you were enduring. Caleb doesn't understand right from wrong when it comes to such things. He will, but right now he doesn't. He was sad because his mom was sad. In his mind, the terrible actions he witnessed by those two men were completely unrelated."

Patrick was stiff, upright. "I'm sorry, but that doesn't make sense to me."

"You're not a four-year-old child, Mr. Lambert. Your brain is fully developed. You know that when the cartoon coyote is flattened with an anvil one minute, then alive and chasing the road runner the very next, that it's all fantasy. You know such a thing couldn't occur in real life."

"Caleb knows that cartoons aren't real," Amy said.

"I'm sure. And it was only an analogy. I don't need to tell you, however, that what Caleb witnessed that night was no cartoon."

Amy and Patrick fell silent.

Patrick eventually said, "It's just so tough to swallow."

Dr. Bogan said, "You stated that your daughter's been suffering from nightmares ever since you returned home from the lake."

"That's right."

"Yet Caleb's been okay."

"Yes."

"You and Amy have *not* been okay."

The couple snorted in agreement.

"Yet I'm willing to bet you've let Caleb *believe* that you were okay. Would I be correct in that assumption?"

Another bout of silence before Patrick said, "Yes."

"That's why your son is sleeping through the night and puttering around as if all is well. He thinks *you're* well. In his mind, what happened three months ago had no lasting effect on his mother and father whatsoever. You were flattened by the anvil but ready to chase the road runner as soon as you got back home."

Dr. Bogan closed his notebook, uncrossed his legs and leaned forward. "Now— your daughter just turned seven.

She has a stronger understanding as to what was happening during the ordeal near the lake. It's why she's plagued with nightmares."

"So our behavior towards our son has actually been detrimental? It *led* to him putting tacks inside my slipper?" Amy asked.

"No—absolutely not. Even if you sat Caleb down and explained everything to him, it would be exceptionally hard for him to comprehend." Dr. Bogan thumbed his wedding ring and took a breath. "Caleb wanted to play a joke on his mommy. He wanted to make her laugh. He remembered how much the two men enjoyed themselves doing the things they did. In an ironic sort of way—as is typical with sociopaths—the two who assaulted you never grew out of their ego-centric phase; they see with a similar pair of eyes as your son currently does."

"*Saw*," Patrick said absolutely. "They saw."

Dr. Bogan closed his eyes and held up a hand: a silent apology for a comparison that, while apt, was still too recent. He waited a tick.

"There's nothing wrong with your son, Mr. and Mrs. Lambert. We had a good talk. He's a wonderful child. He had no idea he was hurting you, Mrs. Lambert. He may have suspected the joke was *naughty* . . . but he truly believed you would end up unharmed. He believed you'd find humor in the prank. Had he known—for one second— that he might have been harming his mother, he never would have left his bedroom that night. I'm sure of this."

Amy managed a weak smile.

Patrick's mind started churning—there was something relevant he wanted to voice, but he had lost it, and couldn't snatch it back. His face misted over into a daze as he tried to remember, the elusive thought taunting his mind like a song he couldn't place. And then all at once it came together, and his face bounced back to life. He turned to Amy and blurted: "The 'bastard' incident."

Amy turned to her husband, startled. A lock of her brown hair fell over her face. "*What?*"

"When I was little . . . the 'bastard' incident . . . with my mom."

Amy wiped the lock of hair out of her face. "What does that have to do with anything?"

Dr. Bogan wore a curious smile as he spoke up. "Do you mind if I ask?"

"It's nothing," Amy said. "It's a silly story he likes to tell at parties."

"But don't you see its relevance here, baby?"

Amy sighed. "You just want an excuse to tell one of your corny stories."

He slapped her thigh lightly and she slapped his hard. Had it been under different circumstances, he would have squeezed her leg, made her scream, and then kissed her to death. And she would have laughed wildly while trying to fend him off.

Make no mistake, Amy and Patrick Lambert were soul mates. As crazy as it might sound to others, their survival at Crescent Lake had made their love that much stronger. But Dr. Bogan's office was not the place for a full-on affection assault, and the subject matter concerning their son (despite the doctor's good news that he was not a budding Jeffrey Dahmer) was hardly the appropriate mood. Their mutual love—seemingly with its own mind—recognized this and adjusted their school-yard affection accordingly.

"It definitely wasn't funny at the time," Patrick said to Amy. "But *now* it kinda is. And I think it might be relevant to what Dr. Bogan was just saying."

Amy looked at her husband. His face was suddenly serious, a rarity for someone of Patrick's genial ilk. Her exasperated look faded into a sober one of her own. She understood.

Dr. Bogan leaned forward in his chair, still smiling.

"I was five," Patrick said. "My parents were having a party and I was up late. You know it's funny—when they're sober, adults would find a five-year-old bumping into their knees a nuisance. But when they're drunk, well, suddenly you're entertainment; they can't get enough of you. You know: 'Isn't he a cute kid?' 'He's getting so big.' 'Say something funny, little man.' 'Here, you want a sip? I won't tell.'"

Dr. Bogan smiled knowingly.

"So there I am, loving the attention, listening to a couple above me when I hear the word 'bastard' for the first time. I remember the woman instantly slapping the man on his chest, looking down at me, and then giggling. He laughed too. Something inside me knew I had just heard a bad word, and I guess my face showed it, because to cover his tracks, the man quickly bent forward and told me that the word was no big deal; it wasn't a swear. It just meant a person without a father.

"So, I now had a funny new word in my arsenal . . . and I had the perfect person to test it on. My mother. Why?" He took a deep breath. "She didn't have a father anymore. My grandfather had died from a massive stroke two months prior."

Patrick took a second pained breath, then let it out slow as he said, "So, I marched right up to my mother—and about ten or twelve of her friends—and proudly announced: 'Isn't my mother a *bastard*?'"

Dr. Bogan gave a sympathetic grimace, like one man telling another about a time he was kicked in the balls.

Patrick continued. "Of course everyone's mouth fell open. My father looked like he wanted to punt me across the room. But not my mom. She didn't yell, she didn't cry, and she didn't hit me. She simply said: 'Patrick, Mommy's father is gone. You know that. And now you've made Mommy very sad.' And then she walked out of the room and went upstairs.

"That was thirty-three years ago, and I can still see the hurt look on her face. Sure, I was an ignorant five-year-old kid, and sure my mom and I can joke about it now, but at the time I was so confused. I was *certain* my idea of calling her a bastard was the thing to do. But she was so hurt . . ." His voice went soft. "All I can remember, in retrospect, of course, was not knowing any better. Like I had a new toy that I wanted to show off. I couldn't see how it could affect my mother as badly as it did." He snorted and added: "A part of me thought she might even be *proud* of me for learning a new word."

Dr. Bogan finally spoke. "And yet you couldn't see anyone's perspective but your own."

"Right."

"You knew your mother had recently lost her father."

"Yes."

"I assume she cried over it?"

"Yes."

"You saw her upset, in pain."

"Yes."

"The wound was still very raw. Only two months had passed since your grandfather had died?"

"Yes."

"And yet you still called her a bastard even after discovering what it meant."

A pause, and then: "Yes."

"You're not at fault for what you did, Patrick . . ." Bogan shrugged and gave a soft smile. "And neither is Caleb. The two of you were just too young to understand the consequences of your actions. There was no foresight, no insight—there was only you. The fact that thirty-three years later you still feel remorse tells me a lot about who you are. And the fact that Caleb cried relentlessly after finding out that he'd actually hurt his mother tells me a lot about your son.

"I think that was an exceptionally relevant anecdote, Patrick. Thanks for sharing it."

Patrick sighed, smiled, then nudged Amy. "See? My corny stories can be helpful."

She nudged back harder. "Even a broken clock is right twice a day."

Dr. Bogan smiled at their banter then added: "Who knows? Perhaps the day will come when Caleb is grown, and you can all share these anecdotes with a modicum of humor."

Patrick said, "If I know my wife, she'll be looking forward to the day when Caleb is grown so she can plan her revenge."

Amy snorted, bent forward and rubbed her injured foot. "Amen."

Dr. Bogan laughed for the first time since they'd arrived.

CHAPTER 6

The five minute ride home from Dr. Bogan's office had started quietly. Patrick and Amy were digesting the recent session. Caleb had been through enough for one evening and was a yawning machine, but Carrie, whose inquisitive nature was blunt and gunslinger-quick, was not about to finish the short trip home without having her say.

"So why did Caleb hurt Mommy?"

Caleb looked at his sister. The question had pulled the plug on the yawn machine, and he looked ready to cry.

"*Carrie,*" Amy said.

Her mother's sharp tongue was a minor roadblock, so Carrie opted to take the detour right to the source. "Why did you hurt Mommy?" she asked her little brother.

Caleb started to cry.

"*Carrie!*" Amy yelled.

"You made her foot *bleed,*" Carrie said.

Caleb cried harder.

Amy unbuckled her seat belt, turned, and started rubbing Caleb's legs. His head was down and his shoulders bounced with each sob. "It's okay, sweetie, Mommy's not angry with you—I promise." She looked at Carrie. "Carrie, I told you, your father and I would discuss this with you when we got home. All you're doing now is upsetting your brother."

Carrie's head volleyed from Caleb to her mother, confused. "Why are you yelling at *me*? I didn't hurt you."

"Caleb didn't *know* he was hurting me. And that's all you need to know for now, got it?"

Carrie glared at Caleb. His head was still down, shoulders still bouncing. Tears had wet his cheeks and a line of snot was headed towards his mouth. "You didn't *know*? That's *dumb*."

Amy took a Kleenex from her purse and caught the snot before it touched Caleb's lips. She then folded the tissue in half and sopped up his tears. "Carrie, this is the last time I'm going to tell you: If you want your father and I to talk to you about what happened at the doctor's tonight, you *will* stop harassing your brother, do you understand me?"

Carrie huffed and folded her arms.

"Thank you," Amy said. She turned back around and re-fastened her seatbelt.

* * *

As Patrick pulled the silver Highlander into their driveway, it was now Carrie who started crying. Before Amy could turn back in her seat to console her, Carrie looked at her brother and said: "You acted just like those bad men that give me nightmares every night."

Now it was Patrick and Amy who felt like crying.

CHAPTER 7

Really? Are you really going to leave your car in the driveway all night, Patrick? You're making this too easy. What to do, what to do . . .

She had an objective. Always. It was just a matter of when and how.

Tonight would be when, and a delightfully unexpected piece of cake would be how— assuming he left the car in the driveway.

Why didn't you pull it into the garage? Was it because the kids were crying? Yeah, I think so. You and Amy wanted to stop the car as soon as possible so you could carry them inside, isn't that right? Poor little Carrie and Caleb. I guess tonight's session with the new therapist upset them?

The porch lights clicked on and the front door opened. She watched eagerly.

Oscar.

The Border terrier exploded out of the front door and began his perfunctory laps around the front of the house, satisfying every conceivable olfactory sense before he would eventually re-appear on the front lawn to do his business.

Always the same routine right, Oscar? She looked away for a moment and took in the surroundings of suburbia: rows of colossal homes, smooth black driveways stretching on forever, flawless lawns, hedges, flower beds; fences tall, sturdy, and safe, indulging the residents' superfluous paranoia. She wondered which species was more mundane, humans or canines.

She heard the front door close and she turned. Patrick stood barefoot on the front porch in a pair of Penn State sweatpants and a white tee. His arms were folded to keep warm.

And there he is. Hate to admit it, but he is handsome. Wonder if I could get him to fuck me before I kill him . . . or get him to fuck me while I'm killing him . . . or get him to fuck me while I'm killing him while Amy watches . . .

She felt the familiar tingle warming below.

Patrick called for Oscar.

The terrier finally re-appeared, nose dragging the lawn, finding the ideal spot to do his thing. She looked at the wagging stump where his tail used to be and wondered which one of her brothers had cut it off. The Lamberts didn't know, and therefore Dr. Stone didn't know. *Mind like a sieve, that idiot head-shrinker—writes every single nugget down. Didn't surprise me though; her filing system was an archaic joke.*

Oscar lifted a leg.

So it's just a pee is it? Lucky Patrick—nothing to clean up, and no reason to walk on the freezing lawn in your bare feet. But please do me one favor, will you, handsome? Please leave the Highlander in the driveway tonight. Just this once?

Tucked away in the shadows, Monica Kemp watched Oscar dart back inside. She watched Patrick close the door, the porch lights go out, the downstairs lights click off one by one, and then, with a disciplined patience that fought off the eagerness that beckoned, watched the final light from the bedroom window disappear. Patrick and Amy had gone to bed, and Patrick would not be putting the car in the garage tonight.

Monica smiled. "Thank you, handsome."

CHAPTER 8

The lights in the bedroom were off, but Patrick and Amy weren't sleeping. They lay next to one another, flat on their backs and staring at the dark ceiling as though it might begin to flash answers.

"I thought we were making progress," Amy said.

Patrick kept his eyes on the ceiling. "We *are* . . . Dr. Bogan said—"

"Did you *hear* what Carrie said to Caleb? I've never felt so helpless."

"Her nightmares are nothing new. Dr. Stone said they would eventually fade. What we need to do now is try and explain to Carrie *why* Caleb did what he did, help her understand the way Dr. Bogan helped us understand."

"Maybe Carrie should talk to Dr. Bogan. Maybe he could explain it to her."

"Don't you think it would be better if she heard it from her own parents?"

Amy didn't reply.

Patrick rolled towards her. She spooned into him, and he kissed the back of her head. "We *are* getting better. Dr. Bogan's words were an absolute relief—no question—but you and I both know our son; we know in our hearts that he didn't pull that prank maliciously. We just needed clarification . . . and that's what we got tonight." He kissed her head again.

"I just want it all to be over," she said.

"It *is* over. You think Jim's coming back to life? You think Arty's going anywhere?"

"What about the trial?"

"What about it? I don't care what kind of insanity plea his scumbag lawyer tries. It won't amount to shit."

"I just don't want to have to re-live it all over again."

Patrick squeezed his wife. "It's not gonna be a picnic. But if we can survive what we've survived, then we can definitely endure its memory."

She sighed deep, his arm around her rising and falling. "I guess."

He rolled her over so she faced him. "Let's look at it from a different point of view. Let's look at it as the final 'fuck you.'"

"The what?"

"*The final fuck you.* We already fought those crazy bastards at their own game, and we won, right?"

Amy nodded into her pillow.

"Well then let's not take the stand and show fear or anguish over remembering what happened. You know Arty. You know the kind of sicko he is. He'd love that. It would be the same as congratulating the opposition and telling them what worthy opponents they were. No—we got the last laugh at the hospital when we told the prick he was adopted, and we're gonna get the last laugh *again*. Let's get up on the stand, stick our chests out, and look the son of a bitch right in the eye as we give our testimony. We're not gonna congratulate our opponent, we're gonna shove our victory right down his goddamned throat. We'll even wink at the piece of shit while we're doing it."

She laughed.

"We won, baby," he said. "We won the war. But no war comes without casualties. Right now we're nursing ours . . . but I'll be damned if we're gonna let Arty-fucking-Fannelli know that."

She laughed again and kissed him. "I love you."

He stroked her scarred breast: A raised pink circle the size of a nickel was all that remained months after surgery. "This can be your badge of honor," he said.

"I think you're stroking my badge a little too long. It's becoming inappropriate."

"Just admiring it."

"I heard you've got one of your own," she said. Amy brought her hand under the sheet, and ran her fingers over the scar on Patrick's stomach. "I must say, your badge is rather impressive too." Her hand continued creeping further south.

Patrick's hand had since left her badge and began sliding south as well.

"The final fuck you, huh?" she said.

"The final fuck you," he repeated.

"I like that."

Patrick's hand reached its destination first. "I like *you*," he said, slipping an innocent finger in.

Amy moaned lightly. Her hand then reached *its* destination. "Mmm . . . I like *this*," she said as she took hold of him and began stroking.

For the first time since Crescent Lake, Amy and Patrick had great sex.

CHAPTER 9

Patrick woke up before the alarm. He rolled gently and switched it off.

"What time is it?" Amy's voice was soft, barely a whisper. She didn't dare wake the kids. She would savor the calm before the morning storm that was a school day.

"Six." Patrick's voice was equally soft. He feared the storm as well.

Amy cuddled close to him and buried her lips into his shoulder. She mumbled: "I would give anything to be able to lie in bed with you all day."

He cuddled back and kissed her forehead. "That would be amazing."

Her mouth left his shoulder and started kissing the side of his chest. "I'm still tingling from last night."

"It *was* good wasn't it?"

She rolled over and traced her tongue from his nipple to his belly button. "What time do we have to get up?"

He smirked. "I'm already up."

"I practically gave you that one. No points."

"Fair enough."

"What time?"

"6:30."

She hovered over his naked groin, her mouth centimeters away. He felt her hot breath on him. She gave his engorged head a flick of her tongue and he all but came right then. 6:30? He'd be lucky to last until 6:02.

"Plenty of time," she said.

Patrick thought about this weekend's Sixers game for the first few minutes until he was able to gain some control.

* * *

7 a.m. The morning storm.

Patrick dressing, drinking coffee, and eating a protein bar simultaneously. Amy's voice echoing from the floor below, arguing with Carrie about finishing her breakfast, pitching the empty threat that if she missed the bus she was staying home. Carrie's squeaky voice arguing right back. Caleb silent as always.

Dressed, caffeinated, and full of protein, Patrick headed downstairs. He kissed both kids seated at the kitchen table.

Amy approached him, got close and fixed his tie. "We'll talk to Carrie tonight?" she whispered.

"Yeah."

"You thinking about your presentation?"

He was—until Amy mentioned tonight's conversation with Carrie. "Nah, not really."

"You've still got a couple months," she said.

"I know. I'm good."

She kissed him. "I know you'll kick some ass when it's time. You always do."

He smiled. "What about you? What's on your agenda today?"

"After I drop Caleb off, I've got to figure out how I'm going to unload the rest of that software." She made a dreadful face and added: "Might have to make some cold calls."

"Ewww . . . I'm sorry, baby." He admired his wife's work ethic. There was no *way* he could summon the discipline to work from home. Cold calls without a boss holding a gun to your head? Eff that.

"Be thankful you're in advertising," she said.

"I'll be thankful when this presentation is done. Besides, our jobs aren't so different."

"No?"

"No—we're both trying to sell something."

"Oh, so then you wouldn't mind helping me with some of those cold calls?"

He looked at his watch. "Gotta go."

She laughed and smacked him on the chest. He kissed her, the kids at the kitchen table again, then headed towards the garage.

"Wait."

He stopped and turned.

"We parked in the driveway, remember?"

"Oh—right." He changed direction and went out the front door.

As he backed out, Patrick never noticed the big green puddle of antifreeze on the driveway.

CHAPTER 10

The morning storm had nearly passed. Only one more threat of resurgence loomed.

"I can see the bus! *Let's go!*" Amy stood at the open front door, the flashing red and yellow lights of the school bus visible two blocks up.

Carrie hurried to the front door, backpack stuffed bigger than her torso making her sway, lunch box clattering against her knees.

"Gimme a kiss," Amy said bending forward.

Carrie kissed her mother then hurried out the front door and onto the lawn. A furry bullet shot out after her, barking and moving at such a speed that it matched each stride she took with a full circle around her feet.

Amy smiled as she watched the Oscar the dog bid her daughter farewell for the day. It was their morning ritual.

The school bus arrived, slowing to a crawl before finally stopping. Its small stop-sign flapped open from its side like an octagonal fin, the flashing red and yellow igniting once again. The big rectangular doors folded open. Carrie gave Oscar a final pat, waved goodbye to her mother, and climbed aboard.

Amy waved to the bus driver, who waved back. She watched her daughter move from square window to square window along the bus' length until she took a seat. The flashing lights clicked off, the small stop sign folded back flat, and with a slow rumble, the bus chugged forward until it eventually disappeared.

Amy whistled. "Oscar! You coming in or staying out?"

The dog's head whipped towards his owner, then back towards an oncoming speed walker. A woman—gray sweats, blonde hair, glasses, headphones.

Oscar immediately approached the woman and jumped on her leg. Amy scolded Oscar from the front door, smiled and waved an apology to the woman. The woman smiled back, gave a reassuring wave that it was okay, then bent forward and began petting Oscar.

Amy called Oscar again, harsher this time, and the dog finally left the women in peace before charging off and out of sight to perform his usual inspections of the front half of the house.

Amy waited a tick, then called his name again (by now he would have usually appeared on the front lawn, paused to do his business, and then darted back inside for breakfast). When he didn't reappear, Amy shrugged and shut the door, knowing darn well she would hear his incessant whine in less than two minutes.

* * *

Oscar was busy. He had found something very unusual at the top of the driveway. Something that smelled wonderful and tasted delicious. He lapped away at the green puddle, only pausing for a second to acknowledge the blonde speed walker in the gray sweats approach.

The speed walker had watched and waited from a distance for the Lambert's front door to close. She knew Oscar would be enticed by the antifreeze. Knew Amy would eventually close the door on such a cold morning if the dog did not return right away. She also knew that she couldn't rely on a puddle of antifreeze to do the job. Yes, it only took a few tablespoons to eventually kill a dog, but hopeful eventualities had never graced her syllabus—her job entailed acting certainties. Besides, the puddle's role was not to kill. The puddle was more of a red herring. A red herring that would reek of exceptional guilt when all was said and done.

And so as Oscar lapped away happily at the green puddle, the blonde speed walker squatted down on the driveway, began petting him, looked in all directions, and then pulled a syringe from her pocket and stuck a needle filled with more antifreeze into the meat of Oscar's scruff. The dog flinched and looked up for a split second, mildly annoyed, then resumed lapping. The speed walker patted Oscar on the head, put the syringe back in her pocket, and casually walked away.

Several blocks down and one neighborhood over, the speed walker entered her car, removed the glasses, the blonde wig and the headphones, and tossed them on the passenger seat. She then lit a cigarette before driving off.

CHAPTER 11

Amy looked over her son's shoulder. He sat quietly, staring at the few remaining Cheerios floating in his bowl. She kissed the top of his head and asked, "All done?"

Caleb nodded and Amy took the bowl to the sink. Ordinarily, this would have been Caleb's cue to leave the table and get ready for pre-school. Instead he remained seated, staring at the table.

Amy noticed and left the bowl in the sink without rinsing. She approached her son and stroked his short brown hair. "You okay, sweetheart?"

Caleb's elbows were now on the table, his hands holding up his chin. He nodded into them and tilted his head lower until his palms covered his mouth. Amy reached over and took away one of his hands.

"You don't look okay," she said. "What's wrong with my baby boy?"

She let go of his hand and he immediately brought it back to his face.

"Caleb?"

He shrugged.

"Are you upset about last night?"

Another shrug.

"You know that Mommy and Daddy aren't mad at you after what happened, don't you? We told you that."

Caleb opened both hands a split, and kept his eyes on the table as he spoke. His voice was shaky, trying not cry. "Carrie's mad at me. She says I give her nightmares."

Amy took a seat and began rubbing her son's back. Caleb's eyes became blurred with tears, yet still he would not succumb to a full-on cry. Amy marveled at her son's strength. She was glad his head was down so that he would not spot, and likely misinterpret, the little smile that pride had placed on the corner of her mouth.

"No, honey, that's not what she said."

"I hear her scream at night. It wakes me up."

Amy now rubbed his shoulders. "Yes, Carrie has nightmares, but they're *not* nightmares about what you did to Mommy."

"But she *said* they were."

"No, honey, you misunderstood. Carrie's very confused right now. She doesn't understand why you played that joke on Mommy."

"It was a *stupid* joke . . ."

Amy pulled Caleb into her, and he finally started to cry. "It's okay, honey," she said while he cried into her chest. "Mommy knows you didn't mean to hurt her. Daddy knows that too. Carrie is just confused . . . but Daddy and I are going to talk to her tonight and help her understand."

His brown eyes, glistening wet, looked up at her with a trust and innocence that swelled Amy's heart. "You will?" he sniffed.

She wiped his tears away with her thumbs. "Absolutely. Everything's going to be fine, sweetie—I promise."

He cracked a small smile, and Amy's heart swelled even more. "Who do you love?" she asked.

Caleb turned away.

"Who do you love?"

Caleb turned further away, but she could *feel* his smile growing. She inched closer and started walking her fingers up his back like a spider. "*Who do you love?*" she sang. He started giggling and she immediately snatched him back into her and started tickling him. "*Who?*" she asked again, her son's laughter like a drug.

Caleb eventually squeaked out a "you," and Amy stopped tickling, grabbed his face, flicked her nose back and forth across his in true Eskimo-kiss fashion, and then finished with a real one on his forehead. "I love you too, honey." She palmed the top of his head and rumpled his hair. "Now go get ready for pre-school."

* * *

Amy had just finished tidying up the kitchen when she heard the sound she had expected to hear sooner than later. She walked to the front door and opened it.

"Well look who finally decided to show," she said.

Oscar, who would usually respond with wags of his stump and a brief allowance of petting before hurrying off to all things more important (i.e., food), instead strolled casually inside, walked through the kitchen *past* his food bowl and made his way to his small oval bed in the family room where he immediately curled up and went to sleep.

"Are you kidding me?" Amy said. She turned and looked at his food bowl: a fresh helping of hard and wet food mixed together, prepared only minutes ago—Oscar's absolute favorite. Amy clapped her hands. "Oscar! Come over here and eat." The dog looked up at her for a brief moment before settling back down and closing his eyes.

Amy's chin retracted. "Well that's a first." She shrugged. "Suit yourself. It'll be there when you wake up."

* * *

Amy was two miles from the house after dropping Caleb off at pre-school when her cell phone rang.

"Hi, baby," she answered.

"You won't believe this," Patrick said.

"What?"

"I'm at a gas station downtown. I was five minutes from the office when the coolant indicator came up on the dashboard."

Amy could hear the racket of the gas station in the background. A man was hollering at someone. A loud drill whirred in bursts. She pressed her shoulder over her free ear. "Well that's not a big deal, is it? Maybe you're just low."

"I checked already. I'm not just low, I'm *empty*. The guy at the station says I have a crack in my hose."

"It looked okay to me last night."

"When did you—?" He stopped, sighed.

Amy grinned. Her husband was by far the more juvenile of the two when it came to all things double entendre, but she was in a good mood and couldn't help herself. Biting her tongue and still smiling, she said, "I'm sorry, I couldn't help it."

"It's okay, I'd have done the same," he admitted. "But I have to get this fixed now."

"Okay, so . . . ?"

"I'm gonna be late."

"Honey, I'm sure they'll understand. Just call the office and *ohhh* . . ." Amy trailed off as she pulled up to the top of their driveway. There it was: a puddle of antifreeze the size of a basketball right where the Highlander had been parked the night before.

"What?"

"I see the puddle. The antifreeze. It's at the top of the driveway."

She heard him sigh again. Then more of the whirring drill. Then a horn.

"The hose must have cracked on the way back from Dr. Bogan's. Leaked dry while we slept," he said.

"You didn't notice it when you left this morning?" she asked.

"Did you?"

"Touché."

Amy pulled into the garage and switched off the engine. "It's okay, baby. Just call work, tell them what happened, and that you'll be a little late. No big deal."

"Already did."

"How long is it going to take?"

"Not long—it's only the upper hose."

"Okay—call me when you get to work. I love you."

"Love you too."

Amy hung up and went inside. The first thing she noticed was that Oscar's bowl was still full. She headed into the family room. He was still asleep in his oval bed. She squatted down and started petting him. His eyebrows arched, but he didn't open his eyes. His stump didn't wag.

"What's the matter, buddy?" She scratched behind his head. "Didn't get enough sleep last night?" His eyes finally opened to a meager squint. Amy scratched his head some more. He stood, swayed slightly, then immediately lay back down and closed his eyes. "Too much partying, mister," she said. "Need to watch your drinkin'."

She gave him a final scratch and headed towards her study, the painful irony of her quip coming back in a cruel instant the moment the veterinarian told Amy and Patrick how Oscar died.

CHAPTER 12

The veterinarian left the small white room, leaving Patrick and Amy by themselves.

"I can't believe this," Patrick said. "How could I have been so goddamned stupid?"

"Honey, it's just as much my fault—hell, it's even *more* my fault than it is yours."

"How do you figure that?"

"His behavior. I should have known something was wrong. He didn't even want to eat this morning. And this is a dog that ate a severed finger for God's sake."

Patrick flashed back to Crescent Lake. His family on the dock ready to fish. Caleb pulling what was supposed to be a worm from the bait container. Patrick spotting a fingernail, flinging it to the ground. Oscar approaching the finger and gobbling it up as though it were a cocktail weenie.

He closed his eyes and willed the images away, almost angry at Amy for handing him the reel so he could watch them again. "You couldn't have known," he said.

"But I've heard about it. I know how lethal antifreeze can be to pets," she said.

"You might have known that, but putting the two together . . . ?"

"What?"

"Well have we ever had a dog before? Have we ever had antifreeze leak on the driveway before? Whether you knew about what antifreeze does to pets or not, it isn't a surprise you didn't immediately make the connection. I knew about antifreeze and pets as well, and I never said anything. I could have told you not to let Oscar outside once you spotted the leak."

"But he never *went* back outside after you called. It must have happened right after he followed Carrie out to the bus. He took forever to come back inside. Now we know why. This is more my fault than anyone's." She dropped her head.

He hugged her. "It's nobody's fault, baby. How could you have possibly made the assumption that a puddle of antifreeze was the reason Oscar took so long to head back inside? If we have to blame someone we can blame the stupid car."

"The doctor said if we brought Oscar in immediately they might have been able to save him," she said.

Patrick looked at the oval clock on the wall. 7:15 p.m.

Amy continued. "I should have known something was wrong, antifreeze or not. I should have known—his behavior was so out of character."

Patrick pulled away and looked at her. She had tears in her eyes. "Honey, you can't do this to yourself. It wasn't like he was vomiting or freaking out or anything. You said he was just sleeping, that he looked tired, right?"

She nodded.

"Okay then. I wouldn't have taken him to the vet either. I mean we can blame ourselves—and Lord knows we will—but at the end of the day, Oscar died as a result of an accident."

Amy looked away. When she looked back, Patrick read her mind and his blood ran cold.

"I know what you're thinking," he said, "and you need to stop it *now*."

"What am I thinking?"

"I'm not even going to say it." But he'd be lying if the thought didn't flutter annoyingly around the periphery of his own psyche.

Amy clucked her tongue. "Just more bad luck?"

"Amy, stop. You know as well as I do that this *was* an accident."

She only stared. And it angered him. Yes his fears had indulged the very thoughts she was alluding to, but they were just that: fears. He knew the truth. And they *both* knew Jim was dead. *Both* knew Arty was locked up tight in Pittsburgh somewhere awaiting trial. And yet with that knowledge, after all their therapy, all the progress they had made, *this* is the immediate thing she jumps to after a bump in the road?

Guilt. Yes—guilt was doing it. Her right mind knew that no one could be responsible. "You're feeling guilty," he said. "Your guilt is making you jump to irrational conclusions."

"So you're saying this really is all my fault?"

"No—I already told you, I'm just as much to blame. What I *am* telling you is that this is an accident, Amy. An *accident*." He paused, wondering if he should say it. It was assuredly on both their minds; she had even hinted towards it. But to say it. Oh to *say* it. *Screw this,* he thought. *We are not letting this set us back to square one.* "And I don't mean the kind of 'accidents' we had at Crescent Lake."

Amy twitched a little. Patrick knew it was his wife's indomitable restraint that kept her rooted and composed. It reminded him of the old "two for flinching" game he played as a kid, where someone deliberately swung a hand in your face. If you flinched, two punches were your prize. Keeping still as the hand flew past your face was damned difficult, especially if caught off-guard. Well, Amy was on-guard, but the forever-tainted words that were Crescent Lake were a metaphoric swing from Mike Tyson.

"Okay?" Patrick said.

She did not break his gaze, but her shoulders dropped. "Fine. What are we going to tell the kids?"

"You mean Carrie."

"Well—*and* Caleb." She sighed. "But, yes . . . Carrie."

Patrick took a deep breath, let it out slow. "Well for starters we don't tell her about the antifreeze. We simply tell her that Oscar was old, and . . ." He took another deep breath. "And that it was just his time, I guess."

Amy pulled a face. "Old? He had the energy of a jumping bean."

"Honey, he was a stray. We never did find out how old he actually was."

"He wasn't old enough to die of natural causes."

"Well, yeah, you and I know that. But Carrie doesn't have to."

Amy's shoulders dropped some more and her eyes finally settled. "I know."

"We'll tell her that Oscar was old, it was his time, and that he'll be waiting for her at Rainbow Bridge."

"Where?"

"I'll find it online when we get home. It's a beautiful little piece written by an anonymous author about what happens to pets when they die. It gets me choked up every time I read it." He then added quickly: "But not in a sad way. In a *happy* way. You'll understand when you read it."

Amy sighed. "Okay. Why don't I drop you off at home, you can find the Rainbow Bridge thing, and I'll go pick up the kids at your parents'."

"Sounds good." He held out his hand. She took it, squeezed it, but did not move into him.

"I still can't believe this," she said.

He did not pull her in, just squeezed back and shared her grief with a sympathetic smile. "I know. I can't either."

* * *

Monica sat in the waiting room, a magazine covering her face. The door to the small white room opened and both Patrick and Amy stepped out. The receptionist offered her condolences as they left.

Monica set the magazine on the chair next to her and approached the receptionist. "Sad," she said.

The receptionist, a heavy young girl in blue scrubs, nodded with genuine compassion and said, "Yeah."

"Lost their dog, huh?" Monica said.

The receptionist nodded.

Monica smiled inside. "Shame," she said.

"Yeah," the receptionist whined. "I can't imagine what I'd do if something happened to my baby."

"Me neither," Monica said for some reason.

"What kind of dog do you have?"

"Pug," popped into her head.

"Me too." The receptionist's face brightened. "Boy or girl?"

"Girl."

"*Me too.*" The receptionist was giddy now. "She's the most precious thing in the whole world. Her name's Sophia. What about yours?"

Monica wanted to hit her. To hurt her. This exchange they were having. This . . . *exchange* . . . as though they were the same species.

"Cunt," Monica said.

The receptionist stopped smiling. Softly, she said, "What?"

Monica was not smiling, nor was she brooding. She spoke in a calm, confident manner that held the strange blend of patronizing courtesy. "Cunt," she said again.

The young girl flushed, spoke softer still. "I don't understand."

"What don't you understand?"

"Weren't you . . . weren't you just telling me the name . . . ?"

"The name of what?"

The receptionist cleared her throat, her fair skin looking suddenly scorched by the sun. "The name of your pug."

"I don't have a pug."

"I thought you said—"

"I don't have a pug."

The receptionist broke eye contact, feigned interest in a stack of papers in front of her. Quickly, she said, "Okay, well you have a good day then."

Monica stayed put. The receptionist kept her head down, shuffling the papers aimlessly like an anxious child might twist a lock of hair. She risked a peek up without lifting her head.

Monica was still staring at her.

The receptionist dropped her head into the papers again. There was a silver bell on the counter. Monica hit it and the receptionist jumped. She then started to cry—silent tears from eyes still too frightened to look up, dripping down her full red cheeks.

Monica smiled and left.

* * *

On her way to the car, Monica went for a cigarette but found the pack empty. She cursed, crumpled the pack into a ball, and tossed it to the ground.

"Excuse me."

Monica turned.

A woman, mid-40's, leading a small white poodle by a pink leash. "You just threw your trash on the ground."

"I know," Monica said.

"Well that's disgraceful. You should be ashamed of yourself."

Monica approached the woman until they were a foot apart. She was pleasant when she said: "Say that again?"

"I said—"

Monica slammed her forehead into the woman's face. A dull crack echoed in her ears as the woman's nose exploded. Monica's belly tingled as the woman hit the pavement ass-first and then slowly rocked backwards until she lay like a starfish on the ground. Monica bent over the woman and waved a hand back and forth above her bloodied face. The woman did not acknowledge her. She stared up at the sky, eyes wide and glassy, mouth opening and closing without words like a dying fish. Complete shock.

The only definitive sound thereafter came from the poodle, whose relentless yap seemed its only means of attack as it maintained a guarded distance from the stranger who had floored its master.

Monica glanced at the dog as she brought two fingers to her forehead (it felt wet) and wiped away blood. The stupid woman had bled on her. Monica squatted down and held her bloodied fingers out to the poodle. The dog cautiously approached, sniffed, and then began licking Monica's fingers.

Finished, Monica then guided the poodle with her two fingers towards its still horizontal master's face, where more of the same delicious red goo its palate had been tantalized with was leaking in abundance. The poodle instantly began licking away, and the dazed woman could only lie there and allow it.

Even though she really wanted a cigarette, Monica still drove off thinking today had been a great day.

CHAPTER 13

Patrick and Amy each took a side of Carrie's bed as she sobbed in the middle. Caleb had cried briefly, but it was more a cry of empathy for his sister; he was not as attached to Oscar as she was. He remained in his bedroom while Amy and Patrick took turns soothing their daughter.

"I didn't get a chance to say goodbye," Carrie cried.

Patrick stroked her silken hair. "I know, sweetie. We're so sorry." He glanced up at Amy. Her eyes were already on him, and he'd have bet his left nut she was thinking the same exact thing he was: *Our fault, our fault, our fault.*

Amy took her eyes off Patrick and wiped the tears from Carrie's cheeks. "Have you ever heard of Rainbow Bridge, honey?"

Carrie looked up at her mother with swollen wet eyes and a runny nose. "Huh?"

"*Rainbow Bridge,*" Patrick said. As he had promised Amy, the first thing Patrick had done when they got home was rush to the computer and perform a Google search for "Rainbow Bridge." Sure enough, the anonymous piece appeared on several links. He clicked one, changed a few things—added Oscar's name to make it personal, omitted or substituted words Carrie may not understand—printed it, and now held it in front of his daughter.

Carrie fixed on her father and the piece of paper. "What's that?" she asked.

"Would you like me to read it to you?" Patrick said.

"What is it?" she asked again.

Amy stroked her hair. "It's where Oscar is, sweetie."

Carrie's head whipped towards her mother. *"He's not dead?"*

Patrick felt sick. And once again he felt Amy's eyes leaning on him, sharing the grief. He did not look at her this time; he couldn't. Instead he swallowed (it went down like peanut butter) and focused solely on Carrie.

"No, honey—Oscar is still gone. But he's in a wonderful place. A place called Rainbow Bridge. Would you like Daddy to tell you about it?"

Carrie's head had turned slowly back to her father after he had dismissed the hopeful notion that Oscar was still alive, and her eyes were heavy again. She nodded towards her father and that was all.

Patrick cleared his throat, twice. He almost asked Amy for a glass of water before starting:

"Just this side of heaven is a place called Rainbow Bridge. When an animal dies that has been especially close to someone here, that pet goes to Rainbow Bridge.

There are meadows and hills for all of our special friends so they can run and play together. There is plenty of food, water and sunshine, and our friends are warm and comfortable. All the animals who had been ill and old like Oscar are restored to perfect health.

Those who were hurt are made whole and strong again, just as we remember them in our dreams of days and times gone by. The animals are happy and full of joy, except for one small thing: they each miss someone very special to them who had to be left behind."

Carrie started to cry again. Both Amy and Patrick consoled her until the crying softened to intermittent sniffles. Patrick continued:

"They all run and play together, but the day comes
when Oscar suddenly stops and looks into the distance.
His eyes are bright. His excited body quivers.
Suddenly Oscar begins to run from the group, flying over
the green grass, his legs carrying him faster and
faster.
You have been spotted!

And when you and Oscar finally meet, you cling
together in a gigantic hug, never to be parted again.
The happy kisses rain upon your face; your hands
again caress his
beloved head, and you look once more into the trusting
eyes of your pet, so long gone from your life but
never absent from your heart.

Then you and Oscar cross Rainbow Bridge
together...."

Patrick expected more tears. His delight was off the charts when he saw hope and joy in his daughter's eyes.

"Is all that really true?" she asked. "Oscar's at Rainbow Bridge waiting for me?"

Patrick smiled and nodded. Carrie turned to her mother. Amy smiled and nodded.

Carrie frowned for a moment, her lips tightening. "But when I go to heaven, I'll be *old*. Will Oscar still remember me?"

"Of course," Patrick said. "That's what Rainbow Bridge is all about. Right now he's just playing and having fun and waiting for you to arrive. He will *never* forget you. Ever."

Carrie's frown left. Her tight lips softened and eventually became a smile. "I like Rainbow Bridge."

Patrick didn't know who wrote it, but if he ever found out, he was buying him or her a diamond-studded diamond wrapped in diamonds. "I'm so glad, baby," he said as he kissed her forehead. "You feel a little better?"

"A little," she said. Her eyes were still puffy, but the tears were drying.

Amy took her turn kissing her daughter before she and Patrick tucked her in. When Patrick checked on her ten minutes later, Carrie was already fast asleep. He hoped she was dreaming about Oscar and Rainbow Bridge.

CHAPTER 14

Monica Kemp watched her father appear among the masses at the gates of Philadelphia International Airport. He was not hard to miss. Six-foot-one and two hundred and fifty pounds of solid mass that made men *half* his fifty-two years glance in envy, John Brooks could have easily been mistaken for a retired linemen of the Philadelphia Eagles, returning to his old stomping grounds. A retired linemen who opted for a gym as opposed to a couch after retirement.

Monica, catching glances from young men herself (for exceptionally different reasons), was dressed in posh attire that hugged every curve of her tight figure with a design that allowed teasing glimpses of skin while still maintaining a decent level of warmth during the winter season.

John wore faded jeans, a grey wool coat, and boots.

"You always dress that way?" he immediately asked, setting his bag down to hug her.

She hugged him back and said, "Like what?"

He grabbed her shoulders, held her back at arms length, looked her up down. "*That.* You look like some rich celebrity."

"I *am* rich," she smiled.

He gave her a face. "You're hard to forget looking like that."

"This look," she began contemptuously, "is one of many. I can be a bag-lady with a dead security guard tucked away in a utility closet in under five minutes."

"Scary." He picked up his bag.

She shook her head and could not help but smirk at him. "Such an asshole."

They walked side by side towards the escalators. A man and his teenage son were a step in front, but John shoved them to one side as he and Monica boarded the top of the escalator. The man went to open his mouth, but John need only glance at him before the man snapped it shut.

"What's our itinerary?" he asked as they descended. "When can I see Arthur?"

"That won't be for awhile."

They hit the bottom and headed towards the exit.

"I have to wait until the trial," he said.

She nodded.

They stepped outside the glass doors and stood on the pavement. Men and women in airport uniforms shouted at people who dare ask questions twice. Cars honked and swerved recklessly out of each other's way. A family crossing the strip to get to the arrivals lot on the opposing side was nearly hit by a cab. An officer futilely blew his whistle as the cab sped away, the elders of the family clutching their chests as they watched the taxi disappear up the on-ramp.

"Nice huh?" Monica said. "I've landed in Philly International several times. Believe it or not, it's actually gotten better."

John just shrugged his thick shoulders and began crossing the strip, almost daring a cab to approach them the way it had the family. Fortunately for cab drivers throughout the Philadelphia area, none did.

Monica stopped in front of a shiny black BMW tucked around a small bend in the lot.

"This you?" her father asked.

"For now." She pressed her keychain and the car beeped and flashed twice.

"*For now?*" John grunted and tossed his bag in the back seat. "Hot shot."

They both entered the car. John said, "So I have to wait."

Monica turned the ignition. "I've got plenty to keep us busy until then."

He grunted again.

"We're gonna have a good time, Dad. Trust your little girl."

He threw her a sideways glance and gave a thin smile.

"Much better." She reached to her right, opened the glove compartment, and took out her cigarettes. She lit one and cracked her window.

He waved smoke out of his face. "Come on, can't you wait until we get there?"

"Deal with it, you big pussy."

He laughed as she took the ramp onto I-95 towards Valley Forge.

CHAPTER 15

Once you received a ticket in King of Prussia to enter the Pennsylvania Turnpike, you had only a few hundred feet to make a decision. East and you would find yourself heading towards New Jersey. West and you were heading towards Harrisburg . . . towards Crescent Lake.

The Lamberts were not going to New Jersey. And they certainly weren't going to Crescent Lake. But they *were* headed west. They were headed to a small town outside of Harrisburg, just past Hershey, for a visit with Amy's family.

Every time Patrick had selected west during that brief stretch of turnpike with only two options (and there *had* been a few times since the tragedy, all business-related, which thankfully took him no further than a hundred miles or so), it was absurd to suggest that the memories of Crescent Lake would not come flooding back.

Except it was not the brutal details of his family's ordeal that he remembered most when he chose west. It was not the horrors of watching his children tormented, the knowing that his wife was being sexually assaulted while he remained bound and helpless in the next room, that she was eventually shot and almost taken from him. It was not the horrors of transforming into the monster he had become in order to protect his family: stabbing a man over and over in hopes of reducing him to shreds of tissue and bone (and that, God damn it, was *exactly* what he'd been thinking at the time). Nor was it biting the nose off another man before repeatedly shooting him in the face until the chamber clicked empty and the man was deader than dead. Not the painful, physical rehabilitation in the hospital, or worse still, the mental rehabilitation once they returned home.

It was the *hope* Patrick remembered. He remembered—as clear as he remembered this morning—the hope he had for his family before their weekend trip to the lake months ago. He'd hoped the weather would be nice. Hoped his wife would transcend relaxation during the time away. Hoped his kids would never want to leave. Hoped it would be the perfect weekend with a family he loved more than he ever imagined possible. He hoped it would be a memory they would never forget . . .

Oh, Mr. Irony, he thought, *you can be so fucking cruel sometimes.*

"You're quiet." Amy said.

Patrick took his eyes off the road for a second and smiled at her. "I'm good. Just thinking."

"About what?"

He knew she knew. But he deflected anyway. And when she didn't push, he loved her even more.

"Wondering if you're prepared to play goalie once your dad starts shooting drinks my way," he said.

Amy laughed. "I could be Ron Hextall and my dad would still get a few past me."

Patrick threw her a curious glance. "How do you know who Ron Hextall is?"

"An ex. He was a big hockey nut. Almost as much as my dad. He even tried out for the Hershey Bears."

Patrick grunted.

"Didn't make it though," she said.

"Couldn't cut it, huh?" Patrick said with some satisfaction.

Amy flashed a cheeky smirk. "Oh, I wouldn't say that—he was an amazing athlete . . . rugged . . . hot." Her smirk spread to a grin. "Mmmm, I haven't thought about *him* in awhile—"

Patrick grabbed her knee and she screamed.

Both kids leaned forward in their child seats. Carrie asked: "What?"

"Nothing," Patrick said. "Mommy's just trying to make Daddy jealous."

"Mommy *did* make Daddy jealous," Amy said.

"*Anyway* . . ." Patrick said, getting back on track, "I hope you're prepared to play some solid defense for me this evening."

"Oh stop. You know my dad's idea of male bonding is booze."

"And that's fine, I'll watch him drink all night. Doesn't mean I have to match him drink for drink though."

Amy's grin returned. "Oh yes it does. And God help you if there's a Bears game on tonight."

"You just want me hung over in the morning so you can make my life miserable."

"Correct."

Patrick went to grab her knee again. She saw it coming and dodged. "Too slow."

Patrick placed his hand back on the wheel. "Fine— then you're driving home tomorrow while I sleep."

She shrugged cheerfully. "Okay."

"You suck. Don't expect any later tonight if your dad gets me loaded."

Amy glanced in the back seat. Both kids were oblivious to their father's implication. She faced front again. "Fine by me." She then whispered: "*It's creepy doing it at my parents' anyway.*"

"So what did you do in high school?"

"Oh, so now you *want* to talk about my exes?" She sighed and gazed dreamily towards the roof. "Let's see . . . who to think about first?"

This time her knee had nowhere to hide.

CHAPTER 16

Harrisburg, Pennsylvania

Bob and Audrey Corcoran had company from out of town. The Toyota Highlander parked in their driveway told you that. In this neighborhood, the SUV was an exchange student in a proud classroom of names like Ford, Chevy, and Dodge.

Patrick's decision in choosing the Highlander had little to do with a lack of appreciation for American craftsmanship and more to do with providing conveniences for his family. The Highlander ticked three out of four on that ballot—tons of space, a smooth ride, safe (as far as SUVs go), but damned expensive. And yet he still bought it. Because he could. Patrick had had done well for himself thus far. So had Amy. Their combined income gave their family a comfortable life in a suburb that flaunted fine sushi and martinis with clever names.

And yet when they stepped out of their lavish suburb for journeys elsewhere, there wasn't the slightest hint of unease. Both Patrick and Amy were raised in small blue collar towns throughout the state of Pennsylvania, and despite the amicable friendships formed back in that lavish suburb, which often involved outings at restaurants plentiful with sanctimonious patrons, assuredly there to be seen as opposed to dine, it was not uncommon for Amy and Patrick to go it alone in a quest to seek out less-stifling accommodations—a place that served a steak that wasn't the size of a nickel, a place where you couldn't give two shits about what you looked like, who you saw, and who saw you. Somewhere you could get drunk in public and receive *been there!* giggles from fellow patrons instead of rolled eyes and disgusted clucks of the tongue.

The Lamberts did not resent their luxuries back in Valley Forge; they had worked hard for them. The surrounding school districts were excellent too. Amy and Patrick were comfortable in *both* worlds; it was why they were soul mates. Their marriage wasn't one that saw Patrick sitting on the sofa watching the game, farting and drinking beer while Amy pined to go out to extravagant restaurants and social events. She happily joined him on that sofa. Drank beer and farted with him.

And there were plenty of times when too many nights of sloth tugged at their social needs, and they would happily get dressed up and do the town. The fancy town— the type of town they often resented. It was all about moderation. One type of evening would help them appreciate the other, and vice versa.

So it was no chore to be nestled here in a cozy blue collar neighborhood just outside of Harrisburg. Patrick knew the booze would be poured down his neck the moment he entered, and Amy knew a part of him—despite his flimsy objections earlier—looked forward to it. She would likely let her hair down and have a few too. They all would. Except for Amy's mother of course.

Mrs. Audrey Corcoran did not drink—that was her husband's job. If there was one bit of resentment Amy had concerning her old stomping grounds, it was that the intangibles seemed to remain as traditional as the tangibles. Although never voiced, it was still presumed that the husband was the head of the house, and the wife, while not exactly on her hands and knees scrubbing floors with a pregnant belly, did not hide the fact that her primary purpose was to serve her husband. The husband made the money, the wife took care of him. That's just how it was. Amy didn't necessarily approve, and things were certainly not the same for her and Patrick, but she accepted it. She had no choice. Besides, her father was a good husband. A good father. Rough and stern at times, but good. He could scream and holler like hell, and his fuse could be just as short as the next man's (especially after a few), but Amy could never recall him laying anything but a tongue-lashing on her mother, and the odd spank on the butt to her and her brother growing up.

Carrie and Caleb liked Grandma and Grandpa Corcoran. Not as much as Grandma and Grandpa Lambert, but this had nothing to do with personalities; it was simply a matter of location. The elder Lamberts lived in Conshohocken—a fifteen minute drive from Valley Forge. Harrisburg was an hour and a half away. The kids saw Grandma and Grandpa Lambert more often. Nearly once a week. It was why the elder Lamberts were called to pick the children up after the incident at Crescent Lake. Despite the cabin belonging to the Corcorans, comfort was the order of the day after such a tragedy, and Patrick and Amy had both decided on the spot that it would be better if Grandma and Grandpa Lambert were initially called. The Corcorans showed up the following day after a call from Amy, never once questioning why they hadn't been contacted first. Amy had felt deep down that they understood, and she loved them for it.

Amy stood on the third and final step to her parent's front door. Black iron railings sloped up from the ground and attached themselves to a white brick exterior. Two oval lanterns hung lit on opposing sides of the door. As a child Amy always thought they looked like giant fireflies. This evening was no different, and the nostalgia warmed her heart.

Patrick stood on the second step behind Amy, a hand on the shoulder of each child that flanked him. Carrie picked at a chip of black paint on one of the railings. Patrick tapped her hand and told her to stop. She did for a second, then continued. Caleb shook from a gust of wind and Patrick pulled him close and rubbed his shoulder.

"Did you ring the bell?" Patrick asked.

Amy glanced back at him with a "duh" face. "No, honey—I thought if we just waited out here in the freezing cold, they might eventually come out and greet us." She rang the bell again.

A voice boomed behind the door. "*Who is it?*"

"Dad, open the door, it's freezing."

"*We don't want any.*"

"*Dad!*"

A click of a lock, the sound of a chain sliding, and the door flew open, revealing a man who, if he ever decided to dye his brown beard white, could have doubled for Santa Claus without a hint of scrutiny. His nose was round and red, eyes bunched into slivers from full cheeks and a constant smile, and a frame short and thick with a belly seemingly in its third trimester. He was even wearing a red sweater.

Amy's father barked out what seemed a triumphant laugh, then snatched his daughter into him. He kissed her cheek hard and rubbed his beard against it.

Amy pushed away and wiped her face as a child would. "I hate when you do that!"

He grinned and looked past her. "And who's this big bugger you've got with you? He's a handsome fella. Finally got rid of Patrick did you?"

Patrick laughed. "How you doing, Bob?"

"Gettin' older and fatter." Bob Corcoran then looked over the heads of both Carrie and Caleb, scanning east to west as though searching for something. "Funny," he said,

"I could have *sworn* I saw two little varmints with you when I opened the door." He continued his ruse, searching aimlessly above them. "Guess they ran off. Shame too, 'cause we got cookies and hot chocolate inside."

Carrie blurted out as though jabbed with a stick. "*Grandpa!*"

Bob made a startled face. "Who said that?"

"*Me!*" Carrie shrugged her father's hand off her shoulder and joined Amy's side on the third step.

"Oh, well there you are . . ." Bob bent forward and tapped Carrie's nose with his finger. "Good thing I found you . . ." He stood upright and jiggled his big belly. "I woulda had to have eaten all the goodies myself!"

Carrie giggled, and Bob stroked her cheek before standing up and playing blind again. "Now I could have sworn there was another little varmint roaming around here. Where'd that one go?"

Caleb stayed tight to his father's side but raised a hand. Bob honed in on him. "Ah ha! There he is!" He took a step down and clamped onto the top of Caleb's head. "Guess I won't be getting any cookies at all now that this big fella's on board!"

"I'm big too!" Carrie piped up.

Bob jumped back a step, feigning shock, as though Carrie had suddenly grown a foot. "Darn right you are! I just hope our beds are big enough for you two monsters."

"Dad?" Amy said. "May we *please* come in before we freeze to death?"

Bob Corcoran stepped away from the door, bowed and swept his hand majestically inside. "I'm so sorry," he said. "After you, your highness."

* * *

They all entered. Amy got a second hug (no beard this time), Carrie got hoisted up to the ceiling before her hug, Caleb got a firm "man's handshake" that intentionally shook his whole body and made him giggle, and Patrick got a strong pat on the back followed by an offer for a bourbon. Patrick immediately glanced at Amy and she spun away, her grin visible on the back of her head.

Audrey Corcoran emerged from the kitchen, wiping her hands on the green apron that covered her torso and knees. Her glasses, thick and outdated, magnified the light brown eyes she shared with her daughter. If you asked Patrick, that was the only resemblance between the two. Audrey was shorter, thicker, and her hair was curly and graying. Patrick did not think his mother-in-law ugly, but she was not attractive—certainly no looker like his wife. Even in photos from years past when they were the same age, Amy buried her. And despite his friends' good-natured ribbing, Patrick was certain that the old axiom they loved to drill him with (*"Check out the mother if you want to see what your wife will look like in thirty years!"*) was as false as the teeth he suspected Audrey Corcoran wore. Or so he prayed. Actually, maybe he *would* take that bourbon now, thank you, Bob.

Audrey Corcoran took her turn with hugs and kisses before switching all attention towards her grandchildren, guiding them into the kitchen where copious amounts of sugar were happily administered post-haste.

Bob gave a quick tour of the small house, boasting about the new tile he had recently put in the bathroom. Both Amy and Patrick feigned interest (Patrick touching and gliding his fingertips over the tile with an admiring, approving nod, as if he knew what the hell he was talking about), and when all the formalities were done, the three of them gathered in the den with Audrey still entertaining the kids in the kitchen.

Bob poured Amy a glass of cabernet, then he and Patrick a healthy glass of bourbon, no ice, before sinking into his recliner with a groan and a sigh. Amy and Patrick took the sofa to the right of the recliner. Bob sipped his bourbon, wiped his beard and said to Patrick: "Bears game on tonight."

Patrick threw Amy a sideways glance, and she burst out laughing.

CHAPTER 17

Patrick had graduated from Penn State. He was used to crazed fans. But here now, in this neighborhood bar (which was a neighborhood bar in the truest sense of the word, right down to the aging but cheerful staff who appeared happily confined to an eternal stay in their sheltered box, to fifty years of memorabilia smothering all four walls that would mean jack shit to anyone outside a twenty-mile radius of the place), Patrick was almost convinced that these local residents and their devotion to their Hershey Bears may actually *trump* the phenomena that was Penn State football.

Finding a spot at the bar, or more importantly, in plain view of a television, was no easy task, but Bob Corcoran was as close to a celebrity as one could get at Gilley's Tavern. He was showered with handshakes, smiles, and pats on his thick back as the sea of admirers stepped aside after their greeting in order to clear a path towards two stools at the bar, curiously unoccupied considering how packed the place was.

Christ, I'm hanging out with Norm from Cheers, Patrick thought.

As father and son-in-law settled into their stools, Patrick's attention was anywhere but the television, or what he might want to drink; it was on the eclectic abundance of patrons crammed into the humble bar—kids, the elderly, drunks, business men, manual laborers. People who at any other time in their lives might not even share a friendly glance on the street tonight shared one common bond: their local hockey team. The feeling was instantly contagious. Patrick, who had seen maybe one or two Bears games in the past with an indifferent eye—Bob drunk and screaming at the television back in the Corcoran's home—was now an instant fan. He wanted nothing more than for the Bears to win, to celebrate with these mass of strangers he now felt a connection with. It was a bizarre yet exhilarating feeling that had him wishing Philadelphia fans were not the fickle frontrunners they were so that he might experience this same camaraderie with strangers back home.

"You awake, partner?" Bob asked Patrick with a nudge.

Patrick's daze broke. "Huh?"

The bartender, a balding, heavy-set man with hairy forearms below the curled sleeves of a stained white button-down (complete with damp moons under both pits, rag over the shoulder, and if smoking had not been banned in Pennsylvania bars, Patrick would have bet his life a chewed cigar would have been jammed into one corner of the guy's mouth) was leaning forward on the bar, staring at Patrick.

Bob laughed. "What do you want to drink, space cadet?"

Patrick smiled at the bartender. "Sorry." The bartender nodded back, neither annoyed nor pleasant, just busy. Patrick quickly turned to Bob. "I don't—what are you having, Bob?"

"Whiskey and beer." His curt reply held a self-evidence that was akin to asking Cookie Monster what he wanted to eat.

"That's fine, I'm good with that," Patrick said.

The bartender went to work on their drinks.

"You alright?" Bob asked.

"I can't get over this."

"What?"

Patrick waved a hand around the packed bar. "This. You can literally *feel* the energy in this place."

Bob smiled proudly as though his own child had been praised. The bartender reappeared and placed two neat bourbons and two bottles of beer in front of them. Both men took sips of their bourbon and chased it with a swig from their beers.

"People ever get rowdy?" Patrick asked.

"Oh hell yeah. But no fights. Never any fights."

"Never?"

"No way. You don't disrespect Gilley's, and *especially* the Bears by fighting on a game night. That'd get you black-balled. People would sooner have their legs cut off than be black-balled from Gilley's on game night."

Patrick smiled and took another sip of his beer. "I wish Philly fans could take a cue from this place."

"What you got in Philly aren't fans . . ." And then, as though he had somehow timed his statement to coincide exactly with the start of the game, the bar erupted as the Hershey Bears skated onto the ice. Bob grinned and shouted: "*These* are fans!"

Patrick smiled wide. He then followed his father-in-law's lead and drained his whiskey (the grimace that instantly began the moment the abundance of warm whiskey hit his throat had *no* chance of reaching his face in a place like this, at a time like this—sorry, face), clinked bottles necks with him, then happily doused the fire in his throat and belly with a deep swig of his icy beer.

Bob let out a satisfied gasp, wiped his beard, and immediately signaled the bartender for an encore.

* * *

The Hershey Bears defeated the Norfolk Admirals 4-1 in an experience Patrick wouldn't soon forget. He screamed and cheered until his voice was raw, drank a heck of a lot (although he did have the presence of mind to ask the bartender to find a subtle way to stop sending him whiskey with his beer the moment Bob finally left for the toilet), and seemed to befriend every resident of Harrisburg, Pennsylvania, in the span of three hours.

With the game now an hour gone, the patrons at Gilley's were filtering out. Some stayed behind, recapping the highlights of the game with mimic vigor, and some stayed to chase the liquid buzz they had so delightfully acquired during all three periods.

Bob Corcoran was part of the latter. He waved the bartender over and motioned to both he and Patrick. Patrick eyed the bartender, who returned a faint nod before returning moments later with two beers and only one whiskey. Bob instantly leaned into the bar to object, but Patrick put a hand on his shoulder, patted it, and pulled him back.

"It's alright, Bob, I'm fine with just beer."

"That's about the fifth time he dicked you on whiskey." His voice was slurred, his eyes rimmed red and droopy.

"It's fine, Bob, really. Besides, someone's gotta drive us home."

"Call Amy, she'll pick us up."

Patrick raised an eyebrow. "Just how well do you know your daughter?"

Bob burst out laughing. "She's got you by the short and curlies, doesn't she?"

"If I call her now and ask her to pick our drunken asses up, she will."

Bob gulped his whiskey like it was iced tea and looked straight ahead. "That's my little girl . . ." He took a big pull on his beer, gasped, ". . . tough as nails."

"You're preaching to the choir, my friend."

Bob went suddenly quiet, his garrulous, drunken manner vanishing in an instant. "I've still got her," he said.

"What?"

Bob turned to Patrick. His eyes, still droopy and red from drink, now shined with a glassy coat of tears. "I've still got my daughter. I've got her because of you."

Even if Patrick had the words—and he didn't—he knew they'd never find a way out of his mouth. At least not at this precise moment. The incident at Crescent Lake had already been discussed. Some details withheld, some not. Hugs and more hugs had been given. Audrey Corcoran had cried. Amy's older brother Eric had cried. But a man's man like Bob Corcoran? Crying? Patrick wasn't sure a man like Bob even knew how. Yet here he was, on the verge of real tears. Sure, the excessive booze was the likely catalyst, but since the day he met the man, Patrick imagined it would take a freaking crack pipe to burst his father-in-law's dam.

"Bob, I..."

Bob put his thick hand on Patrick's shoulder and squeezed hard. The dam cracked, and tears rolled down his cheeks, catching on his beard. "I've still got her because of you."

The words came to Patrick now. "You've got her because of me *and* her. She saved my ass just as much as I saved hers."

Bob took his hand off Patrick's shoulder and wiped his eyes. "Yeah?"

The Lamberts had told the Corcorans about Amy holding a kitchen knife to Maria Fannelli's throat, threatening her life in front of Arty Fannelli in exchange for the freedom of her family. Unfortunately, the threat had backfired and resulted in gunfire—Arty shooting both Amy *and* his adopted mother. Amy had survived the wound thanks to Patrick's appearance moments later, where he dispatched both Arty *and* Jim Fannelli in such brutal fashion that he often shuddered at the memory, sometimes genuinely questioning whether or not he had truly done such things to another man.

But he was getting side-tracked now, letting his mind slip into that dark place he was constantly trying to avoid. He was here, at Gilley's, about to divulge something to his father-in-law that he had never told anyone before. Amy would be pissed, but so be it. It was necessary. Yes he was buzzed, but he was not drunk like Bob. And Patrick felt— or at least his buzz felt—that Bob needed to know what his daughter had done. How if it had not been for Amy, his entire family would likely be dead. Patrick may have done the grisly work at the end, but Amy sure as *hell* did some grisly work of her own. Work that many would think even grislier—at least most men would.

"If it wasn't for Amy, I would have never been able to take those two guys out," Patrick said.

Bob gave a final wipe of his eyes and gulped his beer. He burped under his breath and said, "You mean when she pulled the knife on the mother? Made that threat?"

"No—before that."

Bob frowned.

Patrick swigged hard on his beer, second-guessing his decision to divulge.

Fuck it.

"She stuck a big metal nail file into one of the brother's balls. That's how she was able to get free."

Bob's face dropped.

Patrick leaned back on his stool, steeling himself for whatever may come . . . and it sure as hell seemed to take its time.

And then finally, thankfully, an incredulous smile. "She did *what*?!"

Patrick, relieved Bob's reaction was seemingly one of delight, still found himself leaning forward quickly for a respectful shushing. Bob Corcoran was the antithesis of subtlety, and this was *not* a conversation that needed broadcasting. Patrick put a subtle finger to his lips then patted the air. "Keep it down, Bob. This is stuff even the media doesn't know about."

"Why didn't she tell me any of this?"

"I imagine it's not the kind of thing you voluntarily tell your father."

"Tell me everything." Bob was beaming, and Patrick felt some discomfort from his father-in-law's sudden zeal for the grisly report. Still, the man wanted to know, and his response to the previous information could have been a hell of a lot worse.

So Patrick told as much as he could, with as little detail as he could. After all, despite Bob's insistence on hearing "everything," and despite Bob's apparent show of pride for his daughter's ass-kicking abilities, Patrick was sure Bob would *not* want to hear the intricate details of how Amy was forced to give Jim Fannelli a blowjob. Her secret intention of biting his dick off. The plan backfiring horribly. Amy then finding herself being forcefully stripped and bent over a dresser where the savior nail file clattered free, magically presenting itself for insertion into said nut sack. Patrick did, however, happily tell Bob that after Jim doubled over, gripping his wounded balls in agony, Amy hoisted a heavy lamp over her head and brought it crashing down onto Jim's skull, knocking him "the fuck out."

Bob threw his head back and barked a laugh that made the remaining patrons jump. He slapped Patrick's shoulder. "Then what?"

Patrick shrugged. "You *know* the rest. She went downstairs, held the knife to the mother's throat . . ."

"And then got shot," Bob said flatly, his smile gone.

Patrick nodded slowly, confused. He couldn't read his father-in-law's sudden shift in demeanor. *Surely it's not accusatory?* he thought. *Not after the emotional thanks earlier?*

"That's right," Patrick said.

"And then you showed up."

Patrick sipped his beer and nodded.

"You were upstairs?"

"That's right. I was bound to a chair. Carrie cut me loose. We were *all* heroes that night, Bob. Me, Amy, *and* the kids."

"So you were cut free, came downstairs and . . . ?"

Bob already knew this part, knew practically all of it, but much like an unforgettable night on the town, the desire for a second telling—and likely a third, and a fourth, and so on—seemed to change the status of events from utterly horrific to a celluloid gallantry. Patrick didn't like it. It was all starting to play back in his head with a cruel clarity that defied time or alcohol—right down to the last spatter of blood and flesh that flecked his face as he murdered one man, and critically wounded another. His earlier hopes of avoiding the dark place were fading. He needed to end this soon. Amy's bit had been told. No need to go further.

Bob nudged him. "And . . . ?"

Patrick took a deep breath, let it out slow, and in what was nearly a whisper said: "And I took care of the guy."

"*Two* guys," Bob said. He seemed proud again. Proud of his son-in-law.

"Well not at the same time. It was kind of one after the other."

"How'd you do it?" Bob asked.

"What?"

"How'd you take 'em out?" He held up a pair of fists and made a playful fighting gesture, nearly toppling off his stool in the process.

Patrick reached out with a hand to steady him. "You know this already, Bob. Hell, it seems like the whole *country* knows."

Bob smiled. "Yeah, but no one knew about Amy and the nail file in the balls . . . "

Patrick sighed again. "I stabbed one and shot one," he said quickly.

Bob cocked his head, made a disappointed yet friendly face that asked for more. "*Come on . . .*" he crooned.

Give him something, Patrick. Christ, anything so we can squash this.

Patrick leaned in and whispered: "I bit one guy's nose off."

Bob's drunken slits for eyes popped wide. "You *what?*"

Patrick looked around, saw that no eyes were on him, then lifted his shirt and showed the thick purple scar on his abdomen. Bob's eyes zeroed in on it like it was a pair of tits. "I had just been stabbed; I was full of adrenaline . . . so I just grabbed the guy, bit his nose off, then threw him to the floor and shot him to death."

"Jesus . . ."

Let it go now, Bob. Please.

"I think you need a drink," Bob said.

Patrick held up his beer. "Got one."

"A *real* goddamned drink. A drink to pay my respects to you for saving my daughter's life."

Bob's voice was loud and it made Patrick cringe. He scanned the room quickly to see if anyone had heard. With the exception of a few locals clinging to the bar, and a big man sitting alone with a beer at a corner table, the place was fairly empty. No one seemed to have heard.

Patrick leaned into Bob's ear and spoke softly. "Okay—one last drink. Then I'm taking us home."

Bob slammed his hand on the bar and hollered for two shots of whiskey. The bartender gave Patrick a subtle glance, and Patrick returned a subtle nod. The bartender shrugged and poured their shots.

Bob pulled out a wad of bills.

"I got this, Bob," Patrick said, shifting on the stool and reaching for his own wallet.

Bob waived his hand away with the grace of a gorilla. "No way. You're in *my* town. Your money's no good here."

Patrick didn't object.

Let him pay. Just do the damn shots and go. Speaking of which . . .

"Can I have the keys to the car, Bob?"

Bob looked genuinely surprised when Patrick asked. "What for?"

You don't tell a man of Bob Corcoran's ilk that he's too drunk to drive. You'd be better off telling him he had a little dick. Patrick knew that. He weighed a response and settled on: "Because you had more to drink than I did."

Bob grinned. "I can make it home from Gilley's with my friggin' eyes closed."

Patrick chuckled and switched to a more placating approach. He had worked as a bouncer during his time at Penn State, and knew through experience that reasoning with a drunk was a lesson in futility. "I'm sure you can, but if we got pulled over . . ."

Bob shook his head, still grinning. "We'll take Woodmere; we'll be fine."

The bartender brought the drinks, and Bob used the diversion to cut the conversation. He snatched one of the shots, handed it to Patrick, and then grabbed his own, spilling some onto his hand. He raised the glass. "To my son-in-law!"

Patrick quickly leaned into his ear again. "Let's just leave it at that, okay, Bob? Nothing about Amy or what happened."

Bob shrugged, and then once again, louder now: "*To my son-in-law!*"

Patrick was not about to wait and see if Bob would leave it at that. He raised his glass and downed the shot in an instant.

Bob gulped his own, gasped, and then slammed the glass down on the bar. He turned to Patrick and pulled him in for a titanic hug, nearly pulling Patrick clean-off his stool. "Thank you, son," he said in his ear. And then again when they separated, both hands cupping Patrick's face as though he meant to pull him in for a kiss: "Thank you, son."

Bob Corcoran had called Patrick *son*—something he had never done before. Son-in-law, yes, but never just son. Patrick knew Bob was very drunk, but he also knew true gratitude and sincerity when he saw it. It made his response all the more difficult; a lump had suddenly grown in his throat. "You're very welcome," he managed. Patrick then allowed a brief moment to pass before donning a playful smirk. "Now . . . can I please have the keys to the car . . . *Dad?*"

Bob studied him.

Patrick knew he had him on the ropes, and so he added—in the dreadful tone Amy both loathed and loved—a little Harry Chapin's "Cat's in the Cradle" with extra special emphasis on *Dad* and *borrowing car keys*, to finish him off.

Bob finally gave a hearty laugh and admitted defeat. He dug into his pocket and handed over the keys. "You are one piece of work, my boy," he said. "Just promise me no more singing."

"Yup—you're definitely Amy's father."

Both men laughed then stood from their stools. Bob knocked his over and started laughing harder. Patrick picked up the stool, thanked the bartender, and guided his swaying father-in-law out of Gilley's.

* * *

John Brooks sat alone at a corner table. He'd heard the entire conversation between Bob Corcoran and Patrick Lambert: Earlier he had planted a bugging device beneath the bar ledge where the two men had hunkered down. He had planted the device when Patrick had gotten up to use the toilet and when Bob was busy shouting at the television, just after the Admirals had scored their one and only goal.

The conversation was minimal at first. And even if it *had* been substantial, little could be articulated in John's invisible ear-piece. The roar of the patrons was as good as a scrambler. But that was okay. It gave him time to study the pair; watch their body-language; observe their habits. Spot faults. Weaknesses.

When the game ended and the crowd began to filter out, John heard more. He heard and watched it all: the Santa-looking fucker salivating with pride while Patrick told him how his cunt-of-a-daughter had jammed a nail file into his dead son's balls. How Patrick had then bitten his son's nose off before shooting him to death. How he had stabbed Arthur repeatedly.

John sensed apprehension from Patrick when he had relayed the events of that night. If it wasn't in his voice, it was in the way he shifted on his stool as he spoke. Truly he did not derive any pleasure from re-living the tragedy, contain any sense of pride for what he'd done. And that was good. It was a chink in the man's armor. It showed a conscience. John Brooks' only brush with conscience was when he had to spell it.

"You want anything else?" his waitress asked.

John shook his head and handed her two twenties. More than enough. "Keep it."

"Thanks, hon."

He waited for the waitress to disappear into the back before he stood and approached Bob's stool. The bartender was wiping down the counter.

"Never misses a game does he?"

The bartender glanced up. "Who Bob? Not a chance. Rain, sleet, or snow."

John gave a smile. The bartender turned and started wiping the opposite end of the counter. John reached under the bar, removed the bug, and stared at it with bottled rage as though the tiny device in his palm was more culprit than transmitter for the atrocities he'd heard tonight.

He ignored the bartender's goodbye as he left.

* * *

John Brooks sat parked in Gilley's lot, engine idling on a battered Dodge Dakota, bought and paid for in cash upon arrival in Harrisburg. He was playing back the conversation between Patrick and Bob on the hand-held device he had used to record the give and take. When it came to the part about Amy sticking a nail file into his dead son's balls, John hit rewind, and played it again. He listened, immediately hit rewind, and played it again. During an attempted fourth run, John Brooks had a momentary lapse in restraint and squeezed until the device splintered in his hand, setting free a slice of plastic that pierced deep into his palm. He tossed the broken device to the floor, but did not pull the plastic shard out. He pushed it *deeper* into his flesh, swirling it, teasing his nerve-endings. The pain was good; it gave him a sense of control again. He pushed harder on the plastic, blood streaming down his arm, warm and sticky, pulling his sleeve to his skin like cling wrap.

Better now, John Brooks pulled the plastic shard from his hand, wiped his bloodied palm on his jeans, and flicked the shard out his window like a cigarette butt. He pulled away from the bar humming "Cats in the Cradle."

CHAPTER 18

Patrick felt Amy straddling him but refused to open his eyes. He knew he'd be looking up at a devious grin that was more than ready to talk loud and jar the hell out of the bed that was his hangover crypt.

"I know you're awake," she said.

One eye creaked open. "Please let me die in peace."

She yelled: "What's wrong, baby?!"

The one eye snapped shut. He grimaced and moaned.

She bounced on his chest. "Wake up, sleepy head!"

Both eyes creaked open this time. "Why do you hate me?"

Her grin was out of a cartoon. "Good morning, my love. How do you feel?"

"You *know* how I feel. What time is it?"

"Almost ten. I let you sleep in."

"Thank you. Any chance I could go to eleven?"

"My dad's been up since six."

"*What?* He was *hammered* last night. How the hell was he up so early?"

"Up and playing with Carrie and Caleb by seven."

"The guy's a freak. He had twice as much to drink as I did, and I feel like crap."

"Yeah, well, even though I take no pride in saying this, my father is what you'd call a functioning alcoholic."

"He wasn't functioning too well last night. He wanted to drive home, you know."

Amy hung her head for a second. "Yeah . . . he's like that. Taking his keys is like taking his machismo."

"It's dangerous. He was really drunk, Amy. I mean, I'll admit, I had a buzz going, so I'm not trying to act all high and mighty here, but to think of him behind the wheel, in the state he was in . . ."

Amy rolled off Patrick's chest and took the other side of the bed. She seemed to have no other answer but: "I know." After a brief silence that Patrick wished would last an eternity, she asked, "How *did* you get his keys?"

Patrick rolled onto his side and faced her. "I sang to him."

"Oh *God*. No wonder he gave them up. Poor Daddy."

"It worked didn't it?"

"Did you have fun?"

"I did. It turned out to be a really good time. Things got a little serious towards the end though."

"I thought the Bears won?"

"No, I mean between me and your dad."

Amy made a curious face and propped herself up on one elbow. "What do you mean?"

Patrick had no intention of telling Amy he had divulged the taboo specifics about Crescent Lake to her father. Sure, he had to worry about Bob getting loose lips after a few too many somewhere down the road, but that was a bet he had no interest in handicapping right now, especially when it felt like his head was in a vice.

"He started getting pretty emotional about what happened to us. He thanked me for saving your life. I told him you saved mine just as much as I saved yours. He liked that. He even cried."

"My father *cried*?"

"Yup. He even called me 'son.' Twice. I got a little choked up myself."

"Aww, baby . . ." She snuggled in close and kissed him on the nose. "I'll tell you what, I'll leave you alone until eleven, then we have to get going. Caleb has an early appointment with Dr. Bogan tomorrow."

"I fucking *love* you."

She laughed, kissed him on the nose again, and left. Patrick was snoring a minute later.

CHAPTER 19

John Brooks sat on the edge of the motel bed, cell in one hand, Hershey Bears game schedule in the other. He dialed his daughter's number.

"Hello?"

"It's me. We're good. You'll need to be here no later than seven tonight."

"You sound eager."

"I am eager," he said.

She laughed. "See? I told you we'd have fun."

He conceded with his usual grunt.

She laughed again. "Seven tonight."

John hung up and checked the bandage on his right hand. The wound on his palm was still raw from last night. The rage suddenly flickered. He made a fist, squeezing until blood leaked through his massive knuckles. He opened his hand, looked at the Bears' schedule again, wiped blood on it. His rage finally simmered when he entertained feeding the bloodied paper to Bob Corcoran tonight.

CHAPTER 20

Monica stepped out of Gilley's Tavern and lit a cigarette. She stuck the butt between her full lips and wrapped the lapels of her overcoat tight around her neck with both hands to shield the cold.

Idling ten yards away, John Brooks waited anxiously in his daughter's new BMW. Given their current surroundings, the recently acquired Dodge Dakota that looked as if it had been rolled down a mountain would have been far more apt in passing the anonymity test, but for tonight's performance the spotless new BMW was a necessity: It would be playing the distinguished role of bait.

John tapped the horn. She nodded towards the car and took a final drag of her cigarette, flicked it to the ground where it sparked orange then smoldered. She strolled unassumingly towards the car and entered.

"He bought me a drink," she said after shutting the door.

"Oh yeah?"

She smirked and began fiddling with the heat. "Sure did, the dirty old bugger."

"How much time left in the game?"

"Not much. He's pretty loaded already. If he has a few more after . . ."

"He will—especially if the Bears win."

"Can't see how'd they lose. They were beating Adirondack six to nothing when I walked out."

John allowed himself a small smile. "Perfect."

* * *

Just past midnight, Bob Corcoran eventually swayed his way out of Gilley's Tavern. John nudged his daughter. Monica sat up, instantly alert.

"About fucking time," she said.

Father and daughter watched their drunken target manage his way towards a blue Ford Taurus. He dug for his keys, dropped them, bent down, and nearly tumbled scooping them up.

"Wasted," Monica said.

John nodded, immediately hit reverse, and screeched out of the lot. They needed at least a two minute head start to prepare.

Monica eyed her father playfully as he drove. "You better hope he takes Woodmere, old man."

John shot his daughter a look. He knew Bob Corcoran's type—drinking and driving was not oil and water to a man like that. It wasn't lemonade either. It just was. You drank—because that's what you do—and you needed to get home. Designated driver? Fuck off. I can get myself home, thank you.

Still, no matter how hammered, you weren't *completely* stupid. You could take the quick route home, the route on the main road with dozens of street lamps and a cop aching to fill a quota around every bend, or you could be a clever little drunk and take the long way home down Woodmere Road . . . just as Bob had planned to do with his son-in-law last night.

Not long after his stay at Gilley's, John had spent a good portion of last night becoming familiar with Woodmere. He quickly found that the road held an allure for drunk drivers that was the epitome of a paradox: It was narrow and rough, lined with steep wooded embankments, and despite high beams, it was like finding your way through a cave with a dying torch. Yet after fifteen tactical runs last night, John Brooks had passed *zero* cars. Certainly no police. None hiding in dark corners either. And it made sense too: Why fish in a lake with no fish?

Ten more runs were completed today to keep sharp. He'd passed only two cars this time, both going ten miles under the speed limit in broad daylight.

And so now he did not, as his daughter joked, *hope* Bob Corcoran would take Woodmere. He was sure of it.

"How sad it is when the delusional student feels they've surpassed the teacher," he said to her.

"Not nearly as sad as when the archaic teacher refuses to accept the fact that the seedling will ultimately grow taller than the one who planted it," she retorted.

"Keep dreaming, little sapling."

She grinned at him.

He hit the accelerator and succumbed to a grin himself. It was fucking Christmas.

CHAPTER 21

Bob Corcoran took Woodmere Road, just as he had done every night he left Gilley's Tavern for the past umpteen years. Drunk or sober—and he was indeed drunk—he knew every hair-pin turn before he made it, every blind hill before he hopped it, every weathered stop sign before he slowed toward it. He knew the notorious embankments where even his drunken pride could not dispute anything over fifteen miles an hour. What Bob didn't expect was for there to be a flashing car stopped twenty yards ahead, on the edge of one of those embankments. And he *never* would have expected such a car to be what looked like a brand-new BMW.

"Talk about a hard-on in church," he said aloud.

He was hesitant to stop in his drunken state, but when a young woman who might have been the sexiest little thing his old eyes had ever seen stepped away from the car and waved him down, Bob pulled his Taurus right on over.

* * *

Monica had to hand it to her father; he had called everything to a tee. She watched the blue Taurus slow to a stop a few yards in front of her BMW, and waited for Bob Corcoran to exit.

"Now you *must* be lost, young lady!" he called the moment he stepped out. He swayed on approach, the hazard lights on Monica's car flashing rhythmic shots of a bearded smile as he got close. "Wait a second now," he said, scratching his beard. "You were at Gilley's earlier, weren't you?"

"Was I?"

Bob scratched his beard again, smiled and said, "Ma'am, you can be sure I wouldn't forget a face like yours."

Monica stepped closer, into the light. "That's very sweet."

"Well, like I said, ma'am, a fella isn't likely to forget a woman as sexy as you." He looked at her car. "So I imagine you're lost? Not many folks would come through here in a beemer."

Monica leaned against the BMW. "Bimmer," she said.

"Come again?"

"It's actually referred to as a bimmer. BMW *motorcycles* are called beemers. But I wouldn't expect ignorant white trash like you to know that."

Bob's smile slowly faded. He blinked several times. "I'm sorry?"

Monica shrugged. "I called you ignorant white trash. And I don't think your wife would appreciate you hitting on a woman half your age. How would you like it if my father hit on Amy?"

If Bob Corcoran was confused before, his drunken head now looked close to short-circuiting. The pinnacle was when Monica dropped Amy's name. He went to speak, but John placed a sudden hand on his shoulder and spun him.

"That's not a bad idea," John said. "I could finish what my son James started with her."

It was all too much to register right away. Drunk or sober, Monica had expected the pause button to be hit. Expected Bob Corcoran to stare at her father, mouth open a crack in a state of wonder, brow furrowed as the pieces tried to come together. The fact that he was drunk only kept the pause button on longer.

John slapped him.

The blow rocked Bob on his heels. He quickly gathered himself and threw a right haymaker. John side-stepped the punch with ease, and Bob's momentum nearly pitched him over.

"Whoops!" John said.

Monica laughed.

Bob growled, turned, and dove at John's waist for a tackle. He had a better shot at charging through a stone wall. John stood his ground and let the drunken man literally bounce off his massive frame. Monica laughed again. John glanced over at her and smirked. He then jerked Bob to his feet and spun him into a rear choke with his right forearm.

Bob struggled and flailed, but had all the success of a rat in the coiled grip of a python. Monica continued laughing, felt the familiar tingle warming her belly.

"Bob?" John said calmly into his ear. "Bob, hold still. If you keep trying to fight I'll break your neck."

Bob stopped, panting wildly.

"Good boy. I don't want to hurt you if I don't have to," John said.

Bob garbled a question beneath the weight of John's arm: "*The fuck do you people want?*"

John took a long cleansing breath before answering. "We want revenge, Bob. You see . . . Patrick, Amy, hell, even little Carrie and Caleb—they *really* fucked with the wrong family out there by Crescent Lake."

It all sunk in. Bob screamed and spat, stomped and kicked, reached and clawed behind him to get at John's face. His fight was admirable, but John still held onto him with no effort, and Bob's tank soon emptied. His back sank against his assailant in exhausted defeat. Monica laughed some more, but stayed put. This one was her dad's.

"We have to set things right, Bob," John said. "Your cunt-of-a-daughter and cock-sucking son-in-law may have been lucky enough to visit hell once and return . . ." He gritted his teeth. ". . . but they sure as *fuck* won't do it again." He tightened his grip on Bob's neck, placed his lips to his ear. "And you know what? I think I will do as my daughter suggested. I *will* fuck Amy. Your wife too."

John kissed Bob on the cheek then snapped his neck.

CHAPTER 22

Back home, Patrick was dreaming about an alarm clock he couldn't shut off. When Amy's second elbow drilled into his side, coupled with a muffled yell into her pillow that sounded like "*get it!*", Patrick abruptly left the dream world and discovered the stubborn alarm's real-world accomplice was the telephone. He pawed blindly on his nightstand until he found it.

"Hello." His voice was soft and crackly.

"Hi, Patrick. I'm sorry for calling so late."

Who was this? Was this Amy's mother?

"Audrey?" he said.

Amy rolled over.

"Yes, I'm sorry for calling so late," she said again, "it's just that Bob hasn't come home yet and I'm starting to get concerned."

Patrick propped himself up on an elbow and looked at the alarm clock. The green-lit numbers were fuzzy. He blinked hard, stretched his eyes wide, and then looked again. 2:30 a.m.

"Maybe the game went into overtime," he said, swallowing a yawn. "The owners usually let him stay after hours. Did you try calling Gilley's?"

"I already did. They said he left hours ago."

Patrick sat up and clicked on the light. Both he and Amy squinted. There was only one thought in his head now, and he wondered if Audrey shared it with him. Likely, she was not concerned with infidelity—in the waveless world of someone like Audrey Corcoran, infidelity, even if performed smack in front of her, would be quietly repressed until its status inexplicably reached the level of fiction—so what other line of thinking did that leave? Yes, Patrick was sure they were sharing the same fear. But he was damned if he knew how he'd voice such a concern. So he passed it off to Amy and handed her the phone.

"It's your mom. She says Bob hasn't come home yet."

Amy took the phone and sat up. "Mom?"

Amy listened, spoke, listened, spoke. Her voice was calm and decisive. Patrick watched his wife and thought about how life eventually came full-circle. Amy was the mother now; the nurturer, the one keeping it together. But then he had always suspected it had been this way in her family.

"Just call the police, Mom," she said. "I'm not saying anything's wrong, but still, it's our best option right now. Daddy probably just went to another bar to celebrate after the game."

Patrick wondered if Amy believed that.

"Just call the police and tell them what you told me. They all know Daddy; I'm sure they'll find him."

Amy talked and listened a little more, nodding with reassurance into the phone as though her mother could see her. "It'll be okay, Mom. Call us back the second you hear something. I'm sure Daddy's fine."

She hung up and looked at Patrick. Patrick was wearing his apprehension.

"What are you thinking?" she asked.

"I don't know. I'm afraid to say it."

"Say what?"

"Come on, Amy. I told you he wanted to drive home the other night."

"My father's been driving home drunk from that bar since I was a kid."

Patrick couldn't help but snort. "And?"

Her eyes dropped, the flawed logic evident on her face. "I'm just saying I doubt that's what it is."

"Look, baby, I hope it's not that either. I hope he *is* at another bar. It's just . . . I don't know what else to think."

Amy looked away. She fiddled with the phone. It rang in her hands and she jumped. She answered immediately. "Mom?"

Patrick watched his wife, studied her face—praying it didn't droop or pale or burst into tears. He wanted a smile, a sigh of relief, an: *"I told you everything would be okay, Mom."* But all he got was another:

"Okay, well call us back as soon as you hear—"

And then it suddenly came to him like the name of a forgotten song. Patrick blurted: *"Woodmere!"*

Amy's head whipped towards him. "What?"

"Tell her to call the police back and ask them to check Woodmere Road," he said.

"Mom, hold on a second." She covered the receiver with her palm. "What are you talking about?"

"The other night your dad told me he would drive us home on *Woodmere.* At least that's what I think he called it. Do you know a Woodmere Road?"

"Yeah—it's out of the way though. It's all backwoods and—"

"Well that was the point. I told him he shouldn't be driving because he might get pulled over, and he said we'd be fine if we took Woodmere."

Amy put the phone back to her ear. "Mom? Call the police back and have them check Woodmere Road." She listened then said, "I know, but can you just do it please?" She listened a little more. "Okay. I love you. Call us back."

* * *

Patrick was in the bathroom taking a leak when the phone rang an hour later. He cursed his bladder and forced the stream out as quickly as possible, its splash making it difficult to hear Amy in the bedroom.

Finished, he hiked up his boxers and rushed into the bedroom. Amy was still on the phone. She kept saying "okay" over and over in an even tone, and did not acknowledge Patrick standing eagerly in the bedroom doorway.

She eventually said thank you, hung up, looked at Patrick and said, "My dad's dead."

CHAPTER 23

Patrick and Amy arrived at the Corcorans' just after 6 a.m. There were two squad cars out front, lights flashing on one of them. An officer was leaning against the cruiser with the flashing lights. He stood and adjusted his uniform when Patrick and Amy approached.

"Morning. You Amy and Patrick Lambert?"

Amy said, "Can I go see my mother?"

The officer nodded. "Yes, ma'am. Go right on in."

Patrick thanked the officer and led Amy up the three short steps to the front door. He glanced at the black iron railings with the chipped paint and remembered telling Carrie to stop picking at them. The man they were waiting to see that night was now dead. As a child, Patrick always wished for a time machine whenever his luck went south. A way to go back and change things. It was a silly wish that even as a child he knew held impossible merit, yet still he wished for it all the same.

He found himself wishing for it now. Just as he had done after the incident at Crescent Lake. Just as he had done after Oscar died. Lately, Patrick was getting really tired of wishing for a fucking time machine.

The couple entered and spotted Audrey Corcoran sitting on the sofa, being consoled by a female officer. Amy immediately went to her. The two embraced and began crying.

A third officer came out of the kitchen holding a cup of coffee. He extended his hand and Patrick shook it.

"Sergeant Bennett," he said.

"Patrick Lambert." He motioned towards the sofa where Amy was still hugging Audrey. "That's my wife Amy—Bob's daughter."

Amy glanced up at Bennett, and the sergeant immediately took off his hat and nodded.

Amy kissed Audrey, whispered into her mother's ear, then stood and joined Patrick and Sergeant Bennett. The female officer resumed comforting Audrey.

"What exactly happened?" Amy asked, wiping away tears.

The sergeant motioned the couple to join him in the kitchen. Patrick and Amy both nodded and followed.

"So what exactly happened?" Amy repeated.

Sergeant Bennett was curt but professional. "Your father went off one of the embankments on Woodmere Road. Car was upended when we found it by the river."

"And the other car?" Patrick said.

Bennett shook his head. "As of now, it looks like no other car was involved." He nudged his chin towards the kitchen window. It was fairly dark when Patrick and Amy had arrived, but dawn was now seeping in. "We're going to have a better look in an hour or so to confirm."

"I don't get it then," Amy said. "If there was no other car...?"

Sergeant Bennett glanced at Patrick as though looking for support.

Amy said, "Look, I know he was drinking, okay? But, my dad, he . . ." Bennett opened his mouth to speak, but Amy suddenly continued, cutting him off with: "He was a *good drunk driver*." She laughed pathetically at her own words. "I know how insane that sounds, but my dad—" Her voice cracked and she stopped.

"Mrs. Lambert," Bennett began, placing his coffee cup on the kitchen table. "I knew Bob. He was a good man. But he did like to indulge. Nothing wrong with that . . . except for when it's time to head home. Now, I know you're upset—and you have my deepest sympathies, you truly do—but I'm sure a rational woman such as yourself can agree that you can only play with a loaded gun so many times . . ."

Amy looked at the floor. When she lifted her head, she asked: "You're still going back to look again though, right? Back to Woodmere?"

"Yes, we are. But, Mrs. Lambert?"

Amy kept her eyes on the sergeant but said nothing, just folded her arms across her chest: a guarded gesture for him to continue.

"I'm quite certain we won't find anything new," Bennett said. "I don't say that to upset or discourage you— I say it because I owe it to you to be honest. I don't want to instill any false hope. Your father's blood alcohol level was very high. Woodmere Road, as I'm sure you know, is notoriously treacherous—*especially* at night. Now if you take those facts into consideration and look—"

"How did he die?" Amy interrupted.

Patrick squeezed Amy's shoulder and said, "Amy . . ."

She shrugged him off. "How did he die?"

Bennett said, "Your mother already made a positive ID, Amy."

"Why can't I know how my father died?"

"His neck was broken," Bennett said evenly.

Amy took a sharp breath and looked away. Patrick tried putting his hand back on her shoulder. She let him this time. Still looking away, Amy gave one small appreciative nod and said, "Thank you."

With a sympathetic face, Bennett said, "You're welcome." He put his hat back on and tipped it to both Amy and Patrick. "I'll be in touch. I can reach you here?"

"Yeah," Patrick said.

Bennett frowned for a second. "Audrey mentioned she had grandchildren?"

"They're with my parents," Patrick said.

Bennett tipped his hat again and left the kitchen. Patrick could hear him give more condolences to Audrey in the living room before he told the female officer they were headed back to Woodmere. He heard the front door open and close. The house was now exceptionally quiet. Amy's head was down, her eyes glazed—likely trying to process events that could not and would not be processed for some time.

"Baby?" Patrick said.

Amy blinked from her daze but didn't look at him. "I should go be with my mother," she said, beginning to walk past him.

Patrick stopped her march and pulled her close. His chest burned with helplessness as she sunk into him and began to weep. Patrick wished for the goddamned time machine again.

CHAPTER 24

Father and daughter sat across from one another in a small diner in Harrisburg—Monica drinking coffee, John shoveling down enough food for three men. They were both tired and needed rest, but the drug of adrenaline from last night's event was still surging; sleep would be too difficult right now.

"You're not going to eat anything?" John asked, his mouth crammed with eggs and toast.

Monica shook her head and sipped her coffee. John shrugged and continued eating. Last night had gone incredibly well. As individuals they excelled at what they did. As a team they were downright frightening. Staging the scene, posing the body, eliminating all traces, all tracks. It seemed almost effortless, and with a result that was flawless: According to the message that had recently come over Monica's scanner, Bob Corcoran had killed himself by driving off an embankment on Woodmere Road. He had been intoxicated. End of story.

"I want to find out about the funeral," Monica said.

John raised an eyebrow, chased a mouthful of pancakes down with milk. "You think we should risk it?"

Monica looked disappointed with her father. "There's no risk," she said.

"I'm not saying we couldn't get away with it—we've just got a lot of shit on our plate. We need to be looking ahead."

Monica lifted her coffee and spoke just before the rim touched her mouth. "I'm going to the funeral."

John took a bite of his eggs and nodded. He understood. Watching them mourn, tasting their pain, knowing you were the one responsible for it all. The act of killing Bob Corcoran was only foreplay.

CHAPTER 25

There was not much to say on the ride home. All the facts were in, and Patrick certainly wasn't about to lecture Amy on the dangers of drinking and driving, not if he expected to get laid again before his 40th birthday. Besides, Amy was grieving, but hardly ignorant to the truth; she knew the fault lay with her father.

Patrick had sensed anger from Amy when her brother Eric arrived from Akron shortly before they left. He'd sensed it from Eric too. Nothing was blatantly voiced between the two siblings; they shared this anger with the occasional glance or passive-aggressive comment intentionally flown over their mother's radar, yet it appeared in flashing red to a receptive codependent like Patrick, and the message on this radar had been quite clear: Their mother was not strong. It was their father's responsibility to look after her, his recklessness had needlessly taken his own life and left Mom alone. And they were pissed, and sad, and pissed.

Patrick periodically laid a subtle eye on Amy as he drove, gauging her face, trying to determine if his instincts were correct. For now, he read only sorrow. He wondered when anger—voiced this time—might appear. Would there be a third phase after that? Acceptance, maybe? No. Amy was strong. Christ, strong was an insult. His wife was a goddamned oak. He was fairly certain she had accepted her father's death shortly after hearing it confirmed by Sergeant Bennett when he'd phoned back earlier this afternoon. Perhaps anger and sorrow were the only two phases here, one as easily interchangeable for the other, depending on the day.

He placed a hand on her leg. "How you doing, baby?"

She stared straight ahead as she spoke. Her voice was neither angry nor sad. It was almost a dreamy, lazy tone, like talking after a long day at work.

"I don't know," she said. "The usual, I guess."

"The usual?"

She shrugged. "Well how do people usually feel after a parent dies?"

"I would imagine it's different for everybody."

She shrugged again. "I guess."

"So how are *you* doing?" he said.

She looked at him. "I don't know." Her voice was still lazy, lacking inflection. "What do you want me to say?"

Truth be told, Patrick wasn't sure. Usually Amy didn't need prodding in voicing her anxieties. He rubbed her leg softly, and in a tone even softer: "You don't have to say anything if you don't want to. Just checking on ya. That's all"

She rolled to the left and laid her head against the seat. "I'm just so drained." She closed her eyes. "We've been through so much . . ."

Patrick rubbed her leg some more. "I know."

They drove the rest of the way home in silence.

CHAPTER 26

Bob Corcoran was cremated while Patrick and Amy were back in Valley Forge, collecting Carrie and Caleb.

Not the most devout of families, the Lamberts still periodically spoke of God and heaven with their children. Apparently Grandpa Corcoran had been called up to heaven sooner than expected to help God with making angels laugh. Patrick had thought up that little gem on the spot, and it did the job in satisfying Caleb with a perfectly logical explanation. Carrie was not so easily swayed. Her trademark skepticism shot forth an unrelenting supply of dreaded *why?*s and *but why?*s after each explanation, and it took a deeper pocket of gems from Patrick, and finally, some exasperated *just becauses* from Amy before Carrie finally accepted the fact that Grandpa Corcoran wasn't coming back.

The rest of the trip back to Harrisburg was quiet and sad.

CHAPTER 27

A modest church in Harrisburg was stuffed to capacity. Bob Corcoran was indeed a popular fellow. The service over, Amy now felt a pinch of guilt in thinking the condolence line would never end. She would have to accept a million sympathies from a million strangers—beer-and-whiskey-swilling men a good number of them, the cold truth that they could have easily been the ashes in her father's urn never once flickering across their bulbous, red faces—before she could go home and get some sleep.

Patrick and Amy stood close together, Eric and his boyfriend of ten years next to them. Audrey at the very end. Carrie and Caleb were wandering about the church, interacting but not playing with the other children attending. Somehow their young minds, although not yet grasping the gravity of the situation, sensed that playing wasn't right today.

Patrick leaned into Amy's ear before the next sympathizer approached. "How you doing, honey?"

They were holding hands and she squeezed his and whispered: "Tired."

Patrick looked at the remaining line; it was still deep. "Your dad was a popular guy."

Amy only nodded.

A balding, heavy-set man approached. Patrick bent to Amy's ear again. "That's the bartender from Gilley's," he said.

Amy turned her back to the man and said to Patrick: "Maybe I should thank him for getting my dad drunk enough to kill himself."

"*Honey,*" Patrick quickly said with a hush face, his eyes tracing the church to see if anyone had heard.

Amy gave an *I don't give a shit* shrug, turned back towards the bartender, and did not acknowledge his gratitude.

More people came and went down the line. Amy glanced at her mother. She was not crying. Denial? In shock? Flipped her damn cookie? Amy moved a step behind Patrick, leaned forward and tugged her mother's elbow. "How you doing, Mom?"

Audrey Corcoran smiled. "It's a lovely turnout, isn't it? Everyone loved your father."

Amy said, "It's okay to cry, Mom."

Audrey looked almost shocked at the suggestion. "Oh, Amy, stop it."

Amy knew Patrick overheard. "What the hell?" she whispered to him after returning to his side.

"Honey, she *did* cry. She's been crying for days," he said.

"But this is his *funeral.*"

Patrick rubbed the small of her back. "Everyone grieves differently."

Amy took in Patrick's words and looked at her mother again. She seemed proud. Beaming, almost. And it all kind of made sense. Her mother lived in a bubble—nothing bad ever truly seeped in; she wouldn't allow it. Whenever bad news was given, responses were automatic, uplifting, and painfully empty.

"*Everything'll be fine, honey, you'll see.*"
"*I pray for you every night, honey, you'll be fine.*"
"*Oh well . . . what're you gonna do? . . . it'll be*

fine . . ."

When Amy and her family had returned from the ordeal at Crescent Lake, it was her father who had made the fuss.

"Goddamned sons of bitches, hope they rot in hell. Try and take my babies from me . . ."

Audrey had remained mostly quiet, save for a few of her automatic responses here and there. Most of her attention had been geared toward the children—likely because they were not capable of popping her bubble. Their youth did not threaten with questions or comments that demanded sincere feedback. They were happily distracted with sugar and television. And so was Audrey.

So looking now, Amy realized her mother was not in denial or shock or flipping her cookie. She was being herself, living in her world-less world. And so Amy reached behind Patrick and tugged her mother's elbow again. "Sorry, Mom," she said. "It *is* a lovely turnout."

Audrey smiled at her daughter as though she had complimented her dress, then turned to face the next person in line.

Amy took a huge breath, cheeks puffing, then let it out slow. She glanced towards the large oak table by the exit. People were standing around the table, smiling and pointing at pictures of her father. Some were bent forward signing the grandiose guest book Patrick had bought.

"People are signing the guest book," she said to him.

Patrick smiled down at his wife and kissed her forehead.

A big man stepped in front of Amy and Patrick. He was an inch or two shorter than Patrick's six feet-three inches, but had Patrick well beat on shoulder width and chest depth. Amy thought the big man looked uncomfortable in a coat and tie, as did many of the other men. But unlike them, whose buttons and seams struggled to contain bellies and chins, this man looked as if he could tear his attire clean off his torso with nothing more than a quick flex of his muscles.

The big man took Patrick's hand first. "I'm sorry for your loss," he said. Patrick thanked him, and the big man pulled Patrick into a powerful hug, patting his back hard.

Patrick laughed and politely forced his way out of the man's arms. "How did you know Bob?" Patrick asked.

"Gilley's," he said.

The man took one step left and fronted Amy. He held out his hand and Amy took it. It was thick and rough. "I'm very sorry," he said to her. And then suddenly, the man began gnawing on a fingernail on his free hand, grimacing as he worked. "Sorry," he said once finished. "Hangnail."

Amy fought a puzzled look. She exchanged subtle glances with Patrick who looked equally puzzled. The big man moved down the line.

"Hangnail?" Patrick whispered to Amy.

"Dad's friends," she whispered back. "He looked about as comfortable in that suit as he would a straightjacket."

Patrick smiled. And then his eyes dropped and he blushed. Amy instantly saw why. Ordinarily she would have been hit with a twinge of jealousy, but on this occasion, Amy granted her husband a pardon. The woman standing before Patrick was stunning. Even Amy felt like blushing.

The woman extended her hand and Patrick took it. She then extended the other hand and cupped Patrick's hand whole. She looked deep into his eyes and Patrick blushed again. Now Amy was a little jealous.

"I'm so sorry for your loss," the woman said. "I truly am." She kept hold of Patrick's hand, still staring into his eyes, unblinking.

Amy immediately put her arm around Patrick's waist and pulled him close. *Mine!* "How did you know my dad?" Amy asked.

The beautiful woman let go of Patrick's hand and turned to Amy. "I met him a few times at Gilley's," she said, taking Amy's hand now, a one-handed, limp offering, the antithesis of what she'd given Patrick. "I'm sorry for your loss."

"Thank you," Amy said with a quick, lipless smile that appeared just as suitable to follow *"bitch."*

The beautiful woman returned a smile, hers full and true, and then left the line and headed towards the exit. She stopped by the guest book, signed it, and left.

"You can roll your tongue up now," Amy said.

"Oh stop," Patrick said.

"You were blushing."

Eric leaned over. "If I was straight . . ."

Amy shot her brother a look.

Patrick smirked at Eric and then rubbed Amy's neck.

She shrugged him off. "Whatever. I'll tell you this though: no way that girl goes to Gilley's. She'd stand out like a Victoria's Secret model at a sci-fi convention."

Patrick laughed. "Maybe your dad was having a little thing with her."

Amy spun towards Patrick, her scowl like a knife slashing at him. She saw on his instantly somber face that he regretted his words; his censor button was on the fritz again. She loved—and always would love—his dry wit, but she was still jealous of the beautiful woman, and, well, this was her father's funeral for Christ's sake. A few months later? Maybe she'd smirk or chuckle at his quip. Right now? Patrick was knocking on the front door of the dog house, and by the look of him—the appropriate face of a shamed dog through and through—he knew it. And she knew he knew. And even if she wasn't really *that* pissed off at him, she was going to make him sweat for awhile.

"I'm sorry," he said.

She ignored him and checked on her mother again.

* * *

John Brooks and his daughter, Monica Kemp (no disguises today—flawless dark eyes, flawless dark hair, appropriate yet alluring dress painting her flawless body black), walked towards a beaten Dodge Dakota parked in the church's lot.

"You think you're pretty funny, don't you?" she said.

"What?"

"Hangnail?"

John began pulling at his tie. "I was going to ask if she had a nail file I could borrow."

Monica smirked. "I know you were. I'm glad you showed some restraint. That would have been a little *too* obvious, Daddy-O."

They entered the Dakota. Monica lit a cigarette and pulled deep on it. "That was fun," she said.

CHAPTER 28

Patrick wondered if he was still a potential resident of the dog house during the quiet ride back to Valley Forge, which, odd as it may seem, was just fine by him. He really didn't know what to say to his wife. Amy's father was officially dead and gone. Bringing up the hows and whys of his death would be unnecessary and taboo. Bringing up the good times, the good memories, was too soon. The only thing that seemed logical was a periodic rub of the knee followed by a soft: "How you holding up, baby?" These mostly went unanswered, and sometimes got a shrug followed by a long look out the window. Despite the lack of receptivity, Patrick knew they still meant something. Amy had once told him, after a particularly difficult episode with one of her girlfriends (Patrick had given a simple response to her dilemma, as though the answer was self-evident), that he didn't always need to fix things—sometimes she just wanted him to *listen*.

This was no easy task for Patrick. He was the fixer in the relationship. His own trepidations and worries be damned, Patrick would always assure his stressed wife that all was well and that he would fix things, even if he didn't have the slightest freaking clue how. He did not do this with robotic replies from someone like an Audrey Corcoran, but with logic (even if Patrick sometimes had trouble believing that same logic himself) and reassurance. And it always seemed to do the job: Amy would feel better.

This dynamic of their relationship was never more apparent than during the ordeal at Crescent Lake. In hindsight, the writing was on the wall from day one: so much unbelievable bad luck leading up to the tragedy that it simply *couldn't* have been a coincidence. Amy had been wary. She'd wanted to leave. Patrick had assured her—again, despite his own misgivings—that all was well, that they were just having shitty luck, that he would protect her if worse came to worst. But by the time worst did come around, it was too late—Arty and Jim Fannelli had sunk in their pre-meditated claws, and hell was about to ensue.

Patrick liked to think he'd learned from that experience. A hell of a way to learn, but learned nonetheless. Always trust your gut. If it feels wrong, it is wrong. After being discharged from the hospital in Pittsburgh months ago, Patrick and Amy stopped for gas on the ride back to Valley Forge. A young man had asked Patrick if he went to Penn State because of the blue lion emblem on the back of their Toyota Highlander.

Arty Fannelli had kindly asked Patrick that same exact thing during their first encounter.

So Patrick answered the inquisitive young man with a right hook that sent the kid tumbling into an unconscious heap. A bit over-the-top, but he'd rather knockout a million maybes than let one yes fuck with his family again.

Trust your gut. Trust your gut when it comes to the bad stuff. That was the lesson learned. And learned he did.

So what do you make of this then, Patrick? he thought. *How does your gut feel?*

If he was honest with himself, he would admit that a fleeting thought *had* entered his mind earlier. *First Oscar and now this? Is it happening again?*

But that was impossible and he knew it. No need to reassure himself or Amy on this one. Oscar was their fault.

Bob was Bob's fault. There was no need to convince Amy that the boogeyman hadn't returned; he just had to reassure her that the pain of losing her father would dissipate over time, he would always be there for her, and that he loved her very much. And he welcomed that—it was a cake walk compared to the hell he had to deal with months ago.

He rubbed her leg again. This time she gave him a small smile. Patrick felt confident the dog house would have a vacancy tonight.

CHAPTER 29

For the first couple of days, blame had been in abundance. This brought the anger. To Amy and her brother Eric, what had happened to their father felt no different than suicide—his reckless behavior had been selfish, leaving those who loved him behind to suffer in its wake.

It didn't last long though. Anger soon melted into sadness, and Eric and Amy were left with the acceptance of who their father was. Bob Corcoran was not a difficult read. His manner, his lifestyle, his beliefs—all on the table the first five minutes you met him. A fortune teller's wet dream. And it didn't take a fortune teller to see the potential for such a tragic end to the man. Perhaps only Audrey Corcoran was blind to it. Intentionally blind of course. Patrick wondered—fascinated by the mind's ability to block a reality that consistently smacked you in the face—if Audrey would now, in quiet moments of reflection, admit that what had happened to her husband was something she could have seen from miles away, years ago. Or was she such a deeply repressed, suppressed, (*depressed?*) woman that Bob could have blown his freaking head off in their living room, only to have Audrey immediately and forever blame the gun and not the finger that pulled it. Yes—Patrick believed that. If Audrey had a gripe with anyone in her little bubble she called life, then it was not with her beloved Bob. It was with the booze. The booze was responsible. The booze was as deadly as the damned gun. Never mind Bob's choice to always drive drunk. To always take Woodmere. If it wasn't for the booze, those two factors would have been immaterial. The *booze* was responsible.

Patrick remembered seeing a segment on some news show a few years back. A twenty-something kid had blown his head off with a shotgun because his character had been killed off in one of those popular online video games. The segment then milked grieving shots of the mother, blaming the video game for "killing her baby." Of course the mother was suing the mega-successful game for millions, but that wasn't the point was it? The game had killed her only son!

When the news crew had gone to the boy's apartment following the tragedy, Patrick could distinctly remember one member of the crew holding his nose upon entry, and it wasn't the remnants of a dead body that had the crew member wincing. It was pizza boxes, burger wrappers, Chinese takeout cubes, half-eaten anythings stacked as high as book cases and spread throughout the small apartment, forming a revolting maze of sorts. The boy had been a shut-in. Had been living in this squalor for months. Job? He had quit his job six months ago so he could play the game day and night. *Where was mom during all of this?* Patrick remembered wondering. *Did you drop in on him at least ONCE during his deep spiral downward? Christ, a blind stranger could have entered the apartment and at least SMELLED something was amiss. But no, you're right lady; it was the video game that killed your son. His shit was wrapped very tight. His mental stability was as sturdy as an teen's first boner. The GAME is what put that shotgun into his mouth and blew his head clean off his shoulders. Yup. The game.*

"Hey! Are you listening?" Amy said.

Patrick snapped to, the hazy images of the news program disappearing. "I'm sorry, what?"

Amy shook her head and gulped the last of her coffee. She turned her back to him and got a refill from the pot on the kitchen counter. Patrick leaned against the kitchen bar, watching his wife's back, knowing he'd been caught in one of his notorious daydreams. He was a cerebral guy, Patrick was. Amy loved that about him. Quite often, however, it made him drift when drifting was not appropriate. Now was one of those times.

Amy faced him again. She was drinking the coffee black, something she usually never did. "I was saying how Carrie and Caleb don't seem to realize what happened to their grandfather."

"I think that's somewhat normal at their age, honey."

Amy frowned. "Carrie sobbed for days when Oscar died."

"That's a little different."

"*What?*"

"I'm not saying it's more *significant*, I'm saying it's *different*. Try and think like a seven-year-old for a second."

"A dog dying is more important than a grandparent?"

Amy's grief was blocking any chance at rationalization. In any other situation, with any other family in the same boat, Patrick felt she would have comprehended what he was getting at without further elaboration.

"Of course not. You know that, and so do I. But does a seven-year-old child who spent every conceivable moment with said dog know it? She saw Bob how often? Once a month? Maybe less? She's too young, baby. Remember what Dr. Bogan said about stages of development in children? The ego-centric phase? Carrie's world stops at the tip of her nose. Oscar was part of that little world. You can't expect her to absorb the severity of something like this. She's not capable yet. It's way beyond her reach at this stage of her life. And of course Caleb is even less capable."

"So you're saying if it was your parents, then they'd be sad?"

"Did I say that?"

"You implied it."

"Well if I did, it was unintentional. And for the record, no—I still think Carrie would have wept more for Oscar than my parents if they were to have suddenly died."

Amy put her coffee cup down, covered her face, and started to cry.

Patrick pulled her close. He had been waiting for this. Amy had yet to truly let go. He hugged her tight and periodically whispered reassurances to her. She sobbed into his chest for a long time.

CHAPTER 30

Pittsburgh, Pennsylvania

Arty in his holding cell, lying on a cot, staring at the ceiling, not seeing the ceiling, seeing only the woman who visited him in the hospital months ago, fantasizing about what she had planned, believing she was the real deal the moment he looked into her eyes, certain when he got word of his adoptive mother's death, and then, *absolutely certain* when he got the card in his stack of mail this afternoon.

The game wasn't dead. He should have known better.

Jim's death had deflated him. The news of his adoption had all but crippled him. For a time he had to face the likelihood that he was not unique, was not an exception to the rules. Facing life in prison was a cold beer and big tits next to this revelation.

But now. His sister. The woman who could be Jim's twin. Monica, she called herself. In that one brief encounter between the two, she gave him hope. She would resurrect the game. Arty no longer cared about being an exception to the rules. He was *still* unique. *Still* special. How could he not be? Lying half-dead in a hospital, facing an eternity in prison, your brother dead, your life over, and then . . . *and then*, a visit from an angel, assuring him he would have his vengeance. Assuring him that he was *not* done; there *was* a future.

Arty was not a religious man, but he believed in evil. He *was* evil. And to believe in evil he supposed one must believe in good. Was it God and Satan? He didn't know, and he didn't care. But he knew something wanted him to continue his work. Something wanted him to continue the game. And if there was a God, he was betting it wasn't him.

He rolled off his cot, lifted his mattress, took out the card, and read it again. It was a sympathy card. The officers couldn't make sense of it when it had arrived. They had brought it to Arty, asking him what it meant. At first, Arty hadn't known either. The officers were wary—there was no return address on the envelope. The card wasn't signed.

"It's fucking addressed to you in a county jail. How could you not know what it means?" they'd asked.

Arty had just shrugged. He truly didn't know. He didn't know anyone named May. And if he didn't know May, he certainly didn't know her father.

The officers stuffed the card back into its envelope and winged it between the bars, hitting Arty in the shoulder. *"Well enjoy it. It's all the fucking mail you got today."*

Arty had read the card, frowned, and then set it aside. He didn't get it. He had been in the holding cell a few weeks since leaving the hospital and had gotten all sorts of strange mail during that time. Admirers of his work, death threats, love letters—all straightforward in their intent. This was the first that made no sense. Why the hell should he care if some woman named May lost her father? The messenger hadn't even left a name. *A whacko,* he had eventually surmised. *Some schizo who would probably swear in court that his hamster told him to mail the damn thing.* Satisfied, he'd picked his book back up, found the dog-eared page, and resumed reading. He got one sentence in, then slammed the book shut, snatched the card, and read it again:

May.
May's father.
May's father had died.
There was a line about the importance of family.
Family was underlined twice.
May.
Amy.
May = Amy.
Amy Lambert.
Amy Lambert's father had died.
Family was underlined twice.
This was a message from his sister.
His sister had killed Amy Lambert's father.

And now Arty sat, reading the card again and again, caressing it, *smelling* it. Trying to imagine how it was done, how badly the Lamberts were suffering from the loss. The flutter in his belly was so intense it teased his throat, threatening to bring up this afternoon's lunch.

He carefully placed the card in its home beneath his mattress, lay back down, and resumed staring at the ceiling, not seeing the ceiling.

Unique. Special. How could he not be?

CHAPTER 31

6:30 p.m. Patrick entered the mudroom and couldn't kick his shoes off fast enough. Exhausted, tie already pulled loose, briefcase feeling like a fifty pound dumbbell—it wasn't Miller time, it was *Glenlivet* time. Neat, healthy, and straight to the face. Oh and keep the bottle nearby, please and thank you.

Caleb leapt from his hiding spot behind the dividing wall of the family room and attached himself to his father's leg once he came into view. It was ritual, but Patrick always feigned surprise, looking as though he had just gotten the fright of his life. Caleb looked up at his father with loving brown eyes, a big giggling grin, and suddenly Patrick didn't need that scotch as much as he thought. He dropped his briefcase, bent and picked up his son.

"How's it going, brother-man?" he said.

Caleb told his father that he had drawn a picture of a giant bug eating a car in nursery school today. Patrick kissed his son, smiled, and wondered how Dr. Bogan would interpret that one. He set Caleb down and glanced over at Carrie in the family room. His daughter lay smack in front of the TV, hands under her chin, eyes wide and reflecting the screen's images, seemingly oblivious to her father's arrival.

"*Hello, Carrie,*" Patrick hummed, expecting no reply. He nearly fainted when she muttered a "Hi, Daddy" in return, although taking her eyes off the TV was simply out of the question.

"Where's Mommy?" he asked.

Caleb pointed through the kitchen and into the adjoining room towards Amy's office before flopping next to his sister in front of the TV.

"Why don't you guys see if you can actually press your eyeballs to the screen?" Patrick said as he walked towards Amy's office. Both kids blanked him.

Amy swiveled away from her computer screen and faced her husband when he entered. She tilted her chin up as he bent forward for the kiss. He noticed an empty martini glass next to her computer.

He nudged his head toward the glass. "We doing happy hour?" His tone was pleasant, but he could not hide his curiosity. Amy was no virgin when it came to drinking, and it was not unusual for her to have a glass of wine or two in the evening, but a martini? Patrick knew she liked them, but he struggled to recall a time when she ever drank them at home.

"What?" she said. Her cheeks and nose were flushed, and it wasn't from embarrassment. Patrick wondered if that empty glass had seen a refill or two before he got home.

"Nothing," he said. "I just can't remember the last time you drank a martini."

"I always drink martinis."

"Yeah, when we go out . . ." he said. "I've never seen you drink them at home."

"Well so what? I felt like one." She swiveled back to her computer.

Was he making a big deal of this? Her father's funeral was only a few weeks ago. Maybe this was all a normal part of the grieving process. His day at work had been rough and he was looking forward to a stiff drink himself when he got home. Did that make his curiosities hypocritical? Maybe. Except it was not uncommon for him to drink scotch at home. It *was* uncommon for Amy to drink martinis at home.

Stop, Patrick, he thought. *You're thinking too much. You ARE making too big a deal.*

Perhaps he should join her? Or would that be playing the enabler? No—joining her would show he *wasn't* making a big deal, that it was okay to have a martini or two or *three* if she wanted. Hell, as long as they didn't get wasted in front of the kids, he started to think he *would* join her.

Patrick began rubbing her shoulders. "I'll tell you what. How about I go fix you another, pour myself a scotch, and then I'll come back in here and treat your feet to the massaging of a lifetime."

Amy still faced the computer, he continued kneading her shoulders. "What do you think?" he asked.

"The kids haven't eaten yet," she said.

"I'll make dinner. I'll do some chicken nuggets with mac and cheese. They'll be in heaven."

He leaned in and kissed her neck, waiting for her to turn towards him with a devilish smile and then plant a good one on his lips after the irresistible offer to fix her another drink, cook dinner for the kids, and the crème de la crème: the foot massage.

Instead she shocked the hell out of him when she stood and said, "No, that's okay," and left the room, taking the empty martini glass with her.

When a stunned Patrick eventually wandered back into the family room, Amy was sitting in front of the TV sipping a fresh martini. She glanced over at him and asked: "Are you still going to do dinner?"

Patrick mumbled something that was meant to be "yes," then turned and waded into the kitchen. Now it kind of felt like a big deal.

* * *

Amy lay in bed, an open book propped on her chest. The words were fuzzy from too many martinis, and she couldn't concentrate. But it didn't matter. The book was a prop, a visual aid to let her husband know that she was sober enough to read (she wasn't), and that she didn't feel like talking (she didn't). She knew her behavior this evening was odd, and for the moment, even *she* didn't understand why she had behaved the way she did. But she could figure that out tomorrow, and more importantly, they could talk about it tomorrow. Tonight was all about getting her drunken butt to sleep ASAP with as little drama as possible. She had considered rolling to her side and faking sleep, but Patrick would know she was faking. He'd know.

So she lay there, words of the book in and out like a camera trying to focus, listening to Patrick tucking in Caleb, and then Carrie. Listening to Carrie asking to leave her door open, then to leave the hall light on. Listening to Patrick say yes to the door, no to the hall light. Listening to Carrie fake a frightened moan. Pleased to hear when Patrick called her bluff, told her to go to bed, and switched off the hall light.

Patrick walked into the bedroom. She kept her eyes on the book but watched him from her periphery. He did not look her way. Was he pissed or worried? They had not truly talked at dinner; their attention was overtly diverted to the children, making sure food was eaten and manners obeyed, even when it was and they were. An occasional question about his day at work from Amy was asked, and a reply about the rigors of the upcoming presentation, now one month away, was given. There had been no inflection in either of their voices. They were both empty, seemingly rehearsed through years of mundane routine. Except Amy and Patrick didn't have that type of relationship. There was no boredom. Routine, yes—they had a family after all, so some routine was unavoidable. But there were no mundane, ritualistic motions repeated day in and day out as they pined away for a secret life from one another. They *were* each other's life. This awkwardness at dinner may have passed without scrutiny in the eyes of a stranger, but for those that new the couple well, it screamed conflict.

Amy watched Patrick undress down to his boxers and toss his clothes in the hamper. He still did not acknowledge her when he disappeared into the bathroom. She heard the faucet running, Patrick brushing his teeth, gurgling with mouthwash, spitting, running the sink a final time. Here he comes.

Patrick stepped out of the bathroom and joined her under the covers. He lay on his back and looked at the ceiling. *Wait for it,* Amy thought.

"So what's up?" he asked.

Amy paused a moment, then laid the open book flat to her chest and turned towards him as though she had just been interrupted in the middle of an engrossing scene.

"What?"

"You can put the book away now, Amy. I doubt you can even focus on the damn words."

She loved him, but for a split second she wanted to whip the book down onto his face for knowing her as well as he did. Instead she tossed it to the floor.

"Why are you making a big deal out of a few martinis?" she asked.

He rolled to one side and faced her. "You know it's not that—I offered to make you another one."

"So then what's the problem?"

"I want to know why you blanked my offer. I want to know why you're pissed at me."

"I'm not pissed at you."

"Then what? I offer to make dinner, make you another drink, and then offer you a *foot massage* and you turn it down? Then you go and make your *own* drink and wander off to watch TV? What am I to think?"

"Well *don't* think, okay? For once, just don't think."

"What's that supposed to mean?"

"Just don't . . . overanalyze everything so much."

"Amy, I . . . fine, I'll admit, I tend to overanalyze sometimes, but come on . . . even a caveman would be biting his fingernails over this."

Amy thought of the Geico commercials with the prejudice towards cavemen, and before she could stop herself, her drunken mouth let out a giggle.

Patrick frowned. "What the hell is wrong with you?"

"I'm sorry, I'm sorry." She forced her smile down. It surfaced again for a second, and then she pressed her hand to her face and got it back down for good.

There was a long, very awkward pause.

"So are we going to talk or not?" he asked.

Now she rolled to him and they faced one another.

"Patrick, I swear there's nothing wrong, okay? I'm not mad at you. I don't know why I did what I did." She shrugged a shoulder when she added: "I wanted a drink. A *strong* drink, you know? I was edgy and feeling a bit down. I was thinking about all the bullshit we've been through this past year, and then I was thinking about Dad.

"Your offer was very sweet, and you know ninety-nine times out of a hundred I would have gladly taken you up on it. But tonight I just, I don't know . . . I wanted to be left alone I guess. Maybe it's a part of grieving." She rubbed his shoulder and looked sincere when she added:

"Baby, I swear I'm not mad. Please leave it at that. I just needed some alone time. I know that's unusual for me, but tonight I needed it. That's all. I still love you as much—*more*—than I ever did. I swear everything's okay."

Patrick's eyes crinkled with a soft smile. He ran his fingers through her hair. "Okay," he said. "I just love you so much. I was worried."

She rubbed his shoulder some more. "I know." She leaned in and gave him a small kiss. "Goodnight."

Amy rolled away from him and clicked off the light on her nightstand. She stayed on her side, away from him, and wondered if he would try and cuddle up to her. She was conflicted just then: She wanted him to because it would mean she had convinced him all was well, and had put the matter to rest, and she didn't want him to because she still felt like being left alone.

Patrick rolled onto his back, reached over and clicked off his own light. He remained on his back and didn't try to cuddle. Amy reached behind her and took hold of one of his hands, squeezed it, and then held it there. They fell asleep that way.

CHAPTER 32

"Going on a trip?" co-worker Steve Lucas said when Patrick walked into the office kitchen the next morning for his third cup of coffee.

Patrick glanced at Lucas as he stirred in some sugar. "Huh?"

Lucas pointed to his own eyes, then to Patrick's. "Looks like you got some extra baggage there," he said, a smirk following his dime-store wit.

Patrick didn't have a problem with Steve Lucas. The guy was annoying, but tolerable. However, after only a few hours sleep and yet another colossal day looming ahead, he felt the sudden urge to throw his steaming coffee into the man's face.

"Didn't sleep too well," Patrick said.

"Are you still on schedule?"

Patrick tossed the wooden stirrer in the trash. "No, it's not that." He sipped his coffee. "I just didn't sleep too well."

"Maybe you need a *Megablast* instead of coffee." Another proud smirk. "Have you even tried the stuff yet?"

Patrick shook his head and sipped more coffee. "No. Amy and I went out with a younger couple awhile ago and they kept ordering us Red Bull and vodka. I don't think either of us slept for a week."

Lucas kept smirking. "So you're hyping a product you won't even touch yourself?"

Patrick imagined scalding him with the coffee again. The smirk was quickly losing its harmless status and venturing into the realm of patronizing dickhead. "It's called advertising, Steve. We don't have to love the product—just hype it."

Lucas chuckled, opened the fridge, took out a small bottle of orange juice and started shaking it. "Well I hope you eventually get some rest. And it might not hurt to try the stuff at least once before the big day. Could only help. If it was me, I'd be drinking a bottle of the crap *while* I was giving my presentation."

If Steve Lucas hadn't been so pre-occupied with the new foreign language software company he'd recently been working with, Patrick might have guessed that he was trying to worm his way in on the huge account that was Megablast: the first all-natural, all-day energy, almighty heart attack in one 16-ounce can. Patrick had lied to Steve. He *had* tried a can—of course he had. And after about twenty minutes, when he was sure he could feel his pulse in his teeth, Patrick wondered if cocaine wasn't a safer option—and at $8.95 a can, a cheaper one too.

But in this field, it was all irrelevant. Patrick's job was to propose a marketing plan for any and all things that came his way. Who cares he liked it or not? It was his job to make it shine, and he liked his job. In fact, dare he admit it, it was the products he *didn't* care for that were the most fun to market. They produced the biggest challenge. And Megablast was indeed a challenge, especially when you considered the dozens of energy drinks that already flooded the market. The key selling point on Megablast was that it was "all-natural"— whatever that meant. Patrick was very aware of all the ingredients in Megablast, and was also humble enough to admit that he hadn't heard of, nor could hardly pronounce, two-thirds of them. "All-natural," in this particular market, seemed a very subjective term. But that was the main angle he was going with—among others— and he was determined to make this stuff look like it had been poured from the Holy Grail itself. If he succeeded, his already promising status within the company would climb that much higher.

But there was still lots to do. His presentation as of now was akin to a jigsaw puzzle that was complete around the edges—it was the shape of a picture, but the middle still needed work, still needed to be put together just right until it began to look like something beautiful.

And this is one hell of a big puzzle, he thought as he settled into his office chair and clicked open a document on his PC. *One hell of a big puzzle.*

Patrick sipped his coffee, yawned, and then went to work.

CHAPTER 33

Patrick was still yawning at a quarter to five when the phone on his desk rang.

"Patrick Lambert."

"Hey, baby, it's me," Amy said.

She sounded pleasant. Downright happy. It filled him with a wonderful sense of relief and he could feel the remainder of last night's anxiety melting away.

"Hey, honey. How's my girl?"

"Good. I'm standing outside Friday's right now. Me and a few of the girls decided to go out for happy hour. Would you mind picking up Carrie and Caleb on your way home from work?"

The relief was short-lived. Of course he had no problem with Amy going to happy hour with friends; she did it from time to time. But it seemed wrong after what had happened last night. And then Amy's words came back to him, as clear as if she had just spoken them over the phone:

("Just don't . . . overanalyze everything so much.")

So he tried not to. "Happy hour, huh? You aren't still hurting from last night?" His tone was pleasant but forced. He was walking that exceptionally thin line between pleasant and passive aggressive. He steeled himself for a defensive reply.

Except Amy's response was anything but defensive; it was just as happy as her initial greeting. Happier even?

Because she's been drinking.

"Oh stop," she said playfully. "So can you get the kids? They're next door with the Lehman's." She slurred a little when she spoke the last sentence. Many might have missed it. Patrick spotted it immediately.

Not even five o'clock yet and she's got a buzz.

("Just don't . . . overanalyze everything so much.")

Patrick closed his eyes and pinched the bridge of his nose when he said, "Yeah, I can get the kids. What time do you think you'll be home?"

"I don't—hold on." A pause, followed by the muffled then blaring sounds of bar noise as Amy re-entered the bar. Amy yelling over the noise: "Hey! HEY! HOW LONG DO YOU THINK WE'LL BE HERE?" A woman yelled something back and Amy laughed. She was still laughing when she came back to the phone and said, "We have no idea."

"Well how are you going to get home?"

"*WHAT?*"

Patrick pinched harder on the bridge of his nose. "*HOW WILL YOU GET HOME?*" he yelled back, drawing a few looks from colleagues outside his office.

"I'll get a ride. Sarah's not drinking."

Patrick wouldn't testify in court, but he was fairly certain he heard a woman shout: "*YEAH RIGHT!*"

"Amy, I —" He stopped himself. Did he need to point out the obvious? Her dad? Last night? She had to have sensed his concern. But then again, she was on her way to being drunk, and those considerations have the uncanny ability of dissolving with each new drink that slides down the chute.

"What?" she said. And then, her mouth away from the receiver, apparently addressing her crew: "*SHUT UP! I CAN'T HEAR!*" More laughter. "Say that again, baby?"

"Nothing," Patrick said. "I was just telling you to have fun and be safe." His voice was intentionally flat—a somewhat shameful attempt at getting her to shed the party girl for a second and send some reassurance his way.

"Thanks, baby. See you tonight. Love you."

Patrick said "I love you too" into a dead line. He hung up and stared at his desk without blinking for a long time.

* * *

Patrick was going over some notes on the kitchen table. It was after ten, the kids were asleep, and Amy wasn't home yet. He had read the first page of his notes at least ten times. Actually, this was a lie. He had never gotten to the end of the page. He would get halfway, sometimes a quarter of the way, and then his mind would wander and he'd go back to the beginning. He remembered Amy with the book propped up on her chest last night, pretending to read, trying to draw attention away from the issue at hand. Was he so different now with his notes? He was getting nothing done. The notes were a prop, just like Amy's book had been. He wanted an excuse to be at the kitchen table, to be in plain sight when she walked in the front door. Their motives might have been slightly different—she using a book to dilute her intoxication and steer away from heavy conversation, he using his notes as an excuse to appear working as opposed to waiting for her like a worried father whose daughter was past curfew—but if you got down to it, they were both doing something they loathed: they were playing games. After so many years together, after knowing and loving each other more than they loved themselves, did they really need the book and the notes as catalysts to get awkward moments up and running? *Why was a straightforward approach still so difficult?* Patrick wondered. Amy could have waited for him to walk into the bedroom last night and immediately unburdened herself without the book, and Patrick could now be waiting at the kitchen table with nothing but a cup of tea, rightfully concerned about the well-being of his wife.

Patrick heard the automatic garage door begin its metal churn and his worry instantly clicked to anger. She had driven home.

Screw the notes—he needed no prop in the face of this sudden discovery. He pushed back his chair and thumped towards the mudroom, waiting for her to emerge from the garage entrance. Amy's only saving grace at this point would be if one of her friends entered with her after offering to drive the car home.

Amy entered the mudroom alone.

"Hi," Patrick immediately said.

Amy's head shot up and she placed a hand to her chest. She burst into a giggle. "Oh my God, baby, you *scared* me." She was drunk.

"Amy, what the hell?"

She swayed as she took off her coat and hung it on one of the hooks lining the wall. She turned back around and the coat slid off the hook and onto the floor. She didn't notice. "What?" she asked.

"You're drunk, and you fucking *drove*."

"I'm not drunk," she said. She did not look concerned by his accusation—her reply was spoken as innocently as someone saying they weren't hungry.

"Yes you *are*. I thought you were getting a ride home?"

"I did—I *was* . . . but they left." She spoke this with an air of certainty, as if it all made perfect sense.

"Your friends left you there? They left you to *drive home?*"

Amy shook her head intently and swayed. "No—no, no. Sarah was going to take me home, but I started talking to this other girl, and we became friends." She stopped there, once again seeming to presume it all made sense, that Patrick could surely fill in the remaining pieces.

"What the hell are you talking about? What girl?"

Amy walked past him into the kitchen. She reeked of alcohol. She spoke over her shoulder as she took a glass from the cupboard and filled it with water from the faucet. "Just some woman I started talking to. She was really cool. All the girls wanted to leave early, so this woman said she'd drive me home. The girls met her. They thought she was cool too." She drank the entire glass of water in one go.

Patrick's head was spinning. It made sense and it didn't. "But you drove home. *You* drove home."

"I know—bitch left me there."

"She did? A complete stranger?" He put a hand on his chest in mock surprise. "I'm stunned!"

"Whatever, Patrick." She rolled her eyes, turned and placed the glass in the sink.

"Why didn't you call me?" he asked. "I would have picked you up."

"What about the kids? Who would have looked after the kids?" she said.

"I could have gotten at least half a dozen neighbors to stay here with them while I got you. You know that."

Amy made a funny face. "That would have been embarrassing."

"And if you came home in a police car? How would that have been?"

She began pleading her case. "Look, I had a ride, okay? Sarah was gonna drive me. But they left because this other girl said she would drive me. And then *she* left. What else was I supposed to do?"

"You should have called me," he said. "You should have called Sarah. Why didn't you call Sarah to come back and get you?"

"They had already left."

More absurd logic. Patrick was angry. Yes, Amy had the grief card to play, but the horrific irony in utilizing it after such a situation would have likely prohibited even the most wasted of individuals from using it. But Amy did use it—sort of.

"Look, I know I fucked up," she said candidly. "And I know with what happened to Dad it seems especially bad, but . . ." She shrugged. "I just fucked up. I'm sorry. It won't happen again, okay?"

Patrick stared at her. She stared back, defiant, as though mentioning her father had given her a pass for her recklessness—a different, and in Patrick's opinion, worse version of the grief card.

"*Okay?*" she said again, her eyes still frustratingly defiant.

Patrick said, "I'm going to bed." He left the kitchen and headed upstairs.

Amy joined him in bed twenty minutes later. Patrick was rolled over onto his side away from her. The lights were off, save for the lamp on Amy's nightstand that he had graciously left on. Pissed as he may be, he didn't want her stumbling in the dark and banging her head on something.

Amy stripped down to her panties, did not brush her teeth, and then clumsily crawled into bed without saying a word. Patrick heard a drunken snore in less than a minute. He didn't fall asleep until well after two.

* * *

Back at Friday's, Monica Kemp approached the bar and ordered a vodka martini. She had not disappeared as her new friend Amy had thought, merely stepped into the ladies room, switched the blonde wig for a red one, her blue contact lenses for green, and then changed all of her clothes. When she emerged from the ladies room she might as well have been a new patron who'd only just stepped foot into the restaurant. She even sat across from Amy at the other end of the bar and did not receive even the slightest gaze of recognition when their eyes met.

When Amy eventually gave up and paid her tab before swaying out the door, Monica followed. When Amy got behind the wheel, Monica smirked. Her only feeling of sorrow came when she realized she would not be able to hear, nor see, Patrick's reaction to his drunken wife's entrance, mere weeks after her father's alleged drunk-driving death.

Still, it had been a pretty good night. Monica had kept the drinks coming for Amy, knowing it wouldn't be long before small talk about work and men and whatever would gradually dip into talk of personal despair—when the truth-serum known as alcohol made strangers into best friends and a tragic tongue uninhibited. Monica had listened to an emotional Amy with a practiced, somber face. She listened to her weep about Oscar the dog, about her father dying. Amy had even mentioned Crescent Lake. Nothing major though. Monica sensed that an entire bottle of tequila wouldn't have pried open the particulars of that treasure. Amy just gave a quick, brief summary (Monica feigned surprise when she heard, stating she had read about it in the paper and seen it on the news. *"That was you?"* she'd asked, biting back a smile).

But still, despite getting a generous helping of Amy's pain at the bar, Monica *really* wanted to bear witness to the train wreck that would inevitably transpire once Amy stumbled into the house—alone. The whole set-up had been an unexpected and opportune masterpiece on her part, and she wanted to see it to the very end, damn it.

Oh well—it was a luxury she would have to do without. She tongued an olive from her toothpick and supplemented the remainder of her time at the bar reminiscing about favorite kills.

CHAPTER 34

Amy woke just before noon the next day. Her head throbbed and her mouth was dry and gross. The sheets clung to her hot and sweaty skin that seemed to get hotter and sweatier with each wave of nausea that washed over her.

She rolled to one side and glanced at the clock on her night stand. 11:54 a.m. She sat bolt upright in bed, threw off the bed sheets and stood. The room swayed and her stomach was suddenly in her throat. She felt the horrible pooling of saliva in her mouth that meant only one thing: Mrs. Amy Lambert would be having a face-to-face date with the toilet, and if she didn't hurry, she was going to be dreadfully late.

* * *

Patrick's eye luggage was accumulating by the minute. Steve Lucas had quipped about it again when they crossed paths in the office kitchen that morning, except Patrick was less cordial this time. In fact, he did not even respond, merely flashed Steve a look that burned, and when a guy Patrick's size gives you that look, it's time to take your lame jokes elsewhere. And Steve Lucas did, post haste.

Patrick sat as his desk, blowing on his fourth cup of coffee. His stomach burbled, wanting to be fed, but Patrick could never eat when he was upset. He marveled at people who shoveled it down under periods of stress. He was the exact opposite. Even something as simple as juice seemed akin to swallowing cotton. So he had skipped breakfast and planned on skipping lunch. His stomach and head—he always got headaches when he went too long without eating—would no doubt complain incessantly, and his energy and performance today would suffer, but hell, he was pretty damn stressed. And after what had happened with Amy last night he had a damn good reason to be. Last night hadn't been a mild disagreement about wanting to watch the Eagles game while Amy wanted to go for a Sunday picnic instead. That type of debate was almost always resolved before dinner (and usually resulted in Patrick taping the game and avoiding all forms of media and technology so as not to hear the game's result while he and Amy went on the damn picnic).

The truth though? He never minded the picnics. Sure, he wanted to watch the Eagles game. Sure, he bitched and moaned a little. Yet somehow he always ended up having fun. Because he loved his wife. And he loved spending time with her. No other person on the planet could make him smile the way she did. No other person could make him belly-laugh the way she did. After years of marriage she could still make his stomach flutter when she emerged from the bathroom to model a new dress for a night out on the town. And after years of marriage he still masturbated to his wife. Most friends he confessed that fact to looked at him as if he was clinically insane—you jerked off to the idea of *strange* pussy, not your friggin' *wife* for Christ's sake. And yet whenever Patrick was alone and had the urge to treat his body like an amusement park, his fantasies always came back to Amy. He might start with a Victoria Secret model, or maybe some online porn, but it always finished with Amy. He didn't know why. Was that true love? Or was it the simple fact that his wife was just flat-out smokin' hot and their sex was great? It was all three, no doubt, except that notion of true love always felt like the winner, always seemed to burn brightest.

And that was why his stomach now burbled, grumbled, and gurgled. It was why his head ached. Why his eye luggage was accumulating. Patrick was worried. Amy had come through okay—or as well as anyone could—from the tragedy at Crescent Lake. They had all started to make small but steady steps in the right direction.

And then Caleb filled her slippers with tacks, shredding her feet.

And then Oscar died.

And then her father died.

Patrick wondered if Amy—his strong, very strong, wife—was possibly reaching her breaking point. Their psychiatrist had recommended medication after Crescent Lake. Nothing serious, just small doses of antidepressants, or perhaps the occasional benzodiazepine to calm you during extreme moments of anxiety when the inevitable nightmare or flashback occurred. Amy flat-out refused. Her kids were the Prozac, her husband the Xanax.

She was not anti-drug, and she believed wholeheartedly in counseling, psychology, and cognitive behavioral therapy. But Amy had later explained to Patrick that she didn't want to use the drugs because if she did, then somehow the Fannelli brothers would win. She hadn't been able to elaborate much further on her reasoning, it was just something she felt. Patrick had had a hard time grasping where she was coming from, and periodically asked her to elaborate. Finally, she came up with an impressive metaphor that seemed to explain her reasoning fairly well:

"I want to win the gold medal without steroids," she'd said.

Still a little gray to some perhaps, but damn good as far as Patrick was concerned, and he'd let it go at that.

Now, he feared her will was cracking, giving into the pressures in order to win that metaphoric gold. Perhaps alcohol was becoming her steroid. A drug that required no prescription and would not label her a hypocrite by succumbing to the medication she had once vehemently opposed.

He was worried, felt justified in his worry, yet his wife's words still played in his head often:

("Just don't . . . overanalyze everything so much.")

But God damn it. *God damn it.* If she'd only gotten a ride home that night, he could have chalked the whole thing up to a night out with the girls that got a little out of hand. No problem. The night before? She wanted a little alone time, a few drinks by herself to mourn her father. Again, no problem—it could all be rationalized.

But she hadn't gotten a ride home. She drove. Drunk. And now Patrick didn't know what to think. He prayed it was a freak occurrence—a serious and horribly ironic lapse in judgment, something that would never happen again. Patrick had showered, shaved, dressed, and gotten the kids off to school this morning without Amy so much as lifting an eyelid: She was sleeping the dead sleep of the very drunk. And if he knew his wife, when she did wake, she would feel like death. He counted on that. If his words could not make a dent—he had yet to talk to her today; he assumed (hoped) she was still asleep and not avoiding him—then perhaps one hell of a hangover could.

Patrick turned away from his computer and stared at the phone on his desk, willing it to ring. He would not call her, damn it, she would call *him*.

More games, Patrick?

He mumbled, "Shit," picked up the phone and dialed Amy.

* * *

Amy sat slumped over the kitchen table, her throbbing head propped up with one hand, her second cup of black coffee in the other. A silent mantra of "never again" played repeatedly, its gun-point promise bringing zero relief each time her stomach hitched and she felt a *third* cuddling session with the toilet bowl may be in order.

She had screwed up. *Boy*, had she screwed up. Last night was fuzzy, but the big parts, the serious parts, carried unavoidable clarity. Getting wasted was no big deal. Everyone's done it. Driving home while wasted? Huge deal. After what happened to her father? Huge deal with a side order of idiot. Boy, had she screwed up.

She wanted to call Patrick. She wanted to call him the moment she sprang upright in bed and realized what time it was, realized what she'd done last night. Unfortunately, excessive vomiting followed by excessive guilt took precedence. Even after the vomiting, the guilt was still strong. The shame. She was ashamed to call Patrick. He had obviously gotten the kids off to school and himself off to work without waking her, and this made the guilt and shame that much stronger. She envisioned Patrick tip-toeing around and keeping the kids quiet so as not to wake Mommy. Telling the kids Mommy wasn't feeling well, she had a stomach bug. The kids feeling worried for Mommy. Caleb wanting to go in to check on her.

Never again, never again, never again, never—

Should she call him? What would she say? Nothing really *to* say other than sorry and forgive me a zillion times. She would sound pathetic, but then, she felt pathetic. And she was definitely in the wrong—no denying that whatsoever. She could justify the martinis and aloof behavior the other night, no problem. In fact she had justified it, and it wasn't bullshit. No justifying this though. She would plead guilty and hope for leniency.

Amy pushed back her chair and walked into the living room. Her cell phone sat charging on the coffee table. She stared at it. *Maybe he'll call me. Maybe he'll soon get worried if he doesn't hear from me.* She closed her head and sighed. *You're playing silly games, dummy. You need to pick up your phone and call your—*

Her cell phone rang and she jumped. The phone read: Patrick/Office.

Amy's face went sunburn hot, her heart thudded in her chest, and for the first time in her life, she was scared to talk to her husband.

* * *

Amy's phone rang three times before she answered it. Patrick was prepared to leave a voicemail, but when his wife's voice greeted him, he suddenly had to regroup and prepare for a conversation—no easy task when your mind is already in message mode and the subject matter is as awkward as it was.

"Hey," he greeted her. His voice felt sturdy, as he'd hoped. "How are you feeling?" Had it been the night after a party where she'd indulged safely, such a question would have been asked with devilish delight, an unmerciful bout of teasing endlessly following.

None of that today.

"Awful," she said.

"Sick?"

"No. . . well yeah, sick-awful, but . . . awful-awful."

Patrick knew what she was alluding to, but he wanted to hear it. "What do you mean?"

He heard her sigh. Then: "I'm so sorry."

Patrick stayed quiet.

"I don't know why I did it," she continued. "It was a mistake. It was *more* than a mistake. But believe me, nothing you say could make me feel any worse than I'm feeling right now."

He wanted to let loose, to let her know that her reckless behavior might have left him a widower and their kids without a mother. He wanted to know how, *how* could she possibly do such a thing after what happened to her father? He wanted to know, and he wanted to rant. Instead he remained quiet. What would ranting or an endless barrage of questions she'd already confessed ignorance to accomplish anyway? Besides, the main question Patrick wanted answered could not be given with words. It was something only time would reveal. In his heart he believed she would never do it again, but still, only time.

"Patrick?" she said.

"I'm here."

"What are you thinking?"

"I think you already know. Do you really want to hear it?"

Softly, she admitted: "No."

"I'm not gonna lie though, Amy—" He rarely called her Amy. Found it too melodramatic when others used it in serious debate. Today it was out of his mouth without consideration. "—I *am* a little worried about you."

Patrick readied himself for some resistance. He got nothing.

It's the hangover, he thought. *A colossal hangover coupled with major guilt is a punch in the gut that just won't go away.*

Amy said, "I know." And then once more: "I'm so sorry."

A promise to never do such foolishness again (even though he'd admitted to himself only moments ago the futility of such words) would have been nice to hear, but in a way he supposed she was saying it without saying it. Patrick was then surprised to find he was suddenly glad she hadn't resorted to such promises. Had she done so, the words would have been empty, like an addict promising he would never use again, reeking of bullshit to clear the air long enough until the next fix was secured. Patrick knew his wife too well. He knew she would not taint an apology like this with predictable and hollow promises, even if it happened to be the most truthful promise she might ever speak.

Patrick pinched the bridge of his nose, squinted hard, and then blinked several times in an attempt to stem the headache that had been with him since morning. "It's okay, baby," he said, realizing just then that he had called her Amy earlier. "Why don't you go take some ibuprofen with a big glass of water, then go lie down for a bit."

"I can't—I have to go get Caleb soon," she said. "Guess that's my penance, huh?"

"No. If you tell him that Mommy doesn't feel well he'll be as quiet as a mouse when you get back. Now, when *Carrie* gets home . . ."

He heard her groan into the phone. He chuckled. A good ten second pause followed.

"So are we good?" she eventually asked.

"We're good."

"I truly am sorry, baby."

"I know."

"I love you."

"I love you too. I'll see you when I get home."

Patrick hung up and sat for a moment, replaying the conversation over in his head. Content it went about as well as a conversation like that could, he spun back to his

PC and started to do some actual work on the Megablast account for the first time that day.

CHAPTER 35

John Brooks lay on his motel bed watching a nature program about crocodiles stalking and killing their prey. He watched the deadly reptiles and drew comparisons between them and himself and his daughter:

The crocodile would glide beneath the murky water, undetected by its prey taking a drink by the riverbank. The crocodile would glide closer, undetected still. It would then wait. Lie and wait from below for as long as it took. The perfect moment. The perfect strike. The perfect kill.

This was Monica.

And when those powerful reptilian jaws snapped shut on its prey, and the desperate, futile struggle would ensue—the blood, the carnage, the up-close-and-personal joy of destroying your victim . . .

That was him. That was John.

Of course he and his daughter were not completely night and day. They did share the most significant trait of all: the trait of truly loving who they were and what they did. No bullshit psychology or FBI profiling about what caused their behavior required. They were born. The end. This was even more evident now with the discovery of Arthur and James. It was in their blood. John's family was put on this earth for the purpose of bringing death and misery to others—and enjoying the hell out of it.

A knock on the motel door shook John from his thoughts. He had been staring at the television but hadn't taken in a thing since his mind began churning. The nature program was now over and some guy in a light blue suit was asking for donations.

John reached under the pillow next to him and gripped the handle of his custom M1911 pistol. "Who is it?"

A female voice, deep and stern. "Police. Open up."

"Okay, gimme a second." Gun in hand, John eased off the bed and crept towards the door. He turned the lock slowly, slid the chain out of its track without a sound, then pressed himself flat against the wall behind the door. He turned his head towards the bathroom and cupped one hand against the side of his mouth to throw his voice. *"Come in."*

John watched the door handle slowly turn. Watched the door ease open. He gripped his M1911 tight, ready, waiting.

The door was completely open now, John behind it. He did not risk peeking through the crack by the hinges. That would be expected. He stayed put, flat to the wall, straining to hear anything significant. He heard distant traffic, the wind, someone slamming a car door in the parking lot.

The subtle click of a gun.

John whirled from his spot and thrust his own gun into the open doorway.

Nothing.

And then the sound of an empty chamber clicking repeatedly from below. He looked down and said, "Ah *shit.*"

Monica lay flat on her back, head at his feet, her own gun pointed up at her father's groin, an impossibly wide grin on her face.

"I believe this now makes it two-nothing, me," she said, still on her back, still pointing the gun, still grinning like a kid.

John thought of the crocodile lurking below the surface, invisible, waiting to strike. He couldn't help but smile back.

* * *

"Old, Pops . . . you're gettin' old," Monica said as she flopped onto the motel bed and propped her head up with both pillows.

"What's this two-nothing crap?" John said. "When was the first?"

"At your cabin—when I beat you to the draw with the bum. I could have popped you too."

"I told you, I knew you were there."

She rolled her eyes. "Right."

He sat at the foot of the bed. "What happened last night?"

Monica put both hands behind her head, a smirk starting. "An opportunity presented itself."

"Such as?"

"I was following her. She strayed from her usual routine and wound up at a bar with her yuppie chums. I stayed close by, and after a few drinks her body language told me the conversation had down-shifted, and that she was now venting to her friends. I turned up my earpiece and got it all. She was whining about Patrick overreacting to her drinking so much the night before. Apparently she'd been mourning her father."

"Shame," John said.

"A tragedy," Monica said. "So anyway, she'd apparently ended up drinking a bunch of martinis by herself that night and got pretty drunk. She was justifying it all to her friends at the bar, claiming she was sad, wanted a drink and some alone time to grieve, it wasn't that big a deal, but Patrick was making it a big deal, overanalyzing things like always . . .

"Eventually her friends said they wanted to leave, but I could tell she didn't; it was obvious she had a decent buzz going. So I slid down the bar and started chatting her up, bought her a few rounds, and then convinced her stupid friends that I'd make sure she got home okay.

"So her friends left, I kept getting her wasted, and then I eventually went to the ladies room and did a quick change. When I came back to the bar I sat directly across from her. She stared right at me a few times—no recognition whatsoever."

"Probably because she was so drunk," he said, dangling the bait.

She took it, intent on dangling her own right back. "Jealousy is for the weak. Still, I can't blame one's jealousy when his only capable transition is from big oaf with hat to big oaf without."

John rolled his eyes and mimed jerking himself off. Monica gave a disgusted look. He smirked then asked, "So then what?"

"Waited a bit, watched her grow impatient, and then . . ."

John's eyes lit up. "She drove home?"

Monica beamed.

John started clapping, threw his head back and barked a solitary laugh. "Fucking brilliant. Goddamn, you amaze me sometimes, girl."

"Thank you, thank you."

"What was the final outcome?"

"Well I imagine Mr. Patrick Lambert was none too pleased when his wife got home."

"You didn't follow?"

"No."

"Well what if she never made it home? What if she got into an accident or pulled over or something?"

"Really? You're really asking me that?"

"What?"

"You telling me you'd be disappointed if any of that happened?"

He paused for a second, then said, "Yeah, okay. Still, we don't know if she got home."

"She did. I swung by there this morning when Patrick left for work. Her car was in the garage."

John stood, strolled to the room's only window and looked out into the parking lot. "So what now? Arrange another incident like last night?"

Monica shook her head. "No. The damage has already been done—let it fester. She won't be able to have even the most casual of drinks from now on without Patrick having an anxiety attack." She placed her hands back behind her head. "Shame we can't run some kind of practice intended on pulling families apart as opposed to keeping them together. We'd have a line out the fucking door."

John said, "We'd be the next Freuds."

"Freud was a sexist pig. I've never envied a penis in my life, thank you very much."

John snorted. "You fucking women should just know your role."

Monica pulled one of the pillows out from behind her head and threw it at him. He caught it and laughed.

"So—what *do* you think the next move should be?" he asked.

"Amy slurred something last night about Patrick and some big advertising account he's working on. I want to look into that."

"Trial's getting closer," he said.

"I know."

"You don't think we should focus on that?"

"You can't multi-task? Besides, this family is resilient—we can keep bending them awhile."

"As long as Arthur does the final break."

"Have we met?" She lit a cigarette. "You forget who found Arthur in the first place." She exhaled a long stream. "First losing your touch, and now senility?" She shook her head and gave him a pity smile. "Sucks to get old."

Rattlesnake-quick, John snatched his daughter by the ankle and yanked her off the bed as though she were a doll. In seconds Monica was pinned to the floor, his knee in her back, one hand clamped under the chin, the other to the hair on the back of her head.

"Should this senile old man who's losing his touch go snappy-snap?" He gave her head a slight turn with both hands. "You see, you might be the croc beneath the water, but we're out of the water now, and you're stuck in this croc's jaws."

His hand still pressing against her chin, Monica spoke through clenched teeth. "*What the fuck are you talking about? Get off me!*"

John slowly turned her head until it would no longer give. One quick twist and she'd be gone.

"What's the score now?" he asked.

Monica grunted and snorted, her breathing labored from the knee in her back.

"What's the score now?" he asked again.

She managed: "*You win, you win!*"

John smiled and hopped off. "I'm not giving you credit for the cabin," he said. "That was bullshit. So right now we're tied, one-one."

"Fine." Monica gradually stood, dusted herself off and rubbed her neck. She spotted her lit cigarette on the bed, picked it up and held it out in front of her father. "See? This is how you start fires."

"Well if you didn't smoke in the first place then it wouldn't—"

She flicked the cigarette into his face. John flinched away and she immediately slammed a kick into his groin, dropping him to all fours. Monica bolted from the room, her laughter echoing throughout the parking lot as she gunned her engine and peeled away.

One hand on his aching balls, John slowly got to his feet and shut the motel door. He turned back towards the bed and with a proud smirk, muttered, "Sneaky bitch."

CHAPTER 36

Pittsburgh, Pennsylvania

Arty lay on his cot, reading a piece of fan mail. He did not read the letters to boost his ego, he read them for amusement. These faceless drones were trying to connect with him, to relate to him, as if they were actually peers. It was laughable.

Arty heard an officer approaching. He put the letter on his chest and looked up at the clock. Lunch time.

The officer appeared in front of Arty's cell carrying a tray that held a sandwich, a bag of chips, and a small carton of juice.

"Lunch, Fannelli."

Arty clenched his teeth when he heard the name. He felt shame that it still got to him. But it did—and the officers knew it. "You know," Arty began, not angry, polite even, "it's no secret I don't like being called by that name. And I imagine wit is hard to come by for people in your if-you-can-sign-your-name-you've-got-the-job   profession. But maybe, just maybe, if during your next chewing tobacco and desperately transparent homosexual-hating break you guys put your empty heads together, you might be able to come up with something new."

The officer said nothing, his face as placid as the moment it appeared in front of Arty's cell. What he did do, however, was balance the tray in one hand, peel back his lower lip with the other to show Arty the wad of tobacco he was dipping, flip open the top of Arty's ham and cheese, and then drop a healthy brown glob of chew-spit into the center of the sandwich. The officer then placed the piece of bread back onto the ham and cheese and pressed it hard and flat.

"Enjoy," the officer said, leaving the tray on the floor, not bothering to unlock and slide it through the food carrier. "I'd eat it quick before the rats get to it."

Arty felt good after his degrading speech, and he was not naïve enough to think that the officer would not retaliate in some way. But he was hungry, and before he could bring it back he grumbled: "*Cocksucker.*"

The fading click-clack of uniformed heels on concrete came to an abrupt halt. They then started up again, only this time not fading, but growing louder and more purposeful until the officer was back in front of the cell. "Say that again, Fannelli?" he said.

Arty was a blend of anger and shame. Angry at the officer for obvious reasons, shameful that he had let the officer bring him down to his level with primitive insults like *cocksucker*. It showed a lack of control, a lack of restraint—two of his unique attributes he treasured as much as oxygen and water. And yet he was suddenly and strangely fueled by it. Because it had gotten to the officer. One word had stopped the man instantaneously. Was it beneath him? Yes. Primitive? Yes. But Arty supposed it came down to the simple fact that a primitive assault begets a primitive response. So he went with it again.

"Called you a cocksucker," he said pleasantly.

When the officer began to unlock the cell, Arty quickly realized his basic revelation held an unfortunate cyclical truth: A primitive assault may lead to a primitive response, but a primitive response had no problem circling back towards a primitive assault. In other words, Arty was about to get the shit kicked out of him.

* * *

As the officer stepped out of Arty's cell, he stopped, bent and picked up the carton of juice on the lunch tray, opened it, re-entered Arty's cell, and then poured it all over the floor.

"See what happens when you spill your juice, Fannelli?" he said. "You slip and fall and then you hurt yourself." He threw the empty carton at the battered fetal ball on the floor that was Arty. The officer then locked the cell and strutted off down the corridor, whistling a pleasant tune that was assuredly more for Arty's ears than his own—a smug reminder about the lack of empathy he had when it came to giving a beating.

Arty remained in his fetal ball for a moment until he was sure the officer was truly gone. His position was not one of cowardice or weakness, just protection. The first two blows with the officer's night stick had dazed him good. Arty was always concerned about head injuries. Many serial killers had suffered head injuries early on in their developmental years and it contributed to their lack of impulse control. Arty and his late brother Jim were better than that. They had supreme control. Serial killers were pathetic and weak. It was why they were inevitably caught. No impulse control.

So once the first two hits to the skull had Arty seeing stars, he immediately dropped to the floor, covered his head, and opted for a beating to the body, to which the officer happily obliged. It wasn't anything excessive. The officer wasn't stupid enough to think that a simple slip and fall could account for an inmate who looked in need of at least a week's stay in the infirmary. Just a few good whacks and it was done.

Arty slowly uncoiled from his ball then stretched out on his cot. His head throbbed, his ribs ached, and he knew it would be even worse tomorrow. But it was just physical pain that would eventually fade. The feeling of helplessness hurt the worst—the lack of power. If Arty were free, he and Jim would have taken the officer from his home in the middle of the night and removed and cauterized his limbs by now.

Arty slipped into a daze as he recalled a similar incident from years ago. An unfortunate was a functioning torso when the brothers had finished with him. His head constantly cried for mercy that was not forthcoming as he flopped on the floor like a fish.

Then they'd brought in the doped-up hooker.

Somehow she'd managed to get him hard.

And then all three had stepped back and laughed at the weeping torso with the hard-on.

Jim had eventually ended the whole scene with two bullets: one for the torso, and one for the hooker—for being a tease.

"She was being a fucking tease," Jim had said with a smirk to a delighted Arty. "Poor guy's got a hard-on with no arms and legs, and she's laughing instead of finishing him off."

A small nostalgic smile had formed on the corner of Arty's mouth as he recalled the past. Now it was gone, sadness and anger for his departed brother the primary culprit. But what about his sister? Her sudden emergence into his life was a godsend, yet he still didn't know her precise intentions. Discretion was obviously the order of the day, and while she was certainly taking care of things on the outside—his fake mother, Amy's father—he wondered if she had plans to try and free him.

And oh if she did . . .

The Lamberts. The things he would do. He would kill the children this time, no question. Ordinarily he and Jim would leave children be. They often used children as instruments to heighten torment for their subjects, but they never planned to kill them. They had left many traumatized orphans in their wake, and he supposed that was often a fate worse than death (to which he felt nothing), but intentional killing of children was against their rules. Not for reasons of empathy, but for reasons of caution. Murdered adults? Horrible. A shame. Murdered *children*? The world stopped. You *would* be found, and you *would* be punished without mercy. Even the most hardened and brutal of inmates adhered to this code.

So they never killed children. But the Lambert kids?

Arty clenched his fist until his knuckles went white and his fingernails cut into his palm. Jim was gone now, and if his sister *was* planning to free him (and in his heart, he knew she was), he was going to make some new rules.

He would kill the Lambert children. He would kill them *first*. Slowly. And he would make Amy and Patrick watch—even if he had to glue their eyelids open.

CHAPTER 37

It had been a week since the incident Patrick and Amy
seldom referred to as "that night." Things did not go back
to rainbows and kittens right after—Bob Corcoran was still
dead after all, and Amy was still grieving—but they were
okay, and the Lamberts were very familiar with okay.
After what they'd been through this past year, *okay* was
the silver medal of status updates. *Good* was the
prestigious gold. *Great*? They'd experienced sporadic
moments of *good* since Crescent Lake, but the enigmatic
great was becoming a memory. A memory that, lately,
carried more melancholy than hope.

Patrick was pouring coffee into his travel mug when
Amy came up behind him and wrapped her arms around
his waist. He looked back over his shoulder and said,
"Morning, love."

She laid her cheek in the center of his back and
mumbled a good morning.

He turned into her. He was cleaned and dressed for
work, she was in a big tee-shirt and sweats with rumpled
hair and puffy eyes. He went in for a kiss.

She turned away and covered her mouth. "Haven't
brushed my teeth yet."

"Oh shut up." He gripped her chin with his thumb and
index finger and pulled her lips to his. She obliged, but it
was only a quick peck.

"Did you make me some?" she asked, peering around
him towards the coffee maker.

"Yeah, but it's not that hippie shit you drink. It's a dark roast."

Amy let go of Patrick's waist and opened the cabinet. She took out the bag of dark roast. "When did you get this?"

"Couple of days ago. I need every conceivable advantage if I'm going to get this Megablast account polished by next month."

"Why not just drink Megablast?"

"Very funny."

She smirked. She knew how vile the stuff was. Amy began looking deeper into the cabinet. "Where'd you put my hippie shit?"

He palmed the top of her head and guided it away from the cabinet and towards the countertop where a bag of organic coffee stood.

"How silly of me," she said. "Looking for coffee in the coffee cabinet."

"I took it out for you so you wouldn't *have* to look in the cabinet."

"If you were hoping to be such a saint, you could have poured the rest of your swamp water out and made me a fresh pot of *my* stuff."

Patrick kissed her on the back of the head and then pinched her butt. Amy jumped, turned, and took a swipe at him. He dodged, laughed, and hurried towards the mudroom with his coffee and briefcase.

* * *

It was 5 p.m. Patrick was intending on staying until at least seven. His neck ached, his eyes burned, and he was hungry. A brief diversion from his PC right now would be nice.

Steve Lucas did a quick rap on Patrick's office window and immediately poked his head in before being invited. Patrick's mind flashed to the TV show "Laverne and Shirley." Whenever Laverne or Shirley had just finished stating something creepy, slimy, revolting, or just flat-out annoying, their apartment door would always fly open on cue, revealing the two loveable doofuses that were Lenny and Squiggy, who would then simultaneously belt out their nasally trademark: *"Hello!"*

Except Steve Lucas was not a loveable doofus. He was just a doofus.

"How they hanging, big man?" Lucas asked.

Patrick took a deep breath, let it out slow through his nose, forced a smile. "It's going fine, thanks." He did a quarter turn back towards his PC, hoping Lucas would take the hint.

He did not. He pointed at Patrick. "You . . ." He pointed at himself. "Me . . ." He grinned. "Happy hour. Right now. What do you say?"

The mere mention of happy hour reminded Patrick of the incident with Amy, and his annoyance meter shot up a notch. "I'm good, man, thanks," he said.

Lucas stood in front of Patrick's desk. "Aw, come on, man. Look, I'm buying, okay? Besides you gotta meet this girl I've been seeing. *Smokin'* hot." He lowered his voice and raised his eyebrows like a car salesman about to whisper an unbeatable offer. *"Fucking crazy in bed too, I'm tellin' ya."*

Patrick took another deep breath. "That's great, Steve, I'm happy for you." He threw a thumb over his shoulder towards his PC. "I've just got way too much stuff to get done."

"Come *ooooon* . . . it's Friday. Give Amy a call, she can join us."

Patrick's annoyance meter jumped another notch. "I don't think so."

Steve cocked his head. "Everything okay?"

Patrick nodded once. "Fine."

Steve put his hands on Patrick's desk, leaned in and said, "You know, if you and Amy are having problems, I can see if my new girl has a friend . . ."

Patrick was not consciously aware of the look he gave Steve Lucas just then, but when Lucas held up both hands and stepped back as though a gun had just been pulled on him, Patrick was certain that the fire that had instantaneously erupted in his gut had climbed and ignited his face, smoking nostrils, red eyes, the works.

"Whoa, relax, man," Lucas said, his hands still up. "Forget I said anything." He slipped out of Patrick's office without another word.

Whatever rage Patrick had just felt towards Steve Lucas delightfully faded when he watched the man shit himself and scurry out of his office. Patrick allowed himself a brief smile then went back to work.

CHAPTER 38

Samantha Hurst, also known as Monica Kemp, sat on a barstool in Bravo's Tavern, drinking a vodka martini and waiting for Steve Lucas to arrive. She was wearing her blonde wig, her green contacts lenses, a thick layer of eyeliner, and an outfit that screamed sex from the rooftops—the exact persona she had donned when she had met Steve a week ago.

Monica had been waiting for Patrick in the parking garage of his office building—basic surveillance, using the time to contemplate some type of innocuous *in* to Patrick and the big advertising account Amy had mentioned. She found it with Steve Lucas. Monica could read body language as well as she could English, and what she'd read as Patrick hurried to his car with Steve Lucas grinning and chatting away endlessly at his heels was written in a bold 72 font: Steve Lucas was an annoying prick, and Patrick couldn't stand him. And oh yeah, they worked together.

Courting Steve hadn't been difficult. The man was the type to take the bait from anyone with a heartbeat, let alone a knockout like Monica. It was the sex that tested her resolve. Much to his delight, she had slept with him the first night they met and it proved more difficult than she had predicted. The bastard had decent staying power. She had nearly dried up several times on that first night, and the only thing that had kept her wet were the graphic visions of what lay in store for the Lamberts once her brother was free.

The seven days and nights that followed had been much of the same. It had been an effort, but Monica managed to dispense enough convincing sex into the eager hands of Steve Lucas to keep him blissfully ignorant to her ulterior motives. A quick lunch-time pop-in at the office on the fourth day had been followed by another on the sixth. Both times Patrick had been out of the office (she had checked in advance), and by the end of that sixth day Monica had the complete layout of the building's interior and could find Patrick's office walking backwards.

All she wanted now was a key, or more appropriately, a magnetic key card—a magnetic key card that registered the name Steve Lucas every time it was swiped. She didn't *need* it, of course; she could get into the office another way if she wanted, but talk about two for the price of one. She smirked and sipped her martini.

Steve arrived a moment later. She ordered him a double bourbon then put her lips to his ear. *"I feel like getting crazy tonight,"* she whispered, her hand tracing the inside of his thigh beneath the bar.

Steve grinned and looked as though he might squeal. He grabbed his bourbon and downed it in three gulps. Monica immediately ordered him another. He grinned again, and she grinned back—no faking this time.

* * *

Steve Lucas sat slurring and leering like a drunken fool on his sofa. He kept mumbling something about fooling around, yet Monica's only reply was a playful bat of the eyes coupled with promises of a reward for patience. That and another large bourbon, his eighth of the night. And if one were to look close enough at bourbon number eight, one might see a few undissolved particles of the benzodiazepine Klonopin floating around in the amber liquid. Not that Steve was capable of noticing. She could have dropped the pills in whole and he likely wouldn't have noticed. As far as tasting something odd about bourbon number eight? Well, drunkenness was her friend, as was Klonopin itself. Monica had chosen Klonopin over Xanax because Xanax had an exceptionally bitter taste. Klonopin was no puff of air, but it was mild enough for someone who was well and truly shit-faced not to give a crap.

* * *

It was less than thirty minutes before Steve Lucas was snoring on his couch. Monica slapped his face and he never so much as twitched. She slapped him once more for fun and then began rifling through the wallet he had placed on his coffee table. She found the key card in seconds, picked up her cell and dialed. A male voice picked up on the first ring.

"Code in."

"Neco. 8122765."

"Waiting for voice authentication . . . clear. What's up?"

"I need 7146."

"Hold."

A click, a pause, and then a different male voice. "What is it and how soon?"

"Security card. Standard magnetic stripe. Nothing crazy. I need it tonight. Multiple copies."

The male voice gave a confirmation number and an address in Philadelphia. Monica hung up and called her father.

"I need you to come get the card and then take it to get copied. It's in the city so I need you to leave now." She gave him the suburban address to Steve's place, the address to the place in the city, and then the confirmation number. "Leave now."

John grunted and hung up. Fifteen minutes later he pulled up to Steve Lucas' home in the battered Dodge Dakota. Monica was outside smoking a cigarette, waiting for him. He rolled the passenger side window down as she approached.

"Here." Monica handed her father the card, then a piece of paper with the address and confirmation number.

"You already gave me all that over the phone," he said.

"You never heard of being thorough?"

He rolled his eyes and took it anyway.

"Hurry back."

John rolled up the window and drove off.

* * *

John Brooks did not like cities. He felt more at home in open spaces, in the wilderness. He tended to choose jobs based on this preference, his last being a family on a ranch in Montana. The husband of that family had sold some of his accomplices out in exchange for no jail time. This landed the husband and his brood presumably safe in the hands of a witness relocation program out in the middle of God's country—the last place a wise guy would go looking for another wise guy. Except the wise guys weren't doing any of the looking—John was.

He'd found them in less than a week. After disposing of security, John had cut the husband's head off, shot the wife dead, left the kids unharmed (as instructed), and then packed the husband's head in dry ice and hand-delivered it back to his employer. It went about as perfectly as any job could go.

Now, in a more than unsavory section of Philadelphia, John felt cramped and vulnerable. He'd parked the

Dakota along the street a few blocks back, and took the remainder on foot. He always felt better on foot.

Beaten row homes lined both sides of the street. Some dark and barren, some dimly lit. Flophouses, he thought. Why would Monica have an affiliate do business here? Discretion, sure, but come on, he wasn't buying fucking nuclear weapons or anything.

John had made it two blocks when he was approached—a young black man, late teens to early twenties, heavy coat, both hands in his pockets.

"What's up, big dawg? You need some help?"

John was told he would not be met by anyone. He was to approach the address given and ring the bell. So he looked the kid dead in the eye and said, "No."

The kid gave a casual glance around, inched closer. "You lost, dawg?"

"No."

The kid's right hand shifted in his coat pocket. John hit him immediately. One shot—an overhand right to the jaw with all the force of a train. The kid was unconscious before he hit the ground, the back of his head cracking concrete after descent stiffening him out like a mannequin as he seized. John calmly bent over the kid's body to search his right coat pocket. He withdrew a .22 caliber pistol.

"A twenty-two?" he said, waving the small gun over the kid's unconscious face. "You were gonna mug me with a fucking twenty-two?" John brought his boot up and stomped on the kid's head once, twice, and then a final third. He then tossed the gun into a square of fenced-in yard across the street. "Give that fucking toy to some kid to play with," he said before spitting on the young man in disgust and continuing towards the designated address.

* * *

On his way back to the Dakota with the original key card and now several perfect copies, John found the young man where he had left him. He bent and checked his pulse. Dead. Probably the stomps that finished him, he thought. He shrugged and carried on towards his truck.

CHAPTER 39

Monica was inside keeping an eye on Steve Lucas. He hadn't moved from his spot on the couch—upright, head back, mouth open with a thunderous snore flapping out of his throat. She found it difficult to look at him for any period of time. She knew she was good, but how she managed to screw him as many times a she did without gutting him, she'd never know.

Her cell phone vibrated twice. A text message. She flipped it open.

From: Dad
HERE.

She snapped the phone shut and headed outside. John was parked along the street in the same spot he'd been when he arrived earlier. The passenger window was down. Monica leaned in.

"Here." John leaned over and handed the key cards to Monica.

She took them and gave them a quick inspection.

"Do I get one?" John asked.

"No—why would you?"

"Well you've got three of them," he said.

"Precaution, Daddy-O," she said.

He grunted and leaned back into his seat.

"Wait," she said. "I need you to come inside."

"What for?"

"Can you just do it, please?"

John grunted again and switched off the ignition.

* * *

Monica and John stood staring at the near-comatose Steve Lucas on the sofa.

"Jesus," John said, "How much did he have to drink?"

"A lot. But I slipped him a few mickeys, too."

"Better hope he doesn't fucking die."

"He'll be fine. The-mother-of-all hangovers, but fine." She turned to her father. "I need you to carry him into his bedroom."

"What?"

"I need it to look like we started to fool around."

"Fine—just don't ask me to undress the fucker."

John scooped Steve's limp body up with ease and followed Monica into the bedroom. He dumped Steve onto the bed. "Okay?" he said.

"Don't leave yet," she said. "Wait for me in the living room."

John nodded and left the room. Monica quickly stripped Steve Lucas naked and tossed his clothes everywhere. She reached beneath him, snatched the blankets and pulled them to the floor in a tangled heap. She knocked some pictures over on his dresser and stamped on the frames. She kicked over a lamp, elbowed the mirror on his wall until it cracked, then went to the kitchen and returned with an open bottle of bourbon. She dropped the bottle onto the rug and let the amber liquid soak into the shag until only a swallow or two remained in the bottle.

Satisfied, she eventually returned to the living room. John was sitting on the couch reading a magazine. Steve Lucas' wallet still sat on the coffee table. Monica took it, stuffed the original key card back inside, then placed it back on the table.

"What the hell were you doing in there?" John asked, still thumbing through the magazine. "Sounded like you were trashing the place."

"I was," she said. "Gotta sell it."

"Sell what?"

"I want you to hit me," she said.

John glanced up from the magazine. "You what?"

"We've got everything we need. You didn't think I was going to keep fucking that idiot, did you?"

John glanced back towards Steve's room, then towards Monica again.

"The booze and the Klonopin will erase his memory," she said.

John nodded, stood and said: "Where?"

Monica pointed to her left eye. "Don't go overboard, tough-guy. He's not exactly Bruce Lee."

John smiled, then punched his daughter in her left eye. It was a jabbing blow, but enough to rock her back several steps.

"*Ow, ow, fuck,*" she said, cupping both hands over her face.

"Let me see," John said.

She took her hands away from her face and he studied her eye. He nodded as though appraising an antique. "You'll have a decent shiner," he said.

"Good." She turned and headed back to the bedroom to give it a final going over. Steve was still naked and sprawled out on his back, snoring as loud as ever. She thought of cutting off his prick and shoving it down his throat to stop the snoring. Maybe one day.

Monica joined her father back in the living room. "Come on, let's go. We need to be back here in the morning."

"What? *Why?*"

She pushed him out the door and said, "Because I didn't let you punch me in the face for nothing, dummy."

CHAPTER 40

Steve Lucas woke up naked and disoriented. A quick survey told him he was in his own bed. A second, deeper survey told him his room was a mess. His lamp was on the floor. His mirror was splintered like a spider web in the corner. His dresser top was wiped clean—the pictures frames strewn all over the floor, some cracked and broken. Next to one of those frames lay a near-empty bottle of Jim Beam, a brown stain circling its open neck.

Where was Samantha? He pulled the sheets up from the floor, covered his lower-half and called for her. "Hello? Samantha?"

Nothing. Calling her name sent a shockwave of pain throughout his head and he pressed a palm to it, squeezing his eyes shut. How much did he fucking drink last night? More importantly, he thought, looking around his room, *what the hell happened?*

A sudden bang on his front door startled him. He quickly dressed in last night's clothes and hurried to the living room. He opened his front door, hoping for Samantha, and she was there, but so was someone else—a large someone else who gripped Steve by the throat with one hand and rammed him back inside his home, slamming him up against the nearest wall. The man's grip was impossibly strong; Steve could feel his blood rushing upward, pulsating hot against his face, bulging his eyes. If the man didn't let go, he would be out cold very soon. The large man seemed to sense this too and loosened his grip, but only slightly. He pressed his face to Steve's and roared into it.

"You sick motherfucker! Give me one reason why I shouldn't crush your fucking throat!"

Steve had no words. He only hoped his shocked expression would plead his ignorance.

"You think you can slap around my baby sister and not have it come back to you?!"

Steve hadn't noticed when he first opened the door—everything happened too fast. But now, as he looked over the shoulder of the big man, he saw a furious Samantha glaring back at him with a swollen purple eye.

Steve instantly said: "Oh God . . . oh shit, *did I do that?*" He took his eyes off Samantha and put them back on the big man, praying they shone as big and remorseful as he felt. "I'm so sorry . . . I don't know what happened . . . I . . . everything's a blank. I don't remember—"

The big man tightened his grip again, cutting Steve off. "You listen to me, you sick little fuck. If you come within one hundred yards of my sister again, I *will* be back here and I *will* end your fucking life." Like a shotgun blast, the big man drove his right fist through the wall just inches from Steve's head. He then let go of Steve's throat with his left and watched him slide down the wall until he sat hugging his knees like a terrified child. The big man slapped the top of Steve's head. "Are we clear?!"

Steve nodded quickly, afraid to look up.

The big man turned to leave and Steve's gaze fell on Samantha. He was too afraid to speak to her; he could only stare his regret through desperate, pleading eyes.

"Asshole," was all she said before she turned and followed the big man, slamming the door behind her.

Steve Lucas dropped his head between his knees and started to cry.

* * *

Monica lit a cigarette once they were inside the Dakota. "'Baby sister'?" she said.

"What?" John said, cracking a window. "I could pass for your older brother. Daddy rescuing his daughter felt too cliché."

"But you *are* my daddy," she said in a mocking, child's voice.

"Well that whole scene was a crock of shit anyway, so who cares?"

She inhaled deep, grinned, and blew a stream of smoke at him. He frowned and fanned it out his window.

CHAPTER 41

It was just past ten and Patrick was still clacking away on his laptop at the kitchen table. A glass of Glenlivet neat sat to his left.

"Oh I see," Amy said, sneaking up behind him, kissing his neck, then picking up his drink. "You can drink at home, but I can't?"

Without turning around he said, "I don't plan on going cruising after."

She bonked him lightly on the head, then sat on his lap. He took his hands away from the lap top, wrapped them around her waist and kissed her.

"You're so funny," she said once their lips separated. Amy was glad they were now at a point where they could make light of "that night." It wasn't stand-up material yet, but it had definitely reached breezy status.

He kissed her again and said, "I shouldn't be much longer."

She scanned what he was writing. "Looks like a screenplay."

He chuckled, looked back at the laptop, and spoke while glancing over what he'd written. "Yeah—PowerPoint slideshow will give me a good ten seconds before changing photos, but I need to be smack-on-cue with each frame like I *am* acting. And if I can convince these people that something as lethal as Megablast is the be-all, end-all, I think I'll be ready for Hollywood."

She chuckled softly then kissed his cheek. "You'll be fine."

He took a deep breath. "Hope so. Ten days and counting."

She laid her head on his shoulder. "So are you almost done?"

His left arm still around her waist, he typed a few more things with his right hand and said, "I think so. Why?"

"I thought I'd give you a blowjob before bed to relieve some of your stress."

Patrick clicked save, closed his laptop, and said: "Done."

CHAPTER 42

Patrick was double-checking various graphics on his PowerPoint presentation when co-worker Todd Hartnett rapped on his office window. Patrick spun away from his computer and waved Todd in.

"Hey, Todd, what's up?"

"Wondering if you've heard from Lucas."

"*Steve* Lucas?"

Todd nodded. "Hasn't shown today."

"Somebody call him?"

Todd nodded again. "Just voicemail."

"Maybe he's sick."

"He never called in though," Todd said. "He's got to pitch that software account soon, doesn't he? The foreign language program?"

"Yeah, Friday I think."

Todd said, "I'd have to be on death's door to keep me outta here if my presentation was at the end of the week."

Patrick nodded lazily in agreement. He had fallen into a daze, recalling the incident with Steve Lucas from the previous Friday. Lucas was going to see his new girl. He seemed excited. Maybe they ran off to Vegas and eloped?

Patrick said: "Huh."

"What?"

"Nothing, I'm just . . . Lucas invited me to happy hour last Friday. Wanted me to meet his new girl. I was thinking maybe they eloped or something."

Todd snorted. "Well if they did, then I hope for his sake the girl's got some money—'cause if he doesn't explain his whereabouts soon, he's gonna lose that account."

Patrick nodded in agreement again.

Todd Hartnett left. Patrick gave recent events a few more seconds of consideration, then discarded the issue and went back to work.

* * *

Patrick sipped from a bottle of warm Coke and looked at his watch. It was 4 p.m. Steve Lucas had yet to show today. Why the hell should he care? After what the prick said to him on Friday he's lucky he didn't crack him one.

Patrick took the last swallow of his warm Coke, tossed it in the trash, and spun back to his PC. He stared at the screen. It may as well have been blank. He *did* care. Damn it, for some reason, he did.

Patrick picked up his phone and punched two numbers. "Suzy, can you get me Steve Lucas at home?"

"It's just voicemail," his secretary said. "People have been trying all day."

"What about his cell?"

"We've been trying both."

Patrick sighed. "What about an address? Do you have his home address?"

A pause.

"Suzy?"

"I'm looking . . . here it is."

She read it to him and Patrick jotted it down.

"Are you going to see him?" she asked.

"I don't know. I might. Thanks, Suzy."

* * *

Patrick double checked the address he had written down, looked at the house, then tossed the address onto the passenger seat and stepped out of the Highlander. He walked the path towards Steve Lucas' front door and rang the bell.

No answer.

He knocked hard. "Steve? You in there? It's Patrick Lambert."

The door opened a crack, the chain still on. Patrick took in a slice of Steve Lucas' face.

"Steve? You alright, man?"

"You alone?" Lucas asked.

Patrick looked behind him, then back at Lucas with an odd look. "Uh . . . yeah. What the hell's going on, man?"

Lucas slid the chain and opened the door a little more. "Come in. Hurry up."

Patrick stepped inside. Lucas locked the door behind him and slid the chain back home.

"Steve, what the hell? You're acting like aliens are watching you or something."

Lucas shuffled into his living room and flopped onto his sofa. He was dressed in sweats and a white undershirt. His stubble looked to have several days' growth.

Patrick took a few cautious steps forward. He saw a hole in Lucas' dry wall the size of a small melon.

"Steve?"

Lucas looked up.

"Lots of people were asking about you at work today," Patrick said. "They tried calling you."

"I know."

Patrick made a face. "Okay . . . any reason you didn't answer? Call back?"

Lucas massaged his temples, opened his mouth to speak, but said nothing.

Patrick stepped further into his living room. "Are you sick?"

Lucas shook his head.

Patrick walked further towards the kitchen to his left. "So what's up then, man? Are you gonna say something or what?"

Lucas kept quiet on the sofa. Patrick was in the kitchen now. He opened a cabinet and spotted a bottle of vodka. A drink. Maybe a drink would relax him and loosen his tongue.

Patrick took the bottle from the cabinet and called: "How about I fix us a drink?"

"*NO.*" Lucas' voice was strong and firm. And then a few seconds later, soft and weak: "I'm never touching the stuff again."

Ah, Patrick thought. *Now we're getting somewhere.* He stepped out of the kitchen and sat on the coffee table in front of the sofa. "What happened?"

* * *

Patrick pulled into his garage two hours late. Not a big deal with the Megablast account looming, except that he'd told Amy he'd be home on time. When he walked into the kitchen she was already doing dishes. She didn't look at him.

"It's in the microwave if you want it," she said.

He walked up behind her at the sink and kissed the top of her head. "I'm sorry I'm late. But trust me, I've got a good reason."

* * *

They sat on the sofa together, Amy lengthwise with her feet in Patrick's lap, he upright and massaging her feet—good for a couple of points after being late for dinner.

"How bad was it?" Amy asked.

"He didn't really go into detail," Patrick said. "He claims she showed up with a shiner. That's bad enough I suppose."

Amy nodded. "I remember him from your work parties."

"He claims he doesn't remember anything. Not even a blur." He tugged one of her toes, cracking it.

She slapped his hand. "I hate that."

He smiled knowingly.

"So did this lady call the police?"

"I don't think so," Patrick said. "I think she would have done so by now. Besides, from the size of the hole in his wall, and from what Lucas told me, the lady's brother seems a far scarier threat than the police."

"So then what . . . ? Is the guy just going to hide in his house forever? What about work?"

"That's what *I* asked him. He's got this big account coming up. If it doesn't pan out due to sheer bad luck, then oh well, it happens to the best of us I guess. But if it doesn't pan out because he became an unproductive recluse a few days before the presentation . . ."

Amy slit her own throat with her thumb and made a gurgling noise.

Patrick said, "Exactly."

"And you were worried he was trying to horn in on Megablast."

"I wasn't worried."

She flicked her foot up and nicked his chin.

"I *wasn't*," he insisted. "I just worried he would . . . muddle things for me."

"*Muddle* things?"

Patrick tried for another toe, but she jerked her foot away in time and shot him a look. "Yeah, you know—the guy's a distraction," he said. "I didn't want him watching my every move, maybe dropping a dime on me here and there if I didn't do something he thought I should."

"Well who the hell is he to judge how you handle your accounts?" she asked.

"Nobody, I'm just saying." Patrick then groaned, trying to find the right words. "He's like that annoying friend at the bar who could ruin your chances at getting laid that night."

Amy cocked her head, arched both eyebrows. "Interesting analogy."

"Oh stop—you know what I mean."

Her expression remained fixed on him.

"Look, I've been massaging your smelly feet now for over ten minutes. You can forgive me one questionable analogy."

She shoved her foot in his face, grinding it into his nose. Patrick turned away and pretended to gag.

"Dick," she said.

"I have a big *what*?"

"You wish." She shoved her foot in his face again. Patrick laughed, snatched her ankle, and started attacking more toes.

CHAPTER 43

Steve Lucas eventually showed up for work on Wednesday looking as if he'd just come from a funeral. On Friday, the presentation for the foreign language software company came and went—and went hard. Although Patrick heard it second-hand, the prospective clients had stayed for all of twenty minutes before packing their things and heading out. Lucas apparently crumbled right after, breaking down in tears. Whether it was this pathetic display or not, something tugged on the heartstrings of the powers above and Steve Lucas was kept on board. Granted, his next account was something a sophomore in high school could handle, but it was still work. He still had a job.

Lucas knocked lightly on Patrick's office window the following Monday. Usually, Lucas would just walk on in without an invite. Apparently his reprieve had knocked his bombastic nature down a peg, and that was just fine with Patrick. He waved him in.

"Hey, Patrick," Lucas said softly. "Can I sit?"

Wow, Patrick thought, *the man's been reborn.* "Sure," he said. "Have a seat." And then once they settled, "What's up?"

"Couple of things really. First, I wanted to thank you for coming by to check on me." He looked over his shoulder despite the closed office door, then lowered his voice. *"I trust you didn't tell anybody anything?"*

Patrick shook his head. "No—I didn't say anything."

Lucas sighed as though he'd been holding his breath. "Thanks."

Patrick nodded once. "No problem, man. I'm glad they decided to keep you on board."

Lucas didn't acknowledge the comment; he appeared pre-occupied with things already spoken. He looked up at Patrick with soulful eyes. "You won't say anything, will you, Patrick?"

Patrick gave a thin smile. "No, Steve, I won't. What's done is done, okay? Let's just focus on the future."

Steve Lucas' face started to brighten. He stood and extended his hand. "That's great. Thanks so much, man."

Patrick shook his hand. "Not a problem. Let's get back to work now, yeah?"

Lucas' face continued to brighten, to change, as if all truly *had* been forgotten. Could that be possible? Patrick wondered. Was the old Steve Lucas back just like that? Patrick felt a twinge of something. Jealousy maybe?

"Got the big Megablast presentation soon, right?" Lucas said, taking a seat again. "Wednesday?"

Patrick nodded slowly and reluctantly. "Yup. Two days."

Lucas leaned back and put his feet up on Patrick's desk. "You feel good?"

"Fine," he said, his eyes on the souls of Lucas' shoes.

"Nervous?"

Patrick's toes bunched together like fists, his jaw clenched until he was aware of it. Again he wondered, why? The presentation was all but done. He was more than prepared—a fighter who had trained harder than he'd ever done his entire life. All there was left to do was step into the ring and do his job. So why was this twerp stressing him? After recent events, Steve Lucas was anything but a threat to his account now. Yet perhaps Patrick's analogy to Amy the other night, no matter how crude, wasn't too far off: He was about to get laid, and he didn't want some cock-blocking idiot like Steve Lucas to ruin it somchow.

"Not nervous at all," Patrick said, his tone flat. "Why would I be?"

"No reason." Steve unwrapped a stick of gum and folded it into his mouth. He chewed and clicked like someone without a care in the world. "It's a big deal is all. Want to make sure you're up to the challenge, feeling good."

Patrick felt his face getting hot, his jaw beginning to ache.

You beat the shit out of some poor woman, blew a huge account, nearly lost your job, and now you're sitting here with your feet on my desk, clicking your gum without a fucking care in the world, as if nothing happened.

Patrick decided right then and there that Steve Lucas wasn't just someone he deemed mildly annoying. He hated him. And as much as it dented his ego, Patrick was now certain jealousy was indeed the primary reason. Steve Lucas had somehow come out of his debacle a rosebud, with only a matter of memory-suppressing time before he flourished again. For Patrick and his family, each passing day felt like a long drive through a dark tunnel—a constant journey of heartache that teased his family with a small square of light in the distance when things seemed to be getting better, only to see that square shrink to nothing without warning, placing them right back into darkness no matter how fast or determinedly they drove on. Steve Lucas was cverything bad that was happening to Patrick and his family. Steve Lucas was the unrelenting hand of bad luck that prodded him without mercy whenever that tunnel seemed it might have a bright end.

(Crescent Lake)

(weeks of healing in cold hospitals)
(months of psychotherapy)
. . . prodding him with his goddamned feet on his desk while popping his gum and smiling . . .
(Caleb and the tacks)
(endless nightmares)
(the infamous trial looming)
. . . as though nothing had ever happened . . .
(Oscar dying)
(Bob dying)
(Amy drinking and driving)

"Yeah, I feel good, Steve." Patrick stood, and with a giant swing, swiped Lucas' feet off his desk with such force, he nearly tipped the man over in his chair. "Why the fuck shouldn't I?"

Steve Lucas stared back at Patrick like a frightened boy, his mouth hanging open in shock, the chewed gum visible.

"How the fuck can you sit there and talk to me like that after what you did?" Patrick said. "You think you get some kind of free pass? You think you're different than everyone else? You were like a little bitch when I went to see you last week. You were like a little bitch a few *hours* ago when you thought your career was fucked. And now you act like it's all okay? You act like I couldn't go out there and tell everyone what really happened? What you did?"

Lucas' lips trembled as he tried for words.

"Why the *fuck* do you care so much about my account, Steve? What the fuck does it have to do with you?"

Any flash of the old Steve Lucas had reverted back to the terrified version Patrick had seen that night in the man's home. He leaned into Patrick's desk and whispered fast and desperate. *"Patrick, I'm sorry, I'm sorry. I didn't mean any harm, man, I was just talking, you know? Just talking. Please don't say anything, man. Please. I was just talking.*" He hurried towards the office door. "*I'm sorry, okay? I'm sorry.*"

"You just can't act like nothing ever happened, Steve. It doesn't work that way." Patrick's face was blood-hot, his chest heaving. The old stab wound on his abdomen throbbed—the first time in awhile—and it only served to anger him further. "Get the hell out of my office, Steve. In fact, avoid me. Avoid me until I tell you *not* to avoid me. Understand?"

"Okay, man. Okay." For the second time this month, Steve Lucas scuttled out of Patrick's office afraid. The first time it happened, Patrick smiled; he had felt justified, had felt good.

He didn't know exactly what he felt now. It certainly wasn't good.

CHAPTER 44

"Whoa," Amy said that night when Patrick told her what had happened.

"I know," he said, taking his plate to the sink. The kids were out of earshot in the den watching TV. "I fucking lost it," he whispered all the same, Carrie possessing superhero hearing abilities when it came to curse words and all.

Amy stayed seated at the kitchen table and handed Patrick her plate. He took it to the sink and started washing while he spoke.

"I don't know what happened. I mean the guy's a tool, but I really laid into him. Everything just seemed to hit me all at once." He turned and faced her, plate in one hand, towel in the other.

"What do you mean *everything*?" she asked.

He shrugged, turned back to the sink and continued with the dishes. "Everything."

Amy glanced over at the kids, then back to Patrick. "You mean CL?"

Patrick faced her again. "No, not just that. Well yeah, that, but everything else, you know? CL and the residual effects are bad enough, but Jesus, have we gotten a fucking break since?"

Carrie's head spun towards the kitchen. "Did Daddy just say the F-word?"

Patrick and Amy simultaneously hummed: "*No.*"

Carrie looked at Caleb, said, "Yes he did," then went back to watching television.

Amy lowered her voice and leaned forward at the table. "Are you talking about woof-woof and Dad?" she said, careful not to say Oscar's name aloud, nevermind her father's.

"Yeah," Patrick said. "I mean are you fucking kidding me? After what we went through we should be getting fucking medals, but instead we get dead dogs and dead parents and more fucking gas on a fire that's been blazing for a fucking hell-of-a-long—"

Amy stomped her foot, cutting him off. Both kids were staring wide-eyed at their father from the living room. No denying the F-word now. "Dead dogs" and "dead parents" weren't exactly poetry either, but it was all but certain those were forgotten instantly after good old Dad started mashing The Fuck Button.

Patrick sighed and nodded at Amy. He stepped into the den. "Daddy's sorry, kids. I did a very bad thing and I used the F-word. Can you forgive me?"

Caleb said: "I forgive you, Dad."

"Thanks, brother-man."

Carrie said: "Will you buy us a present?"

CHAPTER 45

John Brooks was sound asleep early Wednesday morning. Monica could hear him snoring through the motel door. She gave the door a shave-and-a-haircut rap.

The snoring stopped. "Who is it?" His voice was deep and threatening from the other side.

"Room service, dummy."

There was a moment's pause, then the sound of the bolt thumping and the chain sliding. He opened the door and shielded his eyes from the morning sun. "Why so early?" he grumbled.

"You sissy, I've been up all night." She handed him a large coffee and then sipped from her own.

John looked at his coffee then back at Monica. "You haven't slept?"

She walked into the motel room and took a chair. Her left eye was now a decent blue from her father's punch. "Nope."

"Why?"

"You *know* why. Besides, I was too excited." She lit a cigarette and smiled.

John stood by the still-open door—hair rumpled, eyes puffy, wearing only his boxer shorts. He looked at his coffee again as though he didn't know what to do with it.

"Well let's go, Daddy-O," Monica said. "Get dressed and caffeinated so we can begin."

CHAPTER 46

Patrick had trouble sleeping Tuesday night. He dozed briefly and dreamt about his presentation . . .

PowerPoint refused to work.

He jerked awake. Eventually dozed again . . .

He went blank in front of all those important faces, forgetting everything he'd rehearsed.

He jerked awake. Eventually dozed again . . .

He was giving the presentation naked.

He jerked awake. Jesus, did he just actually dream he was naked? Talk about Dream Anxiety 101. He gave a silent laugh and eventually dozed for good.

* * *

Patrick heard the tiny shuffling of feet, heard Amy hushing the children in whispers, the clanking of porcelain, glass, silverware. He felt their presence on him and smiled inside at what he knew was coming.

"Morning, Daddy!" Carrie blurted. Caleb blurted the same a second after, Carrie making sure to get hers in first.

Patrick rolled over in bed. Amy, Carrie, and Caleb stood bedside, Amy holding a tray of breakfast, the kids wearing excited grins.

"Whoa!" Patrick said. "What's this?"

Again Carrie beat everyone to the punch by declaring: "Breakfast in bed!"

Patrick sat up. "Wow! For me?"

Amy sat the tray on his lap and kissed him. He looked down at the bacon, eggs, and coffee, and then back up at his family. His heart swelled. He placed the tray on his nightstand and scooped both kids into bed with him. They giggled and squirmed as he wrestled and kissed them. Carrie wiggled free and began jumping on the bed. Patrick lifted up Caleb's pajama top and blew a big raspberry on his stomach, making him shriek then giggle. Witnessing this, Carrie turned to flee but Patrick latched onto her ankle. She screeched, both terrified and excited. Patrick yanked his daughter back onto the bed and gave her the same treatment as her little brother. She screeched again, impossibly louder than before, and Amy put her hands to her ears.

"*Okay . . .*" she said. "Let's let Daddy eat his breakfast."

Caleb hopped off the bed. Carrie remained, now straddling her father's chest. She bounced a few times, Patrick letting out "*oomphs!*" after each landing. She giggled and continued to bounce.

"Let's go, missy," Amy said.

Patrick shrugged at his daughter, pulled her in for a kiss and said, "Gotta listen to Mommy, kiddo."

Carrie pulled away and slapped a hand over her nose. "Eww, Daddy, your breath stinks."

Patrick looked at Amy. "My breath stinks, baby. You wanna smell?"

"I smelled it already, thank you."

Patrick sat up in bed and pulled the breakfast tray back onto his lap. With a snobbish manner he said, "Fine, you may now all leave Daddy and his stinky morning-breath so that he may eat." He clapped his hands twice. "Be gone!"

Carrie and Caleb left. Amy remained. She leaned into Patrick. "I'll hold my breath," she said and kissed him again.

* * *

The morning storm had come and nearly gone. Patrick had heard Carrie complaining about finishing her breakfast, heard her scurrying frantically throughout the downstairs with a shouting Amy hot on her tail so as not to miss the bus (*had she ever been on time for the darn thing?* Patrick wondered), and now he guessed only Caleb remained, waiting for his mother to take him to nursery school. He pictured his son sitting quietly at the kitchen table, legs hanging from the chair and swinging back and forth, patiently waiting for Mommy. He loved both his kids equally, no question about that, but Jesus, they were night and day.

He rolled over in bed, stretched and yawned. He was going in later than usual because he could. The presentation wasn't until 11:00. He wanted to be well-rested, avoid rush hour, and arrive with enough time to decompress and get in the zone before it all started.

"Knock, knock." Amy stood in the doorway.

He smiled at her and yawned again.

"How you feeling?"

"Good," he said. "Had a few nightmares last night."

Amy made a face. "You did?"

"Not *those* nightmares," he said. "About today. Even dreamed I was giving the presentation naked."

She laughed. "Cliché much?"

"I know, right?"

She sat on the edge of the bed and rubbed his chest. "You'll be fine. You could have aced this thing a month ago."

He took a deep breath and said, "Yeah."

"How was your breakfast?"

He took her hand and squeezed it. "Wonderful."

She leaned over, kissed him, and said, "I've got to go take Caleb. You need anything else before I go?"

"A promise to be naked and ready after my presentation?"

She threw him a coquettish look. "Done."

"Really? That easy?"

Amy leaned in to his ear and whispered: "*After you ace your presentation, I am going to fuck my amazingly talented and successful husband until he forgets his own name.*"

Name? I have a name? And what's all this about a presentation?

Amy left a speechless Patrick. It took a good minute or two before he could get out of bed comfortably.

CHAPTER 47

Patrick sat in his office chair, finishing his third cup of coffee. He looked at his watch. 10:30. Almost time. He stood and walked into the conference room. The large oval table held an extravagant spread of edibles, tea, and coffee. In front of each chair lay a leather-bound folder filled with all things Megablast. The high-tech projector and screen stood proud at the head of the room. A large bulletin board with various Megablast logos and slogans flanked the screen.

It looked good. Damn good. Patrick smiled and went back to his office.

* * *

10:45. Jonathan Miles, president of Miles and Associates, knocked on Patrick's window. Patrick waved his boss in enthusiastically then stood as he entered. Jonathan Miles was a short man, mid-60's, with thick gray hair and a plump belly. He was a friendly man, a fair boss, and all-business. Patrick liked him.

"How you feeling?" Miles asked.

"Good. Real good," Patrick said.

Miles shook Patrick's hand and patted his shoulder. "My man. I've got the utmost confidence." Miles looked at his watch then threw a thumb over his shoulder towards the conference room. "Five minutes?"

"You got it, boss."

Jon Miles smiled and left. Patrick did not sit back down. He remained standing, thought of the analogy he'd entertained the other day about the fighter who'd trained his heart out and was now eager to step into the ring and kick some ass. The analogy proved that much stronger now. He was the fighter, waiting in the tunnel, pacing, bouncing on his toes, a sweat already worked up, eager for his music to sound throughout the stadium so he could begin his march towards the ring. Patrick felt invigorated by these images. He was ready to do battle. Ready to kick some ass.

And then Steve Lucas walked by Patrick's window and glanced at him. And their eyes locked for a moment.

Lucas had done exactly as Patrick had so delicately suggested on Monday, and steered clear of Patrick these last couple of days. Patrick had only bumped into him once in the office kitchen where the two went about fixing their coffee in unbreakable silence—not even the slightest periphery glance had been chanced by Lucas.

Today, things were apparently different. Lucas not only glanced in Patrick's direction, but *held* the glance for a second or two. And it was not a frightened glance either, as Patrick might have guessed. Nor was it a scowl. It was just . . . a glance? The first eye contact they had made with one another since Patrick had told Lucas to stay out of his way.

Stop, Patrick told himself once Lucas was out of sight. *It was nothing. Stay focused.*

Patrick left his office and headed towards the conference room.

* * *

The Megablast clients were seated around the big oval table. Most had helped themselves to coffee. Some had a plate of edibles in front of them. Jonathan Miles sat closest to Patrick, who stood at the head of the room giving his introduction. So far, it was flawless. Patrick periodically glanced at Miles who returned a subtle look of pride. He was rolling.

Patrick hit a remote and the lights dimmed. Time for the PowerPoint presentation.

A moment later, all hell broke loose.

CHAPTER 48

The first few photographs on the automatic slideshow presentation were exactly as Patrick had expected, and he addressed each of them accordingly, perfectly:

The Megablast product being enjoyed by both athletes and regular Joes . . .
Enticing visuals of the "all-natural" ingredients that separated Megablast from the rest of the pack in the energy drink field . . .

And then:

A woman being screwed from behind while giving a blowjob to a second man in front . . .
A tangle of women going down on each other . . .
A close-up of a man's erect penis . . .

The table had collectively gasped after the first image. When shock released its hold on him, Patrick had snatched the projector's remote and began feverishly mashing buttons, hoping beyond hope that erasing the images would somehow erase the collective minds of his prospective client.

When Patrick's fumbling with the remote had failed, it was Jonathan Miles who'd leapt from his chair and picked the projector itself up, smashing it to the ground, even stamping on it despite the fact the images had finally left the screen.

Every member of the prospective client had hurried to their feet and out the conference room door with Patrick and Miles close behind, pleading that there'd been some dreadful misunderstanding, some horrible mistake.

The appalled Megablast tribe had said nothing, only hurried towards the elevators as though fleeing a potential assailant. Desperate, Patrick had attempted stopping the elevator doors from closing by slamming his hand against one of them. A female client slapped his hand away and called him a disgusting pig.

Patrick had brought his hand back as though suddenly burned and then watched helplessly as the metal doors came together until his clients were officially gone. He turned and gaped at Miles.

Miles said, "My office—*right-fucking-now*."

* * *

Patrick sat slumped over in front of Miles' desk, his head down, both hands pressed against it. Miles raged for over twenty minutes:

"Never in my 35 years in the business . . ."

"What the fuck is wrong with you . . . ?!"

"You've really done it, you son of a bitch. You've done it to yourself, and you've done it to ME! Do you know what this will do to us when word gets out?!"

When Miles had eventually finished his fume—and Patrick didn't dare speak a word during its entirety—his face was all veins and purple skin, both hands long since slammed and braced on his desk as he leaned in to hammer home each word. "Say something!" he demanded.

Patrick lifted his head, and a strange calm washed over him. Still upset of course, still confused of course, but . . . it wasn't him. He knew this as fact. And he felt a surge of righteousness in this undeniable truth.

"It wasn't me," Patrick said.

Miles blinked many times. "Come again?"

"It wasn't me."

Miles flumped back into his chair, threw his hands towards the sky. "Well hallelujah! That solves everything." He picked up the phone. "Let me just call them back and tell them that the goddamn skin flick they watched as part of *your* presentation had nothing to do with you. Let me just tell them that and then all will be right-as-fucking-rain." He slammed the phone back down.

Patrick's exterior remained calm while his mind surged with suspicion. "It was someone else," he said. "Someone did this to me. I don't know who, and I don't know how, but someone—"

When Miles and Patrick had first entered Miles' office, Miles had drawn the shades with such force that one shade had fallen closed on a locked angle, giving a small diagonal view into the reception area. And like some gifted clue, Patrick spotted Steve Lucas walking right on by.

That glance earlier. What was behind that glance? What was behind the son of a bitch's glance???

Patrick leapt from his chair and ripped open Miles' door. He was on top of Steve Lucas in two strides and snatched his arm as though grabbing a fleeing thief.

"Hey!" Lucas shouted. "What the—"

Patrick pulled Lucas back into Miles' office, slammed the door shut with the heel of his foot, and then shoved Lucas into the corner of the room.

"*Him,*" Patrick said, his finger pointing at Lucas with such malice it looked capable of firing bullets. "It was him."

Lucas stuttered, "What the hell is—"

"Shut up!" Patrick screamed. He turned to Miles, his finger still pointed at Lucas. "He fucked up that big software account and now he's fucking up mine! He's getting revenge because I know what he did."

Lucas went white. "I don't know what he's talking about, sir. I—"

"Bullshit!" Patrick spat at him. He went back to Miles. "You know why he blew that software account, boss? Because he was busy getting piss-drunk and beating the shit out of a woman. That's why. I'm the only one who knows that, and the little prick can't stand it." He whipped back to Lucas. "Can you? You can't stand knowing I've got one up on you. So you tap into my software and try to ruin me!"

"*STOP!*" Miles yelled. "Just . . . stop." He sighed and shook his head. "Look, I don't know what the beef is between you two, and to be honest, I don't care—in *my* place of work you leave that shit at the front door. Patrick, you pointing fingers isn't going to undo what just happened here today."

Patrick nodded fast. "I know it won't, I know. But it *will* prove that I didn't do this. That account meant everything to me." He pointed his finger at Lucas again. "And *he* knew that. *He's* responsible for what happened."

Miles hung his head, sighed, raised it and looked at Lucas. "Steve?"

Lucas looked terrified. "What?"

Miles splayed a hand. "Do you have anything to say?"

"*No.* I don't even know what's going on!"

"Somebody sabotaged Patrick's presentation. Some pornographic images were inserted into the automatic slideshow. The account is blown."

Patrick studied Lucas' reaction. Despite his rage, he could not help but acknowledge that Lucas wore a convincing look of shock. He was a wimp—he did not handle confrontation well. To think that he may be lying so convincingly now was difficult to accept.

Could it have been someone else in the office? Perhaps. Problem is, Patrick thought, contrary to Hollywood's lust for the beaten-to-death twist-ending, in real life it usually *is* the most likely suspect.

"It was him," Patrick said. "It had to be. Who else would have access to my office?"

"Patrick, I swear—"

"*Shut up,*" Patrick said without turning, his eyes fixed on Miles the whole time he spoke.

Miles sighed yet again, looked at both men with a show of contempt. He then picked up the phone and punched a few numbers. "Stan? It's Jon Miles. I need you to check all security codes entered into the system in the past—hold on . . ." Miles placed a hand over the receiver. "When was the last time you ran a check on your software, Patrick?"

Without hesitation, Patrick said: "Right before I left last night. After six."

Miles took his hand away from the receiver. "Yeah, Stan, you still there? Check and see if anyone came in after six last night."

"I left at five last night," Lucas blurted. "My brother and his kids are in from out of town!"

Both men ignored him—the holy grail of truth lie on the other end of the telephone receiver.

Lucas continued pleading. "I'm telling you, I—"

Miles held up a hand, silencing him. "Yeah, Stan, I'm here . . . uh huh." His eyes fell hard on Lucas. "Thanks." Miles hung up. "Steve, our security system says you entered the building at exactly 12:15 a.m. last night. The officers ended their shift at 12. System says you swiped your way out at exactly 3:47 a.m. You mind telling me what you were—"

Patrick spun and hammered Lucas in the face, shattering his nose into a bloody mess. Lucas fell back against the wall and slumped to the ground in a daze.

"*You motherfucker!*" Patrick screamed, burying his foot into Lucas' ribs. The man cried out, moaned and rolled over into a fetal ball.

Patrick kicked his spine.

He kicked the back of his head.

He kicked his spine again.

Miles hustled from behind his desk and grabbed Patrick from behind in a bear-hug. Patrick threw him off with ease and continued to kick Lucas anywhere he could. Miles gave up, turned and yanked open his door. "*Call security!*"

A beast Patrick long-thought dead—a beast he sometimes refused to believe he had once embodied—had been resurrected, and when security rushed in to try and restrain him, Patrick actually roared.

It took four guards to finally subdue him.

CHAPTER 49

They were not back in Miles' office after the fray. They were in the security office on the bottom floor. Patrick sat in a chair, a security guard on either side of him. Miles was on his feet, pacing back and forth in front of Patrick as he spoke.

"Lucas is on his way to the hospital," Miles said. "He looks like a goddamned bus ran him over."

Patrick stayed quiet, looking at the floor. His rage was not gone; common sense just had a hold on it.

"His story checked out you know," Miles said. "His brother and kids in town and all."

Patrick lifted his head. "What?"

"We checked into it. His brother and kids *were* at his place last night."

Patrick frowned, dropped his eyes for a moment as he searched for reason. When they snapped back up on Miles, he said, "The system said he got here after twelve and stayed until almost four. He could have snuck out after they went to sleep."

"His brother claimed they were up until *two*, catching up. He's willing to testify to that."

Patrick was adamant. "But that's not—then how else do you explain . . ."

Miles stopped pacing and faced Patrick. "I don't know how to explain it, Patrick."

Patrick slapped his own chest. "You still don't think *I* had anything to do with this, do you?"

Miles closed his eyes and shook his head. He looked earnest. "No."

"Well then what the hell could have—"

Miles held up a hand. "Cool it, Patrick. Just cool it." He waited a tick. "The only logical thing I can think of right now is that someone got a hold of Lucas' key card."

Patrick dropped his eyes in thought again. In his haste to blame Lucas he had never considered such a possibility. "Okay . . ." he said. "So then who would have—?"

"*Except,*" Miles interrupted, "Lucas had his key card on him when he was carted off to the ER. We checked."

"So then both Lucas *and* his brother are lying," Patrick said.

Miles grabbed a chair and pulled it close to Patrick's. He sat facing him, looked Patrick in the eye with equal parts sympathy and severity. "I don't think they are, Patrick." Miles lowered his voice—the guards could still hear, no doubt, yet he lowered it all the same for what Patrick guessed was the *man-to-man, let's cut the bullshit* spiel to come. "Look, Patrick, I'm not an ignorant boss. I'm not blind. I know my employees, and I know Steve Lucas can be a pain in the ass sometimes. But I also know he wouldn't do something like this. He doesn't have it in him, he doesn't have the balls. He's a decent employee, and he can get the job done, but there's a reason he never gets the really big accounts." Miles leaned in closer. "Now, having just admitted that to you, can you honestly tell me you think Steve Lucas is capable of pulling something off like *this*? Something of this magnitude?"

Patrick flashed on Lucas in his apartment last week. How scared he looked. How child-like. Patrick flashed on the times he told Lucas to get the hell out of his office. Again, how scared, how child-like. Miles was right: Steve Lucas was an annoying douche, but not the type to pull off something like this. What happened required planning, significant tech-knowledge . . . and a serious set of balls. Once again Patrick had to concede to Miles: Lucas didn't have big balls. Average ones even.

Patrick pinched the bridge of his nose. "Okay," he said. "So what now? Is the blame back in *my* lap?"

Miles leaned back but did not move his chair. "No," he said. "I don't believe the Patrick I knew had this in him either."

Patrick frowned. "The Patrick you *knew?*"

Miles looked at both guards. "Can you leave us alone for a few seconds, fellas? It's okay."

The guards exchanged glances then left.

Miles continued. "I know about what you and your family went through, Patrick."

"Jon—"

Miles held up a hand. "I mean who doesn't, right? The media didn't exactly try to keep it a secret. And the public, they watch the news, they're horrified for a bit, and then just like that it's over and forgotten. Kind of like watching a movie. But it doesn't work that way for you—it's not forgotten just because it's over. I'm not an ignorant boss. Something happens to a man after war. It changes him. Some say that war is the easy part. It's the after that tears you up."

Patrick went to speak, but Miles raised his hand again.

"But you're a strong son of a bitch, Patrick. Not just here . . ." He touched Patrick's thick arm. "But in here . . ." He touched Patrick's heart. "And up here . . ." He pointed to Patrick's head. "I wouldn't have brought you back if I didn't think you were ready. And I gave you Megablast because I *knew* you could handle it. Hell, maybe part of me suspected you *needed* something that big to occupy your mind. It wasn't pity though. Christ, no, it wasn't pity. This is my company after all; I can't afford to be gracious at the expense of my wallet." He smiled.

Patrick didn't.

"And then I hear about your father-in-law," Miles continued. "I even hear about your dog."

Patrick's chin retracted.

"I'm not an ignorant boss, Patrick . . ."

Yes, you've made that quite clear.

"I haven't been in this business as long as I have without keeping solid tabs on all my employees." Miles leaned back in his chair. "So I'll be honest with you, Patrick. A part of me thought about taking Megablast away from you. I gave it to you in confidence when you came back to work. But after what's been happening the last few months . . ."

"*What's* been happening?"

Miles held up both hands and patted the air. "Relax, Patrick. I'm just saying every man has his limits."

"Limits? You think I'm cracking up? You think I put porn in the biggest presentation of my life as some kind of joke?"

"Did I say that?"

"You're implying it."

"I don't imply, Patrick. I *say*. And if I thought you were cracking up I would have taken you off the Megablast account immediately."

"So then what's all this, 'the Patrick you knew' stuff? Are you saying I'm not the same guy?"

Miles was beginning to look annoyed. "I'm saying you need some time off."

"You're firing me."

"No—I'm saying you need some time off."

Patrick's breath quickened. "Tell me something," he said.

Miles straightened his posture. "What?"

"Tell me what you think happened. You don't imply, you *say*, right? So say what you think happened. Say what you think happened to the presentation I *killed* myself over for *months*. You wanna have those guys come back in and check the security system again? Have them check and see how late I've been staying here every night? How much time I invested into this project, only to put a *giant fucking cock* up on-screen—"

"Patrick!"

Patrick stopped, his breath ragged, pulse hammering his skull.

There was a moment of pause as both men collected themselves.

"Okay," Patrick eventually said. "So I need some time off. What—two, three weeks?"

"More like *months*, Patrick."

"Months." Patrick flashed a contemptuous smile. "If you're going to fire me, Jon—"

"You're not fired, Patrick. But you *will* take some considerable time off."

Patrick looked away.

"You'll be compensated of course," Miles said. "No change in benefits."

Patrick wanted to scream. To punch holes in all four walls. Instead he swallowed bile, turned back to Miles and said, "Okay."

They both stood and shook hands. Miles usually patted Patrick on his broad shoulders after a handshake. Not this time.

* * *

Patrick shoved the glass doors of the office building open as he made his way outside, a cardboard box of certain belongings tucked under one arm. The winter air bit into his nose and watered his eyes, and he believed it happened on purpose.

Patrick moved quickly through the lot towards his car, the cardboard box nearly slipping out from under his arm. He caught it just in time, but a stapler still fell and hit the concrete. Patrick believed this happened on purpose too. He kicked the stapler across the lot, sending it skidding beneath a car. He spotted a man and a woman watching him in the distance.

"What the fuck are you two looking at?!" he yelled.

The couple turned their backs to him and began a huddled chat as though they'd never dared look at him in the first place.

Patrick opened the Highlander, chucked the box into the passenger seat, then screeched out of the lot and sped for home.

* * *

"Here he comes," Monica whispered to her father.

They stared as Patrick kicked the stapler across the lot.

"What the fuck are you two looking at?!"

They turned away from Patrick and huddled together, giggling silently like kids. When the Highlander was gone they erupted in laughter.

When they stopped, Monica lit a cigarette, inhaled deep and said, "I wonder how bad my lover-boy Steve is."

John smiled. "He didn't look so hot when they wheeled him out." John's smile changed to a sly smirk as he eyed his daughter. "You knew he'd snap and throw him a beating right then and there didn't you?"

Monica exhaled a long stream accentuated by the cold, then batted her eyes. "I'd hoped. Call it a pleasant bonus."

He grinned. "Have I ever told you how proud of you I am?"

"Not today."

"Apple of my eye, baby girl."

CHAPTER 50

Patrick and Amy were on the sofa. Patrick had told her everything.

"Something's going on, Amy." He shook his head, flustered. "*Something.*"

Amy had been prepared for two basic outcomes after her husband's presentation: pass or fail. She was confident in pass, and was prepared for a hearty celebration. Fail was of course a possibility, but even if you took away her bias and optimism and laid out simple truths, it seemed unlikely Patrick *could* fail given the time and work he had invested in Megablast. Not to mention his consistent rise within the company since the day he'd signed on. And even if he did fail, so what? It wasn't for lack of trying. There would be other accounts.

Except Patrick *had* failed. And all of the rationale Amy had gathered to cushion such potential bad news was immediately tossed when it was revealed exactly *why* Patrick had failed. Sympathy and compassion and reassurance had been replaced with *what* and *the* and *fuck?* as Amy struggled to digest such an outlandish tale. She believed her husband's story though. Never once doubted him. Truth, as the old saying goes (and after what her family had been through, she sure-as-shit believed it), was stranger than fiction.

Amy rubbed his leg. "What do you mean? Something like what?"

"This is no longer bad luck," Patrick said. "Oscar? Your dad? Bad luck, I can admit that. But this? No fucking way."

Amy steadied herself. "Well what do you think happened?"

"I would have sworn it was Steve Lucas. Would have sworn on anything. But now . . ."

Amy really didn't know what to say. She shared her husband's sentiments—Oscar and her father had been bad luck. These new events were deliberate. There was no other explanation. "So now you're not sure it was Steve?"

Patrick laid his head back against the sofa and sighed. "I don't know. Who else could it have been?"

"Is there anyone else at the office you suspect?"

"No. Besides, how could they have done it? How could they have gotten into the system with Lucas' identity? Cracked my files and altered my presentation as smooth as they did? As far as I know, Jason Bourne doesn't work at the office."

Amy smiled even though she knew the quip had no intention of producing one. "Maybe you should go see Lucas."

Patrick lifted his head off the sofa. "*What?* What makes you think he's gonna want to see *me*? Shit, I'm still praying he doesn't press charges."

Amy knew her husband too well not to suggest it again. She knew the idea had crossed his mind. "Do you really believe it was him?"

Patrick stared at the ceiling for a silent moment. "No," he eventually said, dejected. "Jon was right. Lucas is a pain in the ass, but he doesn't have it in him."

Amy continued to stare at Patrick, her look repeating her previous suggestion.

"What would I say?" he asked.

"You could start with 'I'm sorry.'"

"Fine—I go say I'm sorry and kiss his ass so he won't press charges. Then what?"

"What do you mean?"

"Well, I can't just let this drop. I have to find out who did this." Patrick stopped, his fist tightened. "I swear that son of a bitch is behind it somehow."

"You just said—"

"Not Lucas."

Amy read his mind. "Patrick . . ."

"*What?*"

"You know that's impossible."

"So who was it? His asshole-brother's ghost?"

"Go see Lucas," she said. "And then after that, I think you should go see Dr. Bogan."

"*Dr. Bogan?*"

"You respect him. You've told me a dozen times you think the guy is a genius."

"He works with *kids,* Amy. Besides, we've got Dr. Stone."

"So then just talk to him. Invite him over for a chat. Nothing official."

"What about Dr. Stone?"

"Dr. Stone is great—but she's for us. This is for you. It wouldn't hurt to call and ask. Tell him what happened. Ask him to drop by for a man-to-man chat. Tell him you value his insight."

"I don't know." Patrick's eyes scanned Amy's face. "Doesn't this bother you? You know I didn't do it. Don't you want to know who *did*?"

"Of course I do, baby." And then a sudden voice in her head asked: *Could* it be Arty? Amy's paranoia since the moment they'd arrived home from the hospital was no less severe than Patrick's, perhaps more so, but the possibility that Arty was somehow behind this, locked up hundreds of miles away in Pittsburgh, seemed impossible.

She buried the thought instantly and continued. "And ultimately I think we'll find out who's responsible. In the meantime, I think it might be wise to make amends with Steve Lucas. We've already got one court hearing coming up, the last thing we need is to look forward to another. Besides, maybe he'll have a few theories of his own about what happened. It might shed some light on a possibility you haven't considered yet."

"I've considered everything."

"You're also upset. Your anger's probably clouding your mind."

Patrick sunk into the sofa and rubbed his eyes. "Okay, fine."

"And you'll call Dr. Bogan?"

"I don't know if they can do that—make house calls."

"You can still try. Again, nothing official—just someone you can vent to. How many times did you tell me you wished he was *our* therapist?"

"Okay, I'll try."

CHAPTER 51

Steve Lucas had been released from Chester County hospital the same day he'd arrived. He had a broken nose, two broken ribs, and a jacket of bruises.

To Patrick's surprise, Lucas let Patrick into his home and offered him a seat without a fuss. Lucas' nose was plastered with a white dressing and both eyes were already black. He winced as he took a spot on his sofa. Patrick sat in a chair to Lucas' left.

"I'm not pressing charges, Patrick, if that's what you're worried about," he said. "I thought about it, believe me I did, but you were the only one who came to check on me after . . . you know."

"I'm sorry, Steve. I have no excuse for my actions." This wasn't exactly true. At the time, Patrick felt he'd had a damn good excuse. "I had just worked so goddamned hard on that account. What happened . . . what happened was . . . Jesus, I don't even know what to call it."

Lucas nodded. "It was fucked up."

Try, Patrick thought. *What have you got to lose?* "Can you think of anyone at work who might have been capable?"

Lucas shook his head. "No. And I especially can't think of anyone who could get hold of my key card, use it, then slip it back into my wallet hours later without my knowing it."

That was a big piece of the puzzle. If the key card was missing, then they'd be scratching the surface—someone had stolen his card and they'd be off to some kind of start. Problem was, the card wasn't missing—Lucas still had it; apparently always did.

Someone could have hacked into the security system in order to frame Lucas, Patrick supposed. It was possible. But it raised some questions. The first being why frame Steve Lucas? Because Lucas can be an asshole. That was easy enough. The second question was not so easy. Why sabotage Patrick's account in one's efforts to frame Lucas? What was the connection? Someone with the know-how on hacking into a high-tech security system could almost certainly think of better ways to mess with Steve Lucas than ruining Patrick's account in the process. Perhaps Lucas and Patrick shared a common enemy at work? Who, though? Patrick liked to believe he got along well with everyone. And he was more than confident that if he had done something to upset someone in the past, it certainly didn't warrant a retaliation in the vein of what he'd received. No. It didn't add up. None of it added up.

"Who do *you* think it might be?" Lucas asked. "Besides me of course."

Patrick gave a little smile, grateful Lucas had already resorted to levity. "I have no idea, man."

They sat in silence. Patrick looked around the room and saw that the big hole in Lucas' wall had not yet been fixed. Should he change gears and mention it? He knew Lucas didn't like to talk about it, but perhaps if Patrick expressed more interest in the debacle that had ensued with the girl Lucas had been seeing, it would cement Patrick's status as the caring individual who'd checked up on him, lest the man ever change his mind about pressing charges.

"Any updates on . . ." Patrick pointed to the hole in the wall.

Lucas didn't have to turn around and look. "No, thank God."

"You really don't remember anything about that night?"

Lucas shook his head. "I remember meeting her at the bar. The rest is a blank."

"Maybe someone slipped you something."

Lucas shrugged. "Too late to check now—if they did it would already be out of my system. I can tell you one thing though, Patrick: you can think whatever you like of me, but I have never laid a finger on a woman in my life. I'm no angel, I'll admit to that, but even at my worst, I have never, *ever* . . ." He dropped his head and ran a hand through his hair. "Something weird happened that night. Something I had nothing to do with." He brought his head back up and locked eyes with Patrick. "I'd bet my life on it."

Patrick looked at the coffee table and spotted Lucas' cell phone. "Did you go through your phone? Look for any numbers dialed? Weird text messages? Pictures?"

Lucas nodded. "Yeah—nothing. Just the one photo I took of us when we first got to the bar. *That* I remember taking."

"Let me see," Patrick said.

Lucas held his ribs and winced as he leaned forward and grabbed his phone. He punched a few buttons then handed it to Patrick.

It was a picture of Lucas, grinning in all his glory, his arm out of the frame, holding the camera phone. His other arm was around a gorgeous blonde. She looked familiar.

"Huh," Patrick said.

"What?"

"She looks familiar."

"She does?"

"Yeah," Patrick said, frowning at the phone. "Where though?"

Lucas said nothing.

"Where did you meet her?"

"At a bar around the corner. Bravo's."

"What's her name?"

"Samantha."

Patrick stared at the image until it fuzzed. He blinked hard and continued looking. Where had he seen her? It had been recent. He knew it was recent. Maybe he had seen her at Bravo's too. Except he had only been to Bravo's once—a long time ago.

Recent. Recent. Where? Whe—

Patrick's heart skipped. Bob's funeral. He was looking at a picture of the gorgeous woman from Bob's funeral.

"*Can't be,*" he whispered.

Lucas said, "Huh?"

Patrick ignored him. It couldn't be. He remembered that woman as having dark hair, dark eyes. This woman was blonde with (he squinted) green eyes. Besides, Bob's funeral was in *Harrisburg*. That woman claimed she was a local, knew Bob from Gilley's Tavern. Steve's photo was taken *here*.

It couldn't be her. No way.

"Nothing," Patrick said, shaking his head, handing the phone back to Lucas. "She reminded of someone I recently met."

"You met her?"

"No, no. The woman I met lived in Harrisburg. She was at my father-in-law's funeral. Besides the woman I met had dark hair and dark eyes. They just look a lot alike I guess."

Lucas said, "Well, if you ever do run into her, steer clear. The girl is bad news."

CHAPTER 52

Amy was heading out for the night with friends. Patrick told her not to drive home drunk. She punched him in the chest and told him he was hilarious.

An hour later the doorbell rang. Dr. Bogan wore a pleasant smile as Patrick invited him in and took his coat.

"I really appreciate you coming, Dr. Bogan. I know this isn't usually the norm."

Dr. Bogan waved away Patrick's comment. "Not a problem."

They left the foyer and entered the den. "Can I get you a drink?" Patrick asked. "We've got scotch, gin—"

"I don't suppose you have any V8 Juice?" Dr. Bogan asked.

"I . . ." Patrick turned towards the kitchen. "I'm not sure. Let me check." Patrick hurried towards the kitchen and checked the fridge, hoping to spot Dr. Bogan's request. No luck. He checked the pantry. A large bottle stood tall and unopened. Nobody in their house drank V8, but there it was. Sadly, Patrick thought, this plastic bottle of vegetable juice might be the only pleasant surprise he'd had all week. "Eureka," he called into the den. "It's warm. Do you want ice?"

Dr. Bogan, who had been puttering around the den, fingering books on shelves and smiling at family photos, said he would.

Patrick returned to the den with a tall glass of V8 with ice. "You don't mind if I fix myself a drink, do you?" Patrick asked.

"Of course not."

Patrick opened the liquor cabinet adjacent to their largest book case, poured himself a Glenlivet neat, and motioned for Dr. Bogan to sit anywhere he wished. Dr. Bogan took the chair next to the sofa. Patrick took the sofa.

"Cheers," Patrick said.

Dr. Bogan smiled with his eyes and clinked Patrick's glass.

They sipped, sighed, then sunk into their seats.

Patrick had explained everything to Dr. Bogan over the phone, even his paranoid fears that in some inexplicable way, Arty Fannelli was responsible for recent events. Initially he had no intentions of briefing Dr. Bogan over the phone, but at the time it felt necessary, perhaps trying to convince Bogan to show in case the good doctor thought it best otherwise.

Despite the briefing and the obvious subject at hand, Patrick felt he should begin by wading into the shallow end. "Caleb is doing great," he said. "Better than great. He looks forward to your visits."

Dr. Bogan set his V8 on the coffee table. "Tell me about you," he said.

Patrick smiled. He should have known small talk was off the curriculum with Dr. Bogan.

* * *

"What you're suggesting is somewhat fantastic, Patrick," Dr. Bogan said.

"I know—I don't see how it could be possible either. Christ, I even called Pittsburgh this morning to see if he was still locked up."

Dr. Bogan accommodated him. "And is he?"

Patrick smiled. "Yes."

Bogan returned the smile and sipped from his second glass of V8.

"It's just this whole thing—everything that's happened after Crescent Lake—it's something *he* would do."

"The sabotage of your account?" Dr. Bogan said.

"No. Well, yes, but . . ." Patrick gave a frustrated sigh. "Okay, here's the thing: before everything got really bad at Crescent Lake, there was all this . . . bad luck. I mean it's all hindsight now, and I've been trying desperately not to kill myself over it, but we should have left that goddamned place *long* before everything went to hell. You see, that's how they worked, him and his brother, they played *games*. They probably could have killed us whenever they wanted to—Christ, from the day we first arrived there for all I know. But they toyed with us. Even when they had us captive they still . . ." Patrick clenched his fist. "They still had to have their fun, still had to play their little games.

"Before we even met them they were already planning, had already chosen us. And they were *smart*. Apparently they'd been doing this shit forever. They play little tricks and set little traps. They make you doubt yourself; chalk everything up to bad luck. Every-single-little-thing that happened—and again, I'm talking before we were tied up, before shit got *real* bad—was planned by them. From the moment I met the bastard at the gas station, their game had already begun. It just grew and grew from there, and before my stupid ego accepted the fact that this was *not* just bad luck, that these were *not* freak occurrences, it was too late. They had us." Patrick drained his second scotch. "They fucking had us."

"And so now you think this bad luck—everything you've experienced since you've returned from Crescent Lake—is *not* bad luck," Dr. Bogan said. "That it's Arthur Fannelli managing to orchestrate some type of *new* game from behind bars in Pittsburgh."

"Ignoring my gut last time got a knife rammed in it," Patrick said. "I almost lost my family. I won't—it's *not* going to happen again."

Dr. Bogan stood and began wandering around the den as he spoke. "The blown account does raise cause for concern. But the dog? Your father-in-law?"

"*And* Amy's drunk driving after her father's *drunk-driving-death.*" Patrick added.

Dr. Bogan shot a curious look over his shoulder. "Grief, followed by bad judgment?"

"See that's just it, Dr. Bogan. It doesn't seem possible, it doesn't make sense. But after what I've been through, after being up close and personal with this psychopath, I can now—without a fucking doubt—tell you this: It *can* make sense. It *can* be possible." Patrick stared at his empty glass. "I just don't know how."

Dr. Bogan began fingering the books on Patrick's shelves again. "A fan perhaps?"

"What?"

"It's a sad truth that serial killers have an enormous fan base. Perhaps Arthur Fannelli is pulling the strings of some admiring puppet on the outside."

Patrick was stunned. He feared Dr. Bogan was doubting him, filing him under paranoia as ninety-nine percent of other shrinks likely would have. But now he gratefully remembered why Dr. Bogan was not like ninety-nine percent of other shrinks, why he'd called him in the first place. The man had no preconceived notions. He did not jump to textbook conclusions. He eliminated the impossible, and whatever remained, however improbable, would likely be the truth. A modern day Sherlock Holmes . . . who drank V8.

"I never thought of that," Patrick said. "Jesus Christ, I never even *thought* of that."

Dr. Bogan continued puttering around the den as he spoke. "Many serial killers have copycats," he added. "A sick homage to their idols."

Patrick hopped to his feet. "Well that must be it then! He's got some crazy fan who—"

Dr. Bogan held up a hand, then kindly waved Patrick back into his seat. "It's a possibility, Patrick, that's all. We know someone ruined your presentation, that's irrefutable. But the other occurrences? To make them look like bad luck and accidents? That would take a significant degree of cunning. I question whether the type who would deify a character of Arthur Fannelli's ilk would be capable of such feats."

"Well like you said yourself—what if Arty's pulling the strings? *Telling* the guy what to do?"

"Well then that brings us to the issue of communiqué. How would Arty be pulling these strings? I would be shocked if all his incoming and outgoing mail wasn't thoroughly scrutinized."

"Maybe Arty paid off one of the officers. I've read about corrupt guards helping prisoners. They do all kinds of crazy shit for them. Even help them escape."

Dr. Bogan nodded. "Possible."

Patrick felt a queer sense of excitement, like a detective on the verge of cracking a case. "So what can we do?"

Dr. Bogan picked up the guest book from Bob's funeral. Audrey Lambert did not want the book; its reminder would have forced sincere grief, popped her little bubble-world of repression. So Amy had taken it.

Dr. Bogan smiled at the larger-than-life photo of Bob Corcoran on the cover of the guest book. "Well we can contact the prison again," he said as he began leafing through the book. "Ask if any mail has seemed out of the ordinary."

"Should we call now?"

Dr. Bogan flipped another page. "I think it can wait until morning."

"The trial is this Monday."

"He's not going anywhere, Patrick."

"But if we find something, we can use it—his insanity plea won't stand a chance."

"Most insanity pleas don't stand a chance anyway." Dr. Bogan flipped another page of endless signatures. "Your father-in-law was a popular man."

Patrick felt a twinge of irritation at Dr. Bogan's diversion; he wanted to stay on topic. "I know, but listen, if we call now—"

Dr. Bogan said: "*Stop.*"

Patrick thought Dr. Bogan was somehow reprimanding him for his incessant questioning. Yet the doctor's eyes remained on the guest book, his index finger marking something.

Dr. Bogan's expression rarely changed; it was always calm and assured. Pleasant was the closest he came to excitement, and anger did not exist. His expression now was different, something Patrick had yet to see in the man. It crackled with intensity and focus. Dr. Bogan handed Patrick the open guest book and pointed to a name:

A. Fannelli.

Patrick lifted his eyes off the page and locked them with Bogan's. Patrick got it now, the doctor's new expression: Holmes had found his improbable truth.

Patrick said, "You've got to be fucking kidding me."

* * *

Amy was pleased to see Dr. Bogan's car still in their driveway when she came home. She hoped the doctor's long stay was a sign that things were going well, that he was helping Patrick in ways she felt she couldn't.

Amy pulled into the garage and hit the automatic door. It hummed shut behind her. She entered the mudroom and only had time to remove one shoe before Patrick rushed forward and shoved the guest book into her face.

* * *

"I knew it," Patrick said. "I fucking *knew* it. Same thing at Crescent Lake, Amy. Same exact thing."

Patrick and Amy were on the sofa. Dr. Bogan was back in his chair.

"All this bad luck—it was impossible," Patrick added.

Amy kept her eyes on the signature in the guest book. "I don't get it. How?"

"We think it's a fan. Someone Arthur Fannelli is manipulating on the outside," Dr. Bogan said.

"But *how*?" Amy asked again.

"Well, that's the mystery," Dr. Bogan said.

"But that signature in the guest book proves that *someone* was at your dad's funeral," Patrick said.

Amy considered everything. "Maybe it was a sick joke. Someone with a very bad sense of humor."

"Come on, Amy. It was your father's *funeral*. I don't care how messed-up your sense of humor is, nobody's gonna do something like that. Whoever wrote that knew what they were doing. Even more unsettling—knew exactly where we'd be that day."

"So then why didn't he do anything?" Amy said. "If he knew where we were, why didn't he try and hurt us after the funeral?"

"Because it's all a fucking game!" Patrick yelled. "Why didn't they kill us straight away at Crescent Lake? You know how that son of a bitch works!"

Amy's pulse quickened. "So is this signature a sign of more to come? Do we have to worry about someone else now?"

Dr. Bogan looked at Patrick. "I think we should call Allegheny County. Ask about fan mail. See if anything out of the ordinary has stood out."

"Don't you think they would have contacted us?" Amy asked.

"Not necessarily," Dr. Bogan said.

Patrick said, "I'm calling right now."

* * *

Patrick snapped his phone shut, reentered the den shaking his head. "They said nothing out of the ordinary, all things considered. Said the only thing that had them scratching their heads was a sympathy card."

"A what?"

"A sympathy card addressed to Arty. No return address. Consideration for the passing of Mae's father."

Amy fell momentarily silent.

Patrick reiterated: "The jail said that was the only item that stood apart from the rest of the sick fan-mail he gets."

Dr. Bogan suddenly stood. The Holmes expression was back. "I wonder if the smug bastard had the audacity to spell it with a y."

Patrick said, "Huh?"

Amy locked eyes with Dr. Bogan, became his Watson. "I'm May."

Dr. Bogan nodded. "Indeed you are." He looked at Patrick. "May is an anagram for Amy. Either way you spell it—M-a-e, or M-a-y—the message is still very clear. The sympathy card was telling Arthur Fannelli that Amy's father was dead."

* * *

Patrick slammed the phone down onto its receiver. He had phoned the Allegheny County Police again, explaining their discoveries, and then phoned the local police explaining the same, demanding protection for his family. The Allegheny County Police assured Patrick that Arthur Fannelli had no outgoing mail. Was even denied internet access. That ruled out any prompting on Arty's end. The Allegheny County Police surmised that the "fan" had simply heard of Bob Corcoran's unfortunate accident and reached out to Arty in some ambiguous way to inform him. The local police agreed with the Allegheny County Police, but still agreed to investigate and send a cruiser by periodically to check up on the Lamberts. It could not be ignored that a crazed fan was out there somewhere, and that the Lamberts could be in some type of danger. This held little comfort.

"Fucking bullshit," Patrick said. He paced throughout the den. "The son of a bitch is in jail and he's *still* getting to us. This is a goddamned nightmare."

"Is it possible?" Amy asked. "Is it possible my father was murdered?"

"Why not?" Patrick said. "Whoever the hell it is out there, they could have made it look like an accident." He turned to Dr. Bogan. "Right?"

"I suppose," Dr. Bogan said. "Though it's likely that what the police said is true: the fan read about the death of Amy's father and took the initiative to inform Arthur Fannelli in some cryptic way." Dr. Bogan scratched his bald head then asked: "The police did a thorough investigation of the accident?"

Amy said, "Yes."

Dr. Bogan nodded slowly, silently digesting her response.

"What about Oscar?" Patrick said. "Maybe this fan messed with my car—cut the hose so the antifreeze would leak all over the driveway."

"But then comes the daunting task of ensuring the dog consumes the antifreeze," Dr. Bogan said.

"Except the poor little guy *did* consume it," Patrick said. "So whatever trick he had up his sleeve sure as hell worked."

Dr. Bogan turned to Amy. "At your father's funeral—did anyone stick out? Was there anyone there you didn't recognize?"

"There were lots of people there we didn't recognize," Amy said. "My dad had a million friends."

"Did anyone say anything to either of you? Anything out of the ordinary?"

Both Amy and Patrick said no.

The doorbell rang. Patrick left the den to answer. He returned with an officer from the Upper Merion Police Department by his side. The officer stood as Patrick took his spot back on the sofa.

"I'm Detective Knauer," the detective said. "I'm going to be asking you a few questions, okay?" He took out a small notebook and pen.

* * *

Amy and Patrick recounted everything for Detective Knauer. Dr. Bogan remained silent. The detective asked what Patrick felt were rudimentary, and therefore useless questions:

People following you?

No.

Approached by strangers?

No.

Damage to your property?

No.

Anything at all that may seem out of the ordinary?

It was then that Patrick blurted: "You mean aside from having our dog die, my wife's father die, and someone slipping porn into my presentation?"

The detective appeared unfazed by Patrick's frustrated outburst and continued questioning. "How close of a daily routine do you keep?" he asked.

Amy asked him to elaborate.

"What I mean is—is your daily routine clockwork? Do you take scheduled walks on specific routes? Visit certain places regularly? Leave for work at precisely the same time each day? Things like that."

"This is suburbia," Amy said with a whiff of contempt. "Everyone has a routine."

Again the detective ignored any passive-aggressive remarks and continued jotting in his notebook. "Neighbors," he then said. "Have any neighbors mentioned anything to you? Suburbia tends to have an eye out every window. Have any neighbors reported any suspicious characters in the neighborhood?"

"If they did, no one mentioned anything to us," Patrick said.

"I assume you have a community watch?"

Amy said, "Yes." She then looked at Patrick and said, "Margaret Connors would call 911 if she saw a deer roaming the neighborhood."

Patrick nodded at his wife then looked at the detective. "A neighbor of ours," he said. "A retired woman who, like you said, always keeps one eye out the window."

The detective jotted it down then put his notebook away. "Okay, folks—I've got everything I need for now. I'll be in regular touch with the Allegheny County Police Department, and we'll be doing periodic checks on your home. Meanwhile I suggest you try and deviate from your regular routine as much as possible."

"Won't be a problem," Patrick scoffed. "I don't have a job anymore."

Amy rubbed his leg and whispered, "Yes you do."

"In the meantime, if you spot any suspicious-looking men or women, please call. Nothing is insignificant."

Women? Patrick thought. It never occurred to him that the fan could be a woman, that a woman could be capable of such things. *Wouldn't that be perfect though? Who would suspect? Who would—*

"*Wait.*" Patrick stood. "Wait, wait, wait." He thought of the woman on Lucas' phone. The woman at the funeral. Their likeness. Her beauty. What was it Amy's brother Eric had said at the funeral after they'd met the woman?

If I was straight . . . ?

No, not that. It was *Amy* who'd said what he was digging for:

No way a girl like that goes to Gilley's. She'd stick out like a Victoria's Secret model at a sci-fi convention.

His wife was right. He'd been to Gilley's—the best looking woman he'd seen all night was a five, tops.

"The woman at the funeral," Patrick said to Amy. He thought, fuck it, and added, "The hot one. You said it yourself: no way would she go to Gilley's; she'd stick out like a model at a sci-fi convention, remember?"

Amy nodded. "Yeah. So?"

"I might have seen her again."

"*What?*"

"No, it's not like that. It's—" Patrick rushed into the kitchen and grabbed his cell phone. He dialed Steve Lucas' number as everyone from the den looked on.

"Hello?"

"Steve! It's Patrick."

"Hey, man, what's—"

"The girl. The bad news girl. You say you met her locally, right?"

"Yeah."

"What else can you tell me about her?"

"Why?"

"Please, Steve. What else?"

"I don't know. What do you mean?"

"Anything strange about her? Anything unusual?"

There was a pause.

"Steve?"

"I'm thinking . . . I don't know, she was kind of aggressive I guess."

"What do you mean?"

"Well, she slept with me the first night we met. And she was the one who instigated it. I thought it was a one night stand thing or whatever, but we went out again the next night. She seemed like she wanted to pursue something."

"What makes you say that?"

"Well she dropped by work a few times. Brought me lunch. I figure a girl just looking for a good time wouldn't—"

"*She what?* She was at the office? Where was I? Why didn't *I* see her?"

"I don't know. You were always out I think."

"Son of a bitch. What else?"

"She's got a monster for a big brother. But I already told you that."

He *had* told Patrick that. And Patrick had forgotten. *There's two of them,* he thought. *Christ, there's two of them.*

"He looked older though," Steve added.

"What?"

"The guy said he was her big brother, but he looked too old. I mean, not real old, just too old to be her brother. But who knows?"

"Father maybe?"

"I guess."

"Do you still have that photo of her on your phone?"

"No, I erased it."

"Fuck."

"What's going on?"

"Nevermind. Thanks." Patrick hung up and returned to the den. He dove right in as though everyone had been listening to his conversation and didn't need any briefing. Fortunately, he was right.

"This woman was aggressive with Lucas—courted him and slept with him on the first night. *She* was the one who instigated it. You've seen this woman, baby, she's a knockout. What would you rate Lucas?"

Amy shrugged. "Average at best."

"Exactly. Why would a knockout like her express such dire interest in someone like Lucas? Immediately seduce him?" The room remained quiet. The detective listened on with the anxious look of a civilian now. "Lucas claims she came by the office several times during that week they were dating."

"She did?" Amy said. "You didn't see her?"

Patrick felt an odd surge of delight in relaying the details of the mystery, forgetting for a moment that the whole debacle cost him his account. "No—I was never there. She always showed up when I wasn't in the office. That means she was watching me." He looked at the detective with what felt like a kindred stare and added: "*Studying my routine.*"

Detective Knauer nodded back, eyes affirmative and intense.

"Let's face it," Patrick said, bringing his attention back to the group. "She already *had* Lucas. She had him the first night she slept with him. So why bother coming by to drop off lunch or say hello?" He paused a tick, looked at everyone. When no one spoke up, he said: "She was getting the layout of the office."

"But how would she get in after hours?" Amy asked.

"Lucas blacked out the night of their incident. Says he can't remember anything. My guess? She drugged him and took his key card."

"But you told me Lucas still *had* his key card; it wasn't missing," Amy said.

"Then she probably took it and made a quick copy," Patrick said. "Placed the key back into Lucas' wallet before he woke up."

"Can you copy those things?" Amy asked. "It's not a turn-key."

"Why not?" Patrick said. "With today's technology . . . ?"

The room fell silent for a tick, taking it all in.

Detective Knauer started scribbling in his notebook again. "Can you give me a description of the woman? A name maybe?"

"Lucas said her name was Samantha. I doubt that's her real name though."

"Description?" the detective asked again.

Amy and Patrick looked at one another. "I don't know," Patrick said. "At the funeral she had dark hair and dark eyes."

Amy said, "About five-six, I guess. A hundred and twenty-five pounds."

Patrick nodded in agreement.

"Anything else? Anything distinguishing?" Knauer asked.

"She was beautiful," Amy said. "*Really* beautiful. And she had a way about her—like some sultry model or actress or something."

Patrick chose not to nod on that one.

Knauer jotted more in his notebook.

"However," Patrick said, "the picture I saw of her on Lucas' cell phone was different. She had *blonde* hair and *green* eyes."

Dr. Bogan finally spoke. "A disguise?"

"Probably," Patrick said.

Knauer looked suddenly disappointed. "Those are two very different descriptions, Mr. Lambert."

"It was her," Patrick said. "I'm sure of it."

"Does this Steve Lucas still have the picture?" Knauer asked.

Now it was Patrick who looked disappointed. "No—he erased it."

"So in essence, we don't really know *what* she looks like," Detective Knauer said.

"I'd know her if I saw her," Patrick said.

"That's not too helpful," Knauer said. "We need to get an exact description out for the general public if there's any merit to this."

Patrick felt a jab of annoyance at the detective's sudden skepticism; for a brief moment he believed Detective Knauer was hanging on his every word. "Merit?

How else can you explain this? It makes perfect sense to me."

Knauer nodded. "It does seem plausible, but without a description . . ."

Amy said, "We gave you a description."

"A woman that looks like a sultry movie star, who could have either dark hair and dark eyes, or blonde hair and green eyes?" Knauer splayed his hands.

The detective was right. It annoyed Patrick to no end, but the man was right. He then suddenly remembered Lucas' comment about the big man who punched a hole in his wall.

"There's something else," Patrick said. "I think there are two of them. A man is involved too—a big guy, older. Lucas said the guy claimed to be this woman's big brother, but looked more like her father."

Knauer flipped back pages in his notes. "The man who confronted Steve Lucas the next morning after he blacked out."

"Right," Patrick said. "That could explain Bob's accident. A slight woman would have trouble staging such a thing alone. But with the help of a big guy?"

"I was reliably informed that your father-in-law's death was an accident. His blood alcohol level was .29. That's very drunk."

Amy said, "Yes—we're well aware. But my father's been driving home drunk from that bar for years."

The logic in Amy's statement was as empty as the night she'd said the same to Sergeant Bennett in Harrisburg. Detective Knauer's judgmental expression reflected that empty logic. "It only takes one time, ma'am."

Patrick spoke up. "You're right. We're not condoning anything. But what my wife is alluding to, what our gut is telling us, is that somehow—" He stopped, took a long, necessary breath. "*Somehow. . .*"

Detective Knauer put his notebook away. "We can start with the description of the woman. I'll have some men ask around your office, see if they can add anything to it. It's doubtful we can pursue anything about Mr. Corcoran. He was cremated, yes?"

Amy looked at her feet and said, "Yes."

Knauer nodded. "That rules out an autopsy."

"So basically there's nothing we can do," Patrick said.

"I didn't say that," Knauer said. "Like I mentioned earlier, we'll check in on you periodically, have a cruiser patrol the area. And we'll try for more testimony at your place of work—try and get a better description of the woman."

Patrick wanted to laugh in the detective's face. From the moment his family encountered the bastards back in Crescent Lake they were already two sizeable steps behind, playing their twisted little game without an invite. Why would it be any different now?

No more doubt.

No more chalking it all up to bad luck.

Call him the most paranoid man on earth, but from now on Patrick's gut was better than any possible evidence the police could unearth. His gut was everything.

"Fine," Patrick said. He shook the detective's hand and thanked him but meant none of it. Let them ask questions at the office. Let them patrol the area and pop in from time to time. He knew it would amount to nothing—Arty was pulling the strings, and his puppets seemed exceptionally capable. Initially, Patrick almost insisted they go right to the source and sweat Arty until he bled the truth. But he knew that would be futile—Arty would assuredly deny everything, feign ignorance. And most importantly, the son of a bitch would love it. He would love being so intimately involved, to know the Lamberts were suffering still. Patrick would *not* give the prick the satisfaction.

"You're going to court on Monday, yes?" the detective asked as Patrick and Amy led him to the front door.

"Yes," Patrick said. "We're leaving tomorrow. Going to stay the night."

"I suggest you focus on that," Knauer said. "Once he's convicted, and he *will* be convicted, then I can assure you he'll spend the rest of his life behind bars. Graterford Prison is rough. Maybe you can take some delight in knowing that he'll be receiving some serious karma from his fellow inmates." Knauer smiled and winked.

Patrick's face remained grave while he opened the front door for the detective. "They can send him anywhere they want. It won't matter."

Detective Knauer sighed as he stepped outside. "We'll find whoever's responsible, Mr. Lambert."

"Good luck." Patrick closed the door.

CHAPTER 53

Patrick and Amy arrived in Pittsburgh just after seven on Sunday night. Previously, they had arranged for the kids to stay with Patrick's parents. Now it was out of the question. Patrick and Amy wanted their children with them at all times.

They were greeted at the hotel soon after their arrival by two officers from the Allegheny County Police Department. The officers were scheduled to work in shifts standing guard outside the Lambert's hotel door. A part of Patrick wished this crazy bitch and big guy would show that night and the officers would shoot them dead.

If there really is a crazy bitch and big guy out there doing Arty's bidding, a sliver of his paranoia said.

"No," he whispered to himself. "There is. There is."

* * *

Sleep seemed almost laughable. Still, they managed some. Patrick was awake by six, Amy stirred moments later. The kids remained out cold.

The couple dressed quietly, speaking in whispers. Carrie eventually woke at seven. Caleb stayed zonked.

"We should wake him," Amy said to Patrick. "I want to get them a little something to eat before we leave." The plan was to leave the kids in police custody while Patrick and Amy were in court, and Amy wasn't sure the police would have the presence of mind to feed her kids while they were gone. Chips and soda from a vending machine maybe, but Amy wanted at least one proper meal in their bellies before she and Patrick returned—whenever that would be.

Carrie overheard her mother's suggestion about waking her brother and instantly yelled at Caleb to get up. Amy tweaked her daughter's ear and told her to be nice.

"Go brush your teeth," she told them both once Caleb was on his feet.

Patrick nudged Amy to the far corner of the hotel room, out of earshot. "How do you feel?"

"Nervous," she said. "I don't want to see him again."

"Remember, baby: the final fuck you. We look that bastard dead in the eye and let him know we won."

"Did we?"

"*Yes.* To hell with what's going on now. *To hell with it.* We don't let him see any of our grief; we don't give him the satisfaction. We can do this, baby. We beat him once and we *will* do it again." He then flashed a devilish smirk. "Hell, I'm even starting to look forward to it."

Amy hugged him. Patrick lowered his lips to her ear. "The final fuck you, baby. Just like we planned. He's just a man. A sick, pathetic man . . . and he messed with the wrong goddamned family."

Amy hugged harder. Patrick kissed the top of her head. "We can do this, baby."

* * *

The Lamberts exited the hotel room and were immediately greeted by two officers. Good mornings without smiles were exchanged. The officers then led the family down the hall towards the elevators, a man in front, one bringing up the rear. Once everyone was safely piled inside, one of the officers hit the lobby button, the doors closed, and the elevator hitched before descending.

"Makes my belly feel funny," Carrie said.

One of the officers looked down at her and smiled.

The number eight on the panel above glowed.

Seven glowed.

Six.

Five.

Four.

The elevator stopped. The doors opened. A young man and girl. The officers told them to please wait for the next lift. The officer hit the lobby button again.

Three.

Two.

The elevator stopped again. One of the officers grumbled under his breath. The doors opened. No one was there. An officer poked his head out, looked left and right.

Nothing.

The officer came back inside the lift and shrugged, went to hit the lobby button once again but stopped. The radio on his shoulder had started to crackle then screech. Caleb jumped and Carrie held her ears.

The officer adjusted a dial, tilted his chin towards the radio and clicked it. "Go ahead."

The voice came back stern and sharp. "*What's your position?*"

"Coming down in the elevator now. Stopped on the second floor."

"*Take them back up to the room. Do it now.*"

The officer frowned. "Say again, sir?"

"*Take them back up to the room now. You've got backup coming up the stairwell. Feds are on their way.*"

"*Feds?* Sir, what's the FBI—?"

"*Do it now.*"

"Roger that." The officer let go of his radio and pushed the button for the ninth floor. The doors closed.

Patrick said, "What's going on? Why is the FBI on their way?"

The officer flipped the snap on his holster and gripped the handle of his gun. He looked at Patrick and said: "I have no idea."

CHAPTER 54

Earlier

6 a.m. Monday morning. Arthur Fannelli was still on his cot, wrapped tight in a blanket. A heavy metallic thud echoed down the jail's corridor. He rolled towards the wall. The sound of uniformed footsteps clacked closer until they stopped in front of his cell. Now two dings of a night stick on the cell bars.

"Rise and shine, Fannelli. Big day today."

Arty stayed wrapped in his blanket and glanced over his shoulder. "You finally getting your GED?"

The officer cranked the key, slid the cell door open with a boom. "Fannelli, I really don't want to have to explain how you slipped and fell—*again*—before your big day in court."

Arty stayed put.

The officer entered the cell, began clinking his night stick against the metallic sink. "Last warning, Fannelli. You getting up?"

Arty rolled over, kicked off the blanket, sat up and yawned. He was already dressed—the orange jumpsuit given to him the night before.

"Good boy, Fannelli. If I didn't know any better, I'd say you were almost eager to go and get your ass kicked up and down that court r—"

Arty hopped to his feet. The officer jumped back and raised his baton. Arty smirked, turned around and placed his hands behind his back to be cuffed.

The officer shoved Arty's face into the wall as he cuffed him. "Yeah—you keep smiling, fuckface."

* * *

The gray armored bus transporting Arthur Fannelli to court hit a bump in the road and the vehicle bounced.

"Whoa! Careful, fellas—I'm in no hurry," Arty called from the cage in back. Both his hands and his feet were shackled. Outside the wire mesh cage sat three officers— one close to the cage, one seated towards the front of the bus, one the driver. All but the driver held a shotgun in his lap.

The officer close to the cage glanced at Arty. "How can you sit there and smile?"

Arty shrugged, his cuffs clinking between his knees. "Just feels like a good day."

The officer smirked. "All you freaks act tough . . . until they start carrying you away. Then you start cryin' like the pussies you are."

"Assuming I'm found guilty," Arty said.

The officer snorted. "And you all think you're gonna go free too. Delusional dipshits."

Arty kept smiling.

The driver checked his side view mirror and muttered, "What the hell is this?"

The officer closest to the driver looked out the side window. "What does she think she's doing?"

Arty strained forward until the cuffs bit into his wrists and ankles. Peering out the windows ahead and to his left, he caught a glimpse of a red sports car speeding next to the bus on the rural two lane road. He strained an inch further, glanced down and saw no dotted lines on the road for passing, just two parallel strips of solid yellow. The red sports car eventually passed the bus, then immediately sliced in front, disappearing from Arty's view in a blink.

The bus driver hit the brakes and then his horn. "Stupid rich bitches," he said. "Always in a hurry to get nowhere."

"Should call it in," the officer in front said. "Give her dumb ass a tick—"

The driver stomped the brakes and screamed: "*BITCH!*"

The bus screeched and swerved, nearly tipping to one side as it tried to stop its mass on a dime. The officer by the cage flew into the seat ahead of him. Arty rocked to one side, the cuffs biting deeper into his flesh.

The bus was stopped now, engine idling, all four men—Arty included—breathing heavily.

The officer in back spoke first. "The fuck is going on?!"

The officer in front stood, turned and faced the officer in back, shotgun held tight to his chest. "Some stupid bitch just pulled out in front of us, then hit her fucking—"

The officer's forehead exploded.

Arty watched three more instantaneous pops, each one a tiny explosion of glass and blood. The driver took one in the head. The officer by the cage, the head and neck. All three men were dead. No question.

Arty's breathing was erratic. This was it. This had to be it.

A small detonation at the front of the bus made Arty flinch. The door was now open. A slender woman appeared through a faint cloud of gray smoke. She pointed a pistol at the dead driver and shot him twice more, and then the officer in front twice more. She moved with a hurried calm towards Arty's cage. The woman was wearing sunglasses. She took them off for a moment and winked at Arty. He grinned back.

His sister Monica bent and snatched the keys from the dead officer at her feet. She unlocked the cage and then her brother's cuffs. She pumped two more bullets into the officer and then handed the gun to Arty. He pumped a third bullet into the dead officer, and then a fourth that made him laugh.

Monica smiled, took her brother's hand and led him quickly down the bus' aisle and out to the battered Dodge Dakota that was waiting for them. Monica got into the passenger's seat, Arty in back where what looked like some kind of sniper-rifle lay at his feet.

"Dad," Monica said to the driver. "I'd like you to meet your son, Arthur."

CHAPTER 55

The Lamberts' hotel room on the ninth floor was crowded and noisy. FBI agents and Allegheny County officers walked in and out, their radios constantly crackling information, their chatter amongst themselves sometimes whispers, sometimes loud.

Arthur Fannelli had escaped his transport to court. He was loose. And he'd had help—professional help. A rookie cop on his first call would have spotted this truth after five minutes on the scene. Three officers of the Allegheny County Police had been murdered. The department wanted swift vengeance for their fallen comrades, however there were strong possibilities that Arthur and his accomplices had already crossed state lines. This meant the FBI. So in addition to the noise and chaos filtering in and out of the hotel room, a fog of resentment from the Allegheny County Police was in the air. It was why sometimes there were whispers and sometimes there weren't—the officers whispered to one another (subtle sneers on their faces making one wonder why they bothered whispering at all); the agents spoke loud, establishing a sense of dominance and control over the situation, aware but indifferent to the officers' disdain at their arrival. Patrick guessed they were more than used to it whenever they arrived to assist in an investigation.

Patrick also guessed something else, and it seemed to surprise Agent Chris Miller when Patrick voiced it.

"What makes you think he won't cross state lines?" Miller asked.

"Because I know," Patrick said.

Miller frowned. "You mind giving me a little more?"

"He wants *us*. He doesn't want to hide."

"Maybe. But he'll want to hide for now."

"For now," Patrick said with a shrug. "But he'll find us." The initial panic was gone—for Patrick *and* Amy. A type of defense mechanism had kicked in. An acceptance of sorts. Not defeat, no. Just acceptance.

Agent Miller studied Patrick. Patrick stared right back, his expression calm and indifferent, almost bored. "If he *does* find you—" Miller began.

"He will," Patrick said.

"—then we'll be there to grab him."

"*Them.*"

"*Whomever.* We *will* find them, and we *will* protect you and your family, Mr. Lambert. This is a whole new ball game now."

"Amy!" Patrick called across the room. "Amy, come here a minute."

Amy left Carrie and Caleb with one of the Allegheny County officers and joined her husband's side.

"They're going to protect us," Patrick said. "Apparently it's a whole new ball game now."

Amy said, "That's super!"

Miller let out a long breath, dropped his head and nodded slowly. "Look—I can't even begin to imagine what you folks have been through—"

"No, you can't," Patrick interrupted, his demeanor still calm and certain. "But you go on ahead and do your job. You try and find the son of a bitch and his new buddies. And you try and protect us all you want; we won't refuse. But if it's all the same to you, I'm calling in an old friend."

Miller said: "What?"

Amy said: "Who?"

Patrick said, "I'm calling Domino. If anyone can protect us from those psychopaths, it's him."

"Who's Domino?" Miller asked.

"An old buddy of mine. We played football together in high school. He went into the Marine Corps after that. He's got his own security company now. He's also the toughest motherfucker on Earth. I'm calling him."

"We don't need anyone impeding our investigation," Miller said.

"He won't *be* investigating. He'll be protecting."

"I told you, we'd do that," Miller said.

Patrick gave the indifferent shrug again. "Sorry, Agent Miller, but your words offer little comfort."

Miller let out another long breath. "Mr. Lambert, I appreciate your situation, and I understand your reluctance to trust—"

"No you don't. You just admitted you didn't a few minutes ago. Right now there are precious few people my family trusts."

"But you're willing to trust this Domino."

"Yes," Patrick said without pause.

"Mr. Lambert, we cannot have some rogue tough guy jeopardizing procedure. The people who pulled off this escape appear highly trained."

"Domino's hardly a rogue. He and his team are as professional as they come. Look him up: *Domino Taylor*."

Miller shook his head. "It's a bad idea."

"I'm calling him," Patrick insisted. "Right now I believe he's the only man capable of protecting my family."

Miller threw up his hands. "Alright . . . alright fine—it's your dime though."

"He won't charge me a penny."

"Just make sure he stays out of our way."

"He will," Patrick said. "In fact you'll never know he's there—not if he doesn't want you to."

* * *

Amy remembered Domino Taylor well. It was hard to forget such a man, even after the five years that had passed since he'd last been to the house. Amy had still been pregnant with Caleb then, and of all things impressive about the man, she would always remember his massive frame dropping to one knee so he could talk to Amy's pregnant belly, the whites of his animated eyes heightened in his chocolate complexion, his voice a bass that shook items off tables in contrast to his gentle, nurturing words, telling Caleb he could not wait to meet him, could not wait for the day they could throw the football around together.

And of course there were the stories Patrick had told her. What an accomplished soldier Domino had been, the action he saw, his prowess on and *off* the battlefield with his new career in security, protecting the elite of the elite. It was unparalleled. Yet what Amy would always remember was the way he spoke into her belly that night. And it was why she agreed with her husband's decision to hire Domino to protect them. Because she knew he would—with his life.

"Are you sure he'll be available?" Amy asked Patrick when they stepped out into the hallway of the hotel.

"I don't know. He called to check in on us after what happened at Crescent Lake. He knows what's going on."

"I know. It doesn't mean he'll be available though," she said.

"True. But something tells me he'd find a way for us."

"I hope so."

CHAPTER 56

"Mr. Patrick Lambert." Domino Taylor's voice boomed heavy but pleasant into Patrick's cell.

"How's it going, my friend?" Patrick asked.

"Same old, same old. I was worried you might be calling."

Patrick made a curious face as he took a seat outside the hotel room. "Worried?"

"I heard about what happened. Sounds like your boy had some serious help too—three badges dead, in and out, no witnesses."

"How the *hell* did you hear about all that already?"

"Come on, son," he said, his deep southern drawl slipping out as it tended to do with good friends.

Patrick nodded to himself. "Okay, my bad. I should have known."

"How's Amy?"

"Scared."

"I'm sure she is. Say when, my friend."

"Can you? I mean—you're able?" Patrick asked.

"Always able."

"I guess I should have said *available*."

"For you I am."

Patrick paused a moment, collected himself and said, "Thanks, man."

"You mention me to the Feds?"

"Yeah—they thought it was a bad idea."

He chuckled. "Been there many times. We're good at staying out of their way, lettin' them do their thing. Usually end up parting on good terms. I remind them that they're the hunters; we're just there to hold down the fort. They seem to like that."

"Cool," Patrick said. "So then what now?"

"Like I said: say when, brother."

"*When*," Patrick said. "We're in Pittsburgh now and leaving in a few hours. Should be back in Valley Forge around eight or nine tonight I guess."

"We'll be there. How're the kids?"

"Carrie's been a mess since the whole incident by the lake. Not to mention a whole slew of other shit that's happened since. I'll tell you all about it later. Caleb seems okay, but, at this point . . ." Patrick felt his throat seizing up, and then an immediate wave of shame for allowing it to happen with someone like Domino on the end of the line. He quickly cleared his throat. "Sorry."

"Nothing to be sorry for, my friend. When this is done I'm buying Carrie an ice cream and tossing that football with Caleb, just like I promised way back when. I can't wait to meet the little guy."

Patrick envisioned Domino's scene and found himself smiling. "That would be nice," he said. But the smile didn't last. Current events spit a reminder into Patrick's face. "This guy is dangerous, man. Evil. I can only imagine his friends are just as bad."

"They all are, Patrick. At least they think they are— until they meet me. You just hold tight, brother. Give Amy my best. I'll see you tonight."

"Thanks, man."

Patrick snapped his phone shut. Amy appeared in the hallway a moment later.

"Well?" she asked.

"Says he'll be waiting for us when we get home."

Amy put a hand to her chest. "Thank God."

Patrick looked away. A dark thought had been looming on the perimeter of his mind all morning, yet he inexplicably ignored it. Now, after the phone call to Domino was done, that thought had crept its way forward and demanded to be heard.

"What?" Amy asked. She dragged a chair next to his and took a seat.

Patrick lifted his head. "He's one of my best friends."

"And?"

"What if I get him killed?"

Amy laughed. She then stood, and before heading back into the room said, "Baby, Domino would *floss his teeth* with someone like Arty."

But what about Arty's new friends? he wanted to call after her. *The ones the Feds say must be highly trained? Nobody knows jack shit about them.*

Patrick was certain he wanted Domino's help, certain that if anyone could protect his family, it was him. He was thinking of Domino, the decorated soldier. Domino, the elite security specialist. Domino, the human rhino who broke records and bones on the football field, only to make every college scout collectively weep when he chose the Marine Corps instead of college ball.

Patrick never stopped and thought about Domino the friend.

Yes, Domino was good, and yes, Domino had seen the absolute worst and triumphed. But every man has his day. Every man eventually meets his match. What if he had just set his dear friend up for a showdown with some deadly enigma who might actually be his equal . . . and then some?

* * *

John Brooks stood before the bathroom mirror in a beaten-down motel room in West Virginia. Monica and Arty had gone to pick up lunch. John stared hard at his reflection, his jaw clenched, his black eyes nearly vibrating with a focused rage that he would soon unleash. He ripped off his shirt, his awesome musculature swelling in the mirror with each anxious breath he took. He took a hand and traced it along his torso, fingering each scar: bullet holes, slashes, stabs—each one a reminder of just how hard he was to kill, and of course, what he did to the sorry sons of bitches who tried.

He grinned the devil's grin. *Bring it, motherfuckers.*

CHAPTER 57

New York City

Domino Taylor sat at the head of the table. His two best men, Christopher Allan and Dan Briggs, sat opposite one another in the middle. Domino had laid out the situation's objective for them. Told them to have their ready-bags packed the moment they concluded the briefing here at the office in preparation for an immediate trip to Pennsylvania.

"We putting everything else on hold?" Briggs asked.

Domino nodded once. "As of now, our services aren't available to anyone—indefinitely."

"You guys were that tight huh?" Allan asked.

"Yes," Domino said. "The moment we get there, they're royalty. Clear?"

Both men nodded.

Briggs thrummed his fingers on the table. "Feds know we're coming?"

"Yeah," Domino said. "But it's all good. They weren't happy about it, but Patrick insisted."

Allan said, "Your boy's smart."

All three men smirked at each other. Domino's smirk dropped first as he said, "My boy's been through hell and back. His wife and kids too. His *kids*."

Briggs said, "That's fucked up."

"Yeah it is," Domino said. "And when we meet these motherfuckers face to face, there *will* be a momentary lapse in judgment."

Allan smirked. "I like those."

"We gonna draw straws to see who gets to make that lapse?" Briggs asked.

Domino said, "If it plays out the way I want? My boy Patrick can get first dibs."

Briggs blurted: "Seconds."

Allan said, "Ah shit."

Domino smiled and shook his head. "Ya'll some sick motherfuckers."

CHAPTER 58

West Virginia

Monica and Arty came through the motel door with arms full of takeout. John was lying on the bed watching television, his shirt still off.

"Ew—put a shirt on, muscle man," Monica said.

"What'd you get?" John asked.

"Closest place was a deli," Monica said.

Arty headed towards the motel mirror and took in his reflection. A man with dirty blonde hair and a mustache stared back. "Can I take this stuff off now? I look like a porn star."

John laughed.

"Sure," Monica said. "But if you insist on going out again, be prepared to put it back on."

"You try being locked up for months," Arty said, peeling off the wig and then the mustache. "That little trip to the deli was like fucking Disneyland."

Monica started taking the sandwiches out of the paper bags. "I'm glad you enjoyed it—because from now on you're staying hidden."

"What?"

John got off the bed and took one of the sandwiches from his daughter. "She's right—there's a lotta people looking for you, son. Won't be long before your face is wallpapering the entire east coast." John unwrapped the sandwich without checking to see what it was and took a monster bite. His mouth full, he added, "You gotta be a ghost until we get our shit situated."

Arty said, "Okay—I'll be a ghost. I'll be the ghost of a ghost—as long as it ends up getting me what I want."

Monica lit a cigarette and inhaled deep. "My dear brother . . ." She exhaled with a smile. "You're going to get it all. And then some."

CHAPTER 59

Valley Forge, Pennsylvania

Tension you could cut with a knife, Patrick thought when Domino and his team first introduced themselves to the federal agents who escorted the Lambert family back to their home.

"I assure you," Domino began after the awkward formalities, "we are only here to stand guard. You're running the show, you're doing the investigation."

The agents on duty seemed pleased with Domino's respectful manner and walked past him into the Lamberts' home to get their bearings.

Patrick leaned in and whispered, "That must've been tough to say."

Whispering back, Domino said, "Nah—better to have a potential ally than an immediate enemy. Besides, when all is said and done, they'll know who their daddy is."

Both Patrick and Amy laughed. One of the agents turned his head and they immediately stopped laughing and dropped their heads.

"Ya'll are like kids in a classroom," Domino eventually whispered with a sly smile.

Amy leapt forward and hugged him. Domino appeared a little shocked at first. He looked at Patrick, who just smiled and shrugged. Domino then returned Amy's embrace. "It's alright, sweetheart," he whispered in his deep southern drawl. "It's gonna be alright."

Amy pulled away. She had a tear in her eye and she wiped it away before saying, "I know. I know it will."

Domino smiled. He then turned to Patrick and punched him lightly in the gut. "You looking pretty solid, champ."

Patrick flinched from the blow and said, "Yeah, well when people don't punch me in my knife wound, I'm good."

Domino made an *oh shit!* face. "*Oh!* I'm sorry, my friend!"

Patrick started laughing. "I'm just playin, man." He gave his stomach a few firm slaps. "Better than new."

Domino chuckled and shook his head before turning to Briggs and Allan behind him. "Would you look at this clown?" he said, motioning back to Patrick. "Been here ten minutes and already he's playin. Some things just *do not* change."

Patrick patted Domino's shoulder, then looked past him towards Briggs and Allan. "Apparently etiquette was omitted on Mr. Taylor's security curriculum. I suppose it'll be up to *me* to do introductions." Patrick gave Domino a quick smirk before extending his hand to Briggs. "I'm Patrick Lambert, and this is my wife, Amy."

Domino chuckled and shook his head again as formal introductions took place. Patrick was the tallest of them all at six-three, but he was not the widest. Domino took that honor, looking as if he was assembled by a group of engineers trying to develop the ultimate African-American superhero.

Christopher Allan was the polar opposite of his boss. He was pale and very thin. But every now and then, Patrick thought, a man comes along with a certain look in his eye. The look of—quite simply—a man you didn't want to fuck with. All the bench presses in the world couldn't give you Christopher Allan's gaze. Patrick had a good five inches and maybe seventy pounds on the man, but one quick glance into Christopher Allan's eyes was enough to let Patrick know that he'd be a ghost scratching his head as to what just happened if he was ever stupid enough to mess with the guy.

Dan Briggs? A combination of all of the above. Five-ten, one-eighty, negative-point-negative percent body fat, and a veteran's thousand-yard stare that Patrick felt was menacingly accentuated by his shaved-bald head. Perhaps it reminded him of Jim Fannelli? No. *Hell* no. To even compare someone on Domino's team to a sick bastard like Jim Fannelli was flat-out disrespectful.

Domino dipped his torso to one side, his eyes aimed at Amy's knees, a playful smile on the corner of his mouth. "And who's that I see hiding behind Mommy's legs?"

Caleb poked his head out from behind Amy's legs for a split second before snapping back out of sight like a timid pet.

Domino dropped to one knee. He spoke in a nurturing tone that could have added nanny to his already astounding resume. "Come on out, little man. I won't bite."

Caleb poked his head out again. Amy reached down and stroked his fuzzy brown hair. "It's okay, sweetie," she said.

Caleb stepped out from behind his mother's legs. Domino extended his hand. "My name's Domino. Your Mommy and Daddy are two of my best friends in the whole world. You think you and I can be friends too?"

Caleb stared at Domino's hand. It was roughly the size of Caleb's head, and Caleb seemed to have no trouble processing that fact. He stayed frozen.

What Domino did next reminded Patrick of the amazing people on television who seemed to charm and handle the deadliest of snakes without so much as a hiss.

Domino simply reached out, took Caleb's hand into his, shook it softly, and then Patrick watched as Caleb succumbed to one of the warmest smiles he'd seen his son produce in quite some time.

"It's a pleasure to meet you, Caleb," Domino said. Still on one knee, Domino pointed over his shoulder. "Those are my friends, Christopher and Dan."

Briggs and Allan both smiled and waved. Caleb waved back.

Carrie had disappeared upstairs the moment everyone entered the house, despite Amy's objection. One of the agents assured Amy she would follow her, and so Carrie was absent during the initial get-to-know-yas. Now, she had inched her way down the stairs and was perched on the fourth step, watching from a distance, but not so far that she would go unnoticed. Especially since Caleb had been introduced ahead of her, God forbid.

"And who's that pretty girl I see over there on the stairs?" Domino said, now smiling in Carrie's direction.

"Come on down, honey. Say hello," Amy said.

Carrie shook her head and stayed put. She held a stuffed animal, a dog, in her hands, and she seemed content on using the toy as a pacifier in her uncertain state, consistently rubbing its ears, tugging its tail.

"Who you got there?" Domino asked. "Does it have a name?"

"It's not real," Carrie said. "My real dog died."

Amy dropped her head; Patrick rubbed her back.

"I'm sorry to hear that," Domino said. "I had a dog once too."

Carrie flopped her bottom onto the third step. "Did he die?" she asked.

Domino nodded. "Yes, he did."

"What was his name?"

"Major. What was the name of yours?"

Carrie hit the second step. "Oscar."

"Like Oscar from *Sesame Street*?"

Carrie's face lit up. "Yes! I called him that because he was all smelly and dirty like Oscar the Grouch when we found him."

Domino's heavy laughter filled the room.

Carrie skipped the first step altogether, hit the landing, and walked right up to Domino. "Oscar and Major are probably playing together at Rainbow Bridge," she said.

Domino glanced at both Amy and Patrick who returned a *we'll tell you later* look.

"I bet they are," Domino said, "I bet they are." He held out a hand. "I'm Domino. Do you remember me? I met you when you were very young."

"Domino like the pizza?" Carrie asked, taking his hand and ignoring his question.

Domino smiled. "Just like the pizza."

"I like Pizza Hut better." Carrie pulled her stuffed animal to her chest and headed off towards the den without another word.

Patrick rolled his eyes and shook his head.

Amy said, "Yup—that's our daughter."

Domino started laughing again.

CHAPTER 60

West Virginia
One Month Later

Monica Kemp zipped up her bag. It had been a month since Arty had escaped custody. Eyes would still be there, but they wouldn't be everywhere. Monica and John felt enough time had gone by to start gathering more intel—patterns, routine, gifted opportunities.

"Got everything?" John asked.

"Almost." Monica walked across the hotel room towards the dresser and checked her Canon and its 600 mm-f/4 lens. She lifted the camera towards father and brother and said, "Could get a close-up of Saturn with this baby."

"Do I even want to know how much it cost?" John asked.

"Not if you want to feel good about yourself."

"Funny girl."

"You sure you shouldn't be going with her?" Arty said to John.

"She's better at the whole surveillance thing than I am. Don't have the patience for it. Besides—I gotta organize the new van. If all goes well today, it'd be nice to have it sooner than later."

Arty glanced at Monica, then back to John. "What if 'sooner' does happen? What if she needs help?"

Monica smirked at her father who smirked back.

"You're still getting to know the family, son," John said. He then pointed at Monica who was now adjusting the suppressor on her beloved Glock. "That lethal bitch is one daughter I'll never have to worry about."

CHAPTER 61

.A month had passed. A quiet month. At first it was good. At first there were hints and (loose) hopes that Arty and *whoever* had vanished for good.

The FBI continued their search but had found nothing thus far. Domino's security had been top-notch; the Lamberts were never alone. This was comforting for awhile, but once that first quiet month rolled over into a second, and once it seemed as though they had ordered takeout from every conceivable restaurant in Pennsylvania, and had rented every movie ever made, Amy started to become irritable.

They were not *complete* prisoners in the house—there were supervised leaves. They'd had dinner at their friends' house one night, however Amy suspected the Browns were uncomfortable most of the evening, and she didn't blame them one bit. Two imposing bodyguards shadowing Patrick and Amy throughout the night? The awful possibility that the *bad guys* could show up and catch the Browns in the line of fire, not unlike the Mitchells at Crescent Lake? The Browns knew all about the unfortunate Mitchells and their untimely demise—that is, their grisly murder.

So that had been the one and only dinner invite thus far. There were brief morning trips to the park with the kids—both Carrie and Caleb were being home-schooled for the time-being—and occasionally, if she begged, Domino himself would escort Amy to a small strip mall up the road—the enormous King of Prussia Mall a mere five minutes away was out of the question.

"I need to get out," Amy eventually said to Patrick as they sat at the kitchen table with morning coffee. Domino had taken his mug and gone to the den to do some work on his laptop. Briggs and Allan were at the park with the kids.

"Out?" Patrick said after a sip. "Out where?"

Amy waved an arm across the kitchen. "Of here. I need to get out of here."

"You want Domino to take you to the park to meet up with the kids?"

"No—I want to go somewhere else."

"Like where?"

"I don't know, just . . ." Amy ran both hands through her hair, trying to keep cool, refusing to snap at her blameless husband.

"Baby, what are you—"

At the peak of stroking her hair, Amy intentionally pulled upwards and let go, dark strands falling down over her face. "Look at my hair," she blurted, cutting Patrick off. She wiped the hair out of her face, took the pads of her fingers and tugged down on the skin beneath both eyes. "Look at my eyes, my face."

Patrick did. He then shrugged. Amy knew what he was thinking, and on any other day, in any other time, she would have loved him for it. Today, it only served to irritate her further. She did *not* want to hear that he found her beautiful no matter how many split ends that frizzed her locks needed trimming. No matter how many roots were reclaiming their gray. No matter how many dark circles were gathering beneath her eyes, clogged pores circling her nose. She did not want to hear it because today, God damn it, she would never believe it. She felt awful. Felt she *looked* awful. Looked like some bag-lady sleeping on a vent near Market Street Station. A man would never understand this—the need for a woman to look and feel like a woman. A man, if society allowed it, would likely march around in sweats and a stained tee, seven days a week, shaving only when his face itched too much, showering only when his odor became a nose-sore to even himself. A man would live in his man-cave with his DVDs, his beer, his porn, his junk-food, and lose track of time. Forget the day, the month, maybe even the year if the supplies were aplenty.

At least this is what Amy thought. And right now she thought it more than ever. Because, as Mr. John Gray so aptly put it, *men are from Mars, and women are from Venus.* And Amy had been on Mars long enough, thank you. She pined for a trip back to her home planet of Venus, if only for a few hours. She doubted Patrick or Domino (*or any man*, her temporary bias insisted) would understand, but that wasn't going to stop her from trying.

"I need to get out," she said again, disappointed something more articulate didn't come out.

"What are you suggesting?"

"I wanna feel human again. A haircut, a facial . . . maybe even a massage." She rubbed her neck. "My neck and back are a mess. I must have a million knots."

"I can give you a massage."

"No," she said quickly, knowing he would reply as such. "I want a *good* massage." And then feeling a slight hint of guilt, added: "A professional massage, honey. One with a table, and scented oils, and soft music. I want to see Lana at Image."

Patrick sipped his coffee, taking it in, seemingly looking for the right response. "Domino would never allow that," he eventually said.

"Why don't we ask him?"

Patrick pushed his mug aside and leaned in. He dropped his voice, his expression stern. "Are you serious, Amy? Are you forgetting why we're in this position in the first place?"

"It's been over a month," she said. "Nothing has happened."

Patrick's stern expression was teetering on anger. *"Are you kidding me?* Am I the only when who remembers what that sick bastard is capable of? Look how long he waited before he escaped."

"He had no choice but to wait. He was in jail. And he needed help to escape."

Patrick laughed incredulously. "Which proves my point even further. If he's got help, he's even *more* of a threat. And if he had help, why didn't they break him out right away? Why wait so long?"

"Because whoever his help was, they obviously weren't stupid enough to risk breaking into a jail loaded with police. They waited until he was transported, when their odds were better."

"Exactly—they *waited.*"

"Because they had no choice," Amy repeated.

Patrick gritted his teeth and breathed hard through his nose. He was shaking his head when he said, "I can't believe this. A month ago you and I were on the *exact* same page. We *both* wanted Domino here. We *knew* Arty wasn't going to run and hide. We *knew* he was going to be coming for us. Now you're changing your tune just so you can get a massage?"

"And a facial," she added with goading defiance.

"*Amy.*"

"I'm not changing tunes, Patrick. I know who we're dealing with."

"No you don't," Patrick said. "*None of us do.* We know Arty. But his help could be anyone. They could be fucking ninjas for all we know. If we start getting lazy, if we start assuming it's all over and they're gone for good, that's when . . . that's when—"

"He's right." Domino's deep voice from the kitchen entrance turned both their heads. "I know what you're feeling, Amy. But believe it or not, that first week we were here? That first week when you and Patrick slept maybe one out of every three nights? That was the time when you were safest. People like this—bad people, *smart* people— they don't rush things. Patience is their best weapon. It's when shit starts getting boring, when shit starts getting quiet, mundane—that's when you need to be prepared, girl. Because that's when these bad people *use* that patience. They're not only biding their time, waiting for you to slip up, they're also planning . . . preparing. Remember this: you've got many things in your life that can occupy your mind—your kids, your job, bills, your home, friends. These folks have only one. Vengeance. I've been there myself. And believe me, when it gets hold of you, nothing else matters."

Domino's words resonated (how could they not?), but Amy still saw no difference between a trip to the strip mall up the street and a trip to Image for a simple massage. Of course she would never forget who Arty was, or what their current situation was. She would remember Arty and Crescent Lake until the day she died.

"I am not asking for a weekend getaway," she said. "I'm not even asking for a night out on the town. God knows I have been compliant to all the rules and parameters you've set, yes?"

Domino closed his eyes and nodded once.

"All I am asking for is a trip to a spa that happens to be five minutes away. I can take Christopher or Dan, or *both* with me. They can even be in the room while I'm being massaged. I'll strip *naked* in front of them, I don't care."

Patrick made a face.

"You've kept us safe thus far. I trust you and your team with my family's life. I mean, my God, both your men are at the park with my *babies*—I certainly trust you to protect *me* in a simple spa. And if this is the metaphorical mouse finally poking his head out of the safety of his hole and into the baited trap, then I know your team can handle it. They would protect me."

She was using the flattery approach—with lousy metaphors to boot. She also knew Domino was clever enough to see through this and make up his own mind without influence. All she could do was sit and hope at least *some* of her words had made a dent.

Domino sipped his coffee. "Wait until Briggs and Allan come back with the kids. You then call your spa and see if they can take you today. Not tomorrow, *today*. If they can't—tough luck. If they can, you schedule the soonest available time; spontaneity is our ally. No pre-planning. I'll have Briggs tailing you there. Allan will drive you and be with you the whole time. I hope you weren't kidding when you mentioned stripping naked in front of them."

"I wasn't," Amy said.

Patrick made another face.

Amy reached across the table, took Patrick's hand and squeezed it.

"So that's how it's gonna be," Domino said. "If they don't have an opening today, it's like I said—tough luck. Take it or leave it."

"I'll take it."

Amy smiled for two reasons. First, she had been a loyal customer to Lana for years, and knew her massage therapist would fit Amy into her schedule somehow. Second, well . . . she was getting a massage.

Domino looked at Patrick and nodded reassuringly. He then looked at Amy and nodded once, gravely. "When my team is back with your kids you can make your phone call. I'm not gonna lie though—this goes against my better judgment."

"Mine too," Patrick added.

Amy squeezed her husband's hand again then looked at them both. "It'll be fine."

* * *

Dan Briggs did a quick check of his watch between pushes on the swing. Carrie kept urging him to push harder but he would not. Briggs glanced to his left where Allan was standing over Caleb in the sandbox. Briggs clicked the mic on his collar. "You almost ready?"

Allan palmed the invisible receiver in his ear. "You want me to do a sweep first? I can walk the boy over."

"Nah—it's freezing. Plus I only spotted the same three the entire time."

"Eleven and three?" Allan asked.

"Yeah—old couple at the picnic table with coffee, and the teenager shooting hoops."

"Wanna approach? See if they jump?"

"No. I've kept an eye on them the whole time. The kid can play—sunk ten in a row. Low odds there. Old couple's feet were pointed towards each other the entire time they spoke." Briggs always looked at the feet of potential suspects. The feet never lied. Faces could be deceptive; it was why some excelled at poker. But the feet always pointed towards their target. He, Allan, and Domino always had a hearty laugh about this fact whenever they'd stop for a drink, find some couple on a date, and then spot the clueless guy rambling on and on while the desperate woman's feet shot laser beams towards the nearest exit despite looking the fella in the eye.

"Okay then," Allan said. "Let's go."

* * *

One hundred yards away, parked safely beneath a large oak, Monica pulled her eye away from her Canon and lowered the lens. She could tell the two men with the kids weren't Feds—their manner suggested a more militant vibe, a more impenetrable demeanor. They certainly weren't local police. So who were they? Monica set the camera on the passenger seat and started the engine. Time to go find out.

CHAPTER 62

The front door of the Lambert home opened and both Carrie and Caleb sprinted inside towards the television. Christopher Allan and Dan Briggs appeared immediately after.

Domino approached. "All good?"

Briggs said, "All good."

Domino turned and Amy was behind him, smiling like a teen asking for the car keys.

Domino handed her his cell phone. "Go ahead—make your call."

"I can use my phone," she said. "I've got the number to the spa saved in my contacts."

"You'll use *my* phone," he said. "Anyone tries to home in on this and they'll hear a scramble that sounds like a cross between Chinese and Latin."

"Oh," Amy said softly as she took the phone from him. "Well I still need to get the number from my phone."

"Get your number. *But you dial from mine, alright?*"

Amy nodded and headed towards the kitchen.

Allan patted Domino's shoulder. "What's up?"

Domino kept his eyes on Amy in the kitchen as he said: "Tell you in a minute."

* * *

Monica did not have to worry about her tail being spotted by whoever these two guys were. She didn't have to worry because she'd gotten to the Lamberts' before them.

She sat parked two blocks over, her equipment fanned out on her dashboard and on the passenger seat next to her Canon. A cop might call it a stakeout, but unlike a cop, Monica had access to equipment that would make any cop or Fed cream his pants. Unfortunately, the problem with these specific types of stakeouts was that there was seldom a hit for hours. They were not about observation, they were about listening. You were waiting for some kind of technological communiqué, be it telephone, radio, internet, whatever. It could get damn boring. She recalled a target she was paid to eliminate a few years back. The target's main contact was addicted to internet porn. Monica must have listened to a thousand hours of forced moans parked outside the contact's home before the bastard finally took a break and called the target, which resulted in an immediate address. She shot her main guy six times—all in the head. Then she went back to the porn guy and shot him six times too—all in the groin.

Monica lit a cigarette and cracked her window, preparing for a long day, maybe night. Instead, she got a pleasant surprise. A signal was coming from the Lambert house. An outgoing call. She tossed the cigarette out the window and immediately punched a few keys on her laptop. The metallic chirp of a ringing phone filled her car. She waited for the click, the "hello." There was a click, but there was no "hello," just a steady stream of gibberish. Her signal had been scrambled.

"Fuck!" she yelled. She punched more keys, looking for a number, tracing the call. Ten foreign symbols came back—no decipherable numbers.

This was impossible. *Who the fuck are these guys?*

She frantically punched more keys on her laptop, cranked two dials on another device, adjusting frequencies.

Still gibberish.

"Fuck!" she yelled again.

Monica picked up her own cell, hit a number on her speed dial.

"Code in," a male voice said.

"Neco. 8122765."

"Waiting . . . clear. What's—"

"I need an immediate trace," she blurted. "Sending you the signal now."

Monica knew the call would end before she could get the right frequency to unscramble and listen to the call, but she knew they could trace it.

"Got it," the male voice said. "Hold . . ."

Monica lit another cigarette, inhaled deep. Her equipment was the absolute best. This had never, *ever* happened before. *Who the fuck are these guy—*

"Okay," the voice said. "We have the trace. The number is being sent to you now."

Monica didn't thank him, just hung up. She flung her second unfinished cigarette out the window and punched up the number. The gibberish had been over for almost a minute; the call was finished. She dialed the number.

"Image Spa, may I help you?"

She hung up. *A spa? A fucking spa? Why the hell would—*

A piece clicked:

Amy.

Another piece clicked:

The men at the park . . . the high-tech equipment that matched hers . . .

The Lamberts had protection. Real protection. People like her and her father.

Both pieces clicked *together*:

The Lamberts have been prisoners in their own home. Amy needed to get away. Needed to be pampered for a day. Lord knows, Monica understood that.

Monica raised her Canon. Adjusted the lens. Looked in the Lambert's kitchen window from over one hundred yards away as if she were standing right outside their home. She saw Amy. She saw Patrick. The two guys from the park—skinny and baldy. And then she saw the third. A big black fella who looked like the main man by the way he spoke and gestured to everyone in the kitchen one at a time, clearly giving orders.

My dear sweet Amy, once again you've come through for me. And Dad's getting the van today. It appears as if 'sooner' might just be happening after all.

Monica smiled and dialed the spa's number again.

"Image Spa, may I help you?"

"Hi," Monica said, "this is Amy Lambert. I just made an appointment, but I forgot to write it down." She gave a silly chuckle. "Can you tell me when I'm due in again?"

"Four o'clock this afternoon, Mrs. Lambert."

"Great, and that's for . . . ?"

"A ninety-minute massage with Lana."

"Right. Couldn't remember if I booked sixty or ninety. Wouldn't want to deprive myself those extra thirty minutes."

The receptionist laughed.

Monica looked at her watch; it was 10:30 a.m. "See you at four," she said.

"See you then," the receptionist said.

Monica hung up, punched in the name of the spa on her laptop, got the address. She then dialed the same number from a few minutes before.

"Code in."

"Neco. 8122765."

"Waiting . . . go ahead."

"I need blueprints. Sending you the address now."

Monica lit a third cigarette. She would savor and finish this one. When she was done, she would get her photos developed, and then make sure her father had the van secured. Then a nice lunch somewhere. Broiled salmon maybe. After that? Why, after that she was heading to the spa, if you please.

CHAPTER 63

The Image Spa had once been a sizeable one-story home, long since renovated to accommodate its needs. Monica entered just after 3 p.m. Her hair was red, her eyes blue.

"May I help you?"

Monica approached the front desk where a single receptionist stood smiling. Monica performed a quick read of the woman: late 30's, brunette, average features, way too tan, way too much eyeliner, tabloid magazine next to the appointment book, the newest Droid smartphone next to the magazine, no ring on her finger. Two or three more bad dates away from platinum blonde hair and fake tits.

Monica smiled genuinely. "Hi. I just moved into the area and was wondering if I could take a look around."

"Absolutely." The receptionist handed Monica a brochure. "Here is a list of all the services we offer."

Monica took the brochure and pretended to scan it with interest before turning her back to the receptionist and wandering off.

"If you have any questions," the receptionist called to her back, "please let me know."

Monica waved a thank you over her shoulder, her mind too preoccupied to speak. She was comparing the blueprints in her mind to the layout before her. Massage should be to her right, deeper into the spa, past reception. She strolled onward, opened a door with a sign that read: *Shhh . . . Quiet Zone,* and then stepped into a waiting room that was all things serene. A woman sat in a cushy chair dressed in nothing but a white robe, her face in a magazine. The woman lifted her head and smiled at Monica.

Monica smiled back and whispered, "Waiting for a massage?"

The woman nodded.

"Lana, right?" Monica asked.

"Yes."

"Is she any good?"

"She's the best. I won't go to anyone else."

Monica made a surprised face that said *wow*, the blueprints still sliding throughout her mind like an old microfilm reader:

One door to the only massage room—you see that. You also see the fire exit at the extreme end of the waiting room. Behind the fire exit will be the spa's less-than-glamorous side—a dumpster, a recycling bin . . . the new van.

You see the second door—the showers. Crucial. Its interior should have a connecting door leading directly into the massage room, so clients won't have to walk back out into the waiting room before taking a shower after their massage. People feel disheveled after a massage; their hair is greasy and mussed, their faces mushed and half-asleep. They aren't ready to meet the world yet. They need the rejuvenation that is a hot shower. And conversely, many are self-conscious of odor, therefore showers are often desired before a massage. Win-win.

Still, she needed to double-check on the connecting door between the two rooms.

"Is there a shower?" Monica asked.

The woman said there was and pointed to the second door.

Monica put on a worried face and pretended to run a hand through her hair (wig), as if she'd sooner die than be seen with a messy coif. "You mean you have to come back out here before going into the shower?"

"No," the woman said as if she understood Monica's concern completely. "Lana walks you into the showers. There's a connecting door in her room. The tiling is exquisite."

"I'm sure it is. Are there lockers?"

The woman nodded.

Monica smiled, said thank you, and then left the waiting room and approached reception again.

"Any questions so far?" the receptionist asked.

Monica only said, "It's *beautiful*," and kept walking, the blueprints sliding through her mind like the old microfilm reader again:

Facial and body treatments should be through the doorway to the left—right near the spa's entrance.

She made a left.

* * *

Monica appeared at the front desk five minutes later. The receptionist was checking her smartphone.

He hasn't called yet, has he? Probably shouldn't have slept with him on the first date, ya dumb slut.

And then, like so many spontaneous opportunities in her career, a beautiful one hit Monica square on. She'd needed a distraction before leaving the spa. There was already one planned she felt confident in, but this new one was just too irresistible to pass up.

The receptionist quickly put her smart phone back on the desk as if caught by her employer. She smiled wide at Monica. "So what do you think?"

"It's absolutely beautiful," Monica said again. "I will definitely be coming back soon to schedule—" She stopped there on purpose, her eyes fixed excitedly on the smartphone resting by the receptionist's right hand. "Is that the new Droid?"

The receptionist picked up her phone and displayed it proudly. "Yeah—I just got it last week."

"I've been looking into those. Can I see it?"

"Sure." The receptionist handed it over.

Monica gave it a harmless going over, leaned her elbows on the counter, and knocked a container of brochures onto the desk. A good many fluttered to the floor. "Oh! I'm so sorry!"

"It's okay, it's okay," the receptionist said as she squatted down behind the desk to collect the brochures.

Monica went to work on the smartphone—found Contacts, found the phone's vCard, memorized a number, brought the screen back to where it had been when she'd first handled it.

The receptionist rose from behind the desk with all the brochures.

Monica faked embarrassment. "I'm so sorry," she said again.

The receptionist smiled as she placed the brochures back into their container. "It's okay. No problem whatsoever."

Monica held the smartphone in her right hand, in the receptionist's line of vision. Below the desk, in her left hand, Monica was punching a number into her own phone without looking.

"Here's your phone," Monica said when the girl was finally done with the brochures. "It's nice. I may just have to get one."

The receptionist took her phone back. "Thanks. Did you want to schedule something today?"

"Not yet. I want to go home and check my schedule first. But you can rest assured I'll be back."

The receptionist smiled. Monica said goodbye and headed for the entrance. She had planned on dialing the front desk en route to the door in hopes of a distraction, fairly confident it would work. If it didn't, she could have easily talked her way out of any actions that followed. Now, she dialed the receptionist's smartphone instead, positive the blocked number flashing on the screen of her Droid (*perhaps it was HIM, calling from some private line at work!*) would elicit hope and excitement . . . and a turn of the back for some privacy.

It did. The receptionist snatched her phone and immediately gave Monica her back before answering. Monica opened the entrance door to make it sound as if she'd gone, then banked left into the facial and body treatments area. She immediately brought her phone to her ear and began listening to the eager receptionist's voice go on like a skipped record: "Hello? Hello? *Hello?*"

Monica grinned and hung up.

CHAPTER 64

"You ready?" Domino asked Amy.

It was like asking a kid if she was ready for ice cream. Amy, dressed in humble sweats and a sweatshirt with her purse over one shoulder, nodded immediately.

Four of them were at the front door: Domino, Amy, Briggs, and Allan. Patrick watched from the kitchen.

Domino touched Allan's shoulder. "*Anything* seems funny you pull out. I want you frosty every second. A goddamned snowman."

Allan said, "Yup."

Domino turned to Briggs. "Keep the tail as far back as you can—watch for anyone following. Stay in the lot for a spell after they arrive and do a sweep. Call in when they've arrived safe."

Briggs nodded.

No one but Amy was smiling. Patrick spotted this and shook his head from the kitchen. Amy approached him.

"Would you stop worrying?" she said.

Patrick was out of words. He had made his point—several times. Over the course of their relationship he'd always made a concerted effort to see things from his wife's point of view during a debate, to be an understanding husband. But this—this he just didn't understand. And Amy said he wouldn't understand. Because he wasn't a woman. Deep down Patrick wondered if that was a line of manipulative bullshit his wife was feeding him. Or maybe Amy's reasoning held some merit, and short of switching brains with her, he'd *never* understand. But did that change anything? Whether he understood or not, the issue—the main issue—was that she was taking what he felt was an unnecessary risk for something as menial as a massage.

No, he didn't get it at all. But it was happening all the same. She was going.

"No, I won't," he replied.

"Patrick, this is no different than going to the park, or going shopping. I think it's safer even."

Patrick's expression demanded elaboration.

"I'll be in one spot the whole time. When we're in the park or in a store we're moving around, there are tons of people . . ."

"You're safer in crowds. Domino said so."

Amy stood on her toes and kissed him. He accepted the kiss but did not pucker.

"I'll be back soon. I'll be back a new woman, you wait and see."

Patrick's expression stayed flat.

"And I'll be so relaxed and rejuvenated," she continued in a sensual whisper, "that I just may reward my understanding husband with something special tonight."

Their sex life had been less than eventful since arriving back from Pittsburgh—no easy feat for an uninhibited couple that had once managed to have sex on a public beach during the day. Patrick's libido *had* started to nudge anxiety aside these last couple of weeks, if only for a nice quickie. But what Amy was doing now put everything below his waist on lockdown. She was using sex as a tool. It angered him and he wouldn't accommodate her.

Patrick took a step away from her and said, "Enjoy your massage."

Amy cocked her head, studied him, but ultimately shrugged and said, "Okay. Love you."

His anger swelled from her indifference to his manner. He did not reply as she turned and left with Allan and Briggs.

CHAPTER 65

A slender woman stepped out of the facial and body treatment area inside Image Spa. She wore a white robe with white slippers (both bearing the Image Spa emblem), had a white towel wrapped around her head, and her face was covered in a green mud mask.

The woman walked with a casual grace towards the massage area at the far end of the spa, glancing at the reception desk as she passed. The receptionist, busy with a potential customer, never once glanced in the robed woman's direction. The robed woman smiled and opened the door with the sign that read: *Shhh . . . Quiet Zone.*

CHAPTER 66

Christopher Allan and Amy Lambert were waiting for the OK from Dan Briggs. Briggs was doing a sweep of the lot and surrounding areas.

"Looks good," Briggs' voice echoed into Allan's earpiece. "I'm still going to hang around for a bit though."

Allan tucked his chin and spoke into his collar. "Okay. We'll be here for a bit—probably around two hours. Give me a head's up when you're heading back."

"Will do."

Allan opened the front door to the spa and entered first. He and Amy approached the front desk.

"Hi, Amy, how are you?"

"I'm doing okay, Julie. Really looking forward to my massage."

Julie's eyes ping-ponged between Amy and Allan. "Well Lana should almost be ready for you, you can head on back now if . . . um . . . are you two together?" Her eyes locked on Allan. "Are you scheduled for something too?"

Amy shook her head. "No, he's a friend of my husband's—visiting from out of town." Amy felt fine telling the lie, and yet, uncomfortable with the actual truth dressed up as breezy wit that followed. "He's my bodyguard for the day." She smiled wide and it felt all wrong, like her teeth had gone crooked.

Fortunately, Julie returned a genuine smile, looked at Allan, and motioned straight ahead towards the chairs that occupied reception. "You can have a seat there if you like, sir. Would you like some tea or—"

"Water, please," Allan said. "But I'd like you to bring it to me once we're settled. Thank you." Allan spoke with such assuredness that Julie immediately began nodding, as if she'd received an order as opposed to a request.

"No problem," Julie said. "If you two head on back, I'll bring you your water in a minute."

"Thanks, Julie," Amy said.

Allan nodded a thank you then led Amy towards her massage.

* * *

Amy and Allan entered the tranquil waiting room. The space was empty and Allan used the opportunity to pull his gun from his belt and give it a quick check. Amy watched the man with a hesitant eye as he stuffed the gun back into his waist line before whispering into his collar.

"We're inside, Briggs. You there?"

"*Here. She getting her massage?*"

"Not yet. I'm gonna secure the massage room first. They have a waiting room right outside. I'll be on guard there. I'll hit you up the moment I've checked the massage room and she's on the table."

"*I'll be here.*"

The door to the massage room opened and a short woman dressed in dark blue scrubs stepped out. The woman had blonde hair and pale-blue eyes with only the faintest of lines in her milky skin, despite her fifty-plus years.

"Hello, Amy," Lana said, her Russian accent thick, but more exotic than a burden; she spoke strong English. "It is good to see you."

"Hi Lana, it's good to see you too." Amy looked at Allan, then at Lana. "This is my husband's friend, Christopher."

Lana extended her hand and Allan took it. She shook it hard. "It is nice to meet you, Christopher. Are you interested in massage?"

Allan said, "I am, actually. Would you mind if I had a look?"

Lana smiled. "Of course you may."

All three entered the room. It was quaint but purposeful. A massage table dressed in sheets and blankets stood in the center. Candles already lit in three of the four corners flickered the only source of light. A sound system overhead whispered out gentle beats and rhythms coupled with ocean waves, and a tall rectangular dresser in the fourth corner presented an array of oils and creams on its countertop. What you saw was what you got— underneath the massage table was clearly visible, and the drawers that ran the length of the rectangular dresser would fail to house a small dog, never mind a person. Only one potential risk stood out: another door on the opposite end of the room, and Allan pointed to it.

"What's in there?" he asked.

"Shower room," Lana said. "My clients like to sometimes shower after or before massage."

Allan squinted. "Before?"

Lana only nodded.

"What if you're with another client?" he said.

"There is another entrance outside in waiting area."

"Was that the second door I saw?" he asked.

Again Lana just nodded.

"So if someone wanted to, they could enter this room through that second door?"

"If I am with client? No—I lock the door."

"Is there anyone in the showers now?"

"Yes—my last client should be." Lana studied Allan. A tiny smile appeared on the corner of her mouth. She turned and looked at Amy as she continued. "You do not have to play this 'he is my husband's friend' game with me, Amy. I know you well. You are good, faithful client. I know what happened to you. And I know what happened just." Lana looked at Allan but continued speaking to Amy. "He is your protection until the bad man is caught, yes? It is okay, I do not mind. I am not afraid."

Amy glanced at Allan, then back at Lana. "Yes," she said. "Yes, he's my protection."

"Okay then," Lana said. "And I am guessing you want to look in shower room now?"

"Yes," Allan said.

"Okay. Give me a minute. I will go in and tell my client. Then you come in and look."

"Thank you," Allan said.

Lana walked through the connecting door to the showers.

* * *

Lana walked past a row of lockers and onto the tiled floor. Three shower stalls were straight ahead. Left and right were empty, the curtains bunched to one side on both stalls. The middle stall's curtain was drawn tight. The water was running.

Lana approached and raised her voice to the curtain. "Elizabeth?"

"Yes?"

"I have a man coming through." She did not want to tell the truth and scare her client. "He is looking for his wife's ring. She left it here maybe. Are you almost done?"

"Actually, I'm not. I only just got in. He can come in and look, I'll just stay in here."

"Are you sure?"

"Yes. Just please let me know when he's gone."

"Okay, I will."

Lana returned to the massage room.

* * *

"Okay, so my client, she is in the shower," Lana began. "I tell her you are looking for your wife's ring she lost. My client, she says she will stay in the shower while you look and I will tell her when you leave."

Allan said okay, and followed Lana into the showers.

* * *

Monica was pleased Lana had not questioned her identity as Elizabeth when she spoke to her through the shower curtain. As she had predicted, the running water and a cupped hand over her mouth had dulled the intricacies of her voice.

Monica was not beneath the running water— Elizabeth's corpse was. Monica was dry and off to one side, her gun also dry and resting on one of the porcelain shelves. The other necessary items were locked safely away in one of the lockers. When she heard Amy's protection enter and begin opening and closing a few of the locker doors, she felt a brief jab of worry, but the metallic echoes of his indiscriminate opening and closing of the doors made his actions sound more arbitrary than necessary—kicking over stones even though he knew nothing of worth was beneath them.

When the protection's footsteps drew nearer, Monica lifted her gun off the porcelain shelf and quietly steadied it in her hand. When his silhouette—tall and lean—appeared in front of the curtain, she pointed the gun at its head.

The silhouette stood there for a beat. Monica held her breath, finger stroking the trigger, waiting for any sudden movement. The silhouette finally moved past her, checked the next stall over, turned and walked past again without pausing in her direction.

Another beat of silence followed. Was he waiting? Testing to see if she'd poke her head out? That's what *she* would do—and so far these guys proved to be good. She stayed put.

The connecting door into the massage room finally opened. Monica heard Lana's Russian accent echoing from the massage room, asking if all was okay. The protection's deep voice responded, but the particulars were cut off by the closing of the door. She was alone again—save for Elizabeth at her feet of course.

* * *

"Everything appears fine," Allan said upon his return. "I'll be out in the waiting room. What kind of traffic does that fire exit outside get?" he asked Lana.

"Traffic?" she asked.

"How often is it used? By employees? Can I expect anyone coming through there?"

Lana smiled and shook her head. "No—I go outside sometimes to get air. No one comes in though."

"Okay," Allan said. He looked at Amy. "Enjoy your massage."

He left.

"Okay," Lana said to Amy. "You can get undressed and get under the sheets. I think I will start you face-down today." Lana pointed to the head of the table where a face-cradle protruded, allowing clients to lie completely face-down without having to crane their necks uncomfortably to one side. "I am going in to tell Elizabeth the man is gone and it is safe to come out of the shower."

CHAPTER 67

Lana Rabinovich closed the door behind her as she entered the shower room. The water was still running in the middle stall. She approached.

"Elizabeth?"

No response.

Lana rapped her knuckles on the strip of tile separating the stalls. "Elizabeth?" She paused, listened, heard only the consistent rushing sound of the showerhead hitting the same spot. No splashing, no movement.

She slid the curtain open and looked down at Elizabeth's dead body, fetal on the tiled floor. There was little blood—the shower continuously washing away the red leak from the hole in Elizabeth's forehead.

Lana did not recoil in horror. She did not scream for help. Did not even turn around. She lifted her head, straightened her back, and with both eyes fixed straight ahead, she began to speak. "I am a Russian Jew. Growing up in Moscow I watched many of my people die. When I was a child I watched my best friend kicked to death by two men—I could not recognize her face when they had finished. I have been prepared to die my whole life—I am not afraid. I only ask that you do not be a coward. Do not shoot me in the back." Lana turned slowly and faced a woman with dark hair and dark eyes. The woman had a gun pointed at Lana's head.

"I can't say I've met anyone as brave as you," the woman said. "I almost regret having to do this."

Lana's pale blue eyes stayed fixed and fearless on the woman. "I have seen your kind before. You are not capable of regret."

The woman smiled. "I guess that's true. And I guess that's why I said *almost*." The woman pulled the trigger and shot Lana in the head, killing her instantly.

CHAPTER 68

Amy was face-down and under the sheets on the massage table. Head secure in the face cradle, her only view was the rug. She pulled her arms out from under the sheets and brought them beneath the cradle to study her fingernails. She wondered if she would have time to sneak in a quick manicure. Well . . . time she had, the question was whether or not she could convince Domino to let her stay a half hour longer after the massage to get them done.

Amy heard the connecting door from the showers open and close. She brought her arms back to her side and took a deep, nurturing breath.

"Are you comfortable?" Lana asked.

"*Very,*" Amy said into the cradle. "You have no idea how bad I need this, Lana. Thank you so much for squeezing me in."

"It is my pleasure. You are a good client. I am happy to do it."

Lana's feet appeared beneath the face cradle, her two familiar blue slippers side by side on the rug, facing Amy. Then a gentle hand touched her neck and began to knead. "You have much tension. I can feel already."

Amy chuckled softly. "Tell me about it."

"You want me to tell you about it?"

Amy chuckled again. "No, no—it's just an expression, Lana."

"Oh, I see. I thought maybe you were serious," she said. "Because I *can* tell you why you've got so much tension if you like." Her accent seemed suddenly thinner. "I'm sure you've had quite a bit on your mind lately, yes?" Much thinner now. And there was something else.

She said "you've," not "you have," Amy thought. *"I'm," not "I am."*

In all the years Amy had been coming to Lana, she'd never heard the woman use a contraction when speaking. She'd even mentioned it to Patrick once, wondering if it was a product of respect, or the hurdles of the English language.

Lana's feet moved out of sight, her hand remaining on Amy's neck. Amy went to speak, but a photograph hit the rug below the cradle—a close-up of both Carrie and Caleb in the park, Dan Briggs close by. A second photo dropped an instant later—a close-up of Carrie and Caleb in the park again, Christopher Allan close by this time.

It took a moment for Amy's eyes to adjust to the photos in the dim lighting of the room. By the time the third and fourth photo dropped—much of the same—it was all so excruciatingly clear. Amy jerked and went to sit up but the hand on her neck forced her face back down into the cradle. A second later she heard the click of a gun and felt the barrel press hard into the back of her head.

"Seems like you've got *a lot* of tension now," an American woman said. "Am I stupid to think you've got enough common sense to keep your mouth shut?"

Amy shook her head into the cradle, heart hammering in her chest.

"Good," the woman said. "Maybe you'd want to risk your own life, but I doubt you'd want to risk Carrie and Caleb's."

My God, she knows their names.

"Yes, I know your children's names, Amy. They told me themselves less than an hour ago."

What? What?!

Amy cleared her throat, ready to attempt a desperate whisper. The woman's hand gripped her neck tighter, pressed the gun barrel into her head harder.

"Don't speak. At all. Not until I tell you. Do you understand?"

Amy nodded into the cradle. She felt tears coming but refused to cry.

"We have your children, and we have Patrick. They are still alive, but their pending status is up to you."

Is Domino dead? Is Dan? What about Christopher? Is he still outside the door? Only a few feet away?

"I'm going to take my hand off your neck and you're going to slowly lift your head up and call to your little buddy standing guard outside. Ask him to come in for a second. Nice and calm, nothing suspicious. I want some Meryl Streep shit here, Amy, do you understand? If you scream or sound weird in any way, you're dead. Then Patrick. And then your kids. And I'll tell them Mommy could have saved them if only she'd done what she was told. That will be the last thing they hear before I shoot them both in the head: Mommy could have saved you, but chose not to."

Amy started to weep silently; she couldn't help it.

"Are we clear, Amy? Do you think you can manage what I've just asked from you?"

Amy sniffed and nodded into the cradle.

The woman pushed the gun barrel harder still into Amy's head. "Stop crying. If it sounds like you're upset . . ."

Amy took a deep breath and nodded again.

"Well let's go then, Mrs. Lambert," the woman said.

The pressure of the gun barrel eased off the back of Amy's head, the hand slid off her neck. Amy raised her head and stole a glimpse of the woman—she remained at the head of the table, dressed in Lana's blue scrubs, hair as blonde as Lana's, her face down and hidden behind the hair, gun hand (her right) down and to the side now, out of plain sight, left hand now gently rubbing Amy's shoulder, seemingly ready to mime a scene of no concern.

Amy cleared her throat a final time, went to speak, and stopped. It suddenly occurred to her that if she managed the ability to sound "nice and calm" right now— managed some "Meryl Streep shit"— it would assuredly get Christopher killed. Could she live with leading an innocent man to his death?

And then, as this evil woman hovering above her leaned forward and brought her lips to Amy's ear, Amy wondered—incredulously, and yet, somehow not—if the evil woman could somehow look *through* her ear and into her mind, reading her very thoughts. Amy wondered this because the evil woman whispered: "Would you really rather save the life of a stranger than your own children, Amy?"

Amy didn't have to think. She shook her head.

"Smart girl," the evil woman whispered.

"Christopher?" Amy called. She prayed it sounded okay. "Christopher, are you there?"

Both women kept their eyes fixed on the door. It was difficult for Amy to register minute sounds; her pulse thumped in her ears like a distant drum. She watched the door knob instead, waiting for it to turn. It did not.

The woman nudged Amy's shoulder. "Call him again. Louder."

"*Christopher? Hello?*"

"Right here."

Amy's head whipped around. The evil woman spun on the spot. Christopher Allan had entered the massage room through the connecting shower room door without so much as a click. His gun was pointed at the evil woman's chest.

"If you even try to raise that arm," Allan said, nudging his chin towards the evil woman's gun hand, "I *will* shoot you—many times."

The evil woman smiled. "I guess you're going to tell me to drop it?"

Allan steadied his aim on the woman's chest. "Yes."

The evil woman kept smiling. "And suppose I—"

Allan pulled the trigger. Two muffled thumps from his pistol made Amy flinch. The evil woman stumbled backwards, hitting the wall, sliding down the wall, eyes wide with shock, then blinking fast, then blinking slow, then closing. She finally slumped to her right where she lay motionless.

Amy could only stare at her. She knew the woman now. She knew it was the woman from her father's funeral. The woman who got her drunk at the bar and bailed on her. The woman Patrick eventually recognized on Steve Lucas' phone as likely saboteur of his big account. Always different hair, always different eyes, always different whatever—it didn't matter. Amy knew who she was now.

Except she didn't really know. *I recognize her. Can identify her. Accuse her. But who is she? Who the hell is she?*

Allan inched towards the evil woman's body, gun still pointed at her.

"She said she has my kids," Amy said. "She said 'we have your children.' There are more. *They have my kids.*"

Christopher looked over his shoulder. "Relax, Mrs. Lambert. I'm going to contact Domino now and—"

Amy heard a thump, watched the left side of Christopher Allan's head pop open and spray blood on the wall before his body crumbled.

The evil woman got to her feet. "Always go for the head shot," she said as she began removing her top, two bullet holes clearly evident in the fabric. "He was good; I'm surprised he didn't."

The woman tore off the blue top, revealing the thin Kevlar vest beneath it. A different gun was in her hand. Amy looked at the new weapon without logic. The woman noticed, smiled, and lifted her pant-leg for Amy, revealing the holster attached to her ankle. She then brought both hands back to her torso and began un-fastening the Kevlar vest. "Bastard shot me in one of my tits." She dropped the vest to the ground and stood in just a sports bra, massaging her right breast. "Hurts like hell." She looked at Amy and motioned to the vest on the floor. "It still hurts when you get shot in one of those you know. Especially when you get shot in the tit." The woman inched closer and pressed the gun to Amy's head, leaned in and whispered: "But hey, I don't need to tell *you* that, do I? I heard my brother already shot you in one of your tits."

Amy's mouth fell open on the word "brother," and the evil woman who just claimed to be Arty Fannelli's sister started to laugh.

CHAPTER 69

"Tea?" Patrick asked Domino.

Domino turned away from the living room window and gave a silly frown to his friend. "Since when do you drink tea?"

Patrick shrugged. "I don't know. Is that bad?"

Domino walked into the kitchen with a smile. "No. I suppose not."

"I knew a lot of guys who drank tea in college," Patrick said. "British guys that played rugby. They were tough as nails."

Domino held up both hands. "Okay, old chap. You can make me some tea."

Patrick smiled and put the kettle on. "You want milk and sugar?"

"However you usually make it."

Patrick reached for the cupboard when his cell phone beeped. He grabbed a mug and checked his phone. The mug in his hand hit the floor and shattered when he saw the picture staring back at him.

* * *

Domino ripped the phone from Patrick's hand, courtesies for his friend snubbed by emergency. Domino stared at the text-photo of Amy Lambert—bound and gagged to a chair in the back of a van, her face a tear-stained mask of fear and shame.

Domino cursed, pulled out his own cell with his other hand and dialed Christopher Allan. He hung up after four rings; Allan would have answered on no more than two if all was well.

Patrick's phone beeped again. Domino clicked the tiny envelope icon for a new text message and the screen opened up, revealing a close-up of Allan's face—lifeless eyes open, a hole in the side of his head.

"*What is it?*" Patrick blurted.

"Allan's dead." He showed Patrick the photo on his cell.

Dan Briggs appeared in the kitchen. "What's going on?"

Domino said: "Allan's dead. They've got Amy."

"*Fuck,*" Briggs muttered. He dropped his head towards the floor and made the sign of the cross on his chest.

Domino flicked his chin towards the den. "Get back in there with the kids. I'll let you know what the next move is."

Briggs nodded and re-joined Carrie and Caleb. Domino sneaked a peak at the two children from the kitchen—both of them laying on their stomachs, hands propping up their chins, eyes stuck on the television, feet swaying back and forth like cats' tails. Not a care in the world. Their mother was in the hands of psychopaths, one of them the nightmare-man their innocent young minds might finally be starting to forget. And they watched television, blissfully ignorant to it all, as if it were any other day. As if Mommy would be walking in the door at any moment.

Domino glanced down at the photo of Allan again, swallowed bile, hit the send button. The phone started to ring.

"*We Kill and Kidnap Stupid People*, Miss Smith speaking," a woman said in a cheery tone.

"So how's it gonna be?" Domino asked.

"Nice—direct and to the point. I like that," the woman said. "Well, for now, I will be taking the lovely Mrs. Lambert to a reunion of sorts."

"And where might that be?"

"Direct and to the point, but a bit naïve if you think I'm going to tell you that."

Domino breathed fire through his nose. "Just tell me the part when we get involved."

"Well it seems to me like you've been involved for some time now. Bang-up job, sir. The Lamberts might have been better off just buying another dog."

Domino was capable of exhibiting the professional discipline of a thousand pacifists, yet with every word this woman spoke he found himself unavoidably drifting towards demolition mode. He bit the inside of his cheek, tasted blood. "Just talk," he said.

"I don't feel much like talking right now—I've got *sooo* much to do. But please do me a favor and tell Patrick that Arthur will be in touch with him soon . . . after he gets reacquainted with Amy of course. Ciao!"

The woman hung up.

"What'd they say?" Patrick said. "It sounded like a woman. Was it a woman? What'd she say?"

Domino didn't answer right away. Dozens of possibilities and objectives raced through his mind. If these bastards wanted Amy dead, she'd *be* dead, right? So that makes her bait. Problem was, what would these sick sons of bitches *do* with the bait while his team—

(*one good man down now, God damn it*)

—figured out a way to rescue her? They had to find her fast. Because a thought suddenly occurred to Domino.

A thought that tested his earlier logic and made his blood run like ice water:

Bait doesn't necessarily have to be alive.

"It *was* a woman," Domino eventually said. He could not look his friend in the eye when he added: "She said she was taking Amy to see Arthur for a reunion of sorts. Said Arthur would be calling soon."

Patrick dropped his head.

Domino had never felt so awful in his life. For the first time ever, he felt both failure and helplessness. He glanced at his friend. "I'm sorry, man. We *will* get her back."

Patrick lifted his head. There were no tears, no anger. Instead there was an odd look of revelation. "The lady on the phone said *reunion*?" he asked.

Domino nodded.

Patrick said, "I think I know where they're taking her."

CHAPTER 70

Patrick headed West on the Pennsylvania Turnpike in the silver Toyota Highlander. Domino followed close behind in a black Ford SUV with Briggs bringing up the rear in a black Mustang. Patrick's cell phone was between his legs, waiting for the call. He didn't have to wait long.

"This is Patrick."

"Hey, hey now," a man said.

"Arty."

"Wow, first guess. I guess it hasn't been as long as I thought."

"What do you want?"

"No small talk first? No *'How ya doin?'*, *'How ya been?'*"

"Fuck you. What do you want?"

Arty laughed. "Okay, I can take a hint. I want *you*, buddy boy. You *and* your little rug rats. I want a big old family reunion. I recently had one of my own. It was downright titillating."

"Keep my kids out of it."

"Well that's not gonna happen. You've got no bargaining power here, buddy boy—I've got Amy."

"How do I know she's still alive?"

"You don't. Dare I say you'll just have to trust me?"

"Dare I say you can lick the sweat off my sack?"

Arty chuckled. "I can see you're still the same old wannabe tough guy, aren't you?"

"Yes, Arty. I'm still the same guy who killed your brother and put your scrawny ass in the hospital for months."

There was a brief silence before Arty said, "You know, you really should use at least *some* discretion here. I promise that you'll see Amy alive, but if you piss me off, then I can't promise what kind of condition she'll be in when you *do* see her. When Jim and I were kids, we used to pull the arms and legs off of insects and see how long they could live without them. It was amazing—some of them would wriggle around for hours. I wonder if Amy could manage the same? Would you still love her if she was just a torso and a head? You'd still be able to fuck her, you know."

"Tell me what you want."

"I told you—I want a reunion. Any idea where that reunion might be?"

"I've got a pretty good idea."

"Are you heading there now?"

"Soon."

"And will the kids be with you?"

A deliberate pause.

"Patrick . . . ?"

"*What?*"

"Will the kids be with you?"

"I told you to keep my kids out of it."

"And I told you, that wasn't going to happen. I suggest you think about your wife's situation."

"Motherfucker. You *motherfucker.*"

"Can I take that as a yes then? The kiddies will be accompanying you?"

Patrick hissed: "*Yes.*"

"Excellent."

"How do I know Amy will be at Crescent Lake when we get there?"

Arty's voice rose with excitement. "You *do* know where to go! I'm impressed."

"*How do I know Amy will be there?*"

"I give you my word you'll see her when you get here."

"Your word means dick to me."

Another chuckle. "What choice do you have, buddy boy?"

Patrick said nothing.

"Exactly," Arty said. "I'll make sure you see your wife, Patrick, but I do have a condition or two."

"Like what?"

"You come alone. And when I mean alone, I mean *alone*. You and your kids; that's it. I know you've had some hired help, and obviously the Feds are involved. I'll have eyes everywhere when you get close, Patrick. If I even get the slightest hint that you're bringing the law with you I promise Amy will die. And you won't know how. I'll take her body with me. Imagine living the rest of your life wondering how your wife was killed? The things I did. How long it took. How creative I got. You've met me before, you know what kind of imagination I have."

"I'll be alone."

"No Feds."

"No Feds."

"No hired goons."

"No."

"Just you, Carrie, and Caleb. I'm actually looking forward to seeing those two little buggers again. How have they been? Have they grown? Does Carrie still have that weakness for candy? Still trading dolls for a quick sugar fix?"

"Fuck you."

Arty laughed. "So then I can expect the three of you tonight? A nice evening at the lake where it all began?"

"You mentioned you just had your own family reunion," Patrick said.

A pause, and then, "That's right."

"So would I be correct in assuming that the help you've had thus far hasn't been from some deranged fan club—it's been from family?"

"Such a clever boy you are, Patrick."

"So your *real* family found you then. Or did you find them?"

"Does it matter?"

"I suppose not."

"I can tell you this though," Arty said. "They're dying to meet you."

The line went dead.

"I'm dying to meet them too," Patrick said to himself. He called Domino.

"Talk to me, brother," Domino said.

"It's all good," Patrick said.

"Okay. Don't call the Feds until we're close to the lake."

"I won't."

"They'll notify Allegheny County. Those guys are gonna want vengeance for what happened during the court transfer. That means they'll wanna be cowboys."

"You said that could be a good thing, right?"

"In our situation? Yes."

"You and Briggs good?"

"You don't need to worry about us."

A pause.

"They're family," Patrick said.

"What?"

"His help. They're his family. His *real* family."

"He told you that?"

"Yeah."

"He confirm how many?"

"No. But I'm guessing it's just the two—sister and a father. Or maybe he has an older brother. I don't know."

"Okay. How you feeling about your kids?"

"I'd feel better if I knew where they were."

"If you don't know, they won't know."

"*You* know."

"Your kids are my kids. I hope that's enough said."

"It is."

"Alright then. Hit me up again when we pass Shippensburg. Right now I got a Red Bull with my name on it."

"Okay."

Patrick hung up and let out a good five second breath.

CHAPTER 71

Amy Lambert felt the van slow to a stop. The engine click off. Ever since the last picture of her had been taken she'd been blindfolded—likely a necessary precaution, yet she wondered if the precaution had compensations that delighted her captors. Perhaps they knew that the only thing she would likely see on the black canvas of her blindfold was the last gruesome image that was all but impossible to erase: the image of Christopher Allan's head being blown open—product of her selfishness for a stupid massage.

Massage.

Oh God, Lana. It only just hit her. Why so long before it resonated, she had no idea, but Lana must certainly be dead. Lana was dead. Because of her. Lana was dead because of her.

The side of Christopher's head exploding outward.

Lana dead.

How the blood had spackled the walls of the massage room.

Lana dead. Because of her.

Christopher's lifeless eyes open, his blood on the wall.

Patrick, Carrie, Caleb . . .

Amy squeezed her eyes tight, shook her head, desperate to will the images away. She was tough. She knew she was. But how much did she have left? How long before she truly snapped? She wondered about people who went crazy. Was it gradual, or did it happen like a switch? She knew there was much more in store for her. Knew she would be seeing Arty again. She only hoped her guess about one's insanity possibly being decided by a simple flick of a switch was something best left to screenwriters and carried no true merit in the real world. Because if there was anything she wanted more in the real world right now, it was to prevail again. To see Arty dead. Deader than dead. Obliterated. Him and his stupid family. *Fucking dead*. Yes. Yes, this was better. Focus on *this*.

Picture Domino breaking Arty's back with his bare hands.

Picture Dan Briggs snapping the neck of the pretty woman.

Picture you and Patrick kicking a helpless Arty until he stopped breathing.

Picture Domino killing the big guy involved. Shooting him. Stabbing him. Stomping him.

Picture making *sure* everyone was dead. Lighting their bodies on fire. Watching them burn until there was nothing left but bone and ash.

Amy realized she was smiling into her gag as she pictured these things. She was no longer weeping, no longer feeling any remorse—just bloodlust and vengeance. And she wondered if perhaps the aforementioned insanity switch could possibly be a dimmer switch instead. No quick off and on—just a slow, gradual decline into madness. She wondered if her switch was gradually being slid into the abyss.

* * *

Amy heard the back door of the van open. She flinched when it slammed shut a moment later. Someone was in the van with her.

"How you holding up?"

It was the woman. The pretty woman from her father's funeral, from the spa. Arty's supposed sister. Even if Amy didn't have a gag in her mouth, she likely would have said nothing.

"My father and Arthur are taking a leak. Men have bladders like acorns."

So the big guy is their father. She was never one hundred percent sure. And Arty was here. Why hadn't he shown himself yet?

"Do you smoke?"

Amy remained still.

"I've never seen you smoke. But if you sneak them from Patrick I'll let you have one."

Seen you? How long have you been seeing me?

Amy decided to shake her head.

"Okay—just thought I'd ask. Trying to be a good host and all."

Amy heard the flick of a lighter, and soon, the smell of cigarette smoke.

"Big night tonight," the woman said. "It's taking my brother everything in his power to control himself. He's wanted to come back here and say hello so many times. But he's disciplined—like Dad and I. It's what separates us from the rest of the sheep." A pause. The sound of inhaling and exhaling. "So are you excited for tonight?"

Amy stayed still.

The woman removed Amy's blindfold and Amy instantly fixed on the woman. No phony wigs, makeup, or outfits from the spa. The woman had obviously taken the time to clean herself up and was just as stunning as Amy remembered from her father's funeral. The luxuriant dark hair, the full lips, the shimmering black eyes that now reminded Amy of polished coal behind the rising swirls of smoke from the woman's cigarette.

"That's a little better," the pretty woman said. "Felt like I was talking to a dummy." And then letting out a quick laugh she added: "I meant a mannequin dummy. Not an *idiot* dummy." She took a quick drag from her cigarette and blew it away from Amy. "Although I do wonder if you *are* a dummy. Going to that spa was very, very stupid. You got a lot of people killed. And there will be more to come of course."

Amy's guilt became fear. She mourned Lana and Christopher's death, felt impossibly guilty. But the thought of more to come, this woman reading her inner manuscript as though it was printed out in front of her. Previous, comforting thoughts of vengeance, no matter how far they nudged her towards the teetering edge of that abyss, were suddenly losing their appeal, as if that dark side she embraced as an extreme coping mechanism was somehow nullified in the presence of someone else who knew all too well about the benefits of wearing the evil skin. Except this woman did not *wear* anything. She had never taken it off.

Everything but fear was now gone. And Amy's eyes showed it. She shut them like a child willing away the image of the boogeyman standing at the foot of her bed.

The pretty woman saw it all. Amy could *feel* the woman tasting her pain and fear, sipping it as though it were the finest of wines. If this had been Arty or Jim she would have flown into a rage, struggled and spat, fought like an animal, just as she'd done months ago. What was it about this woman that froze her spirit with an icy grip of dread?

"I'm Monica by the way," the pretty woman said. "We never *were* formally introduced. Tell me, is Patrick good in bed?"

Amy's eyes snapped open. She looked hard at Monica.

"Does he have a nice cock?"

A flutter of anger managed to stir. Amy stared at Monica intently.

"He's a very good looking man, Amy. And I can't help but remember the way he kept looking at me at your father's funeral."

The anger grew.

"I mean it was a funeral for Christ's sake. Yet he couldn't show any discretion could he? I caught him staring at my tits more than once. Even my ass as I was walking away. I wonder if he was thinking about fucking me." She took a deep drag of her cigarette and continued, the smoke fluttering out her mouth and nose while she spoke. "Have you guys fucked since the funeral? I'm sure you have; it was months ago. How much do you want to bet he thought about me at least *once* while you were doing it? Men can be like that sometimes, especially after years of marriage. They pump away forever like some poor fool on the handle of a dry well. But then, just when all seems lost, they flash on an image—a snippet of porn, a supermodel . . . a hot piece of ass they saw recently at their father-in-law's funeral . . ." She smirked, deliberately letting it singe for a moment. "And then *woosh!* That well gushes forth as though it had never seen a dry day in its life. And you smile, right? Satisfied? Relieved? As though *you* were the one that got him off." She exhaled in Amy's face. "You know, I wonder . . . under the right circumstances . . . I wonder if I could get Patrick to fuck *me*. I think I could. I can be very persuasive you know. Although by now I'm sure you've probably figured that out." Another drag, another smirk, another exhale in the face. "The only question is: would you want to watch?"

Amy yelled into her gag, jerked against her binds, eyes narrow and fierce. Monica smiled and seemed to drink it in differently than before. Fear and pain had been a sip of fine wine. Anger and rage was a belt of strong whiskey—hot and rough and good.

Amy cursed herself for giving the bitch the satisfaction.

Monica took a final drag of her cigarette and crushed it out on the floor of the van. "Time to go night night again." She reached forward and pulled the blindfold up and over Amy's eyes, patted her on top of the head and said, "I'll wake you when we get there."

CHAPTER 72

They were an hour away. Dusk was almost gone. Patrick called Domino.

"Go, brother," Domino said.

"About an hour to go, give or take."

"Yeah."

"Would I sound like the world's biggest pussy if I said I was scared?"

"You'd sound like the world's biggest *liar* if you said you weren't. Fear is good—it's natural. If you don't feel some measure of fear then you're a sociopath."

"So these assholes don't feel fear?"

"They can feel pain."

"You always know just what to say."

"And I love ya back."

Patrick gave a soft chuckle.

Domino said, "Call the Feds about twenty miles out and give them the rendezvous point."

"What if they jump the gun before I can get there?"

"Make it crystal-fucking-clear that if they do, she's dead. The Feds don't have a big enough shovel to get themselves out of a mess like that."

"And Allegheny County? Cowboys?"

"Promise them first dibs on the assholes; all you care about is your wife's safety. They'll get their chance to come in, guns blazing."

"And then it's on."

"And then it's on, my friend."

CHAPTER 73

Amy heard the back door of the van open again. No greeting this time, just purposeful grunts as her chair was swung around and pulled back on its hind legs before being dragged backwards. More grunts as her chair was lifted out of the van with one swift movement and lowered to the ground.

She sensed only one person behind the effort—likely the father, the big man; he had hoisted her *and* the chair out of the van without much of a struggle. She remembered Arty as lean, not the type of build to perform such a laborious act on his own. Besides, and she knew this in her gut, if it had been Arty, he would not have been able to resist the urge to speak. To mock. To *play*. The father remained quiet. Even when he tilted her chair back again and loaded her onto what Amy could only guess was a dolly—she felt herself being wheeled backwards seconds later—the father still never spoke.

Monica had mocked. Pushed Amy's buttons to keep the game ablaze.

Arty would have certainly said worse. Maybe even hit her.

The father said nothing. All business apparently. Amy began to wonder if this was more frightening: to resist the urge to toy with the helpless prey. To be so focused and disciplined that the objective would never be compromised by even the most harmless of subtleties until the package arrived safely.

Amy felt the dolly slow to a stop. Heard a door open. Felt the dolly bounce twice as it was lifted upward over two small stairs. The cold outdoor air lingered on her skin as a door slammed behind her, shutting out the world. Soon, her once-frosty cheeks flushed to the warmth of indoors. She smelled old wood and dust. And before she was tilted back once more to be wheeled towards her captor's destination, the father finally spoke—the package safely delivered, the objective completed—the time for celebration to begin.

"Welcome back, bitch," he said. "You ready to have some fun?"

* * *

Amy sat alone in silence, the binds on her hands and ankles still strong and stubborn, affording no slack, the gag taking away any articulation from her voice, the blindfold robbing her sight. Smell and sound were her only available senses, and every now and then she thought she heard breathing, someone watching.

Something in the room shifted. Amy cocked her blind head to one side, held her breath. Someone *was* in the room. And she knew who it was. She felt it.

Amy spoke, desperate to manage Arty's name around the gag that stretched her mouth. It came out better than she'd hoped.

Her gag was pulled out and down to her neck. Still blind, Amy said, "Hi, Arty."

"Hi, Amy. Long time."

* * *

Patrick was twenty miles from Crescent Lake. He picked up his cell, hit the speed dial he'd programmed earlier, asked to speak to agent Chris Miller when it picked up on the second ring.

* * *

"Are you comfortable?" Arty asked Amy.

"Yes, thank you," Amy said in the most contemptuous tone she could summon.

Arty slapped her hard. The shock was magnified by the fact that she couldn't see it coming, and the black screen of the blindfold flashed small bursts of purple light as she struggled to keep her head upright.

"That was an appetizer . . . for Jim. A *weak* appetizer. We'll be having more. Drinks too. Then the main course. Dessert. Coffee. After-dinner drinks—"

"Oh shut up," Amy said. "It's old. Your whole shtick is *old*. Christ, any kid with half a brain could come up with a better sequel."

Arty slapped her again. She expected it this time, and the shock was lessened—no less painful, but lessened.

"You've got it all wrong, Amy. This is not a sequel— merely a continuation."

"Tomato, tom*a*to."

She heard Arty laugh. "You really think you're quite the spitfire don't you? Already accepted your fate, yes?"

"Something like that."

"And Patrick?"

Amy's heart jumped. She prayed it didn't show on her face. "What about him?"

"Have you accepted his fate as well? He's on his way you know. Him *and* your kids."

It was impossible for Amy to hide it now. "My husband would never bring our children."

"I suspect you're right. He said he was, but I didn't believe him. Doesn't really matter much anyway—after we're done with you and lover boy we *will* find Carrie and Caleb. And I'll take my time with them."

Amy's rage put a momentary hold on her tongue. All she could do was clench her teeth and snort like a bull.

"I also told Patrick no police. Told him that if we spot them—and we will if they come—you're dead. I mean you're gonna die anyway, but I at least promised him a chance to see you before you die. Before you *both* die. You see I really want it to be like old times. But if we spot the police? The only thing he'll see when he gets here is your corpse. And believe me, sweetums, I'll do a *serious* number on you. He'll have to identify you by the scar over your tit from where I shot you." He laughed.

Amy said, "And when we kill *you,* they'll identify you by the scars on your stomach and chest from where my husband fucked you with a knife."

The third slap knocked her unconscious.

* * *

"*Please* remember to hold at the rendezvous point," Patrick said to Agent Miller. "He said if they spot *any* police whatsoever she was dead."

"We'll hold," Miller said.

"Tell Allegheny County the same."

"Already did."

"I'm sure they're jumpy after losing men during the court transfer," Patrick said. "Tell them they can have first dibs on the assholes, I don't care. I just want my wife to be safe, alright? *Nobody can go in before me.*"

"They won't, Patrick."

Patrick sighed deep into the phone. "Okay. I should be there in about five minutes."

"We'll be waiting."

* * *

Amy came to, disoriented. For a moment she forgot where she was, until Arty's words brought it all back with painful clarity.

"And she's back," Arty said. "Welcome back, Amy."

Amy shook her head, trying to clear it.

"Turned out the lights on that last one, didn't I?" he asked.

"Yes, Arty. You should be very proud of your ability to knock a blind woman unconscious. What a stud you are."

"I guess maybe you need another, huh?"

"Is that your plan? To keep hitting me all night? I remember you being more creative," she said.

"Oh no . . . *oh no*—there's so much more planned, Amy. The hitting? Just getting carried away I suppose. Your smart mouth makes it all but impossible to resist."

"Would you rather I had a dumb mouth?"

"You see? There you go again—so pleased with yourself in the face of adversity. Perhaps our last encounter was a good thing. It seems to have really toughened you up."

"I agree," Amy said. "Sticking a nail file in your brother's little balls *was* very cathartic. Watching my husband blow his head off was even better. Thanks for that."

She heard Arty take a sharp intake of breath, controlling his anger. "Now that *really* deserves another crack upside your cunting head." Another deep breath. "But I won't. I won't because I need you conscious for when Patrick arrives. It won't be long now. I've dreamed of this day, Amy. I'll admit that for a time I had given up and lost hope. But when my sister contacted me, told me who she was, who my *real* father was." Amy heard him sigh contently. "I knew I would have my vengeance soon—

I just needed to be patient. And I knew that *while* I was being patient, my father and sister were picking up right where Jim and I had left off. And *God damn* were they good. Dead dog? Patrick's job? Dead dad . . . ?" He paused as though getting ready to give a punch line. "*Being at the actual funeral and signing the fucking guest book?*" Arty started laughing hard. He tried to continue but had to pause a few times until his laughter finally subsided. "Monica told me she even got you to drive home wasted one night . . . right after your father's drunk driving 'accident.' That is *absolute-fucking-gold.*" He started to laugh hard again, yet managed to finish with: "I'd cut my fucking thumb off right now if I could have seen the look on Patrick's face when that happened."

Arty's words weren't a revelation for Amy. Had she heard them immediately following each incident, especially her father's death, they would have carried the impact of a bullet. Now it was all in the "no shit" column. Amy's face reflected that.

"Abstaining are we?" There was more than just goading in Arty's tone; there was a faint sense of frustration.

"Just bored," Amy said, bracing herself for another possible hit.

"Sure you are," Arty said with a cluck of the tongue. "But you needn't worry . . ."

Amy heard Arty move towards the front of the room. She heard clicks and whirrs—the sounds of some kind of technology.

Arty removed her blindfold. Amy found herself in a room that was nearly bare. The room contained one tall halogen lamp, one window (that, in the dark of night beyond, only served to cruelly reflect her binds), one table, and most significantly, one tripod supporting an elaborate video camera pointing directly at her, a small circle glowing red on its casing, indicating the camera was live and running.

Arty stepped in front of the camera. He and Amy locked eyes for the first time in months. Arty smiled from ear to ear; Amy could not fight a mask of hatred.

Arty's smile shortened into a satisfied smirk. ". . . it's going to be show time very soon."

CHAPTER 74

Patrick switched off his headlights and rolled to a slow stop at the rendezvous point a hundred yards from the perimeter of Crescent Lake. Before clicking off his lights he had spotted three unmarked cars. Patrick was pleased Allegheny hadn't arrived in cruisers; they may have been granted first dibs in taking Arty and his brood down, but it seemed the Feds were still calling the shots.

Agent Miller approached Patrick as he exited the Highlander. It was dark, but Patrick could still make the agent out fairly well. The rest of the car doors behind the agent began opening—federal agents and members of the Allegheny County Police Department filed out, eight in all, geared to the nines in vests and weapons. The officers from Allegheny County were constantly popping, checking, then slamming the clips back home on their Berettas as they paced and twitched like men having to take a piss.

Cowboys, Patrick thought. He didn't blame them though. They weren't here for points or accolades. They wanted vengeance. Same as him. Same as Arty and his family. *Jesus. Today, kids, we're going to learn about something called a theme.*

"How you doing?" Miller asked Patrick.

"Scared. Worried."

Miller patted Patrick's shoulder once. "We'll have the place surrounded, but we'll be out of sight. When you get near—"

"Way out of sight," Patrick interrupted. "He said they have eyes everywhere. If they spot you . . ."

"That was likely a bluff. And even if they do have some type of surveillance they *won't* spot us."

"How can you be so sure?"

"Because I'm sure," Miller said.

Patrick dropped his head and took a breath. "Okay. I'm going to head towards the lake. Cabin eight."

"We'll be close behind, on foot."

"Stay away from my brake lights," Patrick said. "If I hit them and they light one of your faces—"

"We know what we're doing, Patrick." Miller patted his shoulder again. "This will all be over soon; you'll see."

Patrick nodded, entered the Highlander, and began a slow drive down the gravel road leading into Crescent Lake.

* * *

Arty's radio crackled. A deep male voice came through. "Got a car approaching, son."

Arty brought the radio to his mouth. "Make?"

"It's an SUV." A pause, and then: "Highlander. Toyota Highlander."

"That's him," Arty said. "Is he alone?"

"Can't tell yet. Looks like he's about to pull into the driveway."

Arty glanced down at Amy and pulled the radio away from his mouth. "Excited?"

Amy was holding her breath; she said nothing.

Arty smiled and brought the radio back to his lips. "What's going on, Dad?"

"He's alone. No kids."

Amy gasped relief. Arty glanced down at her again and said: "We were expecting that. We'll find them soon enough."

Amy glared up at him with murder in her eyes. He winked at her.

"Any police?" Arty asked.

"None so far. He's heading towards the front door."

* * *

Patrick stood outside the front door of cabin number eight bordering Crescent Lake. Memories came at him unrelenting, each one staying long enough to burn before the next.

He closed his eyes. That only made it worse. He opened them. Shook his head. Slapped his face. Stomped his feet.

Go inside. Do it now.

Patrick turned the handle on the front door. He did not see the shadows of two Allegheny County officers creeping up close behind.

* * *

Arty's radio crackled. "He's at the front door."

"Copy that," Arty said. He licked his lips and readied himself.

"*Except . . .*"

"What?"

". . . it appears our hero brought the police with him after all."

Arty looked down at Amy and grinned. "Well—I guess your hubby doesn't love you as much as you thought." He put her gag back on.

* * *

Patrick opened the front door and walked into the den. He did not survey his surroundings. He did not survey them because the enormous television perched high up on its stand in the middle of the room captured every bit of his attention.

Amy was on that TV screen. The scene was a horrific memory come back to life—his wife bound and gagged and helpless in a chair, Arty next to her, grinning, back in charge. Patrick stared, his mouth gaping.

"I told you you'd see her again," Arty said. He stroked Amy's hair as he spoke. She violently recoiled away from each stroke. "You can speak if you like. There's a mic; I can hear you."

Anger had not hit Patrick's face yet; it was still shock. "What is this?" he said. "You said you wanted us both. You wanted . . . you wanted a reunion."

"Oh I do. Or should I say: *I did*. But I had to test you first, Patrick. And guess what?" He made a boo-hoo face. "You failed."

"*What?* I did exactly what you said! You son of a bitch, I did exactly what you said!"

"Did you? Where are the kids?"

Patrick swallowed hard. He looked away and said, "They're in the car."

Arty made the sound of a game show buzzer. "That's a lie. I imagine you're not much of a poker player."

Patrick's chest was heaving now. "You knew I wasn't going to bring them, Arty. You *knew* that."

Arty closed his eyes and nodded slowly. "I suppose I did." He left Amy's side and approached the camera, his face now taking up the screen. "But what about the *fuzz*? The *pigs*? The *coppers*?"

"What about them?"

Arty tilted his head to one side, pursed his lips and said, "Come on, Patrick. I told you we would know if they came with you."

"There *are* no cops," he said fast and desperate. "I swear, I swear."

"*I swear, I swear*," Arty mocked. "You might want to peek over your shoulder, honest Abe."

Patrick spun. Two Allegheny County Police Officers were behind him, guns drawn, eyes stuck on the television, confused.

"*No!*" Patrick screamed at the officers. "*GODDAMNIT, NO!*"

Patrick spun back towards the television. "Arty, please! Just listen to me!"

Arty shook a finger and made a *tsk, tsk* sound. "Shame. You know, despite my hatred for you, Patrick, there was always a little bit of respect. I thought you had balls. Honor." He shook his head. "You're pathetic . . . and your wife is as good as dead."

"*NO! NO, WAIT! YOU MOTHERFUCKER!!! WHERE ARE YOU?!*"

Arty waved goodbye, stepped away from the camera, and left an image of a sobbing Amy in plain view for a few intentional seconds before the screen went black.

Patrick kicked the television over and roared. The front door burst open and the remaining officers and agents flooded in. Patrick screamed and spat insults at them. Punched holes in the walls. Kicked a table over and stomped it until it was in pieces. No officer or agent dared intervene. Not even Agent Miller.

Patrick let loose one more almighty roar and then ran out of cabin number eight on Crescent Lake like a maniac into the night.

CHAPTER 75

Patrick sprinted through the woods. Branches smacked and stung his face but did not bother him; the pain fueled his charge. It was dark, and at times he doubted his footing, but he knew he was headed in the right direction. If he took a spill, fuck it. He would bounce right back up no matter what the damage and keep on going.

Twenty yards ahead he began to make out the road, and the idling car that was waiting.

* * *

An Allegheny County Officer approached Agent Miller following a thorough sweep of the cabin. "Nothing," the officer said. "Just the TV and some surveillance equipment."

Miller looked at the ground, kicked over a stone and cursed under his breath.

The officer said, "Look, we may have jumped the gun a little, but she wasn't even in there. The sick bastard was playing games. He was gonna kill her no matter what. If she *was* there, we might have been able to save her."

Miller looked away and sighed. "I don't know," he said. "Try and explain that to Mr. Lambert."

The officer looked in all directions. "Where is he?"

CHAPTER 76

Patrick sat in the passenger seat. Dan Briggs sped through the back roads of western Pennsylvania as if he'd lived there his whole life. They were almost there.

Patrick's cell phone rang. The caller ID was blocked, but he knew who it was—he was counting on it. Patrick flipped open his phone. "Hello?"

"Disappointment is an understatement here, Patrick."

Patrick glanced at Briggs, nodded, then replied: "Where are you, Arty?"

"I gave you pretty simple directions. And yet you chose to let your wife die."

"Fuck you. You were going to kill her anyway."

"I wanted to play the game again. I wanted a reunion."

"You've *been* playing the game, asshole. Or should I say, your family has been playing the game while you've been locked away. Living vicariously through them just isn't the same thing though, is it?"

Brief silence. "Are you trying to mind-fuck me, Patrick? Unwise."

"No mind-fuck. Just truth. I have no doubt you would have done the actual deed when the time came, but at the end of the day it would have left you empty inside, wouldn't it? *Just* murder? No fun, no games?"

Arty laughed, but it sounded forced. "Who said no games? We had many, many things in store for you two."

"Bullshit. You're not invisible anymore, Arty. The FBI *dreams* about you. You've got to keep on the move. Your father and sister could plan and spend all the time they wanted. They *still* can. But not you. Nope—your days of fun and games ended the night my wife and I kicked the living shit out of you and your douche bag brother."

Arty's breathing was heavy on the other line. His tone was a modest attempt at controlling his anger. "For a man whose wife is sitting next to me helpless—"

"Whoa, wait a minute," Patrick interrupted. "Where's the man who prided himself on being in constant control? It sounds like I'm getting to you."

Briggs killed the lights on the Mustang and continued driving through night as deftly as he had before. They were less than a football field away now.

"I'm just talking truth here, Arty," Patrick continued. "No need to get riled up. The simple fact is that your family was having all the fun. Sure, they're loyal to you, and sure, they were going to let you be the one to finish Amy and me off—"

"Your kids too," Arty blurted. "Don't forget about your kids. We *will* find them ya know. New rules to the game. Your kids are dead."

Patrick ignored the comment. "Face it, Arty, from here on out you're nothing but a common killer who has to constantly keep on the move. A *common* killer. You love being considered common don't you?" Patrick laughed.

Briggs slowed the Mustang to a stop. They exited. Briggs took lead as they kept their heads down and hurried to their mark on foot.

Arty's attempt at controlling his anger was gone. He did not yell, but spoke with enunciated venom. "You are a very, very stupid man. Would you like to say goodbye to your wife before I torture her to death?"

Patrick glanced over at Domino and nodded. Domino raised his rifle and peered through the scope.

"No," Patrick said. "I'll tell her face to face."

Domino squeezed his trigger four times. All four hits pierced the living room window and hit Arty in every one of his appendages—both arms, both legs. He collapsed instantly. Amy's eyes went frantic with shock and confusion.

Briggs kicked in the back door of Maria Fannelli's former residence—the place where the finalities of the Lamberts' horrific ordeal had truly happened. The place Patrick knew they were taking his wife from the start.

Pistol raised, Briggs swung and spun throughout the downstairs interior of the home.

Domino headed upstairs.

Patrick entered the living room to greet Arty.

* * *

Arty lay on the floor screaming and writhing in pain. Patrick instantly went to his wife and knelt before her. He removed her gag, took hold of her face, and kissed her from her lips to her forehead with feverish relief.

"Listen to me," Patrick said as he worked the last bind free, allowing Amy to get to her feet. "There's a car outside . . ." He pressed the keys to the Mustang into her hand. "A black Mustang about twenty yards west from here. Get inside and drive—and *keep* driving."

Amy looked in all directions. "Where are we?"

"We're at his mother's house. They tried to trick us."

From the floor, Arty managed: "She's not my mothe—"

Patrick lunged forward and punted Arty in the ribs. "Shut the *fuck* up!" He returned to Amy. "Go, baby. Leave now."

"What? Where are *you* going?"

"I'll be here. I'm not leaving until I know he's dead." He looked down at Arty.

"Patrick, no. Come with me. There are more here. The father and sister."

"I know, baby. Domino and Briggs will find them and take care of them." He looked down at Arty again. "I've got *him.*"

"Patrick, please. Just come with me. You don't need to do this. I hate him too. I want him dead too. But it's safer if we both leave. It's been twice now that I thought I lost you. I couldn't bear it again." She started to cry.

Patrick pulled her close. "You won't lose me, honey. Just go. I want you as far away from this mess as possible. We'll be seeing each other very soon. I promise."

Amy went to object again, but Patrick silenced her with a hard kiss on the mouth. "*Please* go," he said.

"Okay . . . okay I will," Amy said. "I'll see you soon?"

"You'll see me soon."

Amy left.

Patrick turned back to Arty, squatted beside him, smiled and said, "Hey, man. You know I'm not one for small talk, but . . . *how ya doin? How ya been?*"

* * *

Domino upstairs, pistol drawn, maneuvering from room to room with swift movements that defied his bulk. Three rooms had been cleared thus far. One remained. Father and sister had not surfaced during the commotion. That was smart. No doubt difficult given family ties, but smart—they were not giving up their position. They were good. Disciplined. He had a true fight on his hands.

* * *

Patrick remained squatting next to Arty's lame body—all four wounded limbs lying useless on the floor like thick slabs of wrapped meat. His head turned and flopped with desperate urgency, his face grimacing in both pain and panic.

Patrick laughed. "You look like some coked-up ventriloquist's doll." And then Patrick's eyes brightened as something came back to him. "No, wait—you look more like an insect with both its arms and legs pulled off." He laughed again, patted Arty on the head and added: "*That, you sick fuck, is what you call* irony."

Patrick pulled a knife from his waist and cut Arty's throat from ear to ear. Blood spurt from both the wound and Arty's mouth as he choked on his own blood. Patrick then straddled Arty's chest and leaned forward as if he meant to kiss him. He stared Arty in his wide frantic eyes, not caring about the spatters of blood that flecked his face from the wet gasps beneath him.

"I'm going to watch you die," Patrick said. "I'm going to sit here on top of you, look you in the eye, and watch you bleed to death."

Arty closed his eyes.

"Open them," Patrick said.

Arty kept them shut tight.

Patrick took the knife, pinched one of Arty's eyelids between his thumb and finger, and sliced it off.

Arty tried to scream. His mouth opened but his voice no longer worked—just more gasps of blood that misted the air and spackled his own face.

Patrick tossed the eyelid away, brought his face back down to Arty's (where his remaining eyelid was now very open) and said, "As I was saying . . ."

Arty took his last breath, a long wet gurgle before sputtering to a complete stop like a dying engine. Patrick pushed off his chest and stood over Arty's corpse.

"No maybes this time, you fuck. Now you are well and truly dead."

* * *

The final room. Domino approached the door, eased it open. The light was on. The three prior rooms had been dark—this one was expecting someone. He peered inside— eyes and gun—before crossing the threshold. It appeared to be a study of sorts. Two bookshelves, one window, one desk, one closet. Everything was in plain sight. If they were anywhere it was the closet.

But it was so obvious. And why leave the light on? It was all *too* obvious. They want him to come to the closet. To walk—

Domino stopped and looked down. He smirked. Of course. Place the prize in plain sight—you'll lose your surroundings once you glimpse the gold. Lose your head and rush forward . . . into a trap. Domino squatted down and ran the tips of his fingers gently along the length of wire strung tight across the base of the doorway.

Enter; trip and fall; weapon becomes compromised; burst from the closet and boom, boom, boom.

Clever. And it might have worked—if you didn't leave the light on. A little *too* obvious, kids. Back to school for you.

Domino kept his gun on the closet, stepped over the wire, and placed his foot on the wooden floorboard that gave way once his full weight was on it.

* * *

Briggs entered the living room. Patrick was sitting in the chair his wife was bound and gagged to only moments ago. Arty's lifeless body was at his feet. Briggs took the scene in and gave Patrick a mild look of amusement.

"Feel better?" he asked.

"Much better, thanks," Patrick said. His blood-speckled face held a look of both sanity and insanity.

Briggs nodded. If war hadn't eroded the ability, he might have smiled at Patrick. "We're clear down here," he said. "I see nothing. Chances are they split when we surprised them." Briggs looked down at Arty. "So much for family loyalty."

"There's a cellar," Patrick said.

* * *

Domino's right leg plunged all the way through the wooden floor. He pitched forward, one leg vanishing beneath him, the other behind him. He felt his hamstring tear, his groin threatening the same. And his weapon—his weapon flew from his hands as he tried to stop his fall. He had failed to maintain his weapon.

And that's when the closet door burst open.

A big man rushed forward and placed the point of his pistol to Domino's head. He did not pull the trigger. Instead, he patted Domino down and checked his body for all weapons. When he found another pistol, he tossed it along with the one Domino had dropped. "Don't be too hard on yourself, boy. I've been hunting since I could crawl. Haven't met anything I couldn't trap yet."

"Good for you." Domino shifted; his hamstring was on fire.

"You alright there, boy?"

"I'd like to get to my feet. Don't suppose that's going to happen though is it?"

"Actually . . ." The big man extended his free hand. "It is."

Domino stared at the man's hand. *They like to play games,* he thought. Was this one of them? Probably. But what did he have to lose at this point? Domino extended his hand, and the big man helped him to his feet, gun still on him.

Upright, Domino rubbed the back of his leg. It hurt to put weight on it. "So I'm guessing you're the father," he said.

"John Brooks," the big man said.

"Domino."

"Like the pizza?"

"Just like."

John nodded, amused.

"So what now, John Brooks?"

"I told you—I'm a hunter." John turned, tossed his gun out the door, then closed it, shutting the two of them inside the room like gladiators in a cage. He then drew a large hunting knife from a sheath on his waist. "I've killed just about every animal there is, but I'll be damned if I've ever bagged a coon as big as you."

* * *

Briggs opened the door leading into the cellar. It was dark and he tried the switch. Nothing. Intentional? Or just a rusty house that has been a realtor's nightmare ever since the tragedy? He clicked his flashlight and crept down all the same.

Reaching the bottom, he waved the light in all directions. Nothing caught his eye. But then he didn't expect anything to. If these guys were as good as Domino said, then they wouldn't exactly be standing out in the open holding a sign.

Gun high and ready, he inched forward. The flashlight was useful, but in the black of the cellar it was a peep hole. Briggs was losing patience. No one was here; they had fled. He returned to the base of the stairs and was ready to ascend when the first silent bullet struck him in the neck.

He clutched at his throat, not believing he was actually wounded, thinking perhaps he had swallowed an insect inside the squalid confines of the cellar instead. The bullets that followed erased all uncertainties. Briggs dropped dead.

* * *

Domino shook his head and chuckled.

"Something funny?" John asked.

"You hunters make me laugh—acting all tough, like it's a big deal killing an innocent animal that doesn't even know it's in the game. I wonder how well you'd fare if a grizzly knocked on *your* door one day."

John sneered. "It wouldn't stand a fucking chance."

Domino kept smiling. "Well I should be easy then."

John lunged forward and slashed. Domino went to dodge but his hamstring betrayed him; the knife caught his arm and sliced deep.

Domino winced and backed up towards the bookshelf. John approached cautiously, waving the knife in front, grinning.

John feinted a thrust. Domino hopped back, his heel hitting the bookcase. He reached behind him, grabbing for anything. His fingers grazed a large hardcover. He snatched it, whipped it towards John's face. John brought both hands up to defend himself. Domino took advantage, pushed off the bookcase and fired a kick into John's groin. John pitched forward from the impact. Domino seized the wrist of John's knife-hand with his left, blasted rapid-fire palm strikes into John's face with his right until both men slammed back against the opposite wall.

Still clutching John's wrist, Domino began banging the knife-hand repeatedly against the wall. The knife clattered to the floor.

John, bloodied and dazed from the palm strikes, still managed to bring a knee up into Domino's groin. Domino groaned and backed up. John instantly launched off the wall and shot a quick double-leg takedown, sending both men skidding along the floor with John Brooks on top. John raised his torso and brought a cannonball head butt down into Domino's face, emitting a sickly crack.

Domino saw stars. Lots of them. One more and he was fucked.

John raised his torso for a second shot. Domino glanced to his left. He spotted the knife, snatched it. John brought his torso back, whipped it forward again, his massive head trailing behind for the knockout blow. Domino stuck the knife upward, and John Brooks impaled himself on it.

* * *

Patrick hadn't moved from his seat in the living room since Briggs had left. His mind felt gone. He just sat, another man's blood on his face and hands. That same man dead at his feet. The second man he had killed in his life. How many go through life killing *one*? How many go through life killing none? A smile that was more a grimace split his mouth. "A lot," he answered himself, the smile now of a man who was colossally drunk and found humor in everything.

Patrick had reached a dark side once. He had saved his family at Crescent Lake less than a year ago. He was forced to kill. To mutilate and savage. Therapy and repetitive self-assurance convinced him it was survival; a defense mechanism to protect his loved ones. No different in the animal kingdom. As time passed he looked back on those horrific acts of survival—infrequently; it was not a nice place to visit—and they became a vivid dream that, while going nowhere anytime soon, possessed the one blessed quality all dreams possessed: they became less vivid in time.

Now the vivid dream was back, and he doubted whether he could wake up. What he had just done—the pre-meditated murder (*slaughter*) of a man. It felt right. Felt great.

Can I go back to being me? he wondered, finally blinking, looking at the blood on his hands. Domino could kill ten men and then hold a kitten. So could Briggs. So could Allan.

Patrick was not those men.

You killed two men. You killed two men and you liked it. You fucking-a liked it.

"If killing motherfuckers is wrong . . . I don't want to be right!" he sang, wearing the drunken smile.

A female voice behind him said: "I agree, Patrick."

Patrick stood and Monica shot him twice in the chest.

* * *

Monica loomed over Patrick's unconscious body. He was still breathing, but it was raspy and shallow. She would call her father (who was no doubt finishing off the big black fella) from upstairs. They would come down and save Patrick. Take him with them. Nurse him back to health. Then keep him hostage until the day he died— which would not be soon. Each day they would find a way to inflict unthinkable agony on his body. Saw off his balls with a dull blade. Sew his lips shut and then rip them back open. Stick needles in his ears until his ear drums burst. Find his wife and kids and slaughter them before his eyes before gouging them out and forcing them down his throat *"to see what you ate for breakfast!"* she would quip with so much glee.

These thoughts filled her with heat and hatred. Heat for the acts themselves, hatred for the motive: the loss of her second and last brother. She had never failed before. Ever. The heat began to fade. The hatred rose.

Monica glanced down at her dead brother, resisted the urge to empty the rest of her gun into Patrick, then lifted her head and called upstairs for her father.

"Dad?"

* * *

The blade plunged handle-deep into John Brooks' throat. Blood gushed and poured from his mouth, his eyes wide in disbelief.

Domino rolled the big man off and hurried to his feet. Adrenaline was masking his wounds, but he would no doubt be feeling them soon.

Domino watched John Brooks die. The big man soon lay dead on his back, eyes open, a pool of blood circling his head and neck. The man was an incredibly worthy opponent, the toughest Domino had ever faced. Had this been on the battlefield or in some other type of circumstance, Domino would have showed his opponent respect and closed his lifeless eyes. An old mentor of Domino's once told him that to die with your eyes open was hell—you would relive your death over and over again for all eternity. To die with them closed was to let God know that you were now at peace and ready to ascend toward heaven.

Worthy opponent or not, this man deserved no respect for the things he'd done to the people Domino loved and considered family. He left the room quietly with John Brooks' dead eyes open.

* * *

"*Dad?*"

No answer. Monica heard someone moving upstairs. "Dad, you there?"

Nothing.

She sighed and glanced down at the dying Patrick.

* * *

Domino retrieved his gun when he heard the crazy bitch calling from downstairs. That was a bad sign. It meant his boys were likely in trouble. He was hurt, but not bad enough for a second attack.

Going hand-to-hand with the daughter would be like a game of checkers after what he had just gone through with the father. Except she would never *do* hand-to-hand, would she? She never needed to. And if she got past Briggs, it certainly wasn't on might. It was the classic brains and brawn. He was up against the brain now. He had to regroup, not succumb to the kind of trap the big fucker had gotten him with.

And then the front door slammed and all plans went out the window. Domino hurried downstairs, gun leading the way.

* * *

Domino saw two things when he hit the bottom of the stairs and entered the living room. One was his friend Patrick, on his back and bleeding badly from his chest and stomach. The other was one word, scrawled in blood on the white wall above Patrick's body:

Ciao.

Domino's instinct was to rush for the door, to follow his target before it fled. Doing that, though, would mean leaving his friend to bleed. And he still didn't know where Briggs was.

She's getting away.

Domino ran to Patrick and placed his hand on his neck. His pulse was very shallow, his breathing barely there.

She's getting away.

Domino stood and ran to the front door, stopped, and returned to Patrick. He called for help on his cell, and then started to perform CPR on his friend.

Patrick died before the ambulance arrived.

CHAPTER 77

Florence, Italy

Four Months Later

A beautiful blonde woman in sunglasses sat at a table in a busy outdoor café. When the waitress approached, the beautiful woman ordered a black coffee in perfect Italian.

While she waited for her coffee, the blonde took a cigarette from her purse, lit it, and inhaled deep. She titled her head back and blew a stream of smoke towards the sky. She kept her head in that position after exhaling, soaking in the morning sun as though she had never had the pleasure of sampling its allure.

The waitress returned with the coffee and the blonde thanked her.

She took a sip, let out a contented sigh, and resumed leaning back in the chair, her face in the sun once more.

She was drawing on her cigarette again when a woman spoke:

"Those are bad for you."

The blonde casually lifted her head and exhaled. "Amy Lambert, as I live and breathe."

"Hey, Monica," Amy said, taking a seat across from her. "Back to blonde again?"

Monica ran her fingers through her hair. "It's real—no wig."

"Looks good. Familiar too."

Monica smirked. "Bringing back good memories?"

"Just memories," Amy said, her eyes never leaving Monica's.

"Now come on, Amy . . ." Monica tossed her lit cigarette to the ground; a patron scoffed at the act. "I always pegged you as rather smart." Monica brought her hand below the table. There was the faint click of a gun. "You know you'd stand no chance against me."

Amy nodded, her eyes no less intense. "I know that."

A powerful hand seized Monica's arm from behind. Effortlessly, the concealed gun was wrenched from her hand and quickly tucked away.

Without turning around, Monica said, "Let me guess—it's the big black fella that killed my father."

"You can call me Domino," a deep voice said.

"I can call you much more than that," Monica said.

Domino bent forward and put his mouth to Monica's ear. "Be quiet and listen to what my friend has to say."

Monica's eyebrows bounced. "Friend? Are you two fucking already? Poor Patrick. It hasn't even been a year and—"

There were two muffled thumps. Nobody in the outdoor café heard them. Monica's head dropped towards the table, towards her stomach. Her face went from shock, to disbelief, to nothing. She fell face-forward onto the table.

By the time anyone noticed, Amy and Domino were faces in a crowd. The gun Amy used was given back to Domino and tossed in the River Arno.

THE END

NOW AVAILABLE!
The third installment in the *Bad Games* series, *Bad Games: Hell Bent*

About The Author

A native of the Philadelphia area, Jeff Menapace has published multiple works in both fiction and non-fiction. In 2011 he was the recipient of the Red Adept Reviews Indie Award for Horror.

Jeff's terrifying debut novel *Bad Games* became a #1 Kindle bestseller that spawned three acclaimed sequels, and now the first three books in the series have been optioned for feature films and translated for foreign audiences.

His other novels, along with his award-winning short works, have also received international acclaim and are eagerly waiting to give you plenty of sleepless nights.

Free time for Jeff is spent watching horror movies, *The Three Stooges*, and mixed martial arts. He loves steak and more steak, thinks the original 1974 *Texas Chainsaw Massacre* is the greatest movie ever, wants to pet a lion someday, and hates spiders.

He currently lives in Pennsylvania with his wife Kelly and their cats Sammy and Bear.

.

Made in the USA
Monee, IL
27 January 2023

26465072R00207